An Ocean Of Blame

A Novel by
Margaret Elizabeth Brook

www.EvolvedPub.com
Evolved Publishing LLC
Butler, Wisconsin, USA

An Ocean of Blame is a work of fiction; however, it draws on real people and historical events, which the author has attempted to be as true to as possible, relying on extensive research. Thus, many of the names, characters, places, and incidents are true representations of historical events. Nonetheless, the general story flow and character interactions are products of the author's imagination, or the author has used them fictitiously in order to plug in the gaps where we have holes in the historical accounts.

Printed in Book Antiqua font.

Dedication

To innocence —
An all too "fleeting" treasure.
Most of all,
to the innocence of all who boarded Titanic.
And to Frederick Fleet himself,
who bore the burden of
An Ocean of Blame.
And to all of us,
as we confront our own loss of innocence.

Silently, one by one, in the infinite meadows of heaven,
Blossomed the lovely stars, the forget-me-nots of the angels.

Henry Wadsworth Longfellow

Prologue

Once the decision was made, it seemed so easy. After all the years of self-doubt, guilt and depression, there was one single, even gentle, answer. At last, he would return to the place he truly belonged, after all these years of questions, replaying the scene in his head for decades, when the answer should have been clear from the beginning on that icy, starlit night so long ago. Frederick Fleet walked to the shed in the back of the garden, pulled the cord on the hanging light bulb and looked around. He reached down and grabbed the step stool from under a watering can. Then he turned off the light, seeing no need to call attention to what he was about to do. He walked to the pear tree.

With determined fingers, he tied a carefully crafted seaman's knot in the heavy rope. Then he tossed the rope over the limb of the tree and stepped up on the stool. Taking a deep breath, he paused for a moment before letting the air out ever so slowly. It was his last hold on this earth, on this cool evening in the south of England. All these years he had stumbled through life, always looking for something that remained elusive. Forgiveness, acceptance, love. Ultimately, he had failed. Now, he was ready. There was nothing left.

He dropped the loop around his neck. The night was surprisingly quiet, no dogs barked, no sound of traffic passing out on the street. But as he stood there poised on the top step, about to change everything, he heard a laugh, a woman's laugh, and the tinkle of glasses, wine glasses, and the sweetness of a violin's song. Confused, he stood there motionless, trying to make sense of it. And then without a doubt, there it was. He recognized it instantly, the siren song that pulled him, the one thing he couldn't escape all these years of running away from himself and from everyone who had ever loved him. But now he had come to this moment of reckoning at last. The bloodcurdling screams of the crowd in the water below, the panic. The unwilling surrender to imminent death. He had run from this sound all these years. It was the sound of *Titanic*. And the sinking was all his fault, he was sure of it.

He closed his eyes and saw himself, as he had been that night, in that last moment of innocence. Although some would argue he was guilty even before he saw the object. That was the crux of their suspicion. He should have seen it sooner. Isn't that what a lookout was supposed to do? Spot an object in their path and react? His failure to do so soon enough had betrayed their trust in him, and his own in himself. If only he had sorted it out right from the first. If only he had known where his poor decisions would take him. If only he'd been stronger. If only. That cold North Atlantic wind bit his face once again. Could that happen? Could the vengeful breath of the universe seek him out and find him after all these years? The desperate screams grew louder. They filled his ears with a deafening roar, laying claim to him at last, after fifty-three years.

Chapter 1

The stars gleamed like beacons in the enormous black sky. They almost distracted him from his task, but unlike the father he'd never known, and the mother who had deserted him when he was just a baby in Liverpool, Frederick Fleet was a responsible man. He never shirked his duty. And so, he pulled his eyes from the irresistible diamond-sparkle above and swept the dark waters stretched out in front of him. That was his charge. Up here in the crow's nest, the icy wind prevailed, but down below, the sea was dead calm. The North Atlantic appeared as a lake, something he had never seen before. He reached up and held on to his cap.

Suddenly, an object appeared dead center, right in front of them. Enormous. Could it be an iceberg, sitting out there close to the horizon, owning the starlit water on this moonless night? He was uncertain. Was it the one thing he hoped he'd never see, not on *his* watch? He *had* seen smaller ones, and some big ones off in the distance, but *none* like this, this close, not ever. And the others had been white, glistening white. This wasn't. Well, whatever it was, this object loomed ahead with no waves lapping at its base, as the calm water refused to offer up a clue. Really, the more he thought about it, all he saw was a dark shape, a *smudge* where sky met water. But it was a shape where only sky belonged. He was confused. He started to grab the crow's nest binoculars, then he remembered, there were none to be had tonight. He reached out and pointed.

"What d'ya think, Reg? See the smudge... over there."

"I'm not sure. Minus the moon, and with that bit of a haze on the horizon, it's impossible to say for sure." Reg stared straight ahead.

The two men were quiet, each hesitant to decide what it might be, unwilling to speak the dreaded word, *iceberg*. But if not ice, what could it be? A ship with no lights? Time slipped by in precious increments.

"We can't take a chance, can we?" Fleet replied. "It could be, well, anything. One thing's for sure, it ain't good news. And it's gettin' bigger every second goes by."

He rang the bell, once, and again, and then a third time. The plaintive sound of the alarm matched the fear streaking through his heart. He wished more than anything that his cold, desperate fingers striking the bell on the crow's nest of *Titanic* could alter her course immediately. He'd wasted enough time.

"Are we going to hit it Fred, wha'ever it is?" his companion asked.

A swirling gust lifted Fred's hat from his head. Before he could grab it, the hat sailed high into the night sky for a moment, only to spiral down, hitting the water and then, instantly, sink into the icy depths below. Just like that, the cap was gone, claimed by the power of the sea.

At last Fred found his voice. "Reg, it must be ice! It's a berg, a black one. I never seen a black one before, but I heard about them once. I *knew* I smelled ice." He raised his hand and pointed once again. This time, his hand shook.

Reginald Lee sucked in his breath.

Fleet yanked at the phone, pulling the receiver to his mouth. The phone rang and rang. Would they answer? Earlier, they'd ignored him when he was trying to say he smelled ice. Then he'd issued warnings a second time, he'd spotted ice, actual bergs, off in the distance. And still he'd received no reply. Now precious seconds ticked off once again, as the ship moved closer to its destiny. Finally, someone answered. Sixth officer, James Paul Moody.

"Iceberg, right ahead!" Fleet screamed, losing control for the first time.

"Thank you," the officer replied calmly. Nothing more was said.

Fleet knew the protocol. The officer would pass the word to First Officer William Murdoch, in charge of the bridge, and then to Robert Hichens who held the wheel and the fate of the ship and 2,228 souls in his hands. Fred slammed the receiver down and shook his head in frustration.

"Reg, I wish I 'ad those *damn* binoculars. You remember 'ow they denied our request, no matter 'ow many times we asked." He reached up to push his cap back, a nervous gesture that wouldn't give him the closer view he so desperately sought. Except of course, the cap was gone.

"Oh my God, look at it now! But *surely* we will miss it." Reg Lee's panicked tone didn't match his words. No ship wants to be lined up, heading for an iceberg. He reached out and grabbed Fred's arm. He was terrified. They both were.

It was worse for Fred. If only he'd rung the bell sooner. Would they find out he'd hesitated?

Chapter 2

Below, in the gloriously decorated, posh, first-class ballroom, the evening was about to draw to a close. The last of the pampered passengers lingered, enjoying the lush music of the orchestra and the conversation of their fellow travelers. The cascading notes almost covered the sound of the alarm, but *not* completely.

"What's that? Did you hear it, Charlotte?" Cybil Stuart tapped at her lips with a linen napkin as she glanced at her friend.

But Cybil could see that Charlotte Fallows was distracted by the handsome man seated next to her. William Pennington extended his hand and invited her to dance. She'd obviously been working toward this moment all evening. As the multicourse dinner had been served and the various wines poured, Charlotte's attention had been caught by his handsome face and the whispered pedigree Cybil had shared with her.

"It's nothing." Charlotte tossed the careless words back at Cybil as she took the hand extended to her, and followed the tall, tuxedoed man onto the dance floor. Immediately they disappeared from view, caught up in the flow of the waltz and the swirling motion of the other elaborately dressed passengers enjoying this lovely evening on the world's most celebrated ocean liner. At least that's the way the White Star Line had sold its pricey first-class tickets for the "opportunity of a lifetime," a "chance to be part of history" on the maiden voyage of the world's first, and only, unsinkable ship.

"You have the most wonderful dressmaker," remarked the woman seated next to Cybil. "I've never seen such beautiful silk."

Cybil gave a coy smile. After the compliment would come a request for the name of the designer. Cybil liked to think of herself as a generous person, when it suited her. Allowing any other woman to attempt to look as beautiful as she imagined she was didn't figure into her level of acceptable largess. Why should it, when they might meet again, at a ball once they had all returned to England? Being recognized as beautiful was extremely important to Cybil.

"Ah yes, the designer is a special treasure, one I keep to myself. Besides, he is picky, he doesn't engage in commerce with just *anyone*." Her seatmate wrinkled her nose, tugged at a glove in a nervous gesture, and gave a quiet sound of disgust as she turned her attention to the rest of their dining partners.

Cybil sat there alone, watching her friend dance with the well-suited Mr. Pennington. She listened to a bell, an alarm perhaps, ringing somewhere far off, it seemed. She couldn't quite place where it came from. What could it mean?

She thought of her son Matthew, back in their stateroom with his nanny, who also served as her maid for the voyage. He was only four, but he'd been so excited to travel with her on his first sea adventure, as he'd called it. Precocious for his age, he meant everything to Cybil. Married to a man twenty years her senior, a wealthy banker with extensive real estate holdings around the world and little time for his wife and child, Cybil sought comfort in the boy. Surely, he was asleep by now, tucked in his bed with the stuffed teddy he'd insisted on bringing along. At the last minute, after the tickets had been purchased, her husband had been too busy to travel with her. Bringing Matthew along had been his idea.

"No need to cancel the trip, my dear. Take the boy. I daresay you prefer *him* to me."

Her thoughts turned uneasy for a moment as she remembered that unpleasant conversation. She had sought to patch things up, and so she had agreed to travel with Matthew instead.

Well, he's safe with Nanny, fast asleep by now, Cybil assured herself. Her fingers reached up and traced the pattern of her exquisite diamond necklace. A gift from her husband, another of his ploys to assuage her disappointment in their empty relationship. He couldn't put up with her tears and complaints in the first year of their marriage each and every time he stepped away from her, always in the name of some vague business obligation. And so, he'd devised a remedy for her discontent. At least *he* must have thought it was a remedy.

On a somewhat regular basis, Randolph Stuart presented his wife with yet another item from his family's collection of heirloom gems. This necklace had been presented to her the day before her departure from Southampton. But on this occasion, the exchange lacked any personal contact between husband and wife. She had found the gold-ribboned box at her place at table, left for her to discover as she sat to breakfast by herself, with the servants bringing eggs and coffee. Randolph had already left, ostensibly for whatever obligation kept him from the sea voyage.

After five and a half years of marriage, there was no doubt that their relationship was a contract between suitable families, and nothing more. By now, she knew full well the deal she had made, but it was too late to do anything about it. Perhaps, on some level the man wished to please his wife, but his chosen vehicle involved no emotional attachment or time spent disrupting what he deemed his personal life, one that did not, and never would, include Cybil. He assumed she would be pleased enough with the exchange of some priceless bauble every now and then. However, for Cybil, each gift had the opposite effect. They reminded her of what she longed for and didn't have—a loving, attentive husband.

She had been profoundly happy upon learning she was pregnant after little more than a year of her empty marriage. They had shared so little time together in the marital bed.

Cybil found great relief from her loneliness in the unconditional love she received from her little boy. Matthew was the one bright spot in her life. She did *enjoy* the jewelry, but her true pleasure came from the reaction it produced in other people. *Your husband must love you so much to shower you with such gifts* were words she lived to hear, even though she knew these sentiments contained no truth.

She sat there, fingering the large diamonds on the necklace and thinking of Randolph, wondering where he *really* was. But that was pointless speculation. The conversation of her companions at table soon distracted her, along with the swell of the violins, and the taste of the sherry on her lips.

She dismissed her marital concerns as easily as a small, far-off bell.

***

In another part of the ship, Captain Edward Smith heard the bell, that he did. Something was happening up in the crow's nest. Surely, they were overreacting, but best to check it out. He shoved aside the papers he'd been working on in his private chart room and stood up quickly, his chair crashing to the floor behind him. *Of all things,* he thought to himself, *those lookouts have no binoculars and we told them they wouldn't need any. And now they're sounding an alarm. Damn! I don't like this at all, I wonder who's on the watch. All the lookouts had been upset,* but most of all, he remembered Fleet's protests when they learned, just after the ship left Southampton, that the glasses were missing. Fleet had been the most outspoken of the lot. He always was.

"Sir, how can I do my job without them?" he'd complained. "I need to see the sea. Surely you know that." Fleet hadn't intended the pun. A totally uneducated man, he wasn't that clever. But he did have some years behind him as watch lookout. He'd had a real concern and justly so. But the glasses stored in the crow's nest, and readily at hand in Belfast, were nowhere to be found once they left Southampton.

He noted the time. It would be Fleet and Lee in the nest. Oh, what the *hell*?" His anger escalated as he recalled, once again, Fleet's fussing three days previously. He threw his hands in the air and ran onto the bridge. He *didn't* want to hear the man's complaints about the missing glasses.

"I can't give him what I don't have," he mumbled to himself. A sudden, unexpected movement of the ship increased his panic. He felt a scrape, and a shudder, a hard-to-discern-what-the-cause-could-be, in-the-middle-of-the-ocean movement. And then, it was the next surprising *action-reaction* shudder that *really* worried him. Why had Murdoch sent the ship into reverse quite like that? Or had he? Too many things were happening all at once, and Smith couldn't process it all. They couldn't be in any *real* danger; after all, the ship was unsinkable.

As an afterthought, he reminded himself that the ship's designer, Thomas Andrews, was on board. Andrews would have to account for anything that might be amiss. Worst case, it could be a dropped propeller. If that, they'd have to limp back to Belfast. *Well, this is at Andrews's feet, all right.* After all, Smith reasoned in a hasty attempt to feel better, it was all Andrews's fault. Anything goes wrong, he designed this lark of a floating castle.

It was the first moment of regret for Smith since he'd maneuvered his way into command of the historic vessel. Shifting the blame for anything and everything was what it was all about. It was Andrews's fault, whatever happened. But then again, he reminded himself, everything was okay. He had no doubt the ship was unsinkable. Maybe Fleet had panicked about some ridiculous nothing; he did seem the overly nervous type. He would put the young snippet of a man in his place.

Smith dusted off his uniform, straightened his gold-braided cap, pulled back his shoulders, and set his chest in a position of command. Then, cursing silently to himself, he set out to do battle with the situation.

"What have we struck?" he asked First Officer Murdoch. Because as soon as he'd stepped onto the bridge, he'd instantly realized this was no false alarm.

"An iceberg, sir," Murdoch replied. As if on cue, drifting off to the starboard side was the biggest mountain of ice Smith had ever laid eyes on. Scattered chunks of ice littered the deck. "I put her hard a-starboard and ran the engines full astern, but the berg was too close. I intended to port around it, but she hit before I could."

"Close the watertight doors," Smith replied automatically.

"The watertight doors are closed, sir."

Well, that shoots to hell my timing to beat the Olympic. Ismay isn't going to like this one bit.

Bruce Ismay, boss of the White Star Line, traveled along for this historic maiden voyage. He was the reason Smith had the ship zipping along at twenty-two and a half knots, near to top speed. Actually, it was Ismay's adamant demand that they beat the maiden crossing record of her sister ship, the *Olympic*. Smith was sure they would, up until this moment. Now at best, they'd be limping along, an embarrassing development to say the least. Shame replaced glory in an instant.

"Murdoch! Explain yourself right this minute." Smith was too angry to take his eyes off the man's face.

"Well, sir, we tried to miss it, the berg. And we didn't." His words were contrite, but his tone of voice and his demeanor, weren't. Murdoch betrayed something else to the captain. Insolence slipped through his lips.

Smith could see that Murdoch was badly rattled by striking the iceberg. The man *could* have slowed the ship as they entered the area with the greatest risk of ice, and he looked extremely annoyed with himself for not having done so. He'd been in charge of the bridge; the immediate call *was* his. But Smith also knew doing so meant spoiling their mileage for the day. If Murdoch had slowed her down, and no ice was spotted, he would have been a subject of blame since Smith had made it clear to Murdoch that he, the captain, and Mr. Ismay expected the ship into port on Tuesday, not the announced Wednesday. Even so, Smith was not pleased.

"How could you let this happen?" He pulled his head back and stared at the massive chunk of ice as his blood pressure shot up and his temples throbbed. He jabbed his finger in the air toward the berg. "How did you manage to fail so completely in your task? Don't you know how to maneuver a ship? We should have missed it easily." His voice was colder than the iceberg practically sitting in their lap. Smith stepped closer, completely invading the man's personal space. He glared at him.

"We were going too fast to miss it, sir," Murdoch responded, defiantly.

"Nonsense. Did you try and turn away quick enough? Did you react at the strike of the bell? Did you?"

"Yes sir, of course we did. I just explained that."

Smith remembered how the other times Fleet warned of ice, he wouldn't allow them to slow her down, not one single knot. But he didn't say a word. He guessed that Murdoch recalled this as well, and all of this had played into his insolence. No doubt about it.

"Really? I know how this ship responds to a turn of the wheel. Don't tell me otherwise." Smith's words were cut off by a crewman running onto the bridge.

"Word has come from Mr. Ismay. We must keep moving. He said, 'Tell Captain Smith, keep moving now.' But, Captain, we're taking on water. We must be! We need to take action!"

"No, we're not taking on water," Smith replied in anger. "Even if we are, we have enough bulkheads to withstand any of it. The ship will not sink. And follow Ismay's order. We have no choice. I may be captain, but he always makes it very clear to me—he wants what he wants. Stay on course, but slow down, five knots at best. We can always radio for help, see what ships are near if we need them, but don't panic the passengers. That won't help at all right now."

Murdoch started to interrupt, something he never would under ordinary conditions, but Smith stopped him. He was having none of it. "This is a minor inconvenience. We'll be fine. Send some crew below decks at once. Tell them to bring back a report immediately. But she is seaworthy, I have no doubt of that."

Either from arrogance or White Star Line propaganda, he truly believed his own words. Besides, Smith's huge ego wouldn't give credence to the possibility that any of the crew on his ship might assume to know more about their situation than he did, even if he'd been off duty in his cabin, sipping scotch whiskey at the moment things went awry.

Smith reached up and tugged at his ear, a new habit he had acquired these last months as he began to suspect a loss in his ability to hear a particular voice when mixed in with the general din on board ship. He could never share this recent development with anyone, not the crew and certainly not Ismay. He had wanted to protest when Ismay told him just a few days ago that he, Bruce Ismay, was the boss. He'd reminded Smith that captain or not, Smith was merely Ismay's employee.

That wasn't how things worked at sea. The captain was always in charge, or was supposed to be. Past history with Ismay, however, had made it very clear that wasn't the case. Ismay insisted he was always in charge of White Star, on land and at sea, and Smith had always acquiesced.

This time, Smith had intended to show a bit more backbone. Once they were in the middle of the sea, there had been several ice warnings from other ships. Smith had wanted to dispute the point of speed. But because of his increasing hearing difficulties, in the rough and tumble noisy atmosphere of the ship, he hadn't wanted to argue with the man just then. *Besides,* he'd thought at the time, *what difference will it make? I've crossed the Atlantic many a time, nothing different about this trip, except for the notoriety of the ship. And this will be my last command. I'm ready to retire, even if, up until now, I've kept this to myself and Ben.*

Only one creature truly knew Smith's heart, his weaknesses, self-doubt, and fears, and that was his closest confidant, his much-loved Russian wolfhound Ben. Ben knew everything, as only a dog can. Smith's great regret was that he had left the dog in Southampton. At the last minute, other arrangements made more sense than bringing him on board for this momentous excursion.

But Smith missed him so much right now. They had become so close. On other journeys, Smith looked forward to going over the events of the day with Ben as he sipped his whiskey, an evening ritual he was fond of repeating as the day came to a close. The dog had been a gift from Benjamin Guggenheim, the industrialist, intended for Smith's daughter Helen, but Edward Smith had quickly grown attached to the pup and kept him as his own. Instead, he'd bought Helen a poodle. He and Ben had traveled together on the high seas many times, but not this time.

Chapter 3

As the ship had traveled ever closer to the iceberg, Fleet and Lee stood side by side, watching the unthinkable descend on them. It seemed like the approach lasted forever, like they were stuck in a terrifying freeze-frame. Just moments before the collision, he had asked Lee to climb down the ladder onto the deck.

"You should get out of here, Reg. Right now, climb down."

"I'm not going to leave you here, Fred. We should both take the brunt of this." He'd rested his hand on Fred's shoulder and looked into the eyes of the younger man. "I'm staying," Reg told him.

But Fleet would have none of it. "There's no sense both of us being up here if we hit the berg. Go. Go on. The foremast might collapse. Anything can happen to the crow's nest. Go on down. Besides, it's all my fault."

"No, it's not."

"We'll talk later, just go."

And so he had. Lee had made his way down the ladder to the deck below, shaking his head all the while.

"Chances are we're in for it now," Fleet mumbled to himself as he chewed on his bottom lip and vigorously rubbed his hands together, trying to get the blood flowing to warm his numb fingers. His gloves were no match for the frigid night air. With his cap at the bottom of the sea, and his hair blowing in all directions, he was chilled to the bone with both fear and the night wind. But, deep down inside, he still held out hope that the ship would manage to turn away in time. He still believed it was possible, and although he knew he wasn't a lucky man, he hoped luck would prevail for all the others caught up in this horrible moment.

Lee popped back up to the nest. He shook his head in commiseration and stood next to Fred, staring straight ahead.

When the impact occurred, Fred was surprised that it wasn't a lot worse. It felt like a scrape, a minor scrape and nothing more. It was only afterwards, when the ship reversed course, and started up again, moving through the water, but slower now, that he was completely unnerved. Lee cut into his thoughts.

"Why especially you, Fred? Why did you say that? Why are you to blame? You aren't, but why did you say that?"

"Well, I've been a lookout longer that you, even though you're an old man compared to me. You've been a lookout how long? Two years?"

Lee nodded.

"Well, I've been in a crow's nest for four years on *Oceanic,* so I'm the senior lookout," Fleet reminded him. "Also, I'm port side, the iceberg side. So, you know that's how it works, plus, they'll say I didn't react fast enough once I saw the ice."

"But you did react fast enough! You did the best anyone could do. And if we had a moon tonight, and some binoculars..." Lee sounded like he was trying to convince himself as well as Fleet.

"People will need to blame someone, and that someone will be me. White Star will never let me off that easy. They aren't going to say, 'Well, it's not Frederick Fleet's fault. After all, we wouldn't give him binoculars.' I'll be their scapegoat. You'll see."

"I won't let that happen, Fred. I swear I won't. I'll back you up. Every day of my life, as long as I live, I'll back you up. No one could have done any better. Don't even think about it. You have to look on the better side of this."

"And what's the better side?" Fleet asked. He was still convinced somehow White Star would find out about his delay ringing the bell.

"If you hadn't reacted as fast as you did, things could be a lot worse. We might have hit the berg harder, and head on. The hull might have buckled. The ship might be taking on water, but none of that happened. Ships do hit ice, and they're all right in the end. It could have been worse." Lee spoke with agitation.

Since they had become partners on the watch, they had grown close. Fleet could see that Lee was trying to help him calm down. And it was true, they would both fare better if they appeared calm. But Fleet knew he was stretching the truth. Could they cover it up?

"Well, I guess you're right. We did hit it, and she jumped around funny. Why in the world did Murdoch put her in reverse?" Fred paused for a moment. "I'll never figure that out, but at least we're all right, so far —"

Lee cut him off. "Hmm, wait a second... I think I take all that back. Just this minute, I think she's starting to list. Look at the horizon, we're tipping..." His tone of voice had changed, just like that.

"You're right. Shit. I knew this was going to be bad."

"But she *can't* sink. She won't."

Just then, the relief crew for the watch showed up at the bottom of their perch. It was well after midnight now, time to change hands.

"What's going on down there?" Fleet asked as he climbed down the ladder, jumped, and hit the deck hard with both feet.

"I'm not sure what they're going to do," Arnold Evans, the elder of the two lookouts said, nodding at both Fleet and Lee. "She's starting to list. I'm sure you can feel it."

"Yes, yes, of course. It feels better up there in the nest, but no doubt about it, on deck here, it's apparent we got an issue," Lee told them.

The four men looked at each other, worry flitting eye to eye. As if on cue, they shook their heads with concern. Arnold Evans reached over and patted Fleet on the shoulder without saying another word. He didn't need to. By now all four of them knew who would bear the blame for the accident, even if the accusation was quite unfair.

Lee grabbed Fleet's arm and urged him to follow his lead. "Let's go down to the deck and see what's happening."

They took the stairs at a fast clip and surveyed the scene.

A small crowd of passengers had formed, and others climbed the steps from the lower deck. They milled about, talking in hushed voices, either out of disbelief, or an unwillingness to accept the possibility that anything serious could be wrong with the ship, or a combination of all of this.

"Women, women and children only, into the boats, come this way. The only men in the boats will be crew manning the oars." The loud, authoritative voice of Second Officer Lightoller indicated the change of mood on the ship, but only slightly. He made it sound like it was just a drill, and for safety's sake, they must do as they were told, no questions asked.

Fred had wondered why they hadn't had a lifeboat drill, he couldn't recall a sailing when this had been skipped. Fleet knew the danger was real. But the passengers didn't.

In the background, mixed in with all the voices, a band played, and the sound of violins filled the air. It lent an unreal atmosphere to the scene unfolding around them. It sounded like a party was afoot instead of a crisis unfolding.

"Sir, no, you cannot get in this boat. You have to wait." Officer Lightoller put his arm on the shoulder of a heavyset young man trying to climb into a lifeboat with his wife.

"But we are just married, two weeks ago. We can't be separated. My wife needs me."

"You can't break the rules, sir. Step out, now. You must wait until later."

The woman was sobbing and shaking, and her husband put his arms around her, trying to give comfort. "Nigel," she begged, "I'm afraid. I really need you, surely you know that. Please, come!"

"I mean it, out now! You are holding everyone else up." Lightoller had lost patience and reached over to pull the man from the boat, but finally the young man did as he was told. His wife grabbed for him as he backed away.

Her tears and cries upset Fleet, but there was nothing to be done. Other passengers gathered about the lifeboat as husbands bid farewell to wives. Their sobs mixed with the music of the violins in a heartbreaking symphony.

"I'll get on the next boat once they start loading the men. Don't worry, I'll see you soon," were oft repeated phrases, although none of them really knew how many boats were available. Were there enough for all the passengers? Most likely, there weren't. But that information wasn't shared.

An elderly couple approached the loading spot. They stood together and watched, as women and children were assisted as they climbed over the side and entered the lifeboats.

"Mr. Straus, sir, due to your age, it is perfectly acceptable for you to enter the boat with your wife," the officer said. "Come, give me your arm. Madam, sir, right this way. I will assist you."

"But the other men are not allowed into the boat?" the old gentleman asked. It was obvious from his voice that he was of the upper classes and was most likely used to receiving preferential treatment.

"No, sir, no they are not. The boats are designated 'women and children only,' but you are so much older, so no problem. Please come on board."

"No, I can't do that. If I did, I'd be taking a place from a woman, or heaven forbid, a child. I would never do that." His voice indicated there was no chance he would change his mind.

"Then, madam, come with me, and I will assist *you* into the boat." The officer reached for her elbow in a kindly gesture.

But she shook her head. "We've never been separated in the fifty-five years we've been married. That has to count for something. I can't get in the boat without him. My place is at my husband's side."

"But you must, madam."

"No, you are very kind, but I'm not going. That's it. I'm staying here, next to my husband, come what may." And she meant it. A finely dressed woman, with elaborately arranged snow-white hair and a velvet nightdress, she planted her feet just so, raised her chin, and took a deep breath.

Watching her, Fleet wondered if she was searching more for courage than oxygen as she drew another deep breath and fixed her eyes on her husband.

"Who are they?" Fred asked a man standing next to him.

"Don't you know? He's the owner of the Macy's department store in New York. They are very upper crust society," came the reply.

"And they are both choosing to stay on the ship?" Fred asked. "Never mind being rich, they are extraordinary people." He shook his head in amazement.

Mrs. Straus's solidarity produced a different response in quite a few of the women already seated in the lifeboat. After all, most had chosen flight and rescue rather than unquestioned loyalty and the unknown. A few of them fussed nervously and patted their hair. One pretty little thing with long, black hair swiped at her cheek as the tears started to fall, but it seemed she could not look at the man standing alone on the deck. No one changed positions, and the boat was declared ready to depart down the side of the ship. No further goodbyes were spoken. There was no need.

Lee and Fleet assisted with the loading of boats. Finally, Officer Lightoller, nicknamed "Lights" by the crew, came over to Reginald Lee. He led him to a boat and pointed, indicating that Lee should climb in. He did as he was told, all the while looking at Fred.

Lightoller pointed at Fleet. "I want you in the next boat, lifeboat number six. You are young and strong, an able seaman. These ladies need your help. Get in now, and row."

Fleet was instantly embarrassed that he and Lee had been singled out, although he knew the man spoke the truth. No way could these fragile ladies navigate the open sea in a flimsy wooden boat. He climbed in, along with another crewman and prepared to do his job. He looked to the boat with Reg. There was no time to say goodbye. He would see him soon.

Fleet's boat started its shaky descent down the side of the vessel; it slid down ropes, called "falls," that seemed highly suspect to carry their full load. The women moaned and fretted, reaching out and grabbing on to one another in fear.

"We should have stayed on board! This is much worse!"

A woman screamed as the lifeboat swayed precariously, catching for a moment then proceeding with a sudden jerky thrust as it plunged to the sea sixty feet below. All the women in the boat were terrified.

"We should have stayed on *Titanic*! This is crazy," was a cry echoed by several of the ladies who held hands, tears falling down their frozen faces.

Now they were surrounded by other boats, some full to capacity, others strangely half empty. Then, all at once, they saw people jumping from the vessel and hitting the water all around them. The scene quickly turned to chaos, and the sound of the night changed, from calm starlit perfection and the music of violins to the vague uncertainty and disbelief on deck as the boats were loaded, to this: sheer pandemonium in the water as those floating in lifejackets experienced the bite of the frigid ocean. Reality struck, as they realized salvation would never come from a floating device that kept their bodies submerged in an ice bath.

"I'm in charge here. Row as fast as you can mates." It was Hichens, the helmsman who'd tried unsuccessfully to steer clear of the iceberg. He manned the tiller and yelled at Fleet and the other man at the oars, a Canadian with a yachting background and seagoing credentials assigned to their boat at the last moment. "We need to get away from the ship as fast as we can."

"But why?" Fleet asked.

"When she goes down, think of the wake," the man said. "We'll be sucked under! Have you no sense of the sea?"

"She's not going down," Fleet screamed back, over the sound of the water and the night. "She's hardly taking on water." At this moment he couldn't accept what was happening. It was too awful.

Hichens yelled at Fred, "Shows what you know! The bulkheads are filling fast. I heard it on good authority."

The women cried and moaned even louder, except for one. She stood, leaving the other women passengers in their crouched position.

"Then we must go back!" she yelled. "We have some room here. Surely we can stuff a few others in the boat. We must pick them up! Look at those people! Can't you hear them? They are screaming for their lives! We can't just let them die!"

Fleet did a quick count of heads in their boat. It was obvious to him even before he was done, there was indeed room for several more passengers, but he said nothing. He didn't wish to antagonize Hichens. The man seemed out of control, near hysteria. Fred couldn't see how he might change his mind. Besides, maybe they were all wrong in their assessment of the situation. A rescue ship could be here quite soon. They were in a busy shipping lane. There must be several vessels in the area.

Hichens echoed his sentiments. "Rescue ships will come," he told her. "As for us, right here, we have no choice, madam. We can't pick them up. We are not going back. Those people are mad out there, they will swamp the boat and drown the lot of us. I refuse to let that happen.

Besides, just who do you think you are? I'm in charge of this boat, not you."

"My name is Margaret Brown, and you don't deserve to be in charge of this boat or any boat. None of you crew members deserve anything at this point. Who got us into this predicament in the first place? The crew! Actually, I put the blame squarely on the lookout. This is all his fault. I swear, if I ever lay eyes and get my hands on that man! What's the use of a lookout if he can't spot a huge thing like an iceberg? What was he doing anyway? Playing cards, or napping? I hope he's the first one on the bottom of the sea tonight. Serves him right."

Fleet was silent. He knew without a doubt, just as he'd predicted, his fate was sealed. Soon enough, everyone would attach his face to his name and his name to the portside lookout, the man everyone would blame for the collision. And his earlier ice warnings would never be acknowledged. He had no status; White Star was in charge. After the collision, who would ever believe him? He could prove nothing. He might not be on the bottom of the North Atlantic, but for the rest of his years, he might wish he was. Most important of all, he had to cover up the time lag before he rang the bell.

Just then, Margaret Brown reached over and, determined as she was to go back and rescue some of the screaming people, attempted to take the oars from the man rowing across from Fleet. A struggle ensued, and the boat rocked back and forth in a most precarious manner.

Fleet was having none of this. He placed his oars in the bottom of the boat and stood up to go to his mate's assistance, lest they be capsized by this ridiculous woman. There was a general state of calamity in the boat. People were screaming. Just as he reached over to grab her arms and subdue her, he saw, not thirty feet away in the water, a very fine lady. That was the only way to describe her. Wearing an emerald-green evening dress and a lifebelt, with a huge diamond necklace trailing what looked like seaweed around her neck, her long red hair floated atop the water. The starlight twinkled off her necklace, and her eyes caught Fred's as she choked on the water lapping at her chin. She called out, begging for mercy.

"Please." She spoke just the one word. They stared at each other for a moment as if they were the only two people in the world. In that split second, Fleet felt the transfer of responsibility for her life shift to him. He was her only hope. She lifted her arms and reached toward him, the sleeves of her gown dripping ocean from the lace trim.

"Save me! Please! Don't leave me here. I'll die, it's so cold, and I must find him —" The rocking of their boat sent a wavelet that washed over her head. She sputtered and choked. "Don't leave me."

Behind her, a mob of men swam about, desperate cries coming from their frozen lips. A few of them looked up at Fred, hoping he would wave them over to the lifeboat.

But again, Hichens was having none of it. He saw the men swimming toward them. He yelled out as a crazed man, "Move ahead! Row now, mates. Go as fast as you can. These are your direct orders. Row away from those men. I forbid you to stop. See that steamer out there, with all the lights on?" He reached out and pointed at a brightly lit ship, maybe ten miles away. "We are to head over there, that was our assignment, from the bridge, from Murdoch himself. She isn't very far. If we stop and pick up anyone, they will all surround our boat, we'll be capsized and that won't do us any good. Move on now."

Hichens's tone of voice left no room for compromise. Besides, Fleet couldn't bring himself to call attention to his identity. What if Hichens asked, "Who are you to tell me what to do? Just who are you anyway? What? You're the lookout? The very one that got us into this pickle."

Fleet followed orders and rowed, but his thoughts were elsewhere. It seemed as if none of the others had seen the emerald lady in that moment before their boat moved on, leaving her to her fate in the sea.

If Hichens had seen her, how could he insist they not pick up just one person? She was so close to their boat, compared to the others. For a second, Fleet even questioned himself if she had really been there at all, struggling to stay alive in the icy water, looking at him and begging him to save her. Perhaps she was a vision, meant to cement his guilt in the events unfolding that night. But then he remembered the pull of her eyes, and the connection they had made with his soul, and he knew she was real, that her very being would live inside him for the rest of his life. He had failed her, and his guilt would stretch on, wherever he might be, content in the subtle sweetness of the new day and any dreams he kept for his life. But he had no dreams for anything, and he certainly deserved less than nothing.

Hichens pointed at the ship near the horizon. "Look, look over there."

They could see more of her bright lights. They could almost make out people on the deck. She was quite large. "She must be what, seven miles away? She will be here in plenty of time to pick up these people from the sea, and the rest of them left on board as well. They will take us on board too. Everything looks good, mates!"

The Canadian pointed. "Look, our ship is sending up white rockets, the universal distress signal. I'm sure the rescue ship will be here in no time! Let's take a rest right now. Hold back, mate. Stop rowing."

Fleet didn't say a word. His hands continued to work the oars in a methodical motion; he'd turned himself into a rowing machine to keep his thoughts at bay. He was lost in the sea with the woman, there was no getting away from it, even as his hands worked to move the small boat away from her.

The Canadian yelled at him, "You there. I said stop rowing! Aren't you paying attention?"

Fleet stopped and let his arms rest, still holding the oars, catching his breath, and surveying the scene. But as he watched, the *Titanic* listed more drastically. Obviously, she was taking on much more water, and filling the bulkheads faster than anyone had imagined as they'd left the vessel. That was the only thing that made sense. The officers, and daresay the captain, had underestimated the damage. It was the only explanation he could come up with because the senior officers had been relatively calm when they loaded the lifeboats. They'd never insisted that anyone climb into a boat. It was left as a matter of choice.

Why would they allow that elderly lady to remain on board with her husband if they knew there was no hope for her survival and the ship was going down? Fleet couldn't get this thought out of his head. Or, had they known the truth, and they were just trying to avert widespread panic? Especially since there wasn't room to rescue everyone. If only they had carried enough lifeboats for everyone on board, but they had not. It wasn't required.

An older woman, with grey hair and a heavy winter coat cut into his thoughts as she pointed toward *Titanic*. "Look there! She's slipping! She really might sink! That rescue ship had better move fast! But, look at it, look at the steamer. Why, she doesn't seem as if she's moving toward us at all! We can't last in this tiny boat out here. We are doomed!" She pulled her hands back and started praying. Tears ran down her wrinkled face.

"That is strange," a woman seated near Fleet said. Her voice lacked all emotion. Most likely, she was in shock. Then tears poured down her face. She pulled her coat around her tightly. A little girl escaped from her safe place under the coat.

"Mummy, I want to see the ship! What's happening? It's going down, isn't it? And Father is still on the ship, isn't he?" She started to scream. Her mother patted at her. She was unable to comfort the child properly.

But then, as they are wont to do, boys being boys, another scene played out. A boy of about eight years was showing his brother a small chunk of ice. He had taken it from the deck, a piece of the iceberg itself.

"What do you have there?" the older brother asked him. "What is it? I want to see. Show me."

"I can't show you. It's mine," the eight-year-old responded.

"I see what you got there. It's a piece of ice, isn't it? Where did you get it?"

"From the deck. It's part of that thing that hit the ship. But it's mine, you can't have it."

"Neither can you, silly. It's going to melt in a minute."

"No, it's not. I want it." A moment later, he said, "You don't really think it will melt, do you? I'll have nothing left of our time on the big ship."

"You boys stop this bickering," their mother said. "There's so much loss tonight. Just be glad you're in this dry boat. Stop your fussing."

Many of the children hadn't taken their predicament on the high seas seriously until now. After all, how could they imagine an event such as this? If anything, it had seemed a great adventure. Now, several of them sobbed quietly and clutched at their mothers. But the little one, the youngest girl, cried the loudest and would not be consoled.

"It's going down, isn't it? And Father, he's still..."

"I'm sure Father jumped from the ship Elizabeth," her mother told her. "He must have. They will pick him up very soon."

"But they told him he should wait on board, they would have other boats for the men, for the fathers. But they don't, do they? It was a lie, wasn't it? Why would they tell my father a lie? He'll die. I'll never see him again."

"Shhh, shhh, you poor sweet girl. You must stop. We will see him again. He'll be fine. Really, he will."

But no one believed her, and certainly not the little girl she sought to comfort. The child's sobs continued, and the cold wind picked up, stinging their faces and robbing them all of any expectations they might have. The most beautiful ship in the world appeared to be sinking.

Things got worse in the next moments. It was growing exceedingly obvious that the closest ship, the one they were sure would save them, moved slowly in the opposite direction, until that brightly lit beacon of hope slipped below the horizon. A few puffs of black smoke remained in its place. The rescue ship was gone, carrying with it all their hopes and whispered prayers, never sensing the burden it bore.

Chapter 4

Just a little while earlier, back on the ship, Matthew's nanny had pulled the boy up to the boat deck, scooting the two of them to safety. Their lifeboat was in the water, just pulling away from the ship. In his fear and excitement, Matthew accidentally dropped the teddy over the edge of their boat.

When he leaned over, grabbing for his bear, he lost his footing and slipped into the sea.

The nanny screamed. She couldn't stop screaming.

Two crewmembers rushed to assist her, but to no avail. The boy had vanished. Matthew was trapped under the lifeboat, clutching his precious teddy, as he and the bear slipped deep into the cold water.

***

The ocean hungered for its next victim. *Titanic* dipped to almost below the water line. The screams in the cold night air escalated to a new pitch. The women in the lifeboat yelled and pointed, Margaret Brown being the loudest.

"That settles it," Margaret Brown's booming voice rang out. It was obvious she had zero trust in Hichens' ability to make a logical decision. "We must go back and pick up some of those people right now. There are even more of them, floating in their lifebelts. How can you hear them screaming like that and choose to ignore them?"

"Madam, I am not ignoring anyone," he replied, "but I am trying to save your life, and the lives of all these other women and poor little children in this lifeboat tonight."

"And maybe, most of all, you are trying to save your own life," she suggested.

"That's enough out of you. You, over there," he pointed at Fleet, "keep that woman quiet."

"Sir, I'm not sure how I can do that," Fleet answered. As he spoke, he wondered if there was truth to the woman's words. Was Hichens looking out for his own well-being as his first priority? Fleet knew that was the exact opposite of the path any crew member should ever take. But then he wondered what he himself was trying to do. Would he willingly die right now, if in doing so he might save any of the others? Could he have traded his life for the woman in the water?

"Well, you better think of something," Hichens chided him. "If she doesn't shut up, I'll toss her over, and then maybe we can go back and pick up a woman from the sea, someone more deserving and easier to deal with."

"I can't believe what I just heard." Margaret Brown was clearly angry, but in spite of that, the sting of Hichens' words caused her to sit down and be quiet. It seemed the inhabitants of the boat were finally settling into their collective situation. An amalgam of patience and hope was the only course to take. The children were quiet, the adults lost in their own thoughts and prayers. And everyone was freezing cold, colder than they could ever imagine.

***

Right after the ship struck the berg, and on the side opposite where Fleet had loaded lifeboats, Cybil Stuart had missed her chance for a seat in a boat. She and many of the other passengers believed the ship would never sink, so they had been in no hurry to leave the warmth of the vessel. Besides, Cybil would never leave without Matthew.

She'd let the others find themselves a place in a boat; she needed to return below decks to her cabin to carry the boy to safety, if need be.

However, the mass of passengers on the stairway moved up, not down. She struggled and pushed, trying to get downstairs. She had to get to Matthew. But it was impossible to breach the crowd.

Eventually, she realized her efforts were useless. Tears poured down her face. What was about to happen to Matthew? Where was he?

By the time she returned to the deck, all the lifeboats were gone. Cybil stood at the rail, looking down at the water, frozen in place, trying to decide what to do.

The screams around her increased, filling her ears with the horrendous sound.

A wave crested over the railing, smashing against her and knocking her overboard.

Even as she flew through the air, her thoughts were of her little boy. Where was he? She smashed into the icy water, coughing and gasping for air as she surfaced again. Panicked, looking in all directions—for a lifeboat, for her Matthew. Which lifeboat was he in? She flailed about in the near-frozen water, trying to grab onto anything that floated by to help buoy her.

Something there, just within reach.

A teddy.

It looked like Matthew's. *But don't all stuffed bears look alike? Is Matthew in a boat?*

***

Now, every head in Fleet's lifeboat, and probably every other lifeboat as well, turned toward the great vessel as the passengers still aboard went into full panic mode, the screams echoing across the water. *Titanic* tilted at an unbelievable angle, with the stern pointed straight up into the sky. Many jumped from the ship. One after another, they leaped or fell into the frigid waters as those in the lifeboats watched in sheer horror.

Under that glittering star-filled sky, the last of the RMS *Titanic*, the ship that couldn't sink, slipped under the waters of the greedy North Atlantic, as the sea sucked up all the lives left on board. Men, women and children of all ages, dogs even. The violins that provided the music, the hands that touched their strings, the silver platters, the crystal goblets, and everything that had carried so many dreams across the sea, was no more. Just like that, the space *Titanic* had occupied, was empty. It seemed impossible.

"That's it, we're going back. Right now." Margaret Brown tossed her blanket to the bottom of the boat and stood up again. "If you don't turn around," she gestured with her arms to illustrate to Hichens just what she expected him to do, "and rescue some of those people in the water, everyone on this boat will know you are a coward. If you don't turn back, I'll throw you over the side!"

It was a do-or-die moment. Hichens searched the faces of his passengers. Most either wouldn't meet his eye or gave a small nod indicating they agreed with the woman. "If you are so strongly in favor of this, then you will help the men row. Mrs. Brown, you're a big strong woman. Show us you really mean it. Start rowing. Give one of those men some relief, they've grown tired and they're slowing down."

Margaret Brown stepped through the boat and stood in front of Fleet, extending her hands.

"Give me those oars. Let me row, you've been rowing long enough. You are holding us back. I should have been in charge of this boat all along. You men are worthless."

Fred didn't say a word as he handed her the oars. All he could think was, heaven forbid if she finds out I'm the guilty lookout. She would toss me into the sea, no doubt about it. She was big enough. She probably could—and would.

Once she was seated and about to begin, she pointed at another woman and told her she would row as well. Soon, Mrs. Brown had things organized and, with a subdued Hichens at the tiller, they turned the boat around and headed back toward what was left of the passengers, a desperate, bedraggled sea of humanity flailing about and screaming in the dark water.

The women rowed as fast and as hard as they could. Precious minutes slipped by. At last, they were close enough to make out the faces of a few people in the water just ahead. The screams had lessened. However, in the time it took them to reach the nearest ones, they had all succumbed to hypothermia. None of them were alive, not a single one. Others still screamed. It became apparent they were all too far away. By the time lifeboat number six might reach them, there would be nothing left to save. And if they tried to pull the water-soaked bodies from the sea, they might very well capsize their own boat, and to what end?

"They are a bunch of stiffs, just as I suspected," Hichens said. "I'm afraid there's nothing to be done here. Do you agree, Mrs. Brown?" He'd regained his surly personality, that was obvious.

"Unfortunately, I do," was her reply. She spoke in a quiet voice, but her eyes blamed him all the same.

"We are heading for the *Carpathia*," Hichens announced. "That's our destination since that other ship refused to come pick us up. C'mon, let's turn this boat around right now."

"*Carpathia*? How far out is she?" Fleet asked.

"About fifty miles," Hichens said. "And she'll be heading this way, fast as she can, top speed. We'll meet up with her eventually. Do as I say, row hard, and have faith. Don't give up."

Lifeboat number six, with Fleet and the others aboard, moved into the dark night. Soon, they spotted another lifeboat moving in the same direction. It had the benefit of a small, green light on board. Their attention, and that of other boats in the vicinity, was caught by the light, and they followed its lead.

As they drew closer to the first boat, the sound of singing drifted across the water. Each of the passengers in boat number six instantly recognized the hymn. Their mouths opened as one person, and they joined in *Amazing Grace.*

Fleet found himself singing along with the rest. He could hardly believe it as the words sprang from his mouth without permission. He had never been a man of strong faith. It went with the territory of being a waif.

At the orphanage, he'd been told his mother had taken him to church to be baptized as a newborn babe. Did that mean she cared about what happened to him? Or was she leaving him in God's hands because she wanted nothing more to do with him?

His voice was joined to Hichens and the Canadian's and the children's and the Brown woman as well, as they sang each and every verse. Orphanage lads were required to attend chapel. The words were buried in his memory. He followed the others when he was unsure of the words. But when they reached the part, *when we've been there 10,000 years,* his voice stumbled and instead he sang, *when we've been dead 10,000 years.*

He wondered, *Will I die tonight? Will we all die? Despite the flimsy little boats supposedly carrying us to safety? Was it possible?*

The thought had never occurred to him, not really, until this moment. His years at sea had stood as a barrier to that possibility. But the exhaustion overpowered him. His will to live grew thin, thinner than it had ever been. But then he thought of the title of the old hymn, and he told himself, because he wanted to believe it more than anything, God's grace *is* amazing, even to a worthless wretch named Frederick Fleet, unloved and unwanted by the world.

And so he sang louder, and stronger, and he realized he wanted to live more than he ever had before. The very real risk of losing his life this night had made it all the more precious to him. The dark shapes of people in the other boats sang as well. Soon the voices took up other hymns.

They passed the time in this manner, until at last, lack of sleep, lack of water to drink, or food to eat, stole the words from their mouths. Silence swept over the huddled, freezing cold occupants of the line of lifeboats moving across the sea. The only sound was the restless North Atlantic wind and the rhythmic slap of oars. Too quiet to be heard was the beating of so many hearts, as their fate remained uncertain.

Through the night and early morning, the rowers made their way around many chunks of ice referred to as growlers, but, for the most part, the people were too tired to notice.

When the first hint of dawn broke, tentative apricot rays of the rising sun glinted off large icebergs scattered all around them. Five hours into their journey, the weary, but lucky lifeboat passengers made their way onto the *Carpathia*. Rope ladders were lowered, and those able to climb the ladders entered the ship through an open hatch. For the children, this was an impossible feat to perform, so they were placed into mail sacks and wrapped in a baggage net and hoisted up from the sea.

All of them reached the deck with legs too stiff to move, and feet too cramped to take another step, but climb aboard they did. Numb to the comforts of life on a warm and secure vessel, they moved in a line and did as they were told. They were oblivious to the stares and scattered applause of the *Carpathia's* passengers as they made their way into a large reception room just off the upper deck.

The officers had spent the last hours preparing for the arrival of the survivors. Now they offered creature comforts to relieve their distress. The horrors of their experience would not be lightly shed, but the new arrivals were quiet and demanded nothing, too weak to make requests.

One elderly woman knelt to the floor. Before anyone could reach her to offer assistance, she leaned over and kissed the deck as she bowed her head in prayer.

"Amen," intoned another woman.

Her prayer complete, the kneeling woman was too exhausted and emotionally overcome to stand up. One of the stewards gently lifted her to her feet.

Once they gathered and sat in comfortable chairs, the crew brought warm beverages. At first, most of the people declined any food, but they did welcome a hot coffee.

Finally, they were ready to eat some of the offerings. A few of the mothers sobbed quietly, hugging their children tightly to them. No doubt more than a few were thinking of a husband left behind on the ill-fated vessel. They had no way of knowing if they might see them again, once *Carpathia* came into port. There was still time for a prayer that another ship had secured their rescue. Even though this seemed very unlikely, these palpable possibilities claimed a space in all their hearts. Hope was hard to extinguish, even and perhaps especially, in the worst of times. And love was impossible to abandon, no matter the circumstances. Even the deep, cold waters could not wrestle those emotions from these bedraggled souls.

Once the survivors were restored a bit, through the drinks and food and the safety of a seat that wasn't in a flimsy boat, they were ushered below to rooms that had been prepared for them. There wasn't space for all, so some stayed in the saloon and were not displeased in the least. Warm, dry clothing and blankets were distributed.

The expression on their weary faces spoke of a long journey and the shock that such an event could have happened to them. Not to someone else. Not to other people they might read about in a newspaper and whisper a prayer for as they sat down to dinner in their warm homes and tucked their children in at night.

Frederick Fleet was one of those left to find his comfort in the saloon. Most of these were men, and some younger women who, at this point, were traveling alone. All of the chairs were occupied, so Fleet reclined on the floor with one wool blanket wrapped around his body, another tucked under his head. He had stuffed his frozen hands in his pockets.

At first, none of the people looked at each other or spoke a word. As the cold seeped out of their veins, they developed some unspoken sense of comradery, having endured the unimaginable together. A few spoke up at last and asked after their companions' comfort.

"I can't believe my husband. I can't believe he actually stayed on board as she went down. He must have jumped. He must be here somewhere." The woman seated nearest Fleet whispered to a lady in a chair on her other side, but Fleet couldn't help but hear her words.

He wondered why she whispered. Everyone here had been through the same experience. There were no secrets except his own. No one knew he was to blame for the whole thing. He looked around the room cautiously to see if anyone stared at him, but no one did. Many of the survivors had found someone seated close by to offer comfort to or be comforted by. He seemed to be the only one who remained on his own.

"Oh yes, you will see him very soon, I would be willing to bet on it," responded the second woman.

"He could have climbed into another lifeboat later on. And surely some boats were pulling people from the water. Please, tell me you think that's possible. Not just possible, but it's true. That's what he did. I'm sure he did. I can't lose my Christopher."

Hearing her words, Fleet thought of his own wife, who eagerly awaited his return in their tiny, rented rooms back in Southampton.

"Give me an extra kiss, Fred. I need one," Eva had begged him as he'd opened the door to the fresh morning breeze ten days previously. He was already leaving later than he'd planned that morning.

"Why is that m' love?" he'd asked as he turned back to face her. "You've never said that before."

"I know, but suddenly, there's a shadow on my heart. I'm worried about you. I can't make it without you."

"Well, 'ere's your kiss, but don't worry about me, lass. I told you when we married, you can't be a seaman's wife and let yerself think of anything but the supper you'll cook when I return, and the kiss you will give me then. Remember?" He leaned over and wrapped her in his arms and kissed her, longer and with more intensity than he had just a few moments ago. After the kiss ended, he'd kept his arms around Eva and leaned back and looked at her. Tears gathered in her eyes.

"Yes, I do remember," she told him, "But you aren't the one left behind. And somehow, this time, I'm feeling so lost and alone as I watch you open that door."

"Well, you aren't lost and alone, so don't feel that way. I'll be back soon, never fear. I'm off now, love." And he was gone, striding down the cobblestone road that dipped into a steep hill as it led to the waterfront. The overcast sky held a raw feeling to the morning air. The gulls swooped low over the street and called out. Their unrelenting caws almost sounded like a distress signal. He tried to ignore them. He tried to think of the voyage before him, but soon realized it was no use. His heart was back in the little kitchen with Eva. And he knew that she would have an impossible task making her way without him, if the unthinkable were to happen and he never came back. To his surprise, tears stung his own eyes. This had never happened before.

Reluctantly, he tucked away that vision of Eva, as once again his attention was captured by the conversation of the two ladies seated near him, as the lady closest to him spoke again.

"But you didn't see any survivors pulled from the sea by the people in the other lifeboats, did you?" Doubt and hope filled her voice at the same time, if such a thing were possible.

"No, I didn't. No wait, I take that back. I'm just not sure what I saw. It was all so confusing and hard to accept that any of that was really happening. It still is. We aren't sure, but we still have hope, don't we? We have to cling to that. How can we live these next days until we arrive in New York, if we abandon our hope?"

"How indeed?" responded the other.

And for Fleet too, he knew he needed to hold on to the possibility that the lady in the emerald dress, the one he had ignored, was somehow rescued and on this boat somewhere right this minute. Well, he hadn't actually ignored her, it might be easier if he hadn't locked eyes with her and then offered nothing in return. If she was alive, somehow it eased his guilt for the whole thing, seeing the iceberg too late, and then, the bloodcurdling screams of all the people he couldn't help. They couldn't have been saved, but that did nothing to lessen his grief. If only he could be certain that this one woman had survived, somehow that would ease his anguish.

He scrunched down lower in his blanket and pulled the top edge to his chin. It helped hide him from his companions, but it did nothing to relieve his guilt. Guilt caused the chill that swept through his body, not the cold night air. He was lying in a warm and pleasant room. Soon his eyes grew heavy and in a quasi-sleep, caught up in a sudden, vivid dream, he imagined the emerald lady walking into the saloon here, on the *Carpathia*, and spotting him at once. What would he say to her? His eyes flew open in distress, but she wasn't there.

After they had rested and eaten a bit of food, Mrs. Brown walked about, calling all of the survivors to a meeting. Fleet didn't want to go, and he was relieved when she specified she only wanted the surviving passengers, not crew members, to join her. The room nearly emptied in a few minutes.

"No telling what that woman is up to. Maybe she'll whip them all into a frenzy, so they can blame us before there's any investigation whatsoever."

Fleet didn't recognize the man who spoke, but he definitely agreed with his comments, and his words brought new worry to the lookout.

"Investigation? I hadn't thought about that." Despite his years at sea, Fleet was naive to the ways of the world. He had been on board an ocean-going ship, first swabbing the decks, and then working his way up to the rank of able seaman, since he was a lad of sixteen. But he had never known anything of formal investigations or trouble on board.

"There's bound to be a huge investigation. I'm guessing we'll all have to answer questions, or at least those of us who were involved with the ship hitting the berg. Were you involved?"

Fleet was speechless for a moment; it was like he had lost the ability to move his lips.

"Well, yes. Yes, I was. I'm the lookout, I spotted the berg. But please, please don't tell anyone. Not here, not now. Especially that Brown woman. What's your name? Who are you?"

"George, George Taylor, a steward I am, or was. And no, I won't say anything to anyone. It's not my place to do that. But tell me, when did you see it? The berg, how big was it?"

"I really don't want to talk about it. Please. I'm so confused now. I wasn't confused then, when I spotted it. I did the best I could, without binoculars. Never mind that, I really don't want to talk about it at all."

"Wait a minute… you didn't have binoculars? How did that happen?"

"I don't know where they went," he said in a quiet voice. He didn't want to draw attention to his words. "We had them for the first leg of the trip, but then, once we left Southampton, they weren't available."

"Whatever you say. What did you call yourself? Who are you? I don't think you told me your name."

"Fleet, Frederick Fleet, able seaman and lookout, until last night." Fleet looked down at his shaking hands. He stuck them back in his pockets. He stared at the ground.

"You're really scared, aren't you? Look, we're safe now. You have nothing to worry about. You did your job." George seemed genuinely concerned.

Something in his voice made Fred look up at him again. The man's eyes held kindness, something he'd known little of in his life.

"Can I tell you something?" Fred asked. "Something I'm not sure I should say? I can only tell you if you promise me, on your mum's grave and anything else you hold dear, that you'll never say a word to anyone."

"Of course you can tell me. On a night like this, special bonds are formed, don't you think? I won't betray you. You can tell me anything." It sounded like he really meant it.

"Well, it's this," Fred whispered. "The iceberg that sunk the ship? It wasn't the first I spotted this night."

"What? What do you mean?"

"I saw three others, far off, and I smelled ice. And I called down to the bridge. And here's the thing. They ignored my calls."

"How can that be?" George asked, his voice raised in surprise, shaking his head.

Fred lifted his hand, urging him to be quiet. "When I call down to the bridge, they don't have to respond. They might listen and hang up with no reply. That's the rule of the ship. I mean, I can't force them to answer me. So, I have no idea why they didn't say a single word. And I can't force them to do anything about my warnings. They just kept the ship going along as fast as it was. But when questions are asked, I'm not sure what to say. I want to tell the truth. I have to. But I'll be in big trouble with White Star if I do. And then there's this. Everyone is ready to blame me for not seeing the last iceberg in time. So, I lose either way. If I snitch on them 'cause they ignored the other three, White Star fires my ass, and if I don't, everyone assumes I'm a bad lookout and caused the wreck. But, I think I must tell about the early ice. I have to save my reputation, and besides, it's the truth."

"Well, I'm sure all will be fine when you testify."

"Testify? You mean, like swear on a Bible or something?"

"I guess that's the way it will work, but I'm not sure."

"I have no bloody idea what's going to happen to me." Fred shook his head and couldn't look the man in the eye.

A fuss in the room caught everyone's attention when a man's voice spoke out, momentarily distracting Fred from his fears.

"Crew? Any members of the *Titanic* crew in here?" Fleet barely recognized Second Officer Lightoller as he strode into the saloon. It was obvious the man had had an extremely rough time of it before ending up aboard *Carpathia*. "All of you need to come with me, right now."

"Here we go, this is just the beginning," George said to the room at large as he pulled himself up from the floor.

Fred stood up, his movements slowed by a feeling of impending doom. His joints were stiff from lying on the floor so long.

His mind switched back to Eva. How would he ever explain to her the role he'd played this sorry night? What would she think of him? There was no telling how much time would pass before he was home again. Between this moment and that, the news would surely carry his name as the lookout. What would Eva think before he was able to stand in front of her and explain exactly what it was like, being ignored in his early warnings, and then, that moment when he first spotted the final smudge on the horizon? Would she judge him before he had a chance to explain himself?

They were all crowded into a room that looked like a smoking room next to a small bar. Again, there weren't enough seats, and Fleet ended up perching on his haunches on the floor. He chose a corner spot where he hoped to remain less noticeable, even though he knew that would be impossible as soon as the meeting, or whatever it was, began. Lights would be looking for him.

Lightoller cleared his throat. "Listen up, men. What I am about to share with you is very important. Do you hear me?" Without waiting for a response from the thirty or so men gathered about, he continued. "I have an official notice for you, from White Star Line. Since it seems I am the highest-ranking officer to survive, and that only because I jumped at the last minute and ended up on an overturned collapsible, I am giving you these orders directly from Mr. Bruce Ismay himself. And his official order is this, short and sweet: Do not talk to anyone about what happened before, during, and after she hit the iceberg, even among yourselves. No gossip. I can't stress that strongly enough. As we journey on to New York, you will be surrounded by the surviving passengers. They will ask you questions, of course they will, and once we get to New York, as we leave *Carpathia*, we will be surrounded by the public, and by the press, the newspaper men. You are not to talk to any of them. Am I making myself clear?" There was no response. He repeated his question.

"Am I making myself clear?" he shouted. "You are to say nothing to anyone."

"Yes, sir," came back at him from each of the men gathered about.

"There will be an investigation, as you can well imagine. How soon it will begin, I cannot tell you at this moment. But those of you directly involved will stay in New York. We will inform your families that you have survived. We will provide lodgings for you, and you will wait there, silently. Remember, you are employees of White Star and so you will do precisely what I say. That's the way things work around here. Most of you know that. It's the rule of the sea. Again, give me a 'yes, sir,' so I know you have heard my instructions. There are to be no exceptions."

This time there was no hesitation.

Fleet headed for the door as it seemed they were dismissed. But Lightoller had one more request. "I need each of you to sign this book so I know exactly who survived and who was in this room right now, hearing my instructions. As you can safely assume, you are not the only crew members rescued. The others are scattered about the ship. I will be rounding them up and giving them the same orders. So, queue up and sign your name. If you can't, put an X and get someone to print your name beside it. Next to that, write your job on the *Titanic* so we are sure who is accounted for."

The men formed a line and did as they were instructed, with Lightoller giving each a perfunctory glance as he filed past. But when Fleet's turn came, Lightoller grabbed his shoulder and looked into the young man's face with deep intent.

"Mr. Fleet, you heard what I said, of course. You are not to talk to anyone. Remember that."

"Yes, I heard. I'm not one to disobey orders."

"Better not. Your future depends on it. You are the key to this whole mess." And he glared at him.

Fleet was frozen in place by the man's words and the hostility in his eyes. But finally, he nodded his head in agreement and willed himself to walk away quietly. He imagined that Lightoller would put as heavy a burden on all the others when he spoke to them, but then again, why would he?

Fred also wondered what Reginald Lee would say when he was questioned about those precious moments of the sighting, and then, of the ringing of the warning bell. If they questioned them separately, as he was sure they would, what would Lee say? How would he account for the time it had taken for Fleet to sound the alarm? If their stories didn't match, what then? And then there was the question of Fleet's earlier, ignored warnings. Fleet knew, if and when he mentioned this, White Star would fry him alive. But if he didn't, in the eyes of the world, he was a worthless lookout. Either way, he was in big trouble. He wished he'd never said a word of this to anyone else. Could he trust George Taylor? And where was Lee? He needed him. He hadn't seen Lee on *Carpathia*. Surely, he was here somewhere.

"Well, I guess we can hardly sneeze, can we?" George offered up once they had made their way back into the large saloon and stretched out on the floor again. "Mum's the word, lips sealed. Lights wasn't kidding around."

"Well, we can talk of home, and that kind of thing, I suppose," Fleet responded, anxious to change the subject. "Do you have a wife?"

"Yes, yes, I do. And you?"

"Yes. Eva, that's her name."

"You sound awfully upset just saying her name. Do you get on well? I don't mean to pry, but you raised the subject of wives, and you seem so undone just saying her name."

"I just wonder what she, and all of the crew families, will hear about the wreck before we can make our way home. Who knows how long this investigation will take? And what will the newspapers print, where will they place the blame?"

"Surely your Eva will wait to hear what you have to say, face to face, once you are home."

"I hope she will, but the newspapers can be very persuasive. She's just a simple, sweet girl from Guernsey. She only just moved to Southampton. She's not a city girl, and she's young, only turned twenty just before I left. She doesn't know the ways of the world. And well, here's the thing, her family doesn't like me much. Because I'm not like them, or like anyone."

"What do you mean, you're not like anyone?"

"I have no parents. Me dad was never there. I have no idea who he is, not really. And me mum left me when I was just a babe. She left England and ran off to America. So when Eva and I asked her family to bless our marriage, they said, 'No, we don't know what his roots are. He has none. He's a waif.' But Eva, she didn't listen to them. She ran off with me and we got married anyway. Her family, they really don't like me."

"Well then, your Eva must love you a great deal. You have nothing to worry about."

"I hope she loves me enough to ignore whatever the newspapers, and her family, especially her brother Philip, will say about me. He hates me inside and out. He has it in for me."

"But why should the newspapers say anything bad about you, Fred?"

"I don't know. The thing is, I don't know what they will say about me, or about anything that's happened. But they must place the blame somewhere. And White Star won't want a black eye, that's for sure. White Star's so powerful, and I'm just one man, with no family to speak up for my character."

"That's what the investigation is for, to determine the whole truth."

"We'll see where that leads," Fleet replied, shaking his head. "And there is the question of my earlier warnings. I can't imagine what's going to happen when I mention that business. But remember, I never told you any of that. Let me tell it my way."

Chapter 5

The rest of the voyage on *Carpathia* was like a surreal dream for the surviving *Titanic* passengers and crew alike. They were in a state of grief and mourning and dread, each and every one of them, for varying reasons and degrees. And yet, an undeniable glimmer of hope was suspended on the high seas and traveled with them all as well, as each was unable to believe that every single one of the poor souls left on board the ship, and those in the water screaming in terror, had lost their lives.

It was in this dreamlike, expectant state that they stood on the decks as *Carpathia* entered New York harbor on Saturday, April 18 just after nine o'clock in the evening. Every possible light in the harbor was lit as tugs surrounded the ship and eased her entrance. Sounds of the harbor reached their ears. Soon a flock of other, smaller boats drew near. They contained members of the press who called out questions to those on board, their voices drowning out one another. A few offered sums of money in exchange for news of the tragedy. Others in the boats were families of passengers begging for answers.

"John Becker, have you seen him? Is he on board? Where is the *Titanic*? Is she coming in for repairs?"

"They really don't know anything, do they?" George looked with amazement at the bevy of boats with people on the decks calling up to *Carpathia*. "Couldn't they send a telegraph? Why wouldn't they?" He raised his hands in disbelief.

"The fate is unknown of so many people, what could they say?" Fleet told him. "We won't have a true accounting until we're ashore. But I can't imagine how anyone thinks *Titanic* is coming along behind us." He put his hand to his forehead and paused, as he tried once again, to accept the events of the last days. "I guess there's just a lot of confusion out there," he said quietly.

A little boy, maybe six years old, followed by a slightly older girl, came up behind them and pushed their way to the railings. The boy jumped up and down, pointing to the brightly lit city stretched out before them. "Woooo, just look, Catherine! It's so wonderful, I can hardly wait! Aren't you excited?"

She did a little dance in response, until a hand reached out and stopped her pirouette. A tall woman with a green cape draped over a heavy woolen coat pulled the children close.

"Peter, Catherine, this is not a time to rejoice. You are too young to understand, but one thing you should do is remember this moment. In the years to come, people will ask you about this night. Take this into your hearts, right now, so you can be a camera to history."

"So, we are to be sad now, Mum?" asked the boy. "Why can't we be happy? I am so excited to see all the lights and this city is so big!" He looked like he was about to break loose and jump up and down once again. But his mother's hand on his shoulder subdued him.

His sister spoke up. "Peter, don't you remember the other people, the ones in the water? Don't you remember their screams as the lifeboats moved away from them and then, when the *Titanic* went down? They aren't here with us. Where do you think they are?" She stuck her hand out and pointed toward the water. She didn't give him a chance to answer. "That is why we shouldn't be happy, I guess. I'm sorry I danced. Is it okay if I'm sorry now, Mum?"

"Of course it is Catherine. You are just a child, both of you are too small. You never should have seen any of this." And she drew them close into her cape with one hand as she wiped a tear from her cheek with the other.

Fred watched them even though he felt the intruder on their poignant moment. But he couldn't stop looking at them as he realized that this one small encounter really reflected the entire tragedy that had befallen all of them.

"I feel so bad for these little ones," he told his comrade. "It's so much worse for them."

"What do you mean?" George asked. "Do you mean it's impossible for them to accept what's happened?"

"Well, yes, but the thing is, they are so young, and unlike us, they have so many years ahead of them, years to doubt everything in life. If the *Titanic* could sink, the most marvelous, and unsinkable ship, how can anyone trust anything or anyone ever again?"

"I hadn't thought of it that way."

"Well, I do. That's exactly the way to think of it. Except we don't have as many years left to suffer as little children do. And, in my case at least, I've never trusted anyone, or anything, least of all myself."

"Why would you say that, least of all yourself? That's not a good way to feel, as a lookout for the ship, and for everything else too. You do trust what you saw that night, don't you?"

"I'm just so confused about the other night. I mean, I know what I saw and when I saw it. I guess they wanted their speed record more than anything else. All they were thinkin' of was the time it took *Olympic* to reach New York her first time out. Oh, but if only I could do it all over, better. Anyway, we ain't supposed to talk about this at all, with anyone. I have no doubt Lights's words came straight from the boss, Mr. Ismay himself."

"You had better decide exactly what happened up on that crow's nest before you sit down to answer questions at the investigation. Have you seen your mate anywhere on *Carpathia*? I think the two of you need to talk a bit, get your act together."

"I've been looking for him. I haven't seen him, but I'm sure he made it safe. I mean, I saw him get into a lifeboat. He was assigned to row, just like you and me."

"But we don't know if all the lifeboats made it, do we?"

"No, we don't. I ain't thought of that, until now. I need Reg to be here. He can back me story up, no matter what. I'm counting on him."

"Counting on me, are you?" Reginald Lee appeared out of the shifting fog on the deck.

"Where have you been?" Fleet asked. His voice had the tone of a petulant child.

"Lying stretched out on a couple of chairs in a ballroom, wondering where you were, mate."

"Well, it's a spot of relief to see you."

"Likewise, mate," Reg replied. He reached over and gave Fred a slap on the back.

"This here is George."

"Steward I am, or was. Good to see you, Mr. Lee." Taylor always had a positive tone to his voice. The three men exchanged nods and looked at the growing number of passengers coming onto the deck as the ship approached the Cunard pier. All eyes were drawn to the docking place.

An expectant crowd filled Pier 54 to overflowing, a noisy throng of what appeared to be tens of thousands of people, awash in cries and calls and tears, and the mist, and the fog, and the rain, in a chaotic, explosive atmosphere. Now and then, a growl of thunder and a flash of lightning sparked the scene. Each person standing there looked for a loved one, a family member. For each one, their lives hinged on the news they were about to receive.

But for Fred, the scene reminded him that no one really cared if he was alive or dead. Oh sure, Eva had loved him, back in England when he left, and he loved her. But again, what would she think when she heard of the accident, and he was the lookout? It was hard for his thought pattern to change. He was used to feeling unwanted, discarded. How could Eva love him enough to ignore all the doubt that would be cast in his direction? And so, there it was, just like when he first found out he didn't have parents and everyone else did, he felt so completely rejected, so bitter, so solitary, and yes, so worthless.

His legs felt like they would give out. He reached for the railing and steadied himself. His parents, ah yes. They had other things they wanted to do with their lives. He wasn't one of those things. He had no memory of either one of them. They were an illusory, faceless presence, and he had never expected them to be there. But still, it hurt almost worse than ever before, as he acknowledged once again that he didn't have what everyone else had always had: people who really loved him, who shared his blood, who cared about what happened to him. Instead, he was something distant relatives had to deal with, after they had tended to what really mattered to them, their own immediate family, their children who had once lived inside their bodies, whose kicks they'd known long before they had seen their wee faces for the first time.

For Fred, there was no one like that. To his only relatives, his mother's kin, he was an added burden. They knew of his existence, but only from a distance. Did they even consider that the world would judge them harshly for completely ignoring him, the "orphan boy," as they had referred to him. He had heard them when he stood outside the kitchen door once, on his one and only visit to his distant cousins when he had a rare day out from the orphanage, or the "Home" as they called it. Except, he wasn't truly an orphan at all. His parents hadn't died. As far as he knew, they were still alive. They just didn't want him, and that hurt even more. And he wasn't invited back to the cousins after that one time, not that he had done anything wrong, other than being born. So, he always expected rejection. He was a nuisance, no more than a pile of refuse.

Eventually, they were herded off the ship and divided up — *Carpathia* passengers, *Titanic* passengers, and last, the crew of *Titanic*. As soon as they filed down the gangway and came ashore, the screams and the overall din of expectation dissolved, as if a giant switch had been flipped in some heavenly place. A silence of great magnitude defined the gravity of the moment. Who had lived and who had died? The answer was now at hand. The only sound was a far-off siren, now and then threading itself through the foggy night air. Its eerie sound heralded the long-awaited news.

Fleet had been in New York a few days each time as he'd waited for the return voyage on the *Oceanic* back to England. But he soon discovered this visit was to be different, as the crew itself was sorted out. Those with a direct connection to the "incident" were to stay behind, confined to another ship, the RMS *Celtic*, while the rest would be sent back to England at once, to Plymouth on the RMS *Lapland*.

As his group was led away, off to the transport that would deliver them to the pier for the *Celtic*, his eyes remained fixed on the *Titanic* survivors as they came down the gangway and were met by family, or the authorities if there was no one to claim them straight off. Through the heavy mist, he still held out hope to see the woman in the emerald dress, not even sure he would recognize her at all. Maybe she would be wrapped in a coat supplied by the *Carpathia* crew. But her long red hair had been distinctive, so he held out hope that he would spot her. But he did not.

Chapter 6

Once on board the *Celtic*, it was apparent that White Star Line had little regard for the comfort of the *Titanic* crew members. Not that he expected much, as crew quarters were never defined as approaching any level of true comfort, but he was used to that. On the *Oceanic*, he had often received the exact same bunk on subsequent journeys, and it was an acceptable spot, sleeping in a huge room with forty other men.

But the *Celtic* was different, smaller than *Titanic* and *Oceanic*. Spartan hardly defined the crew quarters. No telling how long they would be there. Even more disturbing, they were told they were not allowed off the ship, except when they would be escorted to their individual testimony at the investigation.

The gangway was removed as soon as the last of the crew stepped onto the ship. The only bright spot, the realization that he and Lee were assigned to the same sleeping area, and they were alone, so they could talk. And most of all, they could prepare themselves as to their testimony in the coming days.

"Which bunk you want?" Lee asked as they made their way into the tiny cubbyhole of a room.

"Almost looks like it'd be better to sleep outside on the deck," Fleet responded. "Doesn't matter to me. Suit yourself, why don't you?"

They dropped their gear and sat on their mattresses. "This one ain't even got straw in it, if you ask me," Fleet said. "But I hope we won't be here too long. I'm not looking forward to the investigation. How many times can I say, 'I saw a berg and I rang the damn bell three times, I called to the bridge, and the damn phone rang too long!'"

Lee looked at him with concern. "Maybe you don't want to say it quite like that! You might want to watch your tongue!"

"Tell me you're joking! What a bit of bother this is! I rang the damn bell like I was supposed to. That's all that counts, mate."

"Well, you had better get a fresh attitude of what's going on here. These men, these senators, they call them, they're the ones questioning us. I don't think they have much of a mind to take a joke. You know what I mean, mate?"

"Yes, yes, I do. But this whole thing, this query, puts me in a spot of trouble, you know. They want to blame someone, and out of that whole big ocean out there, who you think they're gonna blame? You're looking at 'im."

"Now wait a second. I think the investigators are trying to get to the bottom of this. I mean, they really want to know exactly what happened. And you didn't make that ship hit that iceberg. So don't be jumping to instant, wrong conclusions. And besides—"

"Besides, what?"

"You got me, mate. I was up there in the nest with you when you seen it. I saw exactly what happened and I'll be answering their questions too. I'll see to things, trust me. I won't let them blame you."

"We do need to talk about how long it took for me to ring the bell and call the bridge. And the other times, early on, when they ignored my call when I smelled the ice and saw those other icebergs, you know. How could they do that? And the captain, running the ship so fast on icy waters. Ah, I don't know, as I try to remember things, my thoughts get muddled." Fleet shook his head back and forth and ran his fingers through his tousled brown hair.

"There's nothing to muddle about, mate. You rang the bell for the big berg and called like you were supposed to do. That's all you need to say. If it took us a bit to decide what was out there, no matter. It was a little smudge, at first! Anyone would have wondered on a moonless night like that. Calm down, Fred. You did the right thing." Lee raised his voice and tossed his hands in the air. "My question is, why didn't they slow down in the beginning, as soon as you smelled ice, and saw those bergs? Listen, it's not your fault, mate. You did yer job."

"I just hope they don't twist everything around and say I should have picked out the berg sooner. There was that very slight bit of haze on the horizon."

"That's true," Lee agreed.

"But we both know that didn't make a bit of difference. It was very slight." Fleet was adamant. "If we're being honest, the haze is hardly worth mentioning. I'm not comfortable stretching the truth."

"Well, I'm not sure about that. It does take some of the pressure off both of us. A haze can do that, obscure the view. There was haze and no moon."

"And no binoculars."

"No, strange, that is, no glasses," Lee reminded his buddy. "We had them from Belfast to Southampton. Then they were gone. And we were never in charge of them. It was Lightoller. He was the one in charge of the glasses. Remember? And that other officer, Blair it was, the bloke they removed from the ship when Wilde came on board. Blair had glasses for us."

"Yes, the officers are always the ones with the glasses. Some of the other lookouts, Hogg and Evans, they told me that they had asked him for glasses as well, and Lights told them, 'We don't have any for this part of the voyage, but you won't really need them.'"

"What a bloody thing to say!" Lee exclaimed. "But at least it's not just our word that they wouldn't give us any. Hogg and Evans will back us up. Hey, here's a thought. Whichever of us gets questioned first, we'll share what it was like in that hearing room. You know, what questions they asked, and what our answers were. That way our stories can be the same, not that we have anything to hide. We don't. But still, it's better if things are nice and tidy."

"You're on it, all right!" Fred agreed. "That's a great idea, mate. I'm so glad we're sharing a bunk."

"Yes, spot of luck, ain't it? Besides, you're the worrying kind, I can see. Now you got no worries, mate."

"No worries about what?" Officer Lightoller rolled back the door and glared at the two men.

"Fleet was just worrying about his wife," Lee affected a casual tone to his voice.

"She expected me 'ome on Saturday next, and now we'll all be late, and no telling when we'll make it back to So'ton," Fleet said.

"Well, the sea can be unpredictable, can't she, Mr. Fleet?" Lightoller said. "Do you have to answer to your missus about everything?" His voice indicated he had no patience for subservient men.

"Not at all, Mr. Lightoller, but you know what women are like, I'm sure," Fleet responded, very unhappy with the way the conversation had turned, but realizing it was better than if Lightoller had heard what he and Lee were really discussing, the missing binoculars and ignored warnings.

"Never mind that. That's not why I'm here. Mr. Lee, get your things and come with me at once."

Instantly, electricity charged the air. the two men exchanged a furtive, worried glance.

"Mr. Fleet, you'll be getting another mate for your bunk. Come with me, Mr. Lee. I'm in a hurry, I have other things to do besides resituating you." And just like that, Reginald Lee was extracted from the tiny room.

"See you later, old man," Fleet offered up to the retreating Lee, as the one man who could help him get his story straight disappeared. Fleet was really concerned now. What if Lightoller had overheard them? Maybe he'd been lingering outside the door for a minute or two. What if he'd decided that something must be amiss in their behavior in the crow's nest because of their conversation?

He was in a panic, pacing back and forth, when a few minutes later the door was rolled back once again.

Another man appeared in the doorway, suspended on crutches, both legs heavily bandaged. His mood hardly seemed any better than Fleet's. He carefully maneuvered his way into the small space and dropped his possessions, one small bag to be exact, on the unoccupied bunk. Carefully balancing himself on the crutches, he freed one hand and stuck it out in greeting.

"Harold Bride, Marconi operator, or junior operator."

"Fleet, Fred Fleet. I'm the lookout, iceberg straight ahead." His voice betrayed a certain irony, as if boasting about his post on *Titanic*. Nothing could be further from the truth. Rather, simply stating this one simple fact, he felt depleted. But still, Fred carefully reached for the other man's hand in greeting. They nodded at each other. "I don't want to tip you over there, should you be walking around? That looks bad, all those bandages."

"They put me in hospital on the *Carpathia*, which wasn't too bad. They gave me some drugs to deal with the pain. I was helping their man send messages. But here on this ship, there really isn't a hospital, and no drugs either."

"I hope you'll be okay!" Fred was truly concerned about the man's well-being.

"When I got on board, they wanted to put me in a separate space, with a lock on the door! Can you believe it? They said it would serve as a hospital, but I said no. I couldn't put up with being so restrained. I guess after what's happened, I want to feel like I'm free. You know, we have to be in charge of ourselves." Bride slipped down onto a mattress. "We can't depend on anyone to take care of us. What's happened on *Titanic* taught me that lesson. Don't you agree?"

"I've always felt that way, I've got no family. I always had to take care of me self."

"I'm sorry to hear that."

"I don't think it matters much right now. If anything, I just realized it may have made me stronger than other men. But all that counts right now is we made it off *Titanic,* so we are far luckier than those poor souls lost that night. They never had a chance, did they?" Fleet shook his head, still in disbelief of all he had seen.

"Are your feet hurt very bad?" he asked after a minute or so, seeking to change the conversation. "What happened?"

"They got crushed in the lifeboat. I jumped from the *Titanic.* I had been trying to help some of our mates get a boat, a collapsible, off the deck, but then a huge wave came and washed me and the boat off the deck. My hand was caught on the oar lock, so I went over with the boat and ended up in it. Actually, I was underneath at first."

"You were underneath? You were under that collapsible? What happened next?"

"I knew I shouldn't breathe, or I'd drown. I was trapped underwater! And then somehow, I got out. I had to fight for it, I have no idea how I did it. I just wasn't ready to die." He looked up at Fred, meeting his eyes for a split second before he shifted his gaze. "And I swam again, I swam with all my strength, trying to get away from *Titanic* so I wouldn't be pulled under by the suction. I could see she was starting to sink. And all those voices, all those people screaming to be saved. It was the worst thing, I'm sure you'll agree."

"Yes, yes of course, I can still hear it," Fleet said quietly. "I'll never be free of that sound."

"I know what you mean. I can hear it too, even now. But I can't stop thinking about the voices I could hardly hear at all. The children. They went first, I'm sure. Their voices didn't last but a few minutes." Bride stopped speaking again and looked down at the floor. He shook his head slowly.

He continued in a subdued voice. "Well, I was swimming and swimming, I was so very cold, chilled to the bone, and then I saw a boat. As it happened, it was the very same collapsible, and it was still upside down. By then, it was completely covered over with men. To my surprise, one man reached out and pulled me on board. I managed to roll over onto the very edge and cling to that spot. In a few minutes, another man came along, struggled aboard, and ended up sitting on my legs. I hadn't the breath, or the will to tell him to move, there was no place he might move to. It was a fight for survival, that's for sure. Although, at that moment, I tried to be kind and not force him into a more unsafe spot. I had to do that and put up with the pain. Survival, I had to give him a chance." He paused again.

"So how did you make it, if that boat was overfilled with men, and it being just a flimsy, overturned collapsible?'

"One of the regular lifeboats came along side, and they pulled many of us aboard, even though their boat was already quite full. Somehow, we stayed afloat. Eventually, the *Carpathia* showed up. I had so many miraculous things happen to me out there! Once we are done with this investigation, I'll agree to whatever the doctors have in mind. I want to walk. I want to live my life. That's the main issue for all of us now that we've been so close to the end, isn't it?" He pointed to the ocean, to a fate neither one of them wanted to contemplate. "Survival."

Something in the other man's voice made Fred look up into Harold Bride's face. The man had the strangest eyes. The pupils didn't quite reach the bottom of each eye. They hung suspended from the top lid, as if they were caught up, lingering in some far-off place. It was as if he could see deeper into a different reality than other men.

"Yes, of course it is," Fred said. "But you know, survival has a price attached."

***

"What do you mean, a price?" Bride asked as he leaned over and rubbed his left leg. He was tense but tried not to show it. Fleet couldn't possibly know what he had done in the last minutes on *Titanic*, trying to save Jack Phillips, the senior Marconi man.

"Your leg really hurts, doesn't it?" Fleet asked him.

"Yes. I wish this ship had a hospital. And pain pills. There's no telling how long we'll be here and I'm down to my last tablet. I've been trying to save it, until I can't stand the pain any longer."

Fleet shook his head. "Here's the thing, I just wish I could have done more. I mean, I didn't do anything. All I did was alert the bridge that I saw the berg, and then I helped row a lifeboat. But all those other people, they're gone. And I didn't save a single one of them. And I have to live with that thought."

"What could you have done differently? Nothing." He didn't wait for Fred to reply. He had his own actions to consider, his own guilt. It was himself he sought to console at that moment, not this man he had just met.

Even though he had done it for a good reason, and he knew his action should be seen as justified. The intruder rushed into the room to steal the life vest off the very back of his mate, Jack Phillips, as Jack sent the emergency messages for the *Titanic*, even after Captain Smith had told them they were discharged from their duties and should seek to save their own lives.

Jack had stayed his ground, with no regard for his own safety, and kept sending the SOS. The intruder was a crewman, and so he, like the rest, had been instructed at the start of the voyage to remember where he had stored his life vest. They were not allowed to take another's. Obviously, this man had failed to obey the order, and so he wrestled Jack's vest off his back.

Harold Bride would have none of it. Jack Phillips was a hero, as he continued to send messages rather than save himself. Bride had intervened, with the body of the would-be thief left lying on the floor. Then he and Jack had run to the deck, hoping to get off the ship.

The maritime community on the Atlantic knew *Titanic* was desperate for help. The two men had fulfilled their assignment, and the *Carpathia* was on the way. But a dying man lay on the floor of the telegraph room as the sea rushed in. Bride didn't feel any guilt until now, when his unusual eyes saw a vision no one else had seen.

"What are you thinking about?" Fleet asked. "You escaped. No doubt your legs will heal. I thought you said survival is all that counts."

"Yes, yes, it is. But something happened, back on the *Titanic*. And I guess I should have kept it to myself, but I didn't. You will read about it in the *New York Times*, and so will everyone else."

"*The New York Times*? Didn't you hear that speech from Lightoller? We aren't allowed to say anything, to anyone."

"No, I never heard him say that, or anything else. I was in hospital most of the time on *Carpathia*. Then they needed me in the telegraph room, sending messages for hours and hours. The newspaper reporter found me there and started chatting. I wish I had heard Lightoller's words, I never would have given the interview, no matter how much money they offered me."

"They gave you money? To talk about the accident?"

"Yes," Bride replied in a small voice. "One thousand dollars, US currency. I wish I hadn't said a word. But I was just so happy to be alive, and I was all caught up in that feeling. I guess I was flattered by all the attention. That reporter knew how to pry information out of me. I see that now." He shook his head, thinking of his foolishness.

"My goodness. What did you say that was worth a thousand dollars?" Fleet raised his voice and his eyebrows shot up.

"He was desperate to hear of the last minutes on the ship. How and when did we know she was really sinking? Did we feel the collision with the berg? What was the reaction of the passengers? All those things I really couldn't answer for him because I was asleep when we hit. I didn't feel anything, and even Phillips, who was manning the telegraph key, he didn't know anything serious had happened until the captain came to us. Jack told me he'd felt a slight movement, that was all."

"What did Captain Smith say to you and Phillips?" Fleet asked.

"Just that we'd struck an iceberg, but he didn't sound worried. At first, he said we shouldn't send any messages about it at all just yet, he said they were checking things out and he'd be back. We even made a few jokes about it with him. Then he came back ten minutes later, barely stuck his head in the door and he said, 'Send the call for assistance.' He said, 'Send the regulation international call for help.' Just that. So we sent it, the CQD it's called. It stands for, 'all stations: distress.'"

"And that was all you sent?"

"No. Five minutes later, the captain came back and asked what we were sending. We told him the CQD. Then I made a joke, maybe we should send the newer signal, the SOS. It's only been used a couple of times. I said it may be your only chance to ever send that one! Everyone laughed. And the captain agreed, and we sent it. Again, right then, we didn't know how fast the ship was sinking. No one told us."

"I guess the newspaper man found that interesting. I bet that was just the kind of thing he wanted to hear. You gave him the scoop on using that SOS."

"Well yes, but he really wanted more. Much more. He kept pushing me, what next, what next? I thought I'd said enough. But he pushed so hard he got me talking. So, I said that Phillips only felt a slight jar when we hit. And then, we went from a whisper of trouble to a sunken ship, in a few short hours. And the guy wasn't satisfied with that. He pushed some more. Oh, he was good at it. So then, before I knew what I was saying, I told him how I attacked the intruder." Harold stopped talking. He put his hand to his face, lost in thought.

"What intruder?" Fred asked.

And so Bride confessed the truth to Fred. "I wish I hadn't told the reporter that. I wish I could take those words back. But I'm not sorry I hit the man. I had to save Jack. Like I said, it was all about survival. In this case, survival for a very good man, because Jack Phillips is one of the best."

"So why do you have such big regrets about saying anything, aside from Lightoller, but you didn't hear any of that? What you told the reporter was true, wasn't it?"

"Yes, it was, but that's the problem. Now I'm worried about my own survival. I killed a man. What will they do with me? And what will White

Star do to me? I really like being a Marconi man. It means everything to me."

"But you saved Jack Phillips life," Fleet reminded him. "He would have died if not for you. Surely that counts for something."

"Well, actually, in the end, I didn't. We both turned up on the same collapsible. But by the time *Carpathia* reached our position, there was one dead man on the boat, and that man was Jack. He died of exposure to the cold."

*****

Fred stood up and walked over to Bride. "I'm sorry to hear that, old man." Even though he was feeling awkward, he leaned over and patted Harold Bride on the shoulder.

Fred felt he should do more, but what? Life wasn't filled with happy endings. In his twenty-four years, Fred had no such expectations.

Someone banged on the door and a voice called out. "Supper in the mess in five minutes."

Fleet and Bride broke off their conversation and went in search of the mess area, Bride moving gingerly as he balanced himself on his crutches and slipped through the narrow passageways.

They found their place around one of the tables filled with a host of faces they recognized. The crew members exchanged hasty nods and dug into their food. The conversation was scant, and the voices subdued. Since they hadn't had anything to eat in several hours, the pressed corned beef, mashed potatoes, and coffee were gone in minutes.

Just as Fleet had helped himself to the last of it, two men entered. It was obvious one of them was a crewmember of the *Celtic*, the other man wore a cheap suit with the buttons stretched across his ample midsection and a black fedora perched atop his head. He had an unlit cigar clamped in his mouth under a heavy mustache. The sailor said something under his breath to the man and pointed toward Fleet. In a minute, the man stood in front of Fred.

"Are you Frederick Fleet?" he asked, failing to introduce himself. His manner was most unpleasant.

"What's it to ya?" Fleet responded. He didn't want to be singled out.

"You're the bloke spotted the iceberg?"

"So, what if I am?" Fleet replied.

"Don't take it the wrong way. I am curious to hear your take on things is all. You must be the bravest man of the ship." He adjusted his tone, cajoling Fleet to be more receptive to his questions.

"I was just doing my job," Fleet responded, but the bite was gone from his voice. "There's lots of men who deserve to be called brave that night, not me."

"But you knew everything would change when you sounded the alarm," the guy persisted. "You put your reputation on ringing that bell, old man."

"Well, I guess I did, didn't I?" Fleet was slipping into the one trap he'd planned to avoid. Even though it was immediately obvious the man must be a member of the much feared and definitely dangerous press corps, Fleet took the bait. His hotheaded nature, often his undoing in the past, loosened his lips before he realized what he was doing and saying.

The reporter brought up John Jacob Astor, and how he was lost that night. Several of the crew sounded their opinions of the matter. Fleet broke in and defended Astor's actions, even though he recalled that Mr. Astor had, at first, not been particularly noble, as he tried to enter the boat citing his wife's delicate condition and her need for his care. But then Fred felt that he might get into trouble, defaming the memory of such a powerful man, so he said what he said.

"Seems to me, Mr. Astor only wanted to help his wife. But then when Lightoller told him, get out, he did, no fuss about him whatsoever. He was brave, not like some of the others..."

Fred recalled that he had never intended to break the rules and say anything at all. So rather than finishing his sentence, he raised his coffee mug to his mouth. He drank down to the dregs, until a few stray grounds slipped down his throat. Others spoke with the stranger, but Fleet was silent.

Then the conversation changed, and they were discussing Bruce Ismay. Questions were quickly raised as to the move he'd made to enter a lifeboat and save his own life, in spite of the call that boats were only for women and children.

Again, Fleet took the bait and without thinking, he opened his mouth. But this time there was another reason for Fleet to speak. The stranger had caught sight of his most vulnerable spot, or spots, the dark red birthmark splotches, one on the back of each of Fred's hands.

Fred hated these marks on his skin even more than his status as a waif. They proved to the world, at least in his eyes, that he was condemned from birth. And that pain never went away. As long as the stranger's gaze touched Fred's hand, his skin tingled with discomfort. He raised his voice, hoping to distract the man.

"Mr. Ismay was there as a passenger and nothing more than that. Just you remember that, so he was free to escape in a boat if he could. Of course, it was his choice at the moment, and he got in the boat, even if..." His voice trailed away as he noticed the reporter writing his words in a notebook and instantly, once again, Fred wished he had kept his mouth shut.

The other crewmen stared at Fred. No doubt, they were wondering why he said what he did. Some men needed a bit of alcohol to loosen their lips. Not Fred Fleet. his tongue seemed to have a mind of its own. It was a natural defense mechanism, but one that had served him poorly more times than he cared to admit.

How could I do this? When will I ever learn? Will I lose my job? Will White Star give me the boot? That's what Lightoller had promised if they opened their mouths and said one word. And he had said more than just one.

The sailors then picked up another issue of great interest to all. Money. And the rumor that several of the *Titanic* crew had received substantial cash rewards for stories leaked to the press. Sums as huge as $250 were suggested, and Fleet recalled that Bride had been given, or claimed he had been given, $1000. But Bride didn't say a word.

Bride stared down at the empty dinner plate on the table in front of him. He may have regretted telling the *Times* reporter exactly what he'd done just before he left the telegraph room, but Fleet was still mesmerized by the possibility of a tidy sum making its way into his pocket. Maybe he should be incensed no one had offered him anything.

Not that he would have taken it, he reminded himself. Actually, he chastised himself. *I'm a company man. White Star's all I've got.*

Right then and there, he decided that going forth, he would say, or not say, whatever he needed to keep his job. The challenge would come when he sat down at the formal investigation. He knew the men questioning him would be very smart, men of the world they were, and he was neither of those things, but that didn't mean he had to be stupid in how he answered their questions. He would tell them what they wanted to hear, and nothing other than that. He would do his best to protect himself. He couldn't bear the blame for the iceberg. If he did, he would lose his livelihood. The sea was all he had.

But then it occurred to him, what would he say if they asked him if this was the first iceberg he saw that night. If he said yes, White Star might be saved all responsibility, and he would bear the accusation that he wasn't a very keen lookout, that he should have spotted and reported it sooner.

And then there was the question of how long it took for the bridge to answer the phone. If he mentioned that, White Star would be in the hot seat. And, most of all, if he shared that he'd been completely ignored in his three earlier sightings, all hell would break loose. But how could he not tell about those bergs? Either way, he was done for. Life was never easy. What choice did he really have?

He remembered how uneasy he had been when he was told, not asked, that he was going to sea. Certainly, he had no choice in the matter. To a twelve-year-old boy, going to live on a ship might have seemed like an exciting adventure. But this was different.

"The SS *Clio*, that's where you are headed, Fred," Edward Rudolf told him as they sat together in the musty office under the main stairway at Elm Lodge Home for Boys. "Quite frankly, I tried to get you sent to Tattenhall. You might have liked it there. It's a farm."

It was unusual for the founder and head of the Waifs and Strays Society to speak with any of the boys. But Rudolf was on a tour of the various homes, seeking to straighten out the bad behavior and disposition of some of the most difficult lads. And Frederick Fleet was definitely one of those. As luck would have it, he had arrived at Elm Lodge just a few days after Fred's latest unfortunate incident.

"I like farms, I want to go to that one. Sir, let me go there, please." Fleet always came off as a tough lad with a heavy hint of arrogance. He was a brawler, no doubt about it. But now his voice was reduced to a small, injured child, pleading for help.

"No, that's impossible, Frederick. They have written to us and said you are not the type they can handle. In the past, boys such as yourself haven't worked out at Tattenhall."

"But I'll behave this time, I really will," Fleet protested again. Again, no trace of the tough young man. His voice betrayed his anxiety as to what might happen next.

"If you hadn't gotten into that fistfight with the Webley lad, and that other fight, where you kicked the Hamsford lad and bashed him so badly, maybe they would have accepted you, despite your past history. But two fights in the last month, and now, this last brawl. You put one of the boys in hospital for several days. No, you pushed things too far."

Fred wanted to defend himself, but he couldn't think of anything he might say that wouldn't anger the man further.

"Fred, you have only yourself to blame. The *Clio* is the place for you. It's earmarked for, as we say, the naughty boys."

"But I don't think I'll like being on a ship. I mean, is it for always and ever?"

"It doesn't matter what you like. You have no say in the matter. The only way you might have had a chance to influence your future was by improving your behavior. If you had, you might have stayed here at Elm Lodge with all the lads you've known these past years. But you are a troublemaker. There is no other way of saying it. Tattenhall would have been a good place for you, but as I've explained, that's not possible now. They won't have you. You will be in a more restricted environment on the *Clio*, and most important of all, you will be trained for a life on the sea. Unless you mess that up too. If you do, then the jail is the only place for you, and throw away the key they will."

Fred blinked as, without warning, his eyes filled with tears. All he could think of was nights he'd spent turning and tossing on his narrow cot, always at war with the world. That cot, here at Elm Lodge, was his only refuge. Every morning he rose to see what disappointment would come his way, what small fraction of his limited life would be undone once again by a world that never failed to treat him badly. His poor expectations were rarely wrong. Maybe it would be different, he told himself, if his mother had not run off without him, looking for a new start no doubt, without an eighteen-month-old wee lad to slow her down.

She'd dropped him off at the foundling hospital, not that he remembered any of it. After the hospital had run out of money to care for him, Elm Lodge had become his home, the only place he knew.

Alone in the world, he'd had this one comforting spot, his cot upstairs in the room at the end of the hall on the third floor. It was a place with low ceilings and a lack of heat in the chill of winter, tucked closely under the eaves of the roof. Before the house was turned over to the Church of England, the spot had housed the servants' quarters. That was his tiny place in the world, the place he could tug his blanket over his head, pull his arms to his body, and his knees to his chest as he tried to smother his loneliness in the wee hours of the night.

During the day, he covered his emptiness by punching out at others, a tough shell protecting the hollow boy who existed, who lived, within.

He lived all his days with no one to love him, ever. At the end of the day, like a small baby, he clung to that one, thin, state-issued blanket. Many a night, he lay there wide awake, listening to the other boys breathing as they slept.

Now he was to lose that as well as take up a life on the sea. The thought of salt air stinging his nostrils made him sick to his stomach, sick with apprehension. But he couldn't show that hungry, fragile side of himself. Getting into a tussle was his way of covering up. That hadn't worked out too well for him after all. He raised his hand and swiped at a tear before it could slide down his cheek. He hoped Mr. Rudolf didn't see it.

"You will leave shortly Fred. Perhaps a day or so. Be ready."

How could he be ready? What could that mean? Fred pondered the words. He had few belongings to gather. And if Mr. Rudolf meant ready in his head, he knew he could never find that necessary missing ingredient. He was never ready for anything; life just came at him as a gust of wind moves a branch on a willow tree. At this point in his twelve years on earth, he was barely hanging on.

In three days' time, a man came from the Waifs and Strays Society, a Mr. Griffin, and he proceeded to read off a short list of names of the boys he was to collect. There were three of them, Fred and two others. An hour later, he'd found himself in the back of a carriage.

The driver had said not a word. He'd stared at the boys, almost like he'd eat them for dinner, if he could. Then, with a swipe of his arm he indicated they should hop into the back. The other two lads were older than Fred, and they seemed to be friends. They jumped in first. Mr. Griffin, already seated in the front, called back to Fred. "Hurry up, we haven't got all day, lad."

Fred had barely found his seat and closed the door when they were off, rumbling down the long driveway. At first, Fred didn't turn around for one last look. He couldn't. He hadn't the strength. But then, just as they were about to take the final curve in the road, he couldn't resist. He swiveled in his seat, desperate to steal a final glance of the only home he'd ever known. All at once, the building was awash in a golden light as the clouds parted and the sun touched the old red bricks. It gave the place a warmth Fred had never felt before. Its sudden, unexpected beauty called out to him. He couldn't bear to leave. Most of all, he couldn't imagine what would happen next.

The other boys were bound for Tattenhall, and the small party journeyed there first. After a short train ride, they arrived at a station out in the country. Then, a cart with two strong white horses and a driver, who was quite pleasant, came to ferry them the rest of the way.

As soon as they turned into the long tree-lined drive leading up to the farmhouse, Fred wished there was some way he could persuade Mr. Griffin to just drop him off here. Surely the people in charge would listen to his pleas and let him stay. But it was not to be. The two boys quickly hopped down from the cart and were met by a heavyset older woman with a kind look on her wrinkled face. She escorted the boys up the short path to the house. Fred swiveled about, watching them disappear inside as the driver turned the cart around. Before Fred could say a word, they were clip-clopping back in the direction they had come. A whirl of dust flew up from the driveway.

"If we hurry, we will just make the two o'clock train to Bangor," the driver announced as he tapped the horses with a leather strap.

"Wales?" Fred asked. "We are going to Wales?" He wasn't a worldly boy at all, but somehow, he knew Bangor was in Wales.

"That is where the *Clio* is moored, just off the coast at Bangor," Mr. Griffin answered him in a matter-of-fact tone.

"Don't they speak a different tongue there? I can't speak whatever that is. Welsh, is it? Is that what they call it? I can't say a word."

"Then maybe you'll be better off. I've heard you are a cheeky lad." The man looked at Fleet to see how he took to his words. Not seeing the reaction he wanted, he added, "They speak enough of the King's English there to straighten you out, that's for sure. A good tap with a birch is what you need. No words are necessary for that."

"But I'm hungry. Can't we stop and get something, a cup of tea or something?" Fred asked, trying to delay their journey. Maybe they would miss the train and things would change in his favor.

"We can't," Mr. Griffin replied in a disgusted tone. "Do you think we are out on a spree or something? You have no need of anything, as far as I'm concerned."

When he finally stepped aboard the *Clio* later that afternoon, Fred immediately forgot the ache in his empty stomach. That discomfort was replaced by another. He sensed something different about this place, aside from being on the water. He had never been on a ship before, but that wasn't it. Fred felt uneasy.

And then he realized what it was. The other boys gathered around, watching him carefully as he came aboard. No one greeted him or offered a smile. They all sized him up. Head to toe, they made their read on the new arrival. Fred immediately caught that, unlike Elm Lodge where he was among the toughest and top of the heap, here he'd been assessed and found wanting. He stuffed his hands in his pockets. He felt weak and vulnerable for the first time, as he recognized a new sensation creeping into his chest. Fear.

Looking back twelve years later, maybe it wasn't such a bad thing after all, being sent to the *Clio,* even though the ship was a very dangerous place. Many of the boys, Fred included, had been injured in accidents. Some of the lads lost their lives, ending up in a section in the churchyard reserved for *Clio* boys. Despite all that, Fred had survived. And, at the end of it, he had learned a trade.

His title of able-bodied seaman provided him with a small income, and most of all, it had given him a place where he belonged in the world, up in the crow's nest of a giant steamship, with extra pay attached to his skill as a lookout.

Now, all of that was in danger of being taken from him. If he didn't watch out, he'd be out on his ear with nowhere to go.

He resolved to say nothing more to the reporter.

When Fleet would give him nothing more, the man slid out the door, eager to submit his account of the interview. The next challenge for Fred would be getting through the investigation itself with nary a scratch.

Chapter 7

Early the next morning, there was much gossip going around the ship. The investigation would begin in a couple of hours, in a fancy hotel, the Waldorf Astoria, they were told. Harold Bride was one of the first to be questioned this day. All of the men were uneasy, but Harold and Fred more than the others.

"I did my job, Fred," Bride said, as they sat together finishing the last of their coffee, off to the side of the other men, all gathered in the mess. "I sent and received every message that came my way. So why am I so nervous? As for the bloke in the Marconi room trying to steal Jack's lifebelt, I had no choice, none whatsoever. I just hope everyone else will see it that way. If only I hadn't spilled the story to the *Times*. It wasn't worth the money."

For late April, it was a chilly morning and the wind whistled through the old ship. Harold tied his scarf a little tighter around his neck.

Fred reached in his pocket for his gloves and pulled them on before he spoke. Fred liked gloves. If he wasn't wearing them, he often sunk his hands in his pockets. Many a fight had erupted when he'd been teased about the marks on his hands. He'd been told he had the stamp of the devil on him. In a way, he had come to believe that. He hid his hands any chance he had. Harold had already seen the marks. This cover-up was more out of habit. And the cold.

"You shouldn't be the least bit off kilter, Harold. You couldn't let Jack drown, if you could help it. Other than that sticky point, as a Marconi man, you were like a passageway, weren't you? Your job was to let the news flow through your fingers on the key of the wireless."

"That's perfect! And true. I shouldn't be scared, should I?"

"Of course you shouldn't. It's not like me. I have to make them believe I couldn't have seen the iceberg any sooner than I did. That's tricky business there, all right. I could be in a spot of trouble if they don't agree with me."

"They'll believe you. Why shouldn't they? Besides, you will have Reginald right there with you, backing up your story."

"That's what I thought. But, since Lights pulled him away right after we got on board, I haven't seen 'im anywhere. He's disappeared again, just like he did when we were on the *Carpathia*. The *Carpathia* is a large ship, so it took a while for us to find each other, but eventually we did. But now, 'e just isn't here. I can't imagine what's become of him."

"Well, don't worry about him. You'll get through just fine. Just tell them the truth. You've got nothing to hide, I'm sure of it. When I come back, I'll tell you all about my experience."

"Good luck, old man." Fleet slapped him lightly on the back.

Bride's injured legs made him seem even more fragile than he was. As his new friend limped away, Fleet thought about Bride's last words, about Fleet having nothing to hide. His memory was muddled, but he knew he'd seen the early icebergs. He knew he'd tried to prevent what eventually happened that night. He felt more fragile than Harold Bride, even with his own two healthy legs.

Fleet spent the remainder of the morning sitting with the rest of the *Titanic* crew as they tossed out their concerns for the tedious questioning to come and their desire to get back to England and their families as soon as possible.

For the first time, Fred noticed some of the men looking at him and whispering. At first, they didn't even look away when they realized he was staring at them. After an uncomfortable moment or two, they lowered their eyes. But the damage was done, he knew it. His worst fear was becoming reality; the men were calling into question his performance on the job. They were blaming the collision with the iceberg on him. He was sure of it.

When he couldn't endure their implied accusations any longer, he lunged out of his chair and strode about the ship, climbing from one deck to the next. When that didn't help, he retreated below decks and lay on his bunk, staring at the ceiling. Unfortunately, it wasn't the same as when he had spent those many nights so long ago as a wee lad curled up on his cot at Elm Lodge. Now, comfort evaded him as his anxiety grew.

As the afternoon hours stretched into early evening, Fred pulled himself back to the deck, where he stood alone, leaning over the rail, searching the pier, hoping to catch sight of Harold Bride. Soon the streetlights came on and the activity on the pier diminished. The first stars crept into the sky. Still no sign of the man.

A long, black car drew up and came to a stop. The back door opened, and a figure that could only be the telegraph operator came into view. He limped along, moving very slowly. As he came up the gangway onto the ship, he gave Fred a weak attempt at a grin.

"So, you are still here," Bride greeted him in a tired voice.

"I couldn't exactly leave. You look exhausted. 'ow did it go?

"I could use something to eat. They gave me no food or drink. I'm really worn out."

At the mess, to Fred's relief, the other men had finished their supper and left, but there was still some food on the platters and a pitcher of beer on the table.

"Grab a chair, 'arold, and I'll put together a plate for ya. I'm assuming ya want some beer."

"Beer will be fine. Thanks so much for your help, Fred. I must admit, I'm half dead. It was such a long, long day. If they hadn't located a wheelchair for me to use for the inquiry, I'm not sure how I would have made it through. So many questions, and so much pressure." He paused for a moment and took a long drink of his beer. He coughed for a minute after drinking so fast. Then he cleared his throat. "Yes, I can't deny it, those men are very intense, and well they should be. They announced to the chamber that at least 1,400 people were lost. They are still searching for bodies, so that is just an approximate count. But still, that's the first we've heard of the final number. This hearing is a very demanding undertaking."

"One thousand, four hundred?" Fleet drew in his breath and shook his head. His vision blurred through tears. The people in the water jumped behind his eyes one more time, and the sound of their screams filled his ears. "So I guess we know for certain that the *Carpathia* was the only rescue ship to pick up any survivors." He saw that familiar face again, the one with the long red hair, the desperate gaze, and the diamond necklace attached to a slim, fragile throat.

"Oh yes, absolutely. That was a big part of all the questions they asked me, over and over again. I will say, they never asked about the incident in the telegraph room, with the guy I left lying there. I think all they care about now are things that relate to the actual sinking. Who knows, they may get up to the rest of it later, so I can't relax."

"What did they ask you?"

"They kept asking for the positions of all the ships near *Titanic*, and how they responded to our calls for help. I had to repeat every message I received and each and every one I sent. They dissected every word I spoke. Without Phillips there to tell them of his messages, they are only getting part of the picture today. I'm sure you've heard the old saying, dead men tell no tales. But they are questioning the telegraph men on all the ships who were in communication with *Titanic*, so eventually they will know of the messages Phillips was a part of, and I wasn't. Actually, those were the majority of them, he being the senior man."

"But you were quite busy on your shifts as well, weren't you?"

"Oh yes, indeed I was. But a lot of what I was doing was sending to Cape Race—the telegraph station in Newfoundland. I was transmitting all the messages the passengers were sending to friends and family. That happens on every trip. That's really how Marconi makes its money. The passengers pay for each and every message they send and receive. And we were way behind, because of the system failure earlier."

"What do ya mean, system failure?"

"Late Saturday, the telegraph lost all connection to land. It was a wiring problem in our key. We were told to just leave it be and wait until we reached New York to get it fixed by Marconi. But Phillips wouldn't do that, so we worked for seven hours straight to fix it. Imagine if we hadn't!"

Fleet shook his head. "You never could have called for help. We'd all be out there, even now, and none of us would 'ave survived."

"Lucky thing that Jack wanted the extra money from sending all those passenger messages. The more we send, the more we get paid. That was what drove him to work so hard on the repair, I'm guessing. Of course, it's not acceptable to be out on the ocean with no way to communicate if help were needed. Not that we expected to need any on an unsinkable ship."

"Yes, an unsinkable ship," Fleet replied, the irony thick in his voice. He swallowed a deep drink of his beer and wiped the foam from his lips with the back of his sleeve. He took a small bite of cold chicken, but any appetite he might have had was gone.

"Well, once we got the repair done, we were way behind with sending our backload. Jack left a lot of that work to me. I must admit, I am good at what I do. But really, the number of those personal messages was more than we could keep up with. Through the afternoon, other ships, like the *Californian*, for example, kept cutting in when I was trying to work Cape Race, as we call it. Finally, I got a break to take a nap, so I could relieve Jack for my regular late-night shift. He took over at the key until I woke up and entered the telegraph room, just after we hit the berg. He was exhausted."

"I'm sure 'e was."

"Yes, but he wouldn't stop. Then the biggest challenge, trying to speak with the other ships and send our CQDs and then, our SOS, and the personals. The calls for help, as directed by the captain must take priority over messages from passengers to family, but the thing is, we have a business agreement that requires us to send the passengers' messages, so, I hate to say it... and, hmm, promise you won't say anything of this to anyone else, but it was getting to be a real challenge. Sorting them all out. You see, we can't do both at the same time, one blocks the other."

"Well, that's a bit of a mess there. But wouldn't it be more important to always speak with another ship, who might be warning of ice, or some other important message, rather than 'aving a go at sending, 'Aunt Gracie, I love you'?" Fleet hated to sound critical of Harold, but he was a bit confused. He knew he had no knowledge of such things, but still, it didn't make sense.

"Well, old man, remember, Marconi pays my salary, not White Star."

"Oh. I didn't know that. But still..." Fleet took one look at Bride's face and dropped the conversation.

The two men couldn't look each other in the eye, and an uncomfortable silence filled the room. Finally, traces of sirens and whistles out on the pier eased the tension.

Bride eventually bridged the gap. "So, what I was trying to say to you was, those men, the senators, will be relentless in their questioning. They will ask every tiny detail, every fraction of a second, over and over again. Be prepared for that."

"I'm not sure that I can be. But I do appreciate your advice." Fleet attempted a thin smile, even as his anxiety increased.

So too did his suspicion that there was something about the telegraph transmissions that Bride wasn't telling him. He had implied as much by what he hadn't said as what he had when referring to the need to send as many personal messages as possible to Cape Race so that Marconi could make its money. It almost sounded like, 'So what if a couple of our messages back and forth with the other ships were delayed, or even skipped, because of our passenger backload?'

But how could they do that? Wouldn't the wise thing be to skip all personal messages on a night with multiple ice warnings?

The two men found their way back to their bunk, Bride limping along slowly due to exhaustion and maneuvering through narrow passageways on crutches.

Fred was unnerved by his observations of Bride. He grasped more than ever that getting through the inquiry with these senators would be a grueling, if not impossible, ordeal for a poorly-prepared-for-such-a-strange-event young man such as himself. Even if he couldn't prevent it, he knew that when he opened his mouth, quite often he hurt himself more than anything else. But he wasn't a man raised with any degree of subtlety, not that he even knew such words existed. In the Church of England Home for Waifs and Strays, all he'd known was survival. He wasn't prepared for verbal jousting.

Both he and Bride hardly slept a wink that night. Each heard the other tossing about on his thin excuse for a mattress. But neither one wanted to continue their conversation.

The next morning brought with it at last the perfect weather one might expect of spring. The *Titanic* crew gathered in the mess, hats, gloves, and scarves left behind in their bunks. Perhaps the improvement in the weather lifted their spirits as they were all more accommodating to each other.

All but Fleet. He sat withdrawn at the end of one of the long tables, sipping his coffee and stealing glances at the others, watching for any sign of a renewal of their previous whispered accusations, when they had looked at him with blame dripping from their eyes.

"So, are they letting you go, Mr. Bride?" asked one of the men who had helped load several of the lifeboats. "Are you headed back to England now?"

"Not just yet. They said that anyone who appears for questioning could be recalled as needed. So, you're stuck with me for the duration, even though I need some medical attention paid to my legs, but that doesn't seem to be of concern to those in charge. Also, I heard a comment that there will most likely be a British inquiry to follow this one. So, we will be in each other's company for quite some time."

"You mean that?" the fellow asked, disbelief filled his voice. "I'm sorry about your legs, mate. Oh, by the way, Ryan's the name. Jim Ryan. So, they're going to do this whole thing all over again back home?"

"It makes sense, doesn't it?" Bride replied.

Fleet spoke up. "I'm not interested in wha' makes sense. I just want this to be bloody over and done." His bad mood couldn't keep his lips sealed forever. All heads in the room swiveled toward him. Bride immediately jumped in to deflect attention from his mate.

"Oh, I should have told you this. I heard some talk at the end of the day yesterday that they are sending us down to Washington, DC, to the Capitol of the US, to continue these sessions. They want more senators in attendance, it seems. They didn't actually tell me, but I overheard their comments among themselves. I think we are in for a bit of a cruise today mates."

The others looked at him with surprise, and before anyone could say a single word, almost on cue, the engines hummed. Before, the only sound was small waves slapping the side of the ship, a sound like second nature to them, one they really didn't hear. But when engines engage, the men always switched gear and became instantly alert. It meant there was work to be done. Except not on this unusual, and unannounced voyage. Here, they were passengers, captive passengers.

"So nice of them to tell us." Jim Ryan shook his head.

"We are less than baggage to them," one of the other men muttered.

"That's not exactly true," another interjected. "If they are to figure out just what went wrong, they need us to tell them."

"Well, we won't, will we?" Fred spoke out of turn. Once again, as soon as the words left his lips, he realized what a mistake he'd made. Urging his mates to withhold the truth not only implied there was something to hide, but also pointed the finger at himself as the one with the most to hide.

All heads turned to face him. For the first time, Fleet took notice of who was in the room. No officers were present, as he had expected, but his nerves still played tricks on him. He certainly didn't want Charles Lightoller hearing a word he had spoken.

"Well, they were going too damn fast, weren't they? After all the messages about ice they got, how many did you say you sent up, Harold?" Fleet was thinking fast, trying to divert attention from the actual sighting of any ice whatsoever, when he verbally stepped into murky waters, at least as far as Harold Bride was concerned. Fred knew Harold was hiding another enormous secret. As was Fleet himself, for now.

"We carried a handful of them up to the bridge. They had to know there was serious big ice out there, and we are not just talking growlers," Bride said. "The officers determine the speed. No one in this room could have slowed down *Titanic*, ice messages or not."

Ryan joined in. "Or maybe it was that Mr. Ismay, maybe he insisted that Captain Smith go all out and try to beat the maiden crossing time of the *Olympic*. I actually saw them talking together on the bridge the day before the accident."

"But the captain's the captain!" Fleet sounded off. "Ismay, no matter how big a deal he is, and I know he's the head of White Star, he's not in charge on the sea. I read about him in the So'ton Echo a few weeks ago. The article told all about the excitement for the maiden voyage. But it's the captain who's in charge once we're at sea. All of us who trained as seamen know that. I did my time as a lad, four years on the *Clio* I was, before I came to White Star."

"You were on the *Clio*?" Ryan asked.

"Yes. You've heard of her?" Fred responded, with a cocky look on his face. Enduring and surviving the *Clio* was something to be proud of and he knew it. Some of the swagger attached to his old days as a brawling lad came back to him all at once. He took a deep breath, puffed out his chest and enjoyed the moment.

"Well, I'm Irish, on me pa's side, but my mum's from Wales, so I lived there awhile, right in Bangor actually. So, the *Clio* then, the 'naughty boys ship!'" Ryan had a smart aleck sound in the way he spoke the words.

Fleet narrowed his eyes as he looked him over carefully. So, this was one of the boys he had envied, one of the town boys who had him a pa and a mum, like things ought to be. No discarded waif sitting before him in Jim Ryan.

"You got a problem with that, Ryan? We naughty boys know how t' scuffle, y'know." Fleet's words bit the air between them.

"I've got no problem," Ryan answered in a quieter voice that easily betrayed his backing-down status. The lads in the village had a fear and a begrudging respect for the lads on the ship. The *Clio* boys were known for their toughness, or they would never have survived. Many didn't.

Another young man said, "But getting back to that original comment, so this whole thing could be Ismay's fault. Is that what you're saying, Jim?"

Fleet recognized the young skinny man who spoke. He'd been helping Reginald Lee load a lifeboat the first time Fred had seen him. And then, Fleet had seen him again, chatting with Lee on the *Carpathia*.

"We don't want to jump to any conclusions, do we?" Ryan asked. "There are lots of possibilities as to the cause of the collision with the iceberg." He looked around the room as the words slipped from his mouth, letting his eyes linger longer on Fleet, and then on Harold Bride. It was almost as if, including Fleet in this visual comment, he was trying to show that he could, in a subtle way, stand up to a *Clio* boy. Perhaps it was a jab at the job done, or not done, by the lookout.

Fleet wasn't having any of it.

"You'd better not do that, Ryan. If you're smart, don't jump to anything or you may regret it." Fred felt smug in his reply. He'd never backed down from a fight in his life, which had landed him on the *Clio* in the first place. Often, he went looking for a fight. It was the only way he could hide the scared, lost little boy buried beneath his gruff exterior, but

Fred had no idea such a person existed, even though he looked him in the eye in the mirror over the wash-up sink every morning.

The meal was finished, as was the conversation. The men wandered off to wherever they had decided to spend the next hours as the ship proceeded down to Washington.

Frederick Fleet had in mind to ask the skinny young man if he had any idea what had become of Reginald Lee. Fleet walked about a bit until he spotted him sitting on a chair at the far end of the starboard side of the ship. No one else seemed to be around.

"I'm Fleet, Fred Fleet. I saw you talking with Reg Lee on the *Carpathia*. 'E's me mate, from the crow's nest. Do you know where's he's gone now? He's not on this ship with us anymore, it's fairly obvious. Lightoller took 'im away. We were about to share a bunk. D'ya know anything more?"

The fellow stuck out his hand to shake. Fred held back for a moment, deciding if he'd let the lad see his hands. But the fellow seemed harmless, and so Fred let the lad give a vigorous handshake. "I'm Vincent Adams. I was an assistant stoker. Yes, I was talking with Lee on board *Carpathia*. We'd been in the same lifeboat, both working the oars. I remember he told me on *Carpathia* that he was looking for you. He mentioned you by name. And then, here on the *Celtic*, I caught a glimpse of him for just a second. It was very strange. Lights had a hold of him. He had him by the arm and he was leading him along the upper deck. They didn't see me. I have no idea where he was taking him. I never saw Reg after that."

"That's bloody crazy. The officers told all of us lookouts that we must be part of the investigation, but now Reg has disappeared, and Lights is behind his disappearance. I don't like that."

"Well, maybe he ended up with the rest of the crew, maybe it was a big mix-up and he's back in England now."

"Maybe you're right. I guess that could have happened." Fleet's voice grew more energized. "Maybe Reg will turn up at the British inquiry."

"Most likely he will. I wonder, maybe that's the reason they kept him back now."

"What do you mean, kept him back now?" Fred asked.

"Well, maybe they are going to play his word against ours, to see if we are telling the truth."

That was the last thing Fleet wanted to hear.

Fleet and Adams sat together awhile, watching the sea, and reflecting on the events of the last days, although each of them were cautious of the words they chose. All their raw nerves need not be exposed.

***

Harold Bride sat by himself with his legs propped up on a deck chair. He was too unsettled to allow himself to drift into conversation with any of the men, and so once again, he had found a quiet spot where he could sit alone. His leg hurt, and he was trying to decide if this would be the moment he would swallow his last pain pill. He decided he would not.

He needed a clear mind, so he could think about the main thing that was eating his gut. He had almost, in his easy conversation the previous day, when he let himself relax in Fleet's presence, he had almost mentioned the one word he'd hoped to never hear again, although he knew that was most likely impossible.

The word was *Mesaba*. Rather, it was a name. *Mesaba* was the name of the ship that had sent the most damning message of the entire tragedy. The message cited the latitude and longitude where the *Mesaba* had spotted large icebergs. Neither he nor Jack Phillips knew the exact location of the *Titanic* at that precise moment, but they had a pretty good idea. It wasn't their job to know, and they had no navigational equipment available to them. The messages they sent and received did give them valuable information, and so they did know unofficially.

The message from the *Mesaba* placed a massive iceberg directly in the path of *Titanic*. When Jack received the telegraph, there was plenty of time to alter the course of the huge vessel and completely avoid the berg, if Captain Smith had the warning placed in his hand.

Bride realized he must have been working in the back room when Phillips received that particular message. With all the excitement after he'd come into the main room, right after the collision, Harold had not noticed the *Mesaba* message at all. But then he did catch sight of it. It was the very last thing he saw as he and Phillips fled the Marconi room. The time stamp on the message indicated it had been received at least twenty minutes before the collision. It was stuck under a paperweight, which meant Phillips had never carried it up to the bridge. In Captain's Smith's hands, this information would easily have turned the ship away from the ice in plenty of time, no doubt about it. The message was crucial, even though, at the very last instant Harold had noticed something else. It lacked the required MGS classification. Those letters would have required Jack to provide a response from Captain Smith back to the *Mesaba*. Why had the MGS been omitted?

All Harold could think was how soon until the *Mesaba* telegraph man shares this message with the world. Or would he? It was a message of grave concern. But, the *Mesaba* had omitted that crucial MGS designation. Why?

Harold knew Phillips had been overwhelmed sending all those personal messages to Cape Race. He wouldn't have taken the time to fully digest the dire warning. Now, Harold had absolutely zero doubt that was the fatal berg, the mountain of ice sitting directly in their path. If only Phillips had sidestepped protocol, considered their location, and realized what the situation demanded. He should have paused a moment and put two and two together. Jack needed to make sure the captain saw the message at once. The key ingredient was, Harold realized, Marconi men should always be thinking about the exact location of their ship. But they never did. Maybe, after this tragedy that would change. Most likely, that knowledge would have saved the life of everyone on board *Titanic*.

"Hard times are ahead," Harold said to himself. When he had given his testimony, he had purposely omitted any mention of the *Mesaba* message. Looking back, he realized he had made a mistake. Sharing it would have, in a way, cleared up any chance of suspicion about how well Jack Phillips was doing his job handling the wires, according to the Marconi regulations. Jack's job was sending messages, mainly for the passengers. He had, in effect, saved all their lives by fixing the telegraph when it had failed on Saturday. He fixed it because he had to send those private messages for the passengers. Harold was devoted to preserving the reputation of his fellow worker and good friend. He couldn't bear to see Jack blamed for anything whatsoever.

Harold was glad he had decided to save that one remaining pain pill. No doubt, he would need it very soon.

Chapter 8

Fleet held up the suit of clothes he'd been given. He wasn't sure if he should be pleased or insulted to be treated as a man unfit to enter the hallowed chambers he would visit this morning. In the almost twenty-five years he had been on this earth, Fred hadn't possessed a suit like this. Oh, it wasn't at all fancy, but everything matched, and it was new, or at least as *new* as any he'd ever seen. It didn't come from the Church of England charities that had dressed him as a child, or the bins of handouts left at the Seaman's Union Hall in Southampton. There was a clean, white shirt. It had a celluloid collar, stiff and no doubt uncomfortable, but impressive. A tie and, of all things, a vest! He turned the cap over in his hand, running his fingers over the tweed fabric.

"At least they don't pretend I'm any kinda swell, no fedora like the gents wear. But this is fine, a good workin' man's cap. Better than the last one I 'ad, the one that blew off me 'ead into the sea that night." He slipped into the outfit and carefully placed the cap on his head as Harol Bride limped back into their shared hotel room.

Upon their arrival in Washington, the group had been ushered off the ship and brought here. Fred was concerned about who was paying the bill. He wanted to assume it was White Star, but he had his doubts. Then again, how could they expect him to have enough in his pocket? He didn't have his pay from the voyage. Money was only handed over once they returned to Southampton. It was always done that way.

"Well, look at you, old man! Dressed up a bit, are you?"

"Yes, imagine the likes of me in a suit like this. You wouldn't understand. You come from finer roots. But a bloke like me, all dressed like a dandy. It's 'ard to take in all at once."

"Good luck, Fred. I'm sure you'll do just fine." Bride stared at the clothing Fred was so proud of.

Fred realized that his mate was being polite. Rather than approve of the clothes, Bride had a look of pity in his eyes. He wasn't the least bit impressed, or even approving of the cast off garments. Suddenly, Fleet saw how shabby they truly were, but of course that was his station in life, second best if even that. And that increased his worry.

"I will admit, I am a bit nervous. I ain't never imagined myself in a place like this Senate. I wonder what it will be like. I mean, I don't belong there a t'all. They'll pick me to bits."

"Don't be so sure of that, old man. You can take care of yourself just fine. With your rough beginnings, I'm sure you've been in a tussle or two."

"Oh, you're right about that, 'arold. I'm a fighter, all right."

"Well, there you go then."

Fleet had been impressed the one time he'd been to London and seen the mighty buildings that housed the halls of Parliament. He'd been cowed by his glimpse of Buckingham Palace, with the fancy-dressed guards parading back and forth. He'd known he was less than dirt, standing there in his clothes that reeked of the salty sea. For a moment, he'd pulled the cap from his head in reverence, until he'd realized that no one was watching him, and if they were, they would think him a proper fool.

But the sight of the United States Capitol building was even more humbling, more spectacular. Standing there, gazing at its white shimmer in the sunlight of a spring morning, his knees weakened. The cause wasn't the huge, magnificent edifice itself. It was that he was about to walk in there, against his will, and testify as to the events of the night of April 14. He'd be forced to answer questions as to why he hadn't seen the iceberg sooner. He knew he wasn't up to the task.

What approach should he take? He stood there a moment, trying to decide. The working man in him wanted to cover up about the early ice warnings he'd sent, when the officers on the bridge had ignored his calls. Better not to anger White Star. Better to follow the rule of the sea, take the boss's side in everything.

But another voice whispered in his ear. *Be brave Fred, be really brave. Come what may, be the better man, better than you've ever been before. Tell these pompous men in their fancy clothes the truth, whether they like it or not.*

Titanic had raced through the night, ignored his warnings until it was too late, with the biggest berg sitting in their face. That was what really happened. Yes, he told himself, do that, tell the truth. The world should know that White Star's to blame. The captain should have slowed the vessel at least twenty minutes earlier. And that's the best way to cover up what he must cover up, the pause before striking the bell. With renewed determination, he climbed the steps and pulled open the elaborate and heavy, bronze door.

Once inside on the black marble floor, he was afraid to take a step. Which way to go? He was lost before he started, but a woman sitting at a desk beckoned to him. As surprised as he was, it seemed there was no one else she might be sending a signal. He approached the desk.

"You are here for the *Titanic*, aren't you?" Her eyes raced over his garb, the cheap suit and tie marked his station in life. "Tell me your name please."

"Frederick Fleet."

"Yes, here you are," she murmured as she looked down and found his name on her list. She placed a check mark on the page. "Just walk down that hallway off to the right. Go all the way back and you will find the hearing room. There's a sign on the door."

"Thank you, I'd be lost without I... I mean, I *am* lost." Confused and embarrassed, he turned and took off rapidly down the hallway. He passed several closed doors, none of them with the sign he was looking for.

A door to his right flew open. Standing there, facing Fred, was none other than Mr. Bruce Ismay himself. Fleet had no doubt who he was. He had seen portraits of the man on board ship and in the newspapers sold on every street corner in the days before *Titanic* left Belfast.

"Fleet, come here," Ismay said, as he unceremoniously reached out and grabbed Fred's arm, yanking him into a small room. The door slammed behind him. Ismay pointed to a small, wooden chair. "Sit down." Ismay seated himself in a large wing back.

At first, Fred wondered how the man recognized him and knew his name, but then he realized how stupid that thought was. Ismay would know precisely who had spotted the ice.

"First of all, do you know who I am?" Ismay's voice was filled with authority, with privilege.

Fred wanted to squirm in his chair, but he forced himself to resist the urge. Was he a man or a child? He swallowed hard.

"Yes, I do Mr. Ismay, I mean, yes, sir, I mean..."

"Enough." Ismay lifted his arm to silence him. "Just so you know who you are talking to. Now, I want you to tell me precisely what happened Sunday night. I expect you to be perfectly honest, no matter what. Do you understand?" Fleet stared at him for a second or two, trying to decide what he should say. Then he dropped his gaze and pulled his hands from his pockets as he started to rotate the cap in his hands.

"Do you understand me?" Ismay repeated, the impatience in his voice slapped Fred in the face. And then, Ismay caught sight of the birthmarks on Fleet's hands. Fred flinched as he saw Ismay staring at his hands. All his life they had served as an excuse for other boys to mock him. Whatever self-confidence he might have possessed always vanished when he saw anyone staring at his badge of helplessness.

"Go ahead, tell me what happened."

"Yes, sir, yes I will." Fleet screwed up his eyes, and for that moment he was back in the nest, gazing out at that moonless, starlit night. "It was so cold, almost like the stars themselves were slivers of ice, and there was no moon at all."

"Yes, I'm aware of that. I was there! Get on with it."

"Sometime just after six bells, which is eleven p.m., I saw an iceberg, far off in the distance, maybe two miles. Yes, I could see that far, the night was so clear just then."

"But if it was two miles, and you sounded the alarm, we could have missed it! This makes no sense at all, Fleet. You must be wrong."

"Sir, that wasn't the iceberg that struck the ship. I'm talking of the very first berg I saw." He stared at Ismay, afraid to hear the man's reaction to his words. Ismay's eyes fluttered with discomfort, obviously, the man had been aware of this first iceberg, but he made no reply, other than his eye movement. Fleet was totally unnerved, but he felt compelled to continue.

"I picked up the telephone and I called the bridge. I didn't sound the three bells then, because it wasn't in our path, it was off t' the starboard side, but, as I said, maybe two miles. So I called t' the bridge. But no one answered. Then, maybe five minutes passed, and I saw another iceberg, also off t' starboard, and then, another one, and I called again, and again, no answer. And just a little bit later, maybe three minutes or so, I smelled ice."

"You smelled what? How can that be? What does ice *smell* like?"

It was clear to Fred that Ismay didn't believe his words about smelling ice and was losing his patience.

"It smells like a whole lot of things. Dead fish, salt, and just ice. There's no other way to describe it. It smells foul, and old, and I can't describe it better than that. If you'd been up in a crow's nest, you'd know the smell. I mean, of course you wouldn't be, a gentleman like you, not there, but—"

"Enough. So, what did you do?"

"Well, I called to the bridge again. And a voice picked up. I can't say who it was, I didn't know, all he said was, yes. I screamed at 'im, I screamed, "I can smell ice, and I saw three bergs before, and no one picked up the phone.""

"And then what, what did they say?"

"They didn't say anything. You know they don't have to. All I do, is say what I see, and they don't 'ave to reply."

"No, by the rules, they don't have to."

"And the ship just kept movin' along, just as fast as we were goin' all night. It was as if I'd never warned 'em about anything at all. Then, maybe twenty minutes later, I saw it, the big one, right in our path. And I struck the three bells, and I called to the bridge. The phone rang 'n' rang. Finally, I got the answer, 'What did you see?' And I told 'im, 'Iceberg right ahead.' You know the rest, sir."

"Here's where we are going to make a change, Fleet. Listen to me and listen to me good. Pay attention." Daggers in his voice.

Fred shifted uneasily in his uncomfortable chair.

"You are listening, aren't you? And I hope you are man enough to grasp what I am about to say to you." Ismay looked down at Fred's birthmarks again.

"Yes, sir, yes, I'm listening." Fleet's voice was weak, although he wanted to sound strong.

"You didn't see any of those earlier icebergs, and you never called the bridge about sighting, or smelling, anything up until the big one."

"I didn't, sir?"

"No, you didn't. And here's the reason why. If you decide to be noble, and tell your whole little tale, and oh, you were doing your job so good, and you are the best lookout, and the bridge ignored you, this is what's going to happen to you. You won't have a job. Not on White Star or any other line. I'll see to that, for the rest of your life. Who knows what terrible things will happen to you then? Do you have a family to take you in? Do you have other skills you can use? Do you have money put aside to live off the rest of your life?" He didn't wait for a reply. "I thought not."

Fred lifted his eyes, and for a split second looked into Ismay's face. It was cold and removed. It was obvious Ismay meant every word he said.

"So, here's what's going to happen," Ismay went on. "You will tell them just what happened with the sighting of the last iceberg, and that's all you will say. It was an act of nature, it popped up in the black night with no moon to give you early warning. And if you do that, and if you can keep a secret, I'm going to offer you something in return. Can you keep a secret, Fleet?"

"Yes, sir, yes I can," Fred mumbled.

"I hope you are more certain of that than the way your voice just sounded. Here's the deal. If you say what I insist you say in the hearing, I will give you a job for life with White Star. Even more than that, because I'm in a generous mood, I will give you a pension after you retire. How's that?"

"That sounds better, for me."

"Oh! You are a bright young man, sharper than I figured. Because, Fleet, if you don't do what I say, if you think you can tell anyone your version of what happened that night, you will destroy White Star, and I'm not about to let you do that. If you destroy my shipping line, I will most definitely destroy you. And I can do that—easily. Just so we understand each other. But now that we have established that you will testify the way I want you to, everything's settled. You will have a job on the *Olympic*. And after you retire, a pension for your old age. Just remember, you can tell no one about this, not even your wife. Do you have a wife?"

"Yes, yes I do, Mr. Ismay."

"What's her name?"

"Eva, sir."

"Well then, think of it this way. You are doing this for Eva. Does she come from a rich family, your Eva?" Without waiting for an answer, Ismay continued, obviously pleased with his line of reasoning. "No, I thought not. And you are obligated to take care of her. By doing what I want you to, you will be able to take care of Eva for the rest of your life. So, go now, go on down the hall and into the hearing room. And watch your words. And best tell them that phone call you made was answered immediately. Be very careful how you answer the senator's questions. They may try to trip you up."

Ismay rose from the wing chair and raised his arms, shooing Fleet from the room. "Go, go now. And remember, you never talked to me in your life. Why would a gentleman like me, the chairman of White Star, talk to the likes of you?" Ismay turned his back in dismissal.

Fred stumbled down the hallway, too disturbed by what had happened to formulate anything he might say to the committee other than he must go along with Ismay's demands, but also, if possible, he still wanted to protect his own reputation. If he failed in that, what would Eva think of him?

He came to a door with the sign, "Titanic Investigation." A man sat at a desk beside the door. "Your name?" he asked.

"Frederick Fleet." It was a small voice, a voice Fred hardly recognized as his own.

"You may enter, and hand this slip over when they call your name."

Fred reached out and took the piece of paper. He noticed the expression on the man's face. Obviously, he recognized Fred's name and knew he was the lookout. Blame leaped from his eyes.

As he headed for the door, Fred felt the man's accusation burn into his skin. He looked down at the slip of paper with his name written on it, a check mark next to it. His entry ticket, as it were, to the chamber of horrors. But then he remembered the night and the sea, and the screams, and the voices. Surely that was the true chamber of horrors, not this, not this at all. He must collect himself, and above all else, protect himself in his replies or he might as well have perished in the waters along with all those other poor souls. He entered the room and sat in the back. No one seemed to notice him. The session was already in progress.

Fleet looked around the room. A man was testifying, but Fred could hardly hear his words. At first, he didn't concentrate on any of the faces. His attention was drawn to the room itself. In his years on this earth, he had never seen such an elaborate place. The walls were marble. Marble! The floors as well, and huge crystal chandeliers, a bevy of them, suspended from the high ceilings. Not even in church, where he'd been taken on Christmas by the Home, not even there, had he seen the likes of this. The parish church of St. Mary's in Walton was beautiful to behold, but this was something else. A lump formed in his throat. This was no place for a bloke like him.

"Fleet. Is Frederick Fleet in the room? Next witness, Frederick Fleet. Come to the front at once."

He struggled to find the strength and the will to stand up, but he had no choice. He pulled himself from the chair and made his way to the huge table in the front of the room. He reached out his hand and offered the ticket he had received to the man standing at the head of the table.

The man batted it down, making Fred feel an idiot before he had even begun. "Be seated," he commanded.

Fred sat. He cast a furtive glance at the people arrayed before him. They all wore expensive suits and thick silk neckties, many of them sporting elaborately waxed mustaches. Fred twisted his wool cap in his hands and kept his eyes averted as he examined the pattern of the Oriental carpet at his feet.

"What is your full name?" said the man who had refused his ticket.

"Frederick Fleet."

"Where do you reside?"

"Southampton." For the first time, Fred was aware that he spoke differently than the way other men, educated men, spoke. He knew he had a strong Liverpool accent, but he had never realized how poor his way of talking must sound to others, especially these elegant gentlemen.

"England?"

"England."

The door opened, and Bruce Ismay slipped into the room. He sat down in a chair up front for a moment, but then rose from the chair and paced back and forth.

"How old are you?" The man asking the questions also glanced at Ismay, as he asked Fred the next question.

"Twenty-five next October."

"What is your business?"

"Sailor. Lookout man."

"How much experience have you had in that work?"

"About four years. I was four years on the *Oceanic*, on the lookout."

"Four years as lookout on the *Oceanic*, of the White Star Line?"

"Yes, sir."

"Is that all the experience you have had?"

"Going to sea?"

"Yes."

"Of that, sir, five or six years."

"Besides that?"

"That is all. When I was in the training ship."

"Have you ever been lookout on any other ship?"

"No." That wasn't true, he'd been a lookout on *Oceanic*. He wasn't sure why he'd gotten confused in his reply. He knew he should be evasive in his answers, but there was no reason to lie about that. He was feeling rattled. He shouldn't have said no, but how would he appear if he changed his words?

"You were lookout on the *Titanic*, were you not?"

"Yes."

"And sailed with the *Titanic* from Southampton, or from Belfast?"

"I fetched her around from Belfast, on the lookout."

"And made this voyage from Southampton to the time of the collision—the accident?"

"Yes, sir."

"I want to get on the record the place where you were stationed in the performance of your duty."

"I was on the lookout."

"On the lookout?"

"At the time of the collision."

"In the crow's nest?"

"Yes."

"At the time of the collision?"

"Yes, sir."

"Can you tell how high above the boat deck that is?"

"I have no idea." He did know, however. *Isn't it better if I change things up a bit? Don't let them pin me down.* Somehow it seemed safer to know less.

"Can you tell how high above the crow's nest the masthead is?"

"No, sir."

"Do you know how far you were above the bridge?"

"I am no hand at guessing."

"I do not want you to guess, but if you know, I would like to have you tell."

"I have no idea." Fred squirmed in his seat.

Now, a different senator interrupted. "You hardly mean that. You have some idea?"

"No, I do not." He looked at Ismay again. The man's stare stuck to Fred's face.

The same senator tried again with a different question.

"You know whether it was a thousand feet or two hundred?"

The original man, Senator Smith, resumed the questions. "Was there any other officer or employee stationed at a higher point on the *Titanic* than you were?"

"No, sir."

"You were the lookout?"

"Yes, sir."

"Where are the eyes of the ship?"

"The eyes of the ship?"

"The ship's eyes?"

'"Forward."

"At the extreme bow?"

"Yes, sir."

"And on the same level as the boat deck or below it?"

"Below it."

"How far below it?"

"I do not know, sir."

"Mr. Fleet, can you tell who was on the forward part of the *Titanic* Sunday night when you took your position in the crow's nest?"

"There was nobody."

"Nobody?"

"No, sir."

"Who was on the bridge?"

"When I went up to relieve the others?"

"Yes."

"Mr. Murdoch."

"Officer Murdoch?"

"First Officer."

"Who else?"

"I think it was the Third Officer."

"What was his name?"

"The man that was here, Pitman."

"Mr. Pitman, the man who just left the stand?"

"I do not know all the officers on the bridge." As the words left his mouth, Fred saw the senators exchange a glance. They obviously thought he was an idiot. But what did they know of life on a huge vessel? Nothing. He didn't know the name of every officer.

"You do not recall any more of them?"

"No, I do not know whether he was there or not."

"I do not want any confusion, if I can help it. I want to get this down right. Was the captain on the bridge?" Senator Smith fixed his eyes on Fred.

"I do not know, sir."

"You did not see him?"

"No, sir."

"What time did you take your watch Sunday night?"

"Ten o'clock."

Now another senator cut in with a question, as Senator Smith took a drink of water from a crystal glass. "Whom did you relieve?"

"Symons and Jewell." Fred wished he could have a drink as well, his throat dry with fear. But he didn't ask for one. He knew better than that.

"Who was with you on the watch?"

"Lee."

"What, if anything, did Symons and Jewell, or either one, say to you when you relieved them of the watch?"

"They told us to keep a sharp lookout for small ice."

"What did you say to them?"

"I said, 'All right.'"

Now Senator Smith was back in command of the questions. "What did Lee say?"

"He said the same."

"And you took your position in the crow's nest?"

"Yes, sir."

"Did you keep a sharp lookout for ice?"

"Yes, sir."

"Tell what you did."

"Well, I reported an iceberg right ahead, a black mass."

"When did you report that?"

"I could not tell you the time."

"About what time?"

"Just after seven bells."

"How long after you had taken your place in the crow's nest?"

"The watch was nearly over. I had done the best part of the watch up in the nest."

"How long a watch did you have?"

"Two hours, but the time was going to be put back that watch."

"The time was to be set back?"

"Yes, sir." Fred referred to the need to routinely reset ship's time as she made her way across the ocean.

"Did that alter your time?"

"We were to get about two hours and twenty minutes."

"How long before the collision or accident did you report ice ahead?"

"I have no idea." Fred's hands were shaking. He put them in his lap and clasped one to the other to keep them still.

"About how long?"

"I could not say, at the rate she was going."

"How fast was she going?"

"I have no idea." Or course he had some idea, upwards of twenty knots to be sure, but he wasn't about to tell them. He saw Ismay's eyes cut over in his direction.

"Would you be willing to say that you reported the presence of this iceberg an hour before the collision?"

"No, sir."

"Forty-five minutes?"

"No, sir."

"A half hour before?"

"No, sir."

"Fifteen minutes before?"

"No, sir."

"Ten minutes before?"

"No, sir."

"How far away was this black mass when you first saw it?"

"I have no idea, sir." Fred broke out in a sweat. He glanced about the room quickly and saw Ismay's eyes still fixed in his direction.

"Can you not give us some idea? Did it impress you as serious?"

"I reported it as soon as ever I seen it."

"I want a complete record of it, you know. Give me, as nearly as you can, how far away it was when you saw it. You are accustomed to judging distances, are you not, from the crow's nest? You are there to look ahead and sight objects, are you not?"

"We are only up there to report anything we see."

"But you are expected to see and report anything in the path of the ship, are you not?" the senator's voice belied his growing frustration.

"Anything we see—a ship or anything." Fleet tried to keep his voice as bland as possible.

"Anything you see?"

"Yes, anything we see."

"Whether it be a field of ice, a 'growler,' or an iceberg, or any other substance?"

"Yes, sir."

"Have you trained yourself so that you can see objects as you approach them with fair accuracy?"

"I do not know what you mean, sir." Fred tried very hard not to lose patience. *Of course, a lookout can do this,* he thought to himself.

"If there had been a black object ahead of this ship, or a white one, a mile away, or five miles away, fifty feet above the water or 150 feet above the water, would you have been able to see it, from your experience as a seaman?"

"Yes, sir."

"When you see these things in the path of the ship, you report them?"

"Yes, sir."

"What did you report when you saw this black mass Sunday night?"

"I reported an iceberg right ahead."

"To whom did you report that?"

"I struck three bells first. Then I went straight to the telephone and rang them up on the bridge."

"You struck three bells and went to the telephone and rang them up on the bridge?"

"Yes."

"Did you get anyone on the bridge?"

"I got an answer straight away. 'What did I see,' or 'What did you see?'" Sweat dripped down Fred's back. That was a lie. That night, the phone rang and rang, and for a few moments, Fred had thought to himself, *Are they going to ignore me again? With this huge berg so close this time?*

Ismay gave Fred another sharp glance, indicating, at least to Fred, he was listening closely to his every word and was watching for Fred to tell the lie, to complete the cover-up, to protect White Star.

"Did the person who was talking to you tell you who he was?"

"No. He just asked me what did I see. I told him an iceberg right ahead."

"What did he say then?"

"He said, 'Thank you.'"

"Do you know to whom you were talking?"

"No, I do not know who it was."

"What was the object in sending the three bells?"

"That denotes an iceberg right ahead." He really meant to say, it signals there is an object, any object right ahead, but he didn't want to complicate things, not now.

"It denotes danger?"

"No, it just tells them on the bridge that there is something about."

"You took both precautions. You gave the three bells, and then you went and telephoned to the bridge?"

"Yes, sir."

"Where did you have to go to telephone?"

"The telephone is in the nest."

"The telephone is right in the crow's nest?"

"Yes."

"You turned and communicated with the bridge from the nest?"

"Yes, sir."

"Did you get a prompt response?"

"I did." And there was the lie once again, the response to the phone had not been prompt. He looked up for a second and again he saw Ismay, poised and vigilant as ever, listening carefully to every word he spoke.

"And you made the statement that you have indicated?"

"Yes."

"Then what did you do?"

"After I rang them up?"

"Yes, sir."

"I kept staring ahead again." Fred was amazed the senator had called him sir. He decided it must have been a mistake.

"You remained in the crow's nest?"

"I remained in the crow's nest until I got relief."

"And Lee remained in the nest?"

"Yes." This wasn't true. Fred had begged Reg to climb down, just in case, no need for both of them to be hit if the worst happened. But, how to explain this now? Better to just say yes."

"How long did you stay there?"

"About a quarter of an hour to twenty minutes after."

"After what?"

"After the accident."

"And then did you leave this place?"

"We got relieved by the other two men."

"The other two men came? Did they go up?"

"They came up in the nest."

"And you got down?"

"We got down, yes."

"Can you not indicate, in any way, the length of time that elapsed between the time that you first gave this information by telephone and by bell to the bridge officer and the time the boat struck the iceberg?"

"I could not tell you, sir."

"You cannot say?"

"No, sir." Here, Fred was telling the truth. Watching the iceberg approach had been so terrifying, there was no accounting for the exact passage of time.

"You cannot say whether it was five minutes or an hour?"

"I could not say, sir."

"I wish you would tell the committee whether you apprehended danger when you sounded these signals and telephoned, whether you thought there was danger?"

"No, no, sir. That is all we have to do up in the nest. To ring the bell, and if there is any danger ring them up on the telephone." Fred was getting confused by his own words. Most of all, he just wanted to seem blameless for any outcome.

"You did ring them up on the telephone. Did that indicate that you thought there was danger?"

"Yes, sir."

"You thought there was danger?"

"Well, it was so close to us. That is why I rang them up."

"How large an object was this when you first saw it?"

"It was not very large when I first saw it."

"How large was it?"

"I have no idea of distances or spaces." A ridiculous claim, but Fred knew he had to appear as consistently evasive as possible, mainly to please Ismay, but also to salvage any type of reputation he might have as a lookout. He just figured it was safer not to give out any numbers.

"Was it the size of an ordinary house? Was it as large as this room appears to be?

"No, no. It did not appear very large at all."

"Was it as large as the table at which I am sitting?"

"It would be as large as those two tables put together, when I saw it at first."

"When you first saw it, it appeared about as large as these two tables put together?"

"Yes, sir." Two tables sounded good, like a safe answer.

"Did it appear to get larger after you first saw it?"

"Yes, it kept getting larger as we were getting nearer it."

"As it was coming toward you, and you were going toward it?"

"Yes."

"How large did it get to be finally, when it struck the ship?"

"When we were alongside, it was a little bit higher than the forecastle head.

"The forecastle head is how high above the water line?"

"Fifty feet, I should say."

"About fifty feet?"

"Yes."

"So that this black mass, when it finally struck the boat, turned out to be about fifty feet above the water?"

"About fifty or sixty." As soon as the words slipped from his lips, Fred realized he had revealed he could provide the size, and the number of feet, after he had claimed he was no judge at guessing. He wondered if this was a trap. Would he be called on his previous lie?

"Fifty or sixty feet above the water?"

"Yes." Would they mention his lie? No, they did not. He breathed a bit easier. And again, Ismay watched him carefully. He was breathing fire at Fred with his eyes.

"And when you first saw it, it looked no larger than these two tables?"

"No, sir."

"Do you know whether the ship was stopped after you gave that telephone signal?"

"No. No, she did not stop at all. She did not stop until she passed the iceberg."

"She did not stop until she passed the iceberg?"

"No, sir."

"Do you know whether her engines were reversed?"

"Well, here's what I know, she started to go to port while I was at the telephone."

The questions dragged on. Fred was losing patience and hoped they were nearing the end. So far, they had skipped the items that bothered him most. Maybe they would end now, if he was lucky.

Then Senator Smith leaned forward, his mood shifting.

"What protection against the weather have you in the crow's nest?"

"We have nothing ahead, and there are just two bits of screen behind us." Fred couldn't understand why they cared about this.

"Canvas?"

"Yes, sir."

"And nothing ahead?"

- "Nothing in front."

"So your view is unobstructed?"

"Yes, sir."

"Are you given glasses of any kind?"

"We had none this time. We had nothing at all, only our own eyes, to look out." Fred crossed his legs and started to feel uncomfortable.

"On the *Oceanic* you had glasses, had you not?"

Fred was surprised they mentioned his previous lookout experience, but he decided to ignore it. He just wanted to be done and out of here. There was no use extending the conversation.

"Yes, sir."

"Each of you?"

"There is one pair in the nest." How could he possibly think there would be more than one pair? It was obvious to Fred the man had never sailed any seas!

"One pair of glasses?"

"Yes, sir."

"What kind of glasses are they? Strong, powerful glasses?"

"No, not always, sir."

"What were those on the Oceanic?"

"Very poor. You could see about from here to that looking-glass. But all the same, they served their purpose, Fred wanted to add, but it seemed impudent.

"Did you make any request for glasses on the *Titanic*?"

"We asked them in Southampton, and they said there was none for us."

"Whom did you ask?"

"They said there was none intended for us."

"Whom did you ask?"

"We asked Mr. Lightoller, the second officer." He knew Lights would back him up on this.

"Did you make the request yourself?"

"No, the station lookout men did, Hogg and Evans."

"How do you know they made it?"

"Because they told us." Fred tried not to betray his exasperation, but really!

"Where did they tell you? After leaving Southampton?"

"In Southampton, and afterwards."

"You expected glasses?"

"We had a pair from Belfast to Southampton."

"You had a pair of glasses from Belfast to Southampton?"

"Yes, sir, but none from Southampton to New York."

"Where did those go that you had from Belfast to Southampton?"

"We do not know that. We only know we never got a pair. If we knew where they went, we might have got them back." Fred was trying to behave.

"And you had none from Southampton to the place of this accident?"

"No, sir."

"Suppose you had had glasses such as you had on the Oceanic, or such as you had between Belfast and Southampton, could you have seen this black object a greater distance?"

"We could have seen it a bit sooner."

"How much sooner?"

"Well, enough to get out of the way." Fred was proud of his answer.

"Did you and your mates discuss with one another that you had no glasses?"

"We discussed it all together, between us."

"Did you express surprise or regret that you had none?"

"I do not know what you mean."

"Were you disappointed that you had no glasses?"

"Yes, sir."

Fred talked on and on, answering the rest of their questions. He had passed the sticky part of the interview, or so he thought.

Then Senator Smith fixed him with a sharp glance.

"Did you see any other iceberg, field ice or growlers while you were in the crow's nest Sunday or Sunday night?"

Another bead of sweat slid down Fred's back. He felt Ismay's eyes bite at his face. He willed himself to answer.

"Only the one I reported 'right ahead.'"

He knew his voice sounded weak and a trifle unsure, but it was the best he could do. He felt himself changed by this lie. Oh, he had no illusions about himself being any kind of angel, he was a tough lad, a survivor, and yes, a bully at times. He'd never backed down from a fight, and he'd instigated more than a few of them. But this was different. There was no going back on this descent into hell. The death of 1,500 people hung in the balance, and he felt he'd let them down by withholding the truth from the committee.

"Only that one? You are *sure* of it?"

"That is all." Fred didn't recognize the voice that answered the final question as his own.

The worst of it was over, for now. The only person that could dispute his words was Reginald Lee. Lee knew that Fred's early warnings had been ignored. But Lee was gone, no doubt White Star only wanted one witness available to sit before the Senate, less chance of the two of them getting their stories in a muddle. When or if Fred would ever see Lee again, he had no idea.

A dreadful headache roared in Fred's ears. He hadn't had one like this in years, not since his days on the *Clio*. His nerves had been in poor shape then, in the contentious world of rough lads.

He closed his eyes and rested his head in his hand for a moment until he realized with a start that his testimony was over. He was free to go. Unless objections were raised when the committee met on their own to sum up the day, he was safe, or as safe as he could be.

He had done Ismay's bidding and lied and lied. He had also proved to himself that he was even weaker than he had ever imagined. And he had fed the rumors that would surely spread around the world, the *Titanic*, the most marvelous ship was gone, and Frederick Fleet was to blame. All that was required of him was to see the one iceberg in time. The heavy cloak of guilt descended over him. He was trapped.

Fred had always been a sound sleeper. After a day on a ship with the heavy demands of labor and the sea air in his face, falling asleep was never a problem. But that night, after his testimony before the Senate, all of that changed. Instead of nodding off to sleep easily, he lay on his bunk turning and twisting most of the night.

It wasn't the uncomfortable mattress to blame for his unease. He would fall asleep for a few minutes, ten at most, only to be awakened with a jolt as reality seized hold of him, and the lies and the guilt worked their way through his eyelids. He saw an image of himself at the hearing, speaking the words he knew were untrue, and then right after that the disturbing image of the people in the water, screaming for help, came back to him, over and over.

He had betrayed them, even more than his failure to see the final iceberg in time. He had failed in his duty. He had lived, and they had died. All because he wouldn't stick up for the truth and tell about the ignored ice warnings, or to be more precise, because of his lack of virtue, their demise went unredeemed. White Star Line would get away with everything, and that too was entirely his fault.

Somewhere in life, he had heard the term tormented soul, but he didn't grasp its meaning at the time. But now he did. That was his sentence, the price he would pay, to live out his life as a tormented soul.

He was relieved to hear that Harold Bride would not be bunking with him anymore. Harold was off to hospital, where he needed to be. But more than that, Fred didn't want to discuss with anyone the things he had sworn were true at the hearing. Because they were not.

Chapter 9

Days passed. He was glad when the departure of the *Adriatic* was announced for the next morning. In one day's time, the last of the *Titanic* crew would finally head home to England. He would be traveling with, besides the seamen such as himself, the few surviving *Titanic* officers: Boxhall, Lowe, Pitman, and Lightoller. And yes, Ismay. Fred didn't want to be anywhere near Mr. Ismay.

He longed for England's soil under his boots. Most of all, Fred looked forward to his wife's warm embrace. He needed her so much. Never in his life had he acknowledged a need for or expected such a comfort from another person. Before Eva, he'd had no one who'd loved him, not one single person.

Fred kept to himself on the crossing back to England. The last thing he wanted was to discuss anything with anyone. For this journey, the men from *Titanic* weren't treated as part of the *Adriatic* crew but traveled as third-class passengers. The officers traveled second-class, and Mr. Ismay, first. All except Ismay were required to eat with the *Adriatic* crew.

As the ship left New York, they were told they were not to mingle with any passengers. Fred wanted nothing to do with the crewmen from the *Adriatic* either. He didn't want them asking him about *Titanic*, and what it was like, and why he didn't see the berg sooner. Most of all, the deal he'd made with Ismay must not escape his lips. He knew sometimes he could let his words get away from him, so he made a point of sitting alone, away from all the other men.

On the second day at sea, when he entered the mess for breakfast, Bruce Ismay himself sat at a long table, all alone. *Why wasn't he in the first-class dining room? Ah, maybe he doesn't want the passengers asking him questions.* The two men exchanged a furtive glance and then, leaving his unfinished meal behind, the older man pulled himself from his chair and hurried out of the room.

"What did you do to chase him out?" It was one of the crew members Fred recognized, from somewhere, probably from his years on the *Oceanic*. He tossed a joke at Fred. He wasn't one of the few *Titanic* crew, of that Fred was certain. He looked too calm, too at ease to have been a part of the trauma of *Titanic*. He was *Adriatic* crew.

Fred tried to match the man's mood.

"Wasn't me," Fred replied. "Maybe 'e 'ad to take 'im a leak." The others chuckled at that.

"Not possible" one volunteered. "The boss ain't like the rest of us. He ain't never gotta take a piss."

The rest of the crew laughed. Fred joined in with a weak chuckle. He found the words amusing, but laughing was still hard for him, even two and a half weeks after the sinking.

And still he sat by himself, off to a side once he had fixed a plate off the steaming hot buffet. Fred chewed on a piece of bacon. He wished he hadn't seen Mr. Ismay. He hoped he'd never see him again. Ismay had told him that day in the small, private room in the Senate building that the upcoming job on the *Olympic* and the money for the pension would be set up for him. But Fred never expected to actually see the man face to face again.

A pile of old newspapers was stacked at the end of the table where Fred sat. For want of something to do while he ate, he picked up a paper from the top of the heap. News of the *Titanic's* sinking was plastered across the page. Fred tossed that paper and picked up the next. Same thing, and the next as well. It affirmed his concern that there was no other news in the world on anyone's mind. Why did he, of all people, find himself such a damning spot in history?

He went cold, as if his blood stopped coursing through his body. If *Titanic* was the top story everywhere, and his name was attached to the tragedy—he had seen it, right there on the front page, *Frederick Fleet, Titanic lookout*—was there any chance that somewhere, he had no idea where, his own mum was sitting and reading a newspaper same as this, and learning the news that he, the baby she had left behind, was the cause? What did she think of her wee lad now? Did she regret leaving him so long ago? Or rather, she might feel she had done the right thing, for the lad was trouble from the beginning. That was why she'd left him behind. Such thoughts refused to leave his head. He was frozen to the spot, even as everyone else filed out of the mess and Fred sat there, no telling how long, his eyes shut, thinking about this woman he had never known.

The days drifted past. Rain one day, sun the next, it mattered not to Fred. And then on a fresh morning, with the wind whipping up, Fred's heart beat faster. How would it seem, coming home, after all that had happened?

At last, they were close. England beckoned. At best, they were some two hours out from the entrance to Liverpool waters.

"I can't wait t' see me wife," more than one of the men was heard to say.

Again, Fred wasn't drawn into the group, but his own excitement grew as he put aside thoughts of his mum and thought instead of Eva. He'd never needed to see anyone so much in his entire life. He'd always needed to see his parents, but that was not in the realm of possibility. They had made sure of that. He needed to see Eva. How anxious he would be until he could wrap his arms around her. That's where he would find the healing he needed. Eva held the answer, she had to, because Fred, on his own, was helpless. But first, he had to travel from Liverpool to Southampton. As the ship made ready to fit snug to the pier, Fred was handed a list by one of the crew members, showing the timing of trains to So'ton, as Southampton was referred to by the locals.

"I thought you might need this. Fleet, aren't you? I remember you from my time on *Oceanic*. I'm goin' to So'ton me self. We can catch the train together, if you like."

"Charlie, ain't ya? Charlie Bridger? We sailed t'gether, din' we?" Fred was reluctant to get into conversation, but he was glad to know when the next train was leaving for home. He gave Charlie a weak grin, while he told himself, *Don't start talkin' 'bout Titanic.*

"Fleet, come with us." It was Second Officer Lightoller. "We are all going down the plank together, a show of respect for the people of Liverpool, and all that were lost. You come with us now."

Fred shrugged his shoulders and gave a parting nod to Charlie and hastened over to Lights. He wasn't going to get in any trouble now, not after all he'd been through. Pitman, Lowe, and Boxhall were already standing at Lightoller's side. Feeling like a puppet, not a man, Fred fell in line beside them. With Lightoller leading the procession, they slowly moved down the gangplank. It was a somber moment. The eyes of the crowd watched them.

There was an eerie silence until loud cries rang up from the throng. Fred wondered what was going on, from dead quiet to this uproar. All heads were turned. Fred swiveled in the same direction.

Ismay had appeared, his wife beside him. She had boarded the ship in Queenstown to accompany her husband back to England. "Welcome home! Welcome back, Mr. Ismay!"

Fred couldn't believe it. They were cheering him! *If only they knew the truth,* he thought to himself. They never would.

Just then, Lights ran over to a small woman Fred hadn't noticed before. He had a big grin on his face. The woman moved closer. Fred was surprised by her very awkward limp, and her beautiful face. Of course, Lights had never mentioned his family, but this must be his wife. Fred realized she must have taken the train up from Southampton to greet her husband as quickly as she could. Fred envied her devotion.

"Well, take a look at that, Charlie," he pointed to the couple. As he did so, the woman suddenly looked up, her eyes connecting with his. He couldn't help but wonder if she knew who he was?

"I never would have guessed Lights was a romantic bloke." Charlie laughed as he watched the two of them embrace.

"Hey, we'd better not miss our ride if we are to see our own wives," Fred reminded him.

He and Charlie detached themselves from the rest of the men and headed for the train. If they hurried, they might make the 9:30 and be home for a late morning tea.

The two men found seats together in a third-class carriage. Fred watched out the window, looking at all the ordinary scenes of daily life flitting past. A few children walking with their mum, who pushed a pram with the latest addition to the family. The lads all wore hand-me-down clothes and scuffed shoes. No money for another babe, but there they were. At least they had a real family, Fred thought. The train picked up speed. He closed his eyes, feigning sleep, so Charlie wouldn't ask him any questions. Surely he knew he was the lookout, the one who'd missed the berg.

After an hour's time, the train slowed, hissing and sending up billows of smoke as it drew into the station. The So'ton station was in the area adjoining the waterfront. Fred knew the waterfront at Southampton well. It was his life. But now, as the train pulled in, it was as if he were seeing the place for the first time. The gulls flew up in a rush, only to fall again, circling the ships, swooping and calling out a welcome of sorts. The pier looked much more run down, and smaller than he might have remembered. He'd never been gone so long before. No, it wasn't that.

And that was when it came to him, the realization that he had come so close to death in the frigid waters of the North Atlantic. At the time, as it all unfolded, with the ice, and then loading the lifeboats, and pulling on the oars for hours, and the guilt, and the physical effort required of him, all of this kept at bay the other side of the whole event. He almost died, there was no certainty he would survive. He'd been a bit worried in the lifeboat, but that feeling didn't come close to this. He saw the world in a new way, with a fresh eye. His whole life stretched out before him, if only he didn't feel so guilty. Surely, Eva could help him tamp down those feelings. *Isn't that what a wife will do for a man?* They really hadn't been married long enough for him to have a sure answer to that, but he hoped it was true. He was counting on it.

As they edged out of the train station, Fred caught up with and stayed close to Charlie. A huge crowd stood about. Southampton had turned out to bid them welcome, overwhelming Fred. But the strange thing was, once again, as in Liverpool, it was a silent group. No cheers rang out, no hands were raised in greeting.

Fred could hear sounds of traffic, whistles blowing, and bells ringing, all muted, from a great distance away. Up close, there was not a single sound save the footfalls of the crew as they stepped off the train, touching home soil for the first time. Indeed, it was a solemn moment since the great majority of the crew had been lost. The first wave of surviving crew had traveled on the *Lapland,* and they'd been home for weeks. This smaller bunch, these ragtag men who had been involved in the Senate inquiry, represented the very last of those to return, and their small number summed up the size of the tragedy. Their presence, paltry in numbers, punched lasting holes in the seagoing community.

It was a sober homecoming at best. Southampton was in mourning, as well it should be.

Fred realized that most likely Eva was here, standing in the crowd, searching the faces, looking for him.

Charlie tapped him on the shoulder.

"There's me wife Margaret. I'll see ya later, mate." The young man dashed off to his wife's waiting arms.

Now Fred was even more determined to find Eva. He looked across the waiting throng. *No, that one isn't her, no and no again.* Soon it became apparent, she wasn't here at all. He tried to assure himself that her absence meant nothing. There must be a logical reason.

He hurried along the winding streets, heading up the steep hill, retracing the steps he had taken weeks ago, except everything felt different. Their house, a small, brown, wooden place with a couple of windows that looked out on the road, looked the same. How could it seem so unchanged when the world had turned upside down?

A curtain pulled back for a second, and then slipped back in place. Eva knew he was home! But the door didn't fly open in greeting. It stayed shut. Fred walked the last few steps up the hill and pulled open the door. At least it wasn't locked.

Eva sat in a chair in the front room, her eyes on the door.

Without waiting for her to say a word, he rushed across the room, and pulled her up into a tight embrace. "Eva," he mumbled into her hair. "I missed you so much."

"You're back," she said, the tone in her voice confusing him. It wasn't cold, but it wasn't welcoming. If anything, it sounded as if she was stalling for time, deciding just how she should react to his presence.

But he refused to be denied. He couldn't imagine that she didn't share his joy that they were together again. He gave her a warm and increasingly passionate kiss. He noticed the lack of response. But again, he ignored any signs of warning, his hunger was so great.

"You are all I needed, through all of that, that horror, I can't even begin t' explain what it was like. But you, you are everything t' me, Eva. It's so good to see you."

He couldn't ignore Eva's attitude any longer. He stepped back and looked at her face carefully and started again, taking a gentler tone. "How are you m'love? 'ow 'ave you been?"

"Fred, to tell you the truth, *this* is how I've been. Of course, I'm glad you're home, safe and sound. I wouldn't want it any other way. But all of this, here, it's been a living hell. You can't imagine, but I guess you should know, everyone, the newspapers, and the neighbors, and my family, everyone, they blame you for what happened. How could you not see that huge iceberg in time? How could you fail like that?" The tears dripped down her cheeks. She let them fall, untouched, as she watched her husband's face.

"I was paying attention t' the watch. I was doing me job, Eva, like I always do. But the night, it was moonless, and they had no glasses for us. The glasses were missin' from the nest. We 'ad them at first, when we left Belfast. But after we left So'ton, they told us, they 'ad none for us. They said we wouldn't need 'em. I always had some glasses in me hand, on every trip before this one."

"But still, I..."

"And there were no waves, Eva. The ocean, it was a lake, I ain't never seen it like that before. No waves to break along the front of the berg and give us warning." He made sure not to tell her about the ship's speed, and most important, he omitted his ignored ice warnings. He'd made the deal with Ismay. He would tell no one. Again, he experienced the huge misgivings he'd had at the very instant he'd made the deal.

At the same time, he'd had absolutely no choice when the man grabbed hold of him and told him how it was going to be, how he was going to testify, like it or not. But it was different lying to the woman he loved. He had never lied to Eva before. He hadn't counted on how badly this betrayal of their relationship would feel as the lie was told. He was bringing Eva into the lie. She was married to the man who doomed the *Titanic*. She would bear that burden, which deepened his guilt. He hadn't seen it that way before. A warning tapped deep inside him. This was the wrong thing to say, telling her the Ismay version of the tragedy. But he had no choice. Somehow Eva felt the difference between them. The lie was a new presence in their lives and their marriage, and that was the pity of it.

"I made you some tea, come and sit at the table," she offered, with no enthusiasm in the invitation. "I even baked some scones for you, with jam, if you want them." She put the kettle on and placed the plates on the table as Fred sat down and watched her. She had grown thin and pale, the bloom of youth fading in just a few short weeks.

"I pictured this moment, you know. I've longed for it. Just to sit 'ere with you, Eva, just to 'ave everything as it used to be. Can't we make it so, somehow? You're my girl. You know I love you."

"Things can never be the same, Fred. Yes, I love you too, but things are different." Her voice had a hollow sound, making him doubt she really loved him at all. It sounded as if she just didn't want to discuss how she really felt. "Everyone 'round here is watching me, us, judging and finding fault. And I've had no answer for them. What could I say? When I've had to accept what you did? All those people died."

"Eva, please!" He couldn't disguise his desperation.

"No, you listen to me. With all the crew gone down with the ship, and their poor widows and orphan children, here in So'ton, in Freemantle, our *neighbors*, Fred, and you are the cause of it all. They've told me, 'Your husband took away mine.' I've heard more than enough."

"But Eva," he tried again. "If you were standin' there, watching the sea with me, you would understand how 'ard it was to see anything like a black smudge on the horizon, because that was all it was, at first. Remember, there was no moon. But I rang the bell soon as ever I saw it, and I phoned t' the bridge. It just 'appened, that's all I can tell you."

Rather than respond, Eva lifted her cup and drank some tea. He wasn't sure she was really listening to him at all. He was sure she had already made up her mind long before he came home.

In the days that followed, Eva never mentioned the iceberg again. She didn't have to. Fred could sense in her every expression, in the way she slapped a plate down on the table in front of him, and most especially, in the way she instantly rolled over to the edge of their bed, as far away from him as she could get, that his wife had made use of the iceberg.

It was here in their house with them. She had constructed a wall of ice between them, and there was no chance of a spring thaw. In the past, their relationship had been very passionate. The simple, mild-mannered country girl he had married had, on her introduction to the marital bed, turned into a very willing partner. But that was all in the past. She wanted nothing to do with him, in or out of the bedroom. He lived with a stranger.

On the morning of May 24, Fred got up early. He'd be taking the first train of the day into London. The British Board of Trade inquiry began at nine a.m., and he needed to get there soon after that, with a little time to spare, so he would seem composed and in charge of himself, a reliable witness, or something like that, when they called his name.

He knew they'd pick on him, try to discredit every word. He needed to have his wits about him. No easy thing when he had so much to cover up. He dressed in the suit he'd worn for the Senate hearings and stood in front of the small, cracked mirror in the dingy washroom. He pulled a comb through his dark brown hair and stared into his grey, bloodshot eyes.

He'd spent a sleepless night. The questions they'd likely ask ran through his head, and he'd rehearse his answers, the way Mr. Ismay wanted them answered. He mumbled a prayer under his breath, something he hadn't done in quite a while. *Was it even safe, saying a prayer, asking for help, when you are about to tell a pack of lies?* He hoped God would understand just this once. Maybe it was okay to tell a lie if you've been backed into a corner, your very existence as a man with all you knew to do as a seaman on a vessel about to be taken away if you didn't lie. How could he support his wife without a job?

He wasn't thinking only of himself. Maybe God would understand that. "Amen," he said aloud as he walked into the kitchen.

"What's that? You, praying? And up so early, all dressed up like a regular bloke. What's going on with you, Fred?" Always up at first light, Eva was setting the kettle on the cooker. "Going to see the queen, are you?"

"Not exactly. I'm off to the Board of Trade inquiry. I told you so th' other day. There's a bunch of us, we 'ave to stand up there and relive the whole bloody mess all over again."

"Too bad while you're at it, you can't redo the voyage and get it right this time." She set a cup of tea on the table in front of him, her hands shaking and the tea spilling into the saucer.

"Eva, please. Let it go." His voice echoed his defeat. It seemed as if Eva would always choose the side against him. The trouble was, too many days Fred agreed with her. He was to blame. That she refused to defend him made it all the worse. He finished his tea, crossed the room to the door, and grabbed his cap off the hook.

"I'm off. Don't wait up, no telling 'ow long this'll take," he called out as he slipped out the door. It was still dark outside and very quiet. Just then, a milk cart rattled and horses' hooves stomped on the cobblestones. He turned to take a look before he crossed the road leading down to the train station.

"Mornin', Fred. Is that you?" Mr. Bratchett had been running this milk route ever since Fred could remember. Even though he should have had a small truck by now, he preferred his two old horses, companions of many years.

"Mornin', Mr. Brachett."

"What you doin' up so early? Off t' sea, are ya?"

"Oh no, not today sir. I'm on me way t' London."

"Oh. I shoulda known, you all dressed up like that! Look who I brought with me this mornin'. It's my wee lad, James, but we call him Jamie. Me and the missus, we're so proud of the little fella! Jamie, come say hello to Fred."

"Good mornin', sir." The little lad jumped off the cart and looked up at Fred. He was a sweet boy with red curly hair. A shy smile crept onto his face. Fred reached down and patted him on the head.

"Well, we'd best be gettin' back on our route. Fred, you 'ave a good ride up ta the Smoke and come back safe mate."

The Smoke. The perfect nickname for London, Fred thought, full of fog and smoke.

"Thank you, sir. You too, and Jamie, as well. And keep those horses in check."

The cart started to roll. The large white horse whinnied in response to his words. Fred smiled for a second. *What a comforting way to start this day.* His mood took a more positive turn, as he allowed himself this pleasant thought. Maybe one day in the future, maybe everything would be okay. And maybe he and Eva would have a fine wee lad just like Jamie. Eva would have to forgive him for the iceberg. With a fresh bit of optimism, he wanted to believe that was possible. Although it was hard to imagine himself as a father, the prospect filled him with excitement.

It didn't last long. As he walked along, he mulled over the story he must tell once again to please the boss. In a clear-headed moment, a rarity for him, he saw that all that had mattered to the captain, and Mr. Ismay, was getting *Titanic* into New York on Tuesday, not Wednesday as planned. Ismay no doubt had wanted more headlines and more publicity for the ship. With all the lies he'd been forced to tell, it was becoming harder and harder for Fred to remember the truth. But one sticky point remained. He wished with all his heart that he had seen the smudge on the horizon much sooner. And he wished he hadn't hesitated as he tried to figure out what it might be. If only he'd leaped to the bell at once, with absolutely no delay. If only he'd done something that his future, dreamed-of child might be proud of.

Because they had ignored his early warnings, more than once, he felt he'd needed to be extremely, extremely sure it truly was ice before he rang the bell again. So, there it was. The fault lay to some degree with the ship's officers. If they hadn't ignored him earlier, he would have rung the bell immediately on spotting the smudge. It wasn't completely his fault, but he could never tell it that way. He could never tell the truth to anyone. There he was, a branded man, guilty for the rest of his life, either guilty of being a poor lookout, or guilty of lying, or both. Most of all, he was guilty of weakness, the one thing he'd tried to prevent by being such a bully. That hadn't worked out very well either. He didn't deserve to have a sweet little baby boy looking to him as a father. What kind of father could he ever hope to be? No better surely than the man he'd never known, the one who'd wanted nothing to do with him.

With those damning thoughts in mind, he boarded the third-class compartment on the early train to London.

Chapter 10

Fred didn't know much about the city, but he did remember the way to the palace from years before when he'd had some time to look around. He'd been told that the Board of Trade inquiry was to be held in the Scottish Drill Hall, on Horseferry Road, close to Buckingham, so he had no trouble finding his way. This time, as he passed the forecourt and saw the guards executing their ceremonial march, he wasn't impressed as he had been as a younger man. After all he'd been through in the last few months, such a show seemed unimportant, even pointless, ceremonial gobbledygook at best. *Survival bests fancy pretense* was something worth remembering.

All that mattered was getting through the next few hours. Would they come right out and declare at the end of the hearings in a few weeks' time that he, sorry lookout that he was, the inadequate man on watch, was to blame for the entire disaster? Would it be plastered all over the newspapers, his name and photo affixed to the front page next to an image of the sinking ship? *Lookout Frederick Fleet fails to spot iceberg in time, Titanic sinks.*

Fred took a deep breath, steeling himself to go inside and meet his fate. He climbed the stone steps and pulled open the door. The room was enormous, but dingy and poorly lit. An upstairs gallery stretched across three sides of the space, holding fewer spectators than he had expected. Fred eased himself into a bench in the last row.

As the minutes passed, the room began to fill, until there was hardly an empty spot to be had. But it was hard to hear the questions asked and answered. Fred found himself wondering why they had chosen such an unsuitable hall. It was almost as if they wanted to make it difficult for anyone to hear and see, and most of all, to judge the truth of the tragedy. Darkness had been their goal all along.

When his name was finally called, he walked up to take his seat, surprised by how dizzy he felt. He was lightheaded to say the least. The witness chair appeared in front of him just as he was about to stumble and collapse. He lowered himself carefully, clutching the arms of the chair for support. He looked up at Lord Mersey, head of the Board of Trade and member of the House of Lords, the man in charge of the proceedings. His Lordship returned Fred's glance, glaring down at him through thick glasses, his elaborate wig slightly askew. It was obvious that he believed Fred, or perhaps any simple sailor crossing his path, to be a lesser form of humanity. The air of arrogance emanating from the man gave Fred a clue that he was about to be abused, and, most likely, butchered and transfigured into the sacrificial lamb. The victim, no doubt, of this *impartial* investigation.

But six hours later, as the day's session drew to a close, Fred, having answered questions in the hot seat for only thirty minutes, felt lightheaded again, but in a different way. The sea change, as it were, had occurred when the question was raised of the slight haze that had appeared on the horizon, shortly before Fred spotted the berg. Fred had said, and rightly so, that the haze gave him no difficulty in picking out ice. And it was true. It was a slight mist, really. That was all it had been.

But a point was raised, hinged on evidence given by Reginald Lee to the board. Lee must have appeared before them on a previous day, as Fred had not seen him in the chamber. Fred had not seen Lee since he had disappeared, in the hands of Lightoller, weeks before. They'd been saving Lee, and his testimony, it seemed, for the Board of Trade and Lord Mersey. But again, they'd brought him in on a different day, so the testimony of the two lookouts would be separated, one from the other. Lee had spoken earlier, and now it was obvious Lee had lied.

As soon as Fleet explained there'd been a *slight* haze on the horizon, but it posed no problem, Lee's earlier comments were read aloud to Fred and to the room at large. In them, Lee testified that Fred had told him, in the crow's nest that night, they would have to be lucky to see through the thick haze that had suddenly appeared on the horizon. And so, when Fred testified the haze was light, it posed a problem.

Immediately they asked Fred, "What about that? You told Lee there was trouble because of the thick haze."

"I never said that," Fred had replied honestly. And he'd sat there a moment, wondering who they would believe, him or his mate.

When all was said and done, they had decided that it was Lee who was lying, trying to give an excuse for why the berg hadn't been spotted sooner.

At that moment, Fred wasn't the focus of their anger, and he was lightheaded with relief for a moment. But he felt another sort of guilt. Lee had promised he would always protect him when the time came to testify. He would take any blame away from Fred. Lee had tried to do just that, with his fake story of a thick haze, and Reg had reaped much blame because of his loyalty to his mate. Guilt and relief. Fred was saturated with both. He wondered how he could sustain these disparate feelings. Circumstance would surely tip the uneasy balance.

On the train home, Fred reviewed the day's events. If anything, as the hearing progressed, Lee's lie appeared to be a side issue in the big picture. Of some importance to the Board of Inquiry, in so much as Reginald Lee would tell a lie in their investigation, but, at the end of the day, they wouldn't allow the excuse of a thick haze. Oh no, not at all.

Nor did they ask, as the US senators had, if this was the only ice that Fred had seen that night, so he didn't have to cover up the truth about his earlier ice warnings. All Fred gave them was the Ismay version of only one iceberg. Thus, it was Fred's name that would always be attached to the death of all those poor people. And to make it worse, much worse, he had come home alive. He didn't deserve to be sitting on this train, with the lush green fields, brown and white cows, and golden haystacks racing by, as the setting sun spread a red-orange glow over the countryside. He didn't deserve to draw another breath.

Three men sat across from him. Fred almost expected them to recognize him at any moment, and then, blame creeping across their faces, move away, searching out another seat. But no one seemed to notice him at all. At last, he started to relax. He settled into his seat for the long ride ahead. As he drew a deep breath, one of the men spoke to his traveling companion, a younger man with a ruddy complexion.

"Tommy, I still can't believe this! How could that ship go down? It was completely unsinkable. And the terrible loss of life..."

The older gentleman had barely a strand of hair left on his round head. But his kind eyes peered out through his heavily wrinkled face. He pulled a folded newspaper from the seat next to him and stared at the headline. He showed it to his son and shrugged, saying nothing.

"Well, Father, I guess we'll know soon enough exactly what happened. There are hearings going on. They will get to the bottom of it. No doubt the crew wasn't paying attention. We'll know soon enough which slacker's to blame." The younger man had a no-nonsense attitude about him. "He'll get his just desserts, I'm sure of it."

If he'd any doubt, Fred now had proof positive, as soon as the inquiry was complete, with the results on page one of all the newspapers, things would change. The next weeks would seal his fate.

It had been a long, tension-filled day. Finally, lulled by the motion of the train, Fred's eyes grew heavy. He drifted into a light sleep. In a dream, he saw a baby and a mum and a father. At first, his dream-self told him he was seeing Eva, and he was the father, and he could see their little boy. But when they spoke, it was neither of them, and then a nun appeared, and said, "If you are leaving Alice, just give me the babe. If you really don't want him, we will find a place for him, with the other strays in the foundling hospital." As the sister tried to take the babe, the little one lifted his arms, crying as he reached out for his mum, fighting off the sister's hands.

Alice. All Fred knew of his mum was, her name was Alice, and she'd dropped him off as a discard.

The dream shifted, and the mum, father, and the baby were on *Titanic*, as the waves washed over the deck and she went into her final plunge. Fred woke with a start. He felt chilled to the bone, his face slightly wet from the ocean. How could that be? He was alone, the three men were gone, all that was left was the newspaper, folded back, revealing the headline, "Tragedy Unfolds: Babes Lost at Sea. Board of Trade Hearings Continue. Lookout to Testify."

Fred's first reaction, as he traveled still in that tenuous world between dreams and reality, was a feeling of longing, a feeling so strong he could hardly contain himself. He just wanted everything to be undone. He just wanted to be loved. And it wasn't just his parents' love that he craved. It was Eva's as well. Most of all, he needed to be loved and not judged, because if he were judged, he'd be found wanting. It was a love without conditions that he hungered for, from all of them. It was impossible. He attempted to brush the droplets of ocean off his face, and realized they were tears.

"Freemantle, we're comin' in t' Freemantle," called the conductor in a jaunty voice. Fred pulled himself to his feet, and leaving the newspaper behind, he hopped off the train. It was a gloomy, overcast afternoon that looked like any other as he started the long walk home. His shoes struck the cobblestones and the birds cawed when everything changed.

A cluster of little boys tossed a ball between them, out on the walk in front of a house with a neatly kept garden. A curtain swished in the large window fronting the street, and then the door flung open. A heavyset woman charged out, waving her arms.

"Johnny, Charles, Georgie, come inside, right this minute. Hurry now. It's time for your tea, and I don't want you outside anywhere near that man. He's the one sunk your da's ship." She pointed at Fred in disgust. "It's the lookout brought the iceberg to hit the ship!"

"But Mum, 'e's Fred! It's only Mr. Fleet from up the hill," called out little Georgie in protest.

"And 'e's the one I mean. It's all his fault."

The little boys climbed the steps. Just before he disappeared inside, little Georgie looked back over his shoulder, tossing a brokenhearted glance at Fred.

I would be so much better off at the bottom of the ocean. He was dizzy again. When he reached his house, he walked inside, ignoring Eva, standing at the cooker to prepare their tea.

***

Eva glanced over at him. She opened her mouth, about to ask how the day had gone, but Fred hurried to the tiny bedroom.

Ten minutes later, Eva decided to check on him. Her husband liked his tea, no matter his mood, bad or good. What could be keeping him, even if the day had gone poorly? She couldn't imagine he didn't want a spot of tea to soothe his nerves.

She opened the door.

Fred lay on the bed in a fetal position, rocking back and forth. He stared straight ahead, a fixed look on his face. He still wore his good suit of clothes, his shoes still on.

"Fred, whatever is the matter? Are you all right?" She sat on the bed and stared into his face. His eyes were open, but he seemed unaware of her presence. Wherever he was, he wasn't in the room with her. His gaze focused somewhere very far away and long ago, somewhere Eva could never follow. She wrapped her arms around him, tears pouring down her cheeks. She might be angry at him because of the iceberg, and the shame it brought to both of them, but she was scared. Something was terribly wrong.

"Fred, Fred, I'm here. It's going to be all right, really." She had no idea if there was any truth to her words. She had no idea what to do, so she lay there with her arms around him, waiting quietly for her husband to come back to her, if he ever would.

For all his sea voyages in the short time they had been married, save for the last trip on *Titanic*, she had no doubt he would return to her, walking in the house with a rakish smile on his face, same as always. She remembered the game he liked to play. He would pause in the doorway and pitch his cap to the hook on the wall. He usually made the connection on the first try, and he'd chuckle out loud, even before he said hello and swept her up in a passionate kiss.

Now, with him physically right there next to her, and her arms around him, she had no idea where he had gone and how she could ever get him home again. Eva lay next to a total stranger, not the long absent sailor whose footsteps she waited to hear on the cobblestones outside their door.

His cap was still on his head. He'd even lost the joy to give it a toss and laugh. She gently removed it and ran her fingers through his hair. She touched the rough wool of his jacket and thought how opposite the feel of it was compared to this fragile, lost soul next to her. She pulled him close, concentrating on the beating of his heart against her chest, listening to the sound of his breathing. They stayed wrapped up together as the sun dipped below the horizon and a sliver of moon crept up the twilight sky and showed through the small window.

Fred moved his head. He was back. He looked at Eva as if he wasn't sure who she was for a moment, then slowly pulled himself up from the bed and made his way into the kitchen. The lights were still on, the room the way Eva had left it an hour before. The empty teacups and plates and napkins were on the table. The water in the kettle was cold. Eva followed him into the room, turning on the cooker, unsure what to say.

"Tea will be ready in a couple. Fred, I don't know how to ask this, but what happened in there? You were awake, but you weren't."

"I don't know what you mean. I came home after a long day, and I'm ready for tea." His voice was small, and vacant.

She realized he had no memory of the last hour. None whatsoever. Once the water boiled and the tea steeped, she filled his cup.

"How was the hearing, the thing in London? Did they treat you fair or not?"

"Well, they each had t' badger me some. I finally asked 'em, 'Is there any more likes to 'ave a go at me?' That shut 'em up an' I left. But it seems t' me, as I sat there an' listened through the morning, waitin' for them to call m' name, what they really want is not t' blame White Star or *Titanic* at all."

"Why would they do that? Don't they want to blame someone, in the records?"

"Well, if they blame the whole bloody line, and *Titanic*, they are faultin' themselves too. It's the Board of Trade gave the go ahead for *Titanic* t' sail, remember that. I just don't want 'em to choose one person t' blame, and that be me."

"Well, they might. It's all 'round Freemantle, everyone says you —"

"Eva, just because everyone says... listen to me." He raised his voice when he realized she was about to assert her feelings again and those of the neighbors, and everyone else in Freemantle, that he bore the blame. "It would be wrong t' do that. It was just a bad night, that's what it was. The ice wasn't supposed t' be there, in that lane. Ships travel safe that route all the time. We'd even switched to the more southerly route."

"Fred, now you listen to me. You be quiet for a moment. I went to the church. I was hoping to help with the collections for the crew families lost in the sinking, but no one would sit next t' me. I stayed for some of the meeting, then I left. I wasn't welcome, Fred. Do ya know how bad that made me feel? I come from a family people have some regard for back on the island. People in Guernsey have a good opinion of the name Le Gros. My father was a baker. Everyone needs to eat bread. He was successful. People had respect for us. I'm not used to being shunned. But now I am just that. People, our neighbors, want nothing to do with me. They make a point to avoid me. They lost their families because of that iceberg, because of you." She covered her face with her hands and drew a deep breath.

"If I could change everything for you, Eva, I would. I love you, you know that."

"I hate to say this, but I'm thinking that's not enough. All that is just words. I should have listened to my brother Phil. As soon as we moved into Norman Road, next door to that house where you rented that room, Phil caught me looking at you one day when you were walking up the front walk."

Fred looked like he wanted to interrupt, but she gave him no chance.

"'Stop looking at that man,' he warned me right off. 'When it's time for you to marry, we will go back to Guernsey, and Papa will find the right match for you. Until then, don't think about men, especially that one. He's too good-looking. And all he can do is rent a room in a boarding house. And yet, even though he's poor as can be, he struts up the walk like he thinks he's important, just the way he holds himself, the way he moves along. I can see it, and him dressed in rags from a sea journey. He has nothing to offer you.'"

Eva continued, "But I've always been headstrong and I wouldn't listen. Once he noticed you and I were finding time to talk after dark, out behind your boarding house, Phil wanted to take me back to the island the next day. But he couldn't. He had to be at work. So, we stayed. He told me, 'You are caught up with that man, that Fleet, because he's handsome. You are swept up with those feelings, feelings that a woman shouldn't use to make the biggest decision of her life.' He told me I should let Papa find me a man from a good family, with real roots, something to vouch for his character. Papa knew a man, his family had a business in Guernsey, like our family. Phil sent a letter, saying the match should be made. But I wouldn't go along with it. I threatened to run away."

"You never told me that," Fred said, "about the man in Guernsey. I knew Phil never liked me from the beginning. It was obvious. He's poisoned you against me, he has. But Eva, you know 'ow you feel when we're together. Our love is more than just words. When my arms are around you, holdin' you close, you know wha' I mean." He turned his head slightly toward the bedroom. "You are so alive. I know y' love me, no matter Phil's warnings."

"I'm thinking that kind of love, those feelings you give me, what we share in that bed, it's not enough for a life together. It's all a mistake." Eva burst out crying, resting her head on her hands on the table. Fred jumped up to comfort her. "No, no, don't touch me," she said, shaking her head. "I mean it."

"I'm hoping you'll change yer mind."

"No use wasting your effort. I won't."

Chapter 11

They stayed in the house, sharing the same rooms, sipping tea at the same table, but nothing was the same for Fred and Eva. Fred might have escaped the sinking, but the loss he suffered was tangible. In losing Eva, Fred felt his life was changed forever. If she had believed in him, maybe he could have withstood the guilt he suffered in the court of public opinion, and worse than that, in his own mind.

He did hold out hope that when the decision of the Board of Trade was announced, if somehow, he didn't bear the full brunt of blame for the sinking, in time Eva and everyone else in Southampton might come to forgive him. The weeks went by slowly as he waited and waited for the report.

But first, he needed to earn some money. It didn't seem like the report would be issued anytime soon. He tried asking around the White Star offices, but they could give him no good answer as to the date of the report. He was almost begging them, *"Please assign me to a ship."*

"We have nothing for you," was all the clerk had to say in the cramped crew office.

He wanted to tell the clerk, *"But Mr. Ismay promised me my job, if I told his lies about the ice."* He headed home, feeling less than the husband Eva deserved and less than a man by any measure.

Walking down the street, he fixed his gaze on the pavement and collided with an elderly lady coming out of a shop. She dropped her small bag and looked up at Fred. Lost in his own misery, he walked on by. He didn't even tell her he was sorry. Too late, he realized the gossips in town would pick up on this foolish mistake he'd made, making it worse than it was, if that were possible.

The next day, he made his call once again at White Star. He shuffled into the office, expecting bad news again. He held his cap in his hand, hardly looking up at the man standing behind the desk.

"Fleet, we have something for you," the fellow told him, not meeting Fred's eyes as he glanced down at the sheet of paper in his hand. "The note with the assignment's been sent 'round to your house. Go home and it will be there. Be glad for it, the company wants you back. I'm not sure why."

Fred raced for the door. Outside, almost running along the street, he realized he should have said thank you, but then again, the man had seemed disappointed with Fred's good news.

And so, on the morning of June 26, 1912, Frederick Fleet boarded the *Olympic, Titanic's* sister ship. It was an eerie feeling, since the two ships looked so much alike, identical twins they were, almost. No doubt, it felt like he was stepping back in time. *If only I could go back and get it right this time.*

Fred stood still a moment and glanced up at the huge ship. It was almost as if he were searching for an answer somewhere on *Olympic.* Finally, his eyes were drawn to the crow's nest. But he knew he'd find no answer there. On this crossing, he was no longer assigned as lookout.

Maybe he should have felt relieved. Instead, he felt humiliated. He walked up the gangplank, his duffel bag over his shoulder. The ship was alive with the sounds of preparation for departure. Cargo and crew filled the boat at a steady pace. Birds swirled overhead, a few dipped low, causing Fred to halt for a second, lest he get hit in the face. On any other day, he might have been amused by the bold birds, but today, he was lost in his thoughts. He was thinking of Eva, and how she would question him when he returned. *Did they pick you for lookout? How did they treat you? Is White Star showing you how angry they are?* Up until this moment, he hadn't really thought of White Star as being angry at him at all, but Eva had planted the idea in his head. Fred decided he would watch for signs, see how the officers acted toward him. He felt more uncomfortable than ever.

As the days passed, he mostly did maintenance work, cleaning the decks, repainting railings, and other tasks he had done years before, before he'd been elevated to lookout on the *Oceanic.* As he moved a mop across the deck, he remembered how proud he had felt the moment he'd learned he'd been chosen to climb into the crow's nest of *Oceanic.* It was more than the extra pay that gladdened him, although he liked the idea of five extra shillings just fine. Rather, it was the warm feeling that flooded his chest, when he realized someone had finally seen something good in him, good enough to trust him as the "eyes" of the ship. But all of that was gone. No chance anyone would trust him with anything like that again.

Two days later, with the *Olympic* plowing through deep water and making good time, when the lifeboat drill was announced, it was a difficult moment. *If only we'd had a drill on Titanic, maybe more people would have ended up in the boats and been saved. There'd been room for hundreds more.*

"When does the lifeboat drill start?" he'd asked Reg Lee back on that fateful *Titanic* Sunday morning. "Seems like they are running late."

"I heard there is no drill today, church service instead," Lee replied.

"Really?"

"The captain wants it that way, that's what I 'eard."

"I guess they will do it tomorrow," Fred answered, although Monday seemed awfully late for a lifeboat drill, and then he'd forgotten about it, until the accident occurred. There was no denying, chaos was rampant as the *Titanic* crew and officers had struggled to load the lifeboats. If they had practiced, things might have been different. And the lifeboats were hard to handle, a few of them almost crunching the boat below as each one moved down the falls. *Perhaps, with more training, ah, well,* he told himself, *best not to think of that now, just concentrate on doing your best job, here, today.*

Despite Fred's troubling *Titanic* flashbacks, the journey on *Olympic* was an uneventful crossing. His unrelenting physical labor resulted in deep sleep every night, something he had craved back home in Southampton, as he'd turned and tossed in his bed.

On reaching New York, Fred found a place to stay, as he had done many times before, at the Sailor's Home and Institute. All the lads who knew their way around stayed there. The other places, rundown, shady boarding houses he had frequented when he'd first gone to sea, were dangerous and best avoided. He'd eventually learned this lesson a few years back.

Once, he'd been rolled in the night, and his cash, what little he had, taken from his wallet while he slept. Good thing it wasn't his pay for the entire journey; that was given once they were back on English soil. More so than before, he avoided stopping for a pint in the rough and tumble pubs, or taverns as they called them in America. He didn't fancy getting into a tussle with any who might recognize him as the inadequate *Titanic* lookout. On board *Olympic*, he'd received a few inquisitive stares from his fellow deckhands, but no one wanted to discuss *Titanic* and that awful night, and if they knew who he was, they left him alone.

The days in New York passed quickly. When he wasn't required to be on the ship, engaged in maintenance work, he went for long walks in safe-looking areas. Once again, as he had before, he wished he had a sketch pad in his pocket. He saw some people, some faces he wished to see again. Most of the time, they were mothers and babies, or families just sharing a bit of life together. He daydreamed about being part of such a group, of love and warmth, things he had never known as a boy. If he could have done a sketch, and he thought his hands were capable of it, he would have looked back at his work in a quiet moment and imagined something better. He might have felt loved by them, even though they didn't know him at all. He might be able to put himself in the middle of it, even if it was only pretend. He had sketched a bit in the past, on the *Clio*, although his work had been stolen from him, but that was another story. He'd thought he had kept his passion for drawing a secret. It didn't mesh with his image, but obviously, someone had been watching.

Now, his hands longed for a pencil. He could almost feel them start to move, to begin the drawing of a face. Maybe next time, next trip, he'd bring along supplies. He'd shop around a bit in Southampton and see what he could find. It was better than staying home all day, with Eva giving him disapproving looks.

As the return trip began the next day on a rainy, storm-cast morning, Fred's thoughts returned to his wife. He daydreamed that in his absence, her heart had melted, and she would be glad to see him. As the *Olympic* made her way through turbulent seas, he kept an image in his mind, not of the past but a vision of the future. Eva was wrapped in his arms as they lay together, warm in their small bed, exhausted from lovemaking. His breath caught as he remembered the sweet scent of her skin.

His need was so great, that as the days passed, with no reassurance other than his strong desire, he came to believe he would receive the welcome home he dreamed of.

When he opened the door that Wednesday evening, Eva was not alone. Her brother Phil sat in Fred's chair at the table. They were sipping cups of tea. They stopped their conversation midsentence as he walked into the room. There was an awkward pause.

"D'you want a cuppa, Fred?" Eva finally asked, in a voice that offered no greeting but expressed an undeniable hope that he would decline her offer. But he was worn out, and in need of comfort, even if a cup of warm liquid was to be his only sustenance in place of the loving embrace he craved.

"That would be lovely,," Fred tried to sound positive and in charge of himself, hiding his disappointment as well as his discomfort in Phil's presence. He pulled the one spare chair to the table, finding little room for it, as neither of the others moved an inch to make way for him. In his own house, he felt the intruder.

"So, I understand they let you back on White Star," Phil's voice was cold, his intent clear to make Fred feel worthless.

Eva slapped a sloppy teacup on the table in front of Fred.

"Yes, of course. I 'ave a job with White, they want me there," Fred replied, looking at Eva, trying to gauge her mood. He was looking for some small sign of welcome. At this point, anything would do. He'd never doubted how Phil felt about him. It was all negative. *Titanic* had only made it worse.

"Ah, so you have a regular job now, you say," Phil replied quickly. "Did they want you back as lookout?"

Before Fred could answer, Phil spoke his mind. "Of course, they didn't. You're a failure, that's what you are. And now you bring my sister down, as if you didn't do that already, just by marryin' her. What a sorry bloke you are, Fred Fleet."

Eva was silent, looking down at the table. She might not be willing to verbally disagree with her brother and defend her husband, but now she couldn't even look the man she had married in the eye.

"What were you doing all those days at sea? Scrubbing the deck and earning tuppence?" Phil sounded like he was definitely enjoying himself, demeaning Fred in front of Eva.

Fred stood up abruptly, his chair crashed to the floor. He stormed into the bedroom, slamming the door behind him. He threw himself on the bed. Tears sprang to his eyes, and he struggled to choke them back. He could hear the voices in the other room, but he couldn't make out the words.

The next days passed no better between them, with Phil coming and going as he pleased, sitting with his sister, trying to convince her to take a trip with him back to Guernsey to get away and think things over.

When they were alone, Fred and Eva spoke hardly a word. Fred was relieved when he received a message from White Star. *Olympic* was due to sail in a fortnight and he was expected on board. The 17th of July couldn't come soon enough for Fred, and probably for Eva as well.

On the morning of his departure, just as he was about to walk out the door, he hesitated a moment, working up his courage to give Eva a kiss. If she turned her head and refused his advance, the pain would haunt him for the entire journey. But if he didn't kiss her, would Eva resent that all the days he was gone?

For once, Phil wasn't there, they were alone. Fred summoned his courage and walked across the small kitchen. Eva watched him approach, a noncommittal look in her eyes. He didn't hold back. He put his arms around her and kissed her. In the last weeks, he couldn't find the right words, but now his lips did the job for him. Eva didn't push him away, although he judged her response as less than he'd hoped for, but still, their lips were joined. She hadn't rejected him.

"I love ya, lass," he said as he opened the door. "Remember that."

"Be safe," she replied.

If only they did trust me as lookout again, Fred thought as he climbed aboard the *Olympic*. But they did not. Able-bodied seaman was his designation, and no more than that, with the reduced pay to go along with it. Phil's face back in the kitchen in So'ton flashed before his eyes, the man would enjoy that Fred was stepped on once again by the White Star bosses.

At least I have a job. And, if not for Ismay, I wouldn't. The officers were downright cold and dismissive to the few surviving *Titanic* crew on board. No doubt they were seen as an unpleasant reminder of the tragedy.

Fred found nothing interesting about his duties on board *Olympic*. Besides the promise of extra pay, what he'd really liked was the challenge of searching the seas for danger. Yes, it was cold up there in the nest, and the hours staying alert were exhausting, but it was also so very interesting. Not the looking at empty seas part of it, but the chance, the chance he might see something that no one else had. And the acknowledged responsibility, the trust inherent in being chosen for the job, that side of it held an extra fascination for Fred. Never in his life had he been special in any way. But as a lookout, he had been special. But all that was gone, and he struggled with the emptiness and the personal loss he encountered every day of the crossing.

Sometimes in the middle of the night, as the hour approached when he had seen the berg on *Titanic* two months earlier, he imagined he saw them as they had been that night. All those who died in the frigid cold waters, wearing life vests that were no help against the icy temperature. He could hear them, oh God, how he wished he couldn't, but he could hear them as they screamed with their last ounce of breath, for someone to turn back and come and save them. He remembered the woman with the long red hair, how she'd reached out, begging for help. And they had no help to give her. Hichens wouldn't even consider it.

And then *Olympic* was in New York harbor on a late Wednesday morning that boasted a hot sun. On this crossing, the *Olympic* crew had been a bit friendlier, a couple of his mates even inviting Fred to come have a bite of supper and a pint or two the first evening after they arrived.

Alfred and Horace said they knew a good place to go. Fred said *sure* and followed along.

They all sat together, pulled up to the bar in a spot frequented by working men of their class, most, but not all, on the sea. The air was filled with cigarette smoke coupled with the scent of stale beer. Somewhere in the background, fingers grazed piano keys and a ragtag melody meandered into the room. The barkeep approached the three sailors. The food was ordered, sausages and chips all around, and the overflowing pints of strong ale appeared at once.

"To a wild night, mates!" said Alfred as he hoisted his drink, with a twinkle in his eye. "A night we don't have to tell the missus about!" He howled and slapped Fred on the back.

It wasn't what Fred had expected, but he didn't say anything. He'd been a teetotaler the last couple of years, but, what the hell, he told himself, tonight was different. If needed, he could drink with the best of them, if that was what they had in mind.

"Hey, catch those lasses over there." Horace belched and wiped his chin as he pointed at a couple of women, their looks and clothing indicating they might be on the prowl for a few men to entertain for an hour or so. He asked, "Alf, do ya think the price is right for blokes like us? I could sure use some of what they're offerin'." He laughed.

The two women caught his drift and sashayed up to the three men seated at the bar. Fred stared at them, He couldn't help himself.

"My, aren't you handsome? I haven't seen you here before." The younger of the two, the one with the fullest bosom popping out of her tight red dress, wrapped her arms about Fred's head. She pulled him close to her exposed charms. "Why not come with me? Let the others sort themselves out. I have a little treat for you!"

Fred pulled back.

"What's the matter, sweet?" she asked. "Don't worry 'bout yer friends. Noreen can take care of both of 'em at the same time." She laughed. "But I want you all for meself." She ran her hands through Fred's dark hair and gave a little shimmy-shake. "My name's Moira."

Fred was instantly aroused. All the nights since he'd returned from *Titanic*, Eva had kept her distance in bed. He wanted nothing more at this moment than to follow Moira wherever she wanted him to go, and never mind the cash it might cost. The longer he looked at her, with her full breasts all but totally exposed, her round hips swaying, and the smile on her face that promised everything, the more he became convinced that he deserved some time in her bed. But the thing was, ever since he and Eva had married, when he was lookout on the *Oceanic*, he had never been unfaithful to her. Before they'd met, he'd known plenty of girls, and women, in different ports when he traveled. In England as well. But since he and Eva came together, he'd no need of any other woman. Even when he traveled and was gone for weeks at a time, Eva was worth waiting for. Besides, he loved her.

He pulled back and shook his head.

But Moira would not be put off. She stepped closer to Fred and placed his hand on her breast. His fingers had a mind of their own as they slipped under the plunging neckline of her dress, exploring her body. He hadn't touched a woman in months, and so, in spite of himself, he gasped at the feel of her, his blood running fast.

Moira whispered in his ear, and the touch of her breath on his skin was scintillating. "I won't charge you anything. Don't tell the others. You are my gift to myself tonight, so come, hurry." She grabbed his hand to pull him off the barstool.

Just as he was about to follow her, Fred changed his mind. He couldn't do this to Eva, even though she would never know. He couldn't give up on their love, on their marriage. If he did what he wanted to do to Moira, things would never be the same for him and Eva, and he knew it.

His voice dripping with regret, he told her, "Alf's yer lad, not me, Moira."

She looked annoyed, obviously sure she was about to get what she wanted. In the end, she was a businesswoman, so she turned her attention to Alf.

Alf and Horace moved over, making a place at the bar for the two ladies. They called to the barkeep and ordered for their new friends.

Fred stood up, taking a long drink of his ale. Then he slammed the mug on the bar and turned to walk away.

"What's with yer friend?" he heard Moira ask Alf as she cozied up to him, delivering little tempting kisses to his face and neck, making sure, no doubt, she wouldn't lose this one. "Is he all right in the head?"

Fred slipped out the door, not waiting to hear the answer. He wondered the same thing about himself. What was wrong with his head anyway? He knew he wasn't the same lad who had climbed aboard *Titanic* that morning in April, a day that seemed so long ago, a lifetime ago. Lost in his thoughts, he walked slowly down the unfamiliar street. For now, he would find himself some supper elsewhere.

The rest of the time in New York was mostly filled with his work on the ship. He hoped he wouldn't see any more of Alf and Horace. He could imagine what they were saying about him. He knew at least one of them, Alfred, was a married man, but that didn't seem to enter the picture in a foreign port. Fred guessed that a lot, maybe most, of the crew behaved the same. They would never understand why he wasn't doing what they were doing.

He did have one free day, and this time, he'd brought a sketch pad and a pencil. After walking about a bit, Fred sat on the steps of the Seaman's Institute and watched the crowd flowing about on the street. Mainly they were men, dressed as if they were off to work, but here and there he saw a woman carrying a baby, often with a few small children in tow. He pulled out his sketch pad and started to draw.

When he was done, on the paper before him was a crude sketch of one segment of the scene on the street. A young mum holding a babe, with two little children trailing behind holding onto her skirt, filled the page. A tall man walked along with them. He carried a child, a little boy, wrapped in his arms. As he sketched, Fred could see that he had created a father who loved his little boy. Fred wondered about his father. Had the man ever seen him? Did he even know Fred was alive? It seemed unlikely. There was no chance Fred had ever been loved by that strange, distant man.

He picked up the pencil again and did another quick sketch, and then another. But the charm of the moment was gone. He could make the figures that emerged on the page resemble the people on the street, but it seemed pointless. Fred sought to create something that couldn't come from a pencil and a piece of paper. What he really wanted was to belong to someone who truly loved him. He had thought Eva was that person, but now he had his doubts. If she could be so easily persuaded by the events of the 15th of April, and her neighbors, and her brother, who had never given Fred a fair shake, then she must not have loved him very much from the start. Fred stood up and went inside. He climbed the stairs to his bed and lay down, pulling the blanket over his head. Even though it was July, he shivered with cold.

The very next day at precisely twelve noon, *Olympic* sounded her whistle as the tugboats guided her out from the pier. Fred stood on the boat deck at his assigned position. In his years at sea, he had always felt a thrill once they headed into open water. Now, he was still in a somber mood from the day before. He watched the New York harbor recede and wondered what the future held. All he wanted was a smooth, uneventful crossing. But the more he thought about it, he didn't want the trip to end. He didn't look forward to getting home.

That evening, he was hardly hungry. Even after a long day of work with the sea air blowing at him, he had no appetite. But he decided he'd better go to the mess and have a bite. The food was usually the best the first night out, when everything was the freshest it would be for the next seven days. He wandered in, helped himself to the buffet, and found a seat at the long table of lads. Alf and Horace sat just across from him. They nodded at him, each with a smirk on his face. Keeping his eyes fixed on Fred, Alf muttered something to Horace. Fred couldn't hear the words, but he knew it was something unpleasant. Horace chuckled, and the two men clinked their glasses of ale and enjoyed themselves at Fred's expense, it was quite obvious.

Fred stood up in ablaze of sudden anger. He grabbed his plate off the table. All eyes were on him. He stumbled across the room to a small, empty table and sat down with his back to the other men. Just a few years before, and for most of his life, if someone stirred his anger, he would have yanked the bloke from his seat and beat the daylights out of him. But he thought about Eva again, and how he would explain it to her if he came home without a job. Her reaction to his news, and the scene it would cause, and how Philip would take delight in his fall, all weighed on his thoughts.

Then there was Mr. Ismay. If Fred got himself in trouble fighting, would Ismay feel their deal was off? Would he let Fred go and never offer him another pitch on White Star? And there would be no pension.

Fred sat alone and tried to ignore the rage that filled his head. He picked up a fork and tried to eat his supper, but the food had grown dry and tasteless in his mouth. He was lost in his thoughts, confused as to what he should do next. He picked up his untouched glass of ale and downed it quickly. Someone had left a full pitcher on the table, so he poured himself some more, filling his glass over and over, until all the ale was gone.

When he looked up again, most of the men had left the room. Unsteady on his feet, Fred found his way to his bunk. Never a heavy drinker in the past, now he gave in to the nothingness and slept through the night. For the first time in a long time, he didn't toss and turn. No dreams of the iceberg danced on his eyelids.

The days at sea passed in a blur, and then it was dawn, the last day of the journey home. Fred had always grown excited at this point of the crossing, imagining Eva getting out of bed that morning, and throwing open the shutters as she always did. He saw her standing there, lifting her face to the shimmering early sunlight, breathing in the fresh, morning air. And, on a day like this, she would have been thinking about him, and how excited she was because he'd be home in a few hours, and soon she would feel his arms around her.

That was all in the past. He expected no joyful homecoming. Still, he tried to give himself a glimmer of hope, but all he could summon was the tiniest wisp that Eva might remember the way things used to be and offer him a second chance.

Fred was busy with his duties as the ship pulled into Southampton Water. Hours passed until he could finally grab his duffel bag and leave the boat. In spite of himself, his anticipation built as he walked down the gangplank and breathed in the scent of home. It was a bright, sunny day, hot for England, extra hot, even for the last week of July. The pier was crowded, as passengers and their families huddled together, embracing, and sharing their news. Fred threaded his way through the throng and wondered what it would be like to be a passenger on such a ship, with adventures to share of the crossing and family who took delight in your every word. A magical life it seemed! How was it that some people have that, and then others, like him, end up with so little? He didn't mean things. He didn't care about fancy possessions. It would never occur to him to want such. He had always been on the outside of life, looking in. A leftover, a scrap, and nothing more than that. He walked faster. He needed to see Eva's face, needed to see her so much.

"'ere I am," he called out as he entered the front room, tossing his cap as he'd done before. *Maybe this will be a way to turn back the clock to better times.*

"There's news, Fred," Eva said as she entered the room from the bedroom. She seemed excited. She wore a new, if simple, dress.

Where did that come from? he wondered, but he didn't ask.

"The report's coming out tomorrow, from the Board of Trade. Everyone is talking about it," Eva's eyes flashed at him. "At last, we'll know the truth."

"Tomorrow!" Fred said as he sat down at the kitchen table.

"Yes, everyone is buzzing about the news. The word just came out. Do you fancy a cuppa?"

"Yes, yes, I do. I wasn't quite ready for this, but they've taken their sweet time on writing it, so..."

"Well, it's better to hear, to know what they decided. Isn't it?" Eva asked.

"I'm not sure. I guess I won't know until tomorrow if it's better to know or not." Fred felt a bit dazed after waiting so long. One more day.

Would they blast his name all over England, even more than it already was? Would they blame him for the sinking? *Well, of course they will,* he told himself.

Just then, someone tapped on the door.

"Yoo-hoo, it's me," a voice called out. It was Eva's friend Maisy who lived down the way with her parents. Eva's age, she had yet to find a beau. Eva went to the door and opened it, taking Maisy's hand and ushering her into the house.

"Fred's come home, Maisy!" Eva actually sounded happy, and Fred's mood lifted.

"Hullo, Fred." Maisy didn't look at him. "I came to tell you the news, Eva. The report's coming out, tomorrow... the sinking..." Her eyes cut over to Fred and her face took on an accusatory expression. An uncomfortable silence filled the room.

"Yes, I heard," Eva said, giving a positive note to her voice, trying to salvage something. Perhaps she really didn't want to humiliate her husband in front of her friend.

"Oh, I like your new dress," Maisy said. "You didn't tell me you were getting a new dress. Where did it come from?"

"Phil gave it to me," Eva tried to downplay her enthusiasm as Fred gave her a hard look.

Why was Phil giving her new clothes? The question flashed through Fred's mind.

"You have the nicest brother. I guess I'll go now, since *he's* back." Maisy gave Fred an unpleasant toss of her head and turned on her heel, closing the door with a firmness that made a statement of its own.

"Your friend isn't very subtle, is she?" Fred asked.

"That's just Maisy. She isn't what anyone would call sweet. She never hides her feelings."

"No wonder she hasn't found a husband!" Fred couldn't resist the comment, but Eva didn't disagree with him. He drew courage from that, and so he asked her the question he really wanted to ask.

"Why *did* Phil give you the dress, Eva?"

"I'm not sure."

Fred raised his eyebrows and looked at her.

"Well, maybe it's because he's trying to convince me—it's hard to tell you this, Fred. He's trying to convince me to go back to Guernsey with him for a little while."

"And are you? Are you letting him buy you off with a new dress?"

"He's not going to buy me with any dress."

"Are you going or staying?"

"I... I'm not sure."

"What do you mean, you're not sure?"

"Let's not talk about it now. Let's just wait and see what happens tomorrow." She stopped speaking for a moment, but then she couldn't end it there. "I don't want to go. I don't, you have to believe that, but..."

"But what?"

"Okay then, I'm staying. I just don't want to talk about it anymore, but I'm staying." She put the promised cup of tea on the table in front of Fred. She placed it very gingerly, very carefully on the table, as if she could make something up to him by that simple act. As if the dress and the conversation with Phil had never happened, at least for now. She added the spoonful of sugar to his tea for him, something she never did. And she added the sugar slowly, and she stirred the liquid gently.

Perhaps that was the closest she could come to saying the words he longed to hear, *I love you, Fred.*

But she didn't speak.

Fred lifted the cup to his lips and watched his wife across the table.

Chapter 12

The following morning history would be made, as the Board of Trade was about to break its silence. Both Fred and Eva were quiet and withdrawn as the day progressed. The tension built, not only in their house, but all over Southampton as well. An uneasy feeling hung in the air, like a gathering storm in the Atlantic, and all of England sat directly in its path.

Fred thought it best to get the late edition of the newspaper to be sure he got the whole story. When the time was right, he walked to the docks to buy a copy of *The Echo* and learn his fate. He felt like running, but his nerves got the best of him. He walked slowly, putting off the verdict as long as possible.

He turned the last corner and saw the mob. People were queued up, hungry for the news. Once again, Fred hoped his photo wasn't on the first page with a headline blaming "this man, this lookout, this failure." As he got closer, he caught sight of the front page as the newsboy lofted the paper in the air. One large word comprised the headline: SPEED.

There it was for all the world to see. When his turn came, Fred handed over his coins, almost dropping them in his haste. He grabbed the paper from the boy's outstretched hand. He held his breath as his eyes skipped down the page, stumbling over words, and reading as fast as he could.

His name wasn't mentioned at all. The excessive speed bore the brunt, and if any one person was linked to that, it was the captain, Edward Smith. No mention was made of Mr. Ismay and the role he most likely played in urging Smith to ignore the increasingly dire ice warnings and go for a record. But Smith was dead, and Ismay alive and the owner of the line. So, White Star itself wasn't to blame, not really, and the Board of Trade's decision to approve *Titanic* as fit for travel was without fault. It was speed, pure and simple.

Except it wasn't that simple.

If anything, Fred's strong sense of relief was anticlimactic. He had lied at the hearings. On *Carpathia*, in desperation to set things straight, he'd babbled quite a bit about the early bergs he'd seen before Lights had called them to the crew meeting. Lucky for him, none of the grief-stricken ladies he spoke to seemed to pay him any mind. They were all in a state of distress and confusion. Then Ismay, by way of Lights's instructions to the crew, had silenced any further talk of the sinking. Only Fred knew all the lies that were buried along with the dead.

One thought occurred to him and lifted his spirits. Maybe seeing this summation, with no mention of his name, Eva would back down on her accusations of his poor lookout skills. Maybe the ice between them would thaw at last.

"It's been decided—I'm not to blame," he announced as he walked into the house, closing the door behind him and waving the newspaper in the air. He tossed his cap to the hook, making it on the first try.

"What do you mean?" Eva asked. "Let me see." Her voice was full of excitement. She grabbed at the paper.

"It says right here, if anything, it was Captain Smith's fault fer goin' so fast, after we were known to be entering the area of heavy ice. They mentioned all the messages the ship received. I knew nothin' 'bout them. Seems there were quite a few warnings on the telegraph, big ice ahead, right in our path." Fred had no intention of letting Eva know all he had seen that night.

"But why would the captain do that?"

"Well, ships rarely slow in the area of ice, most of 'em. But not all of them. There was a ship near us, we saw her light when we started to row, and that one had stopped for the night because of the ice field. It's a long story. I'll explain later about that ship. But this is wonderful news, Eva." He was covering over his own inner guilt, but it felt like ecstasy. Fred hadn't felt this much excitement since the day *Titanic* pulled out into Southampton Water when the journey began.

He went with the feeling, especially when Eva wrapped her arms around him and gave him a deep, meaningful kiss. She leaned back in his arms and looked at him, a special smile on her face.

"Supper's almost ready, Fred, but maybe, let's have a little dessert first." She grabbed his hand and led him into the bedroom.

As it turned out, they were both very hungry.

***

So, it should have stopped there, all this blame circulating about, these rumors that Fred Fleet, when he missed seeing the iceberg in time, sank the *Titanic*. That he and he alone was responsible for killing so many innocent people. It should have stopped, but it didn't.

People have a need for revenge. They imagine revenge will help them deal with their loss. Having a target for their misery will ease their grief. Captain Edward Smith, dead and gone at the bottom of the sea, was transformed into a victim, even as the board ignored his role. It was excessive speed that caused the collision. But the people of So'ton still needed a live person to blame.

Making Frederick Fleet feel responsible in the court of public opinion was a necessary step in helping the rest of Southampton accept what had happened, so they could get on with their lives, even though, officially, he bore no blame for the collision with the iceberg.

It worked for everyone. Everyone except Fred and Eva. Once he'd been clothed with the mantle of guilt by his neighbors, there was no shedding his burden. Even worse, they did little to mask their feelings toward him.

Neither could Fred shake loose his own inner guilt. He knew he'd hesitated before striking the bell; it was hard to remember just how long. And he knew he'd been part of Ismay's cover-up. At first, he'd suffered mainly survivor's guilt. But survivor's guilt fades in time.

Fred's guilt went deeper. Deeper than the ocean where *Titanic* lay, dissolving in the elements of the sea and the passage of time. If only Fred's guilt could have met a similar fate and disappeared with time, but it did not.

Many a night he lay awake, replaying the tragedy. When his eyes finally grew heavy and he surrendered to the darkness, he found himself in restless dreams, watching the berg come closer and closer. It gnawed out a bigger piece of him, even as he struggled to carry on with his life. His pain grew, and like the ship, he was sinking.

Eva tried to help him. But she was a young girl who had little idea how to bring Fred around when his spirits slipped, and he became more withdrawn. She tried with mixed success.

At times, Fred could sense her good intentions, but her efforts were eventually impeded by Phil. Her brother kept coming around, casting disapproving looks at her whenever he sensed she was drawing closer to her husband, and away from him. They were engaged in a not-so-subtle tug of war, Fred and Phil, with Eva the prize wrestled between them.

If anything, Fred needed to return to the sea. Maybe it wasn't the best thing for his testy marriage, but it was for his depression.

One afternoon, he decided to go outside and take a walk, which was a big step for him. His nerves had made him a recluse of late, but he'd had enough. He needed some fresh air to clear his head. He walked down the way to buy an *Echo*, only to be met by surly stares and poorly disguised sneers and snippets of whispers as he passed house after house of the *Titanic* crew. Openly talking about *Titanic* in Southampton was taboo but indicting the lookout with stares and whispers was fair game, even necessary business, it seemed. His spirits sank. He was sure things would never improve. His roller-coaster emotions dropped to their lowest point.

Back home again, Fred sat in a chair in the front room, sifting through the pages of the newspaper. Almost immediately, he spotted the item he was searching for. He jabbed a finger at the page.

"It says right 'ere *Olympic's* leavin' next Wednesday, Eva. She's bound for New York once again."

"Do they want you back? That's the big question," Eva replied. The words were barely out of her lips when a thin white envelope slipped through the mail slot in the front door. Fred jumped from his chair and grabbed it. His name was written in black ink on the front. He ripped it open.

Report for duty: Wednesday, 8 August, 1912 at 8 o'clock.
RMS Olympic White Star Pier 44. Southampton. Destination:
New York

"Yes, they do want me back, Eva. It says right 'ere, report for duty, on Wednesday next. I've got me a job again." He pushed the page in her direction, but Eva showed no interest.

"Now you're running away from me, and from all these crew families that lost their loved ones. It's me again, on my own, left to deal with their blame, their turned faces and their anger. I'm the one condemned here in Southampton, and you get to sail away on a big, posh boat."

Fred threw up his hands in disgust. He raised his voice. "Just a moment ago, before the word shot through the mail slot, you were jabbing at me, suggesting White Star wouldn't 'ave me back. Now, they've come through and yer not 'appy all over again. I give up, Eva! What can I do ta satisfy you?" She gave no answer, but walked into the bedroom, slamming the door behind her. *Are we at a breaking point?* he asked himself. He had no idea what he should do. He wiped away a tear that gathered in his eye. His legs felt weak.

Fred sat down and looked at the piece of paper again. The work order could have been written in Mr. Ismay's own hand, as far as he was concerned. *The pay-back from the boss for my lies,* he thought. *They are offering me a job, as he said they would. Even after the report of the Board of Trade, Ismay hasn't broken his word.*

His guilt mixed with relief of a sort, a strange brew indeed. Fred took a deep breath. He needed to be back at sea and he needed to earn a wage. And most important of all, here was his first assignment after the decision of the board. Ismay still intended to look after him. That was the relief he felt.

But it was an odd moment. Guilt versus relief. They balanced equally. Fred sat there, wondering how he could possibly feel these seemingly opposite emotions at the same time. After all, guilt should make him feel uneasy, and it did, but he couldn't deny the relief he felt. He was buoyed up and pulled down simultaneously. Maybe everything would start to turn around for him at last. Could life take a better turn?

Once before, a long time ago, he had known this same combination of feelings.

Chapter 13

Fred was just a lad of twelve, living at Elm Lodge Boys Home in Seaforth. His life was about to take a turn. It was November 1899.

Fred pushed open the back door of the orphanage and headed to the garden. After a break for the midday meal, all of the boys were expected to return to their assigned chores at once. Fred was supposed to finish weeding the lettuce patch before the day was done. Tomorrow, he would start planting potato seedlings. After a few days of on-again, off-again rain, a brilliant burst of sunlight filled the sky, unusual for late November. Fred stood there for a moment, looking up at the sun, enjoying the unexpected warmth on his face.

In the next instant, he was sprawled on the ground, lying on his back in the mud. He hadn't heard the two boys come up beside him. Now they stood over him, laughing. They were new boys, transfers to Elm Lodge in the last week. From the first day he'd seen them, his survivor's instinct told him they could spell trouble.

"Yer not such a big man, are ya now, Fleet?" The larger of the two sneered at Fred as he looked down at him.

Fred struggled to get up, but the lad came at him again, kicking him hard in the ribs, sending him back into the mud.

"That's where you belong, you piece o' garbage. We know, you're a stray, a waif. No one wants you, not even yer own mum."

"That's not true. Me mum is dead. I'm an orphan, like all the rest."

"Ya wish," said the second lad, chiming in and laughing with a cruel chuckle. "We heard the men talkin', the masters. The big fat one, who always smokes that bloody pipe, he told the other one, the bald-headed one, "Freddy has no family. They, his mum, threw him out when he was just a wee babe and she left England.""

"That's not so."

"And how do you know that?" asked the first, as he menacingly stepped closer, standing right over Fred, inches away from his head. "Ya got any proof? Of course ya don't."

"You're the lowest of the low, a piece of trash." The other boy leaned down, hands on his knees, staring at Fred, threatening him, as if he might kick him as well. Then the two lads laughed again.

"You don't run things around here like ya used to Fleet," the bigger one said. "We heard how it used to be, before we came. All that's over and done. Ya got us to tell you what to do now."

They both walked away, slapping each other on the back and having a good time at Fred's expense.

But they hadn't counted on Fred's determination to survive. They had no clue of his desperation. He was the biggest bully at Elm Lodge, and there was a reason for it. Fred was angry at the world. He'd been furious at life as long as he could remember. Being a bully was an outlet for his anger. Beating up a smaller boy calmed him, for a while, until his anger and frustration built again, and he chose his next victim.

His instinct for self-preservation, for dealing with his miserable lot in life the only way he knew how, surfaced once again. His anger pulled him up out of the mud, giving him the strength to ignore the sharp pain in his ribs and the throbbing ache in his head. As he jumped up, he spied a small limb from a tree. In seconds, he was striking his two attackers, hitting one in the head, and then the other, over and over again, until they stumbled and collapsed on the ground, blood spurting from both their noses.

"I think ya got yer answer, the bloody hell with both of ya. Let me know if ya need any *more explainin'*." And then he gave a vicious kick to the ribs of the lad who had kicked him. He felt the crunch of breaking bone in the tip of his boot. The lad cried out in pain, and tears sprung from his eyes. Fred stood over him, watching him suffer. He leaned over and spat in the lad's face. Then he walked away, as if nothing had happened. He knelt once again in the lettuce field, pulling weeds.

In a hidden spot deep inside, a place he'd hardly known existed before, a new sensation settled in. He could only identify it as guilt, even though it made no sense. They'd got what they deserved, both of them, he assured himself. He had to put them in their place. And yet, the seed of guilt was planted. He'd inflicted a terrible beating, the worst he'd ever done. He knew he wished he hadn't turned out this way. But this was his life, and he had no other option.

A question popped into his head. He tried to dismiss it but failed miserably. It couldn't be true, what they had said. All his life he'd been led to believe he was an orphan just like all the other lads, not a discard. Once, he'd had parents who'd loved him, who wanted him. But a wound was opened, and a doubt sprung forth. He had to know the truth.

There was only one way to do that. He would break into the office and find his records. He would have to slip out of the dormitory after bed check and wait until the staff went to sleep. He couldn't wait a single day. He would have to do it tonight, before he was locked up and punished for the fight. If he was punished for the fight. Maybe the two lads would refuse to name their attacker. Maybe they'd be reluctant to talk. Even if they did name him, and he protested, and told the true sequence of events, who would believe him if he said the others had started it first?

They were new boys, with no record as troublemakers, not so for Fred, he'd been in and out of trouble all the time. No doubt he'd be punished, and it would be unpleasant. But if he was lucky, it might take the master a couple of days to sort it all out. He needed to act fast if he wanted the freedom to get into the office unobserved.

As Fred leaned over the lettuce field, he made plans. He felt certain the door to the office was locked at night. It made sense that it would be. Even though he had done many naughty things over the years, he had never learned how to silently break open a locked door in the middle of a quiet night. He had no tools.

He'd have to enter through one of the windows. To find his records, if such things existed, he needed a match and a candle. Not long ago, Mr. Farris had told him they'd added extra pages into his file because of all the mischief he got into.

He decided to find some rocks before nightfall and set them as a hastily erected staircase below the window. He was taller than most of the boys his age, but his legs weren't long enough to climb to the back window. He looked around the field, and when no one was watching, he slipped to the edge of the nearby wood and considered himself lucky to spot a few flat stones. He carried them back to the window, hastily constructing the stairway for his entry point that night.

His heart beat fast. He must get the answer. He must find the assurance that he was an orphan. Certainly, no one had cast him away, an unwanted bit of garbage in the unfair lottery of life. Never before had he thought being an orphan was a good thing, a treasure even.

That night, Fred lay in his cot, listening to the rest of the lads settle in for the night. As usual, he'd blindly recited the bedtime prayer led by the master after bed check. Only this time, at the end, he'd affirmed the amen with fervor, as he knew he needed extra help to accomplish his task.

Although he had looked about repeatedly, he'd failed to see a sign of the two lads he'd fought with earlier in the day. Where were they? He was wide awake, wondering what would happen next. Could he manage to find his records? Would those pages assure him that he was an orphan? Maybe he would even see his parents' names. That would be interesting. Maybe he would learn how and when they had died. With all these possibilities running through his head, he lay perfectly still and waited.

Finally, he heard the muffled sound of the piano in the hall below. Many nights, Mr. Ruggles, the junior boys' master, who played the piano for hymn singing on Sundays, practiced his notes after the lads were out of his hair. Fred would have to wait until the music was over before he crept downstairs and out the front door. His anxiety increased, but he lay still. The last thing he wanted to do was call attention to himself. He hoped everyone else was asleep, but he couldn't be sure, not yet. Listening to the faint strains of the music, he tried and failed to soothe himself.

Then it was quiet. The music had stopped. A moment later, the bench screeched as it was pushed back from the piano, and heavy footsteps sounded on the wooden floor as Mr. Ruggles retreated to the staff dormitory. A place without frills, privacy was unheard of for the boys and for their caretakers as well. Elm Lodge started stirring at six in the morning, so late nights were rare for any of the inhabitants.

At last, somewhat reluctantly, it was time to begin his adventure. He forced himself to think of it that way, because if he didn't, he might slump back in his cot and succumb to his fears. He carefully placed one foot and then another onto the floor, listening for anyone to stir. But no, the large room was silent, other than the same even breathing and a few small snoring noises produced by thirty boys lost in their dreams, or wherever their souls wandered once their eyes were shut.

A strong, well-built boy, Fred struggled to tiptoe lightly across the floor. With his cot in the last row near the back wall, he had to traverse almost the entire space.

A boy across the room turned over in his bed. Fred froze in fear. Was the lad getting up? No, he settled back under his covers without opening his eyes.

Fred moved quickly before anything else might happen, extra nervous, never mind the careful tiptoe. Out the door and onto the landing overlooking the big staircase. He peered down into the darkness. As far as he could tell, no one stirred. Carefully, he descended the stairs, willing his feet to make not a sound as they found one step and then another. Once in the downstairs hall, he made for the front door, opening it, and slipping out fast as he could.

The night was much cooler than he'd expected, and for an instant he wished he'd brought a sweater, but no use worrying about that. If all went well, he'd be inside the office in a matter of moments. He ran around to the back of the building and saw the makeshift stairs he'd built earlier that day.

He stopped dead in his tracks. A light was on in the office. Someone was in there! He hadn't counted on that. He tiptoed to the tree nearest the window, keeping out of sight if anyone should glance out, although what could they see in the black night? He flattened himself to the side of the tree and looked up at the window. He heard voices, at least two people. He would have to wait them out. One voice was a man. He couldn't be sure, but it seemed the other was a boy. Who could it be? All the beds had been full, he was quite sure he'd counted correctly before lights out.

Then he remembered. The two lads he had fought with earlier in the afternoon had been unaccounted for. Were they in there now? Was Fred already in trouble? Would one of the masters, Mr. Farris most likely, climb the stairs to pull Fred from his cot? And when they found he wasn't where he belonged, what would happen next?

Fred did the only thing he could do, he waited, leaning against the tree, and shivering from the cold. After more minutes than he could keep track of, the light went out. It was now or never. He had nothing to lose. If they were onto him, this might well be his only chance to grab a peek at his records. There was no telling how long his punishment would last.

He checked the pocket of his pajama bottoms where he'd stored the candle and the match he had swiped from the kitchen earlier in the evening. He had skills as a sneak, but he'd never broken down a door. But he wouldn't have to. Surely the window would be easy to open. It was time to find out.

He climbed the stone steps and reached up to the sash. His well-muscled arms served him well. After a strong push, the window slid open easily, and he lifted a leg and hopped down into the room.

He grew bold for his task as he didn't hear a single sound in the building. He lit the candle and glanced around the room. On the desk, a beautiful, ornately carved wooden box with a gold cross on the top caught his eye. It was lovely, so out of place in this home where the boys slept under thin blankets and most days ate a soup-like gruel, along with a slice of rough bread for their main meal. He needed to find what he came for and get out of there as quickly as possible, but he walked to the desk. What could be inside the box? He couldn't resist. He opened the lid.

The box was filled with money. Lots of it. He didn't dare touch it. It scared him. He had never seen so much money. There were also a pair of gold cufflinks in the box, square, with the symbol of a cross on them. They were exquisitely beautiful, and Fred wondered who they belonged to. He carefully closed the lid and glanced over the rest of the desk.

He spotted the oft spoken of photo, displayed only on special occasions, that marked the day Elm Lodge had been dedicated as a Church of England Home for Boys. The masters were arrayed on the left-hand side of the group photo. For a moment, Fred felt as if they were watching him, and they had seen him open the box. He felt their eyes upon him. He knew it was impossible but couldn't shake the feeling. In the photo, all the lads were gathered in the front garden, their heads bowed for a blessing. Fred hadn't been here on that auspicious day — he was still in the foundling hospital. He hadn't received the special blessing. That seemed quite fitting.

His eyes flitted across the room as he searched for the likely storage spot for the records. He decided a series of vertical drawers was the place to start. Pulling open the top one, he saw all the last names began with the letter A. He guessed the F drawer must be two down, if he was lucky. And he was.

It only took a moment to find Fleet, Frederick. He pulled out the folder and walked over to the desk. He sat, tipping the candle so he could read. His eyes traveled down the first page, and then the second. It seemed as if they'd written a new sheet for each of the scraps he'd gotten into. There were many of them over the years, he couldn't find the one page he was looking for, the page that had been filled out when he first arrived. *Maybe it would be better to start at the back,* he told himself. And it was. He found the page at once. His hands shook. Try as he might, he couldn't stop them. Written on the page, he found: Mother's name, Alice Fleet. Father's name, Frederick Laurence. *His parents.*

He couldn't believe he'd found them at last. *Alice and Frederick.* He carried his father's Christian name. But seeing he had his mother's last name, and not his father's, he wasn't surprised to see his mother listed as unmarried. So, he was a bastard after all. His father had been in the army, a private in the Fourth Dragoons. A cavalryman. Fred felt like he was reading about a different boy. It was so odd to know anything about anyone related to him. His father was a soldier. Somehow, it wasn't surprising that he had died. Fred kept reading, hoping to find out how he had died.

And then he found what he had hoped wasn't there. But it was. His father was listed as location unknown, so there was no reason to believe he had died. He just wasn't interested in being a father. And his mother had abandoned him when he was just a babe, gone to the United States, to a place called Springfield, Massachusetts. He struggled to read the name of this place. *Mass-a-chu-setts.* He said it over again slowly, examining the feel of it against his tongue. What could be there that she had to leave him and make haste for this oddly named place? *No one wanted me. No one had ever wanted me.*

He felt faint. He couldn't move. He couldn't do anything but sit there, feeling terribly lost, abandoned all over again. He grieved for the lad he used to be, or at least, he thought he'd been. The babe who had parents, parents who had died somehow, and their love had followed him, even after their death.

That boy was gone, and a new one crouched inside Fred's body. And this one had never been wrapped in the love of these people, this Alice Fleet and this Frederick Laurence. They were worse than strangers to him. Strangers don't want rid of a person, they just don't have a connection. But these people, they had wanted rid of the baby Frederick. They hated him. Alice Fleet had dropped him off at a foundling hospital in Liverpool. She'd signed a page, hoping to never see him again.

A tear slipped from Fred's eye.

Before he could wipe it away, footsteps came down the hall. He jumped up, and with shaky hands, tipped the candle, almost dropping it. A stream of hot wax burned his fingers and dripped onto the pages. He stuffed the wax-spotted document back into the file and shoved it into the drawer. He blew out the candle and climbed out the window, pulling down the sash as he leaped from the sill, never mind the stone steps. He waited beside the tree, waited to see if the larger candle sitting on the desk was lit, and it was. He thought he heard laughter, but he couldn't be sure. And then the light went out.

Fred sat down behind the tree, shivering with cold and filled with a feeling of panic and loss such as he had never known before. What was left of him? He wasn't sure. But he knew he needed to get back upstairs, back into his cot, rolled up with his blanket. That small space was the only thing he had in this world. But when would it be safe to try and get in the front door and up the stairs? He had no idea. He sat in the cold and waited, nodding off after a while, exhausted from it all.

He woke with a start sometime later. He was lying on a thick bed of leaves. He looked up and saw the first morning stars. A dim light showed just over the horizon. His fingers still burned where the wax had dripped, but never mind that. He had to get back upstairs unnoticed. Maybe he'd be lucky, just this once.

He raced for the front door and ran up the stairs. He had no idea what he would do if he was caught, but he wasn't. Once he reached the dormitory, he tiptoed back across the room and slipped into his cot. He pulled the thin blanket up to his neck again, as he had hours before.

Things were different now. He was different. He was the empty, unwanted bastard son of strangers who'd kicked him out of their lives. He listened to the other boys, the lucky ones, the orphans, breathe gently in their sleep.

Fred was awakened by the sound of the other lads, as they dressed and readied themselves for breakfast in the dining hall below.

"Get up, Fred. What's wrong with you? Don't you want yer breakfast?" It was Tim, the lad in the cot closest to Fred, and his best buddy. "If'n you don't come down right away, ya know someone will eat ya food. Maybe I will! There's talk we will have us a sausage this mornin'. Imagine that!" Tim laughed and pulled on Fred's arm. "C'mon, mate."

Fred tossed back his blanket and jumped up, giving Tim a poke. "Yer not eatin' me food! Sausage, did ya say? So, there's an unlucky pig this mornin', is there?"

Fred threw his clothes on, and all the lads raced down the stairs, pushing their way into the dining room, until they noticed that Mr. Farris was standing at the table in the front of the room. The boys pulled up short and came to a halt, each one adjusting his clothes and patting his hair in place. This was a surprise they hadn't counted on.

"Come in, all of you. Take your seats. We have something to discuss. But first, we will say our morning prayer, as usual."

The lads filed in and found their places. Heads bowed, the prayer was recited, some of the younger lads stumbling over the words, trying to keep up. Mr. Farris prayed much faster than the usual master, Mr. Robbins, who had deferred to his superior and stayed seated at his own table this morning. Mr. Farris wasted no time.

"Last night, something unprecedented occurred here at Elm Lodge. There was a robbery, a theft of money, from the office. This cannot be overlooked. I will get to the bottom of it, and I will find the person responsible for this heinous deed. Rest assured, the guilty will pay the price, a very steep price indeed. Each of you will be searched and questioned before you leave this room this morning. Right now, the masters are upstairs, searching the dormitory, going through your possessions, and every single spot in the building is being checked."

Fred's heart beat so fast he was sure it would burst from his chest, sprout wings, and fly across the room, informing Mr. Farris that it was

Frederick Fleet who had been in the office last night. Frederick Fleet, who had opened the box containing the money. Isn't it true that our hearts always tell the undeniable, painful truth?

Fred knew he didn't take the money. But who would believe him? No one would. He also knew that whoever had entered the office just after he left, the ones whose footsteps he'd heard, and the laughter, they had taken the money. But again, no one would believe him, there wasn't a chance of it.

He had suggested that a sausage on their plate this morning meant there was an unlucky pig in their midst. But now, it seemed, he was that unlucky creature.

Breakfast was served, but the anticipated sausage did not appear. Once the meal was complete, all of the masters filed into the room and each sat at a table. The lads were assigned to a master and waited in line for their turn to be questioned. Tension hung heavy in the air. Tim stood in front of Fred in the same line. Rather than their usual boisterous banter, both lads were silent, their eyes focused on the first boy in line being questioned by Mr. Ruggles.

"Turn out your pockets now, lad. That's right, let me see what you've got."

"Me pockets are empty, sir. I ain't got a thing in 'em," Nicolas Bannister protested.

"Stop wasting my time, lad. Turn them out and let me see."

Nicolas did as he was told, but instead of having nothing to show as he had claimed, a small knife emerged from his pocket and clattered to the floor.

"What's this? What have you got here, then? This is hardly nothing, Nicolas." Mr. Ruggles reached down and picked up the knife. He turned it over in his hand. "Where did you get this?"

"Sir, it was given to me by my father, just before he died. Please, sir, let me 'ave it back," Nicolas pleaded.

"If you had asked permission when first you received the knife, we might have considered your request and kept it in the office for you, but no, now you cannot have it. You have lied, and you have kept a weapon about you. Hidden away, in fact. So, no, you will not get it back." The man had nothing but venom in his voice.

"But it's just a wee knife. I would never use it to hurt anyone, sir. And it's all I have left, of me da."

"No. I told you my decision. That's an end to it." Mr. Ruggles dropped the knife into his own pocket. "Now, tell me where you were last night, Nicolas."

"Where I was? I was in me bed. Sleeping, sir." A tear glided down the boy's cheek. He sniffled and wiped his eyes.

"Did you hear anything in the night? Any footsteps in the dormitory or on the stairs?" Fred held his breath, waiting to see what Nicolas would say.

"No, sir. No, I was asleep. I heard nothing."

"I hope you are telling me the truth, lad. Now that I know you are not to be believed, I may ask you more questions later. You are excused for now."

And so it went through the line, with the rest of the boys having nothing more than a handkerchief in their pockets and no unusual nighttime noises to report. And then it was Tim's turn.

"Well, Timothy, what have you to show me?" Ruggles asked, his mood growing increasingly foul. His voice showed his disappointment that all he had uncovered so far was Nicolas's knife, although certainly that was better than nothing. Ruggles rubbed his pocket, seeming to relish the feel of the little treasure nested in his pocket. But it didn't point to who had stolen the money. "Be quick about it, lad."

"I have this," Tim said, reaching into his pocket and reluctantly pulling out a small stone.

"Give it here, let me see it. Be quick about it." Mr. Ruggles had clearly run out of patience for the task, if he'd ever had any to start with. "Hmmm, that is a most unusual piece of stone." He turned it over in his hand. "There's a vein in it, quartz no doubt, and mica. It's got a shine to it. I will keep this in the office."

"But, sir," Tim protested, although protest was unheard of in this place. "Why can't I have it back? I found it, and it's mine. It's of no harm to anyone."

"And is the food we feed you, yours? Or does it belong to Elm Lodge? We decide what is yours, Timothy. And the stone, well, it will sit in the office, and I will decide what's to come of it. It is quite attractive." He dropped it into his pocket. The stone clicked as it came to rest next to the knife. "And where were you last night, Timothy? Outside, searching for stones? Or did you, by chance, slip into the office? Did you decide that the money kept in the office was yours as well?"

Seizing the stone and suggesting the scenario of Tim entering the office obviously pleased this cruel, little man. Ruggles had a triumphant note in his voice, as he attempted to prove to the lad, and most of all, to himself, just how clever he was, even though, in reality, in life, he had proven to be neither clever nor triumphant.

"I was asleep in me bed all night," Tim mumbled.

"Speak up, lad. What did you say?"

Rather than reply, Tim looked into the man's eyes with a steady gaze. Fred knew Ruggles had heard every word Tim had said. Tim kept his eyes fixed and did not back down, even though Fred saw him trembling. Fred could tell that something in him, some tiny sliver of self-respect forced him to hold his ground and so he didn't answer the question a second time.

Ruggles flinched first, obviously frustrated. The man snapped his head away from the lad and looked behind him, aiming for whoever was next in line. Fred was drawn into the web of Ruggles's anger and frustration.

"Turn out your pockets, Fleet. Be quick, be quick. Let's see what you've got that you shouldn't have at all."

Fred was convinced Ruggles would find fault with him, even without any proof. The man looked so angry and frustrated. Chances are he wanted to end this long search right here, right now, no matter what, maybe he would win a prize for catching the culprit.

"All I have is me handkerchief," Fred said, as he pulled the item from his pocket and waved it at Ruggles.

"Hmm, let me see your hand. What is that red spot on your fingers? And what's on your handkerchief there, all that white stuff?" He grabbed the cloth from Fred's hand and examined it. "It's wax, that's what it is. Give me your hand." Without waiting for Fred's response, he grabbed the lad's hand forcefully and looked at it. "It's a burn, isn't it? You dripped wax and burnt yourself. How did that happen?"

Just then, Mr. Carter, the office manager burst into the dining room. "Wax, we are looking for evidence of wax. It was dripped on the desk and on the rug in the office last night."

Fred could see Ruggles was filled with a sense of bravado on hearing Mr. Carter's request for a boy incriminated with any amount of wax.

"Here's your thief!" Ruggles cried out. "I've found him just this minute!"

Fred felt sick in the pit of his stomach.

"Yes, he's the one we want," Carter said. "It makes perfect sense. We followed the trail of dripping wax to the record cabinet, and yes, his file was out of place, and there was wax all over it. I'll call the constable. Let them take the lad and lock him up. They will know how to get the truth out of him. We need to know where he's hid the money."

"But I didn't, I didn't take any money." Fred knew it was a mistake to speak up, but he couldn't stop himself. The lads were forbidden to speak unless spoken to. "I wanted to look at me records."

"And why would you want to do that?" Ruggles asked. Of course, he knew this part of Fred's statement was true. They had just heard of the dripped wax and the misplaced file.

"The lads, they've said things about me parents." Fred knew he should not say another word. He had been in a fight linked to the conjecture about his parents. And the fight was the worst he'd ever been in. And he had won. The room was silent, with everyone looking at him. Fred blinked back tears. He couldn't cry. If he did, his tough reputation that he had worked so hard to establish would be gone in an instant.

The head of school, Mr. Somersby, stepped into the room. "Two of the new lads are badly injured. One's on his way to hospital. Let me get ahold of the guilty party right this minute." Without another word, he walked over and forcibly took Fred by the arm.

"You will be whipped, Fleet. Severely whipped. You are a brute, and a thief as well. The new lads have told us they saw you take the money and you beat them up to silence them. But they are good lads, they had to speak up, despite your threats. You'd best come with me, right now." All of the other boys watched Fred follow Mr. Somersby out of the room. Somersby dragged him down the hall, and then downstairs, and into the basement.

"Mr. Ruggles will come down and deal with you shortly." Mr. Somersby's face was contorted with anger and flushed a deep red. He looked like he was about to take a swipe at Fred himself, but he didn't. He left the room.

Fred sank down on the hard dirt floor and leaned against the rock wall. A single candle gave off a dim light. He thought he heard scratching noises, maybe rat's feet. He looked around and didn't see anything he could use to fight them off, if they were rats, and if they were hungry. The boys always said the basement was full of rats, but Fred had never seen any when he was down here before. But then again, the master assigned to administer his punishment had always walked down with him, lifted the paddle, and got down to business. He'd never been left on his own. He thought the scratching noises were getting louder and closer. He'd never been bitten by a rat before.

Just then Ruggles pulled open the door. "You deserve much worse than a beating, Frederick, and mark my word, you will in time get your just desserts. I can assure you of that." He swung the paddle and smacked at Fred's rear end, over and over again. Fred lost count of how many times he was hit. But he wouldn't give in and cry. In all the beatings he'd received over the years, he'd never cried, not once. Though this was the worst ever, he remained silent, willing himself to hold on, just a few more minutes. Finally, Ruggles was finished, or most likely worn out, and lacked the strength to swing the paddle one more time.

Fred told himself again, *Hold on, hold on, he'll be gone in a minute or two.* But Ruggles started to talk. The man was out of breath from the beating, so at first, he had to pause. He glared at Fred. Try as he might, Fred could remain silent no longer and a sob broke loose, and then another.

"That's what I wanted, all these years. I wanted to see you cry, Fleet." Ruggles sounded positively joyful. "Now I'm done with you. Elm Lodge is done with you. May you rot in hell. It's easy to see why your mum threw you out." Carrying the paddle in his hand, he marched out with an air of victory.

Hours later, after Fred had lost track of time, he'd finally been summoned to the office to hear his fate. The only good part of the day was that the rats never paid Fred a visit while he was in the cellar. Those rodents were the only compassionate beings at Elm Lodge that day.

Fred was about to be expelled. Finally, the day of departure arrived. He was told to sit in the main hall and wait. A carriage would arrive soon. The other boys stared at him, but no one came close, no one spoke to him. They whispered among themselves. It was obvious that Fred had yet to recover from the harsh beating, but no one asked how he was or offered any encouragement. When he'd heard the whispers that Sam, the lad he'd kicked, would most likely spend several days in hospital, and the word was he had suffered injuries to his ribs and deep inside his belly, Fred had felt terribly guilty. Beneath his tough exterior, Fred did have a good, if fragile heart, a heart he was terrified to reveal to the world, or even to himself.

Coupled with the guilt, he'd been strangely relieved. He knew he was about to receive the punishment he'd richly deserved all his life. He'd always known he was a miserable human being. He deserved to be punished. At last, that punishment was here, no need to dread the day of its arrival any longer. His relief also came from his escape. It seemed that everyone at Elm Lodge believed he was a thief, that he had stolen the money. He couldn't endure that. He may be a bully, but he wasn't a thief. He was relieved that he would never have to see their judgmental faces again. There he was, awash in guilt and relief, all at the same moment.

***

A few months later, Ruggles discovered Fred wasn't a thief. Reports came to Elm Lodge that the new boys had stolen several items in their previous home. If this had been disclosed in time, they never would have been sent to Elm, and Fred wouldn't have been blamed for the missing items. In fact, the fight never would have taken place.

But Ruggles hated Fred enough that, if anything, he found the whole incident mildly amusing. The bad boys were evicted, and paid the price, but that was the total sum of the new discovery. Ruggles was reluctant to talk about this to anyone; he hated to admit he'd made a mistake.

But one day he sat down for a quick cup of tea with a visitor, Mr. George Killey, from the Home Committee.

"Have your lads been behaving themselves lately?" Killey inquired as he took a sip.

"Oh yes, once we tossed all the bad ones out, things have never been better."

Killey gave him a surprised glance. "I thought you only had one, that Fleet boy. The thief?"

"Oh yes, he was dreadful, always fighting and such. He put a boy in hospital, but that nasty lad kind of deserved it!" Ruggles chuckled, until he realized he'd said more than he intended.

"Wait. What are you talking about?" Killey gave a sharp look. Ruggles guessed that Killey suspected he was holding back on the truth.

"A different boy, well, two boys, took the money, not Fleet. We found out kind of by accident." Ruggles tried to end the conversation.

"Then shouldn't you bring Fleet back from that training ship you sent him to as punishment?"

"Not at all. He was a troublemaker," was the hasty reply. "I won't have him back, don't even ask. Things are better this way." Ruggles stared at Killey. He could see the man wasn't satisfied. He could only hope he would forget about Fred Fleet, and the mistake he had made. He wished he had guarded his tongue more carefully. Just then Killey pulled a small notebook from his pocket and wrote himself a memo. All Ruggles could see was the name of the Fleet boy.

Ruggles was furious, but there was nothing he could do to stop whatever this would bring.

Chapter 14

Fred pulled himself from his memories and considered his current dilemma. He hated the thought of leaving on the *Olympic* with Eva still so angry at him. How could he hope to get through the next days until the ship left with Eva in such a state? How could he concentrate on his job as he watched endless miles of ocean come between them, with this feeling of uncertainty lodged in his throat? He knew he couldn't. So he tapped on the bedroom door. There was no response.

"Eva, please, come out. Please try and see things my way. I need you. But I can't turn down the line when they want me to make this crossing. Eva? Eva?" He tapped on the door again, but no sound came from the room. Unsure if he was doing the right thing, he turned the knob and opened the door.

Eva sat on the edge of the bed with her head in her hands, sobbing quietly. Fred sat beside her. He put his arm around her shoulder, even though he expected her to push him away. But she didn't.

"Eva, don't cry. I don't want ta leave you. You are my life, my everything. I've nothing but you."

"Then stay. Oh Fred, if you really mean it, you will stay here, next to me."

"I can't, lass. We need a way to pay our rent, and you know there's nothing I can do but be on a ship. It's all I'm good for. Remember, when we first met... and when we talked about bein' together always, I told you I haven't anything ta give, as ta money, or fancy things. Only love, that's what I have for you. Only that."

Eva stopped crying and looked at Fred. Pushing her long, blonde hair out of her eyes, she sniffed and tried to gain her composure. "Yes, I remember that. I remember all of it. I'll never forget the first time I saw you, walking out of the house next door to Phil's house, where you rented that little room. It was raining, you remember..."

"I was soaked before I even made it to the street, and I looked back, thinking maybe I should run back in and grab me a jacket, but I was late. I was due at the ship and I should have been there ten minutes past. But then I saw you watching through your front window, and I forgot it was raining, and I forgot I was late."

"And you stood there staring at me, and all that rain pouring down, and all you could do was stand there, without moving, watching me."

"Yes. And then me landlady came out the door, and she looked at me like she had seen a vision or somethin', and she said to me, 'What's wrong with you Fred? I thought ya said you were late ta the docks?'"

"And you took off running and almost slipped in the mud!"

"And all I could think was, I hope that pretty lass didn't see me slip like a fool."

"I did. Of course, I did, but I think that made me love you, right then, even though we had never spoken a word. You were just so, I'm not sure how to say what I felt, but I loved you. I felt so close to you in that moment. Maybe it's this. I've never been filled with self-assurance, and I guess I saw you were so human, just like me. I felt connected to you right then."

"I just wanted to run back and tap on your door. But I couldn't. I was already late. And what would I say if you'd opened the door? 'I'm the bloke who almost fell face-first in the mud and I'd like to introduce meself to ya.' That wouldn't be the best way to meet you. So, I ran down to the docks, thinkin' all the way that I hoped you would forget you'd seen me, so on another day I might find the right way, and the courage, ta get another look at you, and maybe say hello. I just wanted another look, and I wanted to hear your voice. That was it. I couldn't imagine you could ever care about me."

"But I did, right then. And I still do, Fred. Oh, what are we going to do? Things are so, so complicated since the *Titanic*. No one in Southampton is ever going to forgive you. You do know that, don't you?"

"Yes, yes, I do, Eva. None of those people deserved ta die. I should be the one at the bottom of the bloody ocean, not them."

"No, you don't deserve that. No one deserves that."

"But I must not be a very good lookout. I thought I was, but now..." Even as he spoke the words, deep inside, Fred hoped Eva would disagree and stick up for him. He was counting on it.

"Sometimes people make huge mistakes, Fred, and they have to learn to live with the consequences."

Eva probably meant well, but Fred was instantly, mortally wounded by her comment. She did think he was to blame for the sinking. So, he had little defense when she spoke again.

"I think I should move back in with Phil. I think we should give up this little house. We can't afford it, not really. You don't get paid enough. Besides, you're gone all the time. I'm lonely."

Fred was speechless. So, it was over, just like that? On a Friday morning, with really no warning, when they were remembering how they had instantly been pulled together by a single glance, when she confessed she'd loved him from that first moment, in the next sentence, *it's over?*

Eva must have seen the devastation in his face. She reached over and gave him a kiss. But he could sense a change in that simple gesture. Before, her kisses carried passion and invitation. This one bestowed nothing more than pity, and yes, it evidenced a lack of respect for Fred as a man. If a kiss can be an insult, this one surely was.

"Oh, I didn't mean you can't come, Fred," she said with a tone of petulance in her voice. "Of course, you can. What *we* should do is move back there, to Norman Road, and live with Phil."

The way she said her brother's name showed he was the man she respected, as opposed to her husband. She made it sound like Fred was a naughty child who had to be provided for and put up with, even though, at times, he wasn't worth the trouble. Phil would be the center of Eva's world now. After all, it was Phil who was always flush with a bit of cash in his pocket from the LeGros family's bake shop on Guernsey, coupled with his job at the chemist shop. Even though Phil was younger than Eva, their parents sent him the money they always had.

"But Phil doesn't like me, you know that. He told you right from the start, 'Don't marry the handsome bloke who can promise you nothing.' That's how he summed me up, didn't he?"

Without a word, Eva turned away from Fred.

"He's always been against me." There was surrender in his voice.

"I don't want to live here alone, and that's what I'm doing when you're gone all the time. I've no one to talk to, no husband at all. All the neighbors are so unfriendly. They make me feel like I missed that iceberg."

***

The days ran fast until the *Olympic* was due to depart. Fred was torn in two. He knew he had to go, but a voice in his head told him to cancel. But he had no chance at any other job that would provide a single shilling. What did he have to offer Eva in the way of security if he stayed in So'ton?

He was restless and could not sleep. The night before the sailing, he tossed and turned, toward morning he finally fell into a fitful sleep.

***

Eva watched the morning stars creep up the sky through the small window in their bedroom. She lay there, clinging to this instant in time. In a little while, Fred would pull himself from the bed and slip through the door on his way down to the docks. She longed to reach out and touch him, but simply inched closer in the bed, taking care not to wake him. She lay very still and breathed in the moment, trying hard to make it last.

Fred started talking, softly at first. Eva peered at him in the pale light, surprised he was awake, since he hadn't moved a muscle.

"Mr. Ismay... yes, Boss. Yes. Whatever you say. Yes." Fred's eyes were shut. He was talking in his sleep. He had never done this before. His voice grew louder. "Yes, the ice, yes, I know, you are in charge, and I—" Fred thrashed about in his dream, but no more words slipped from his mouth.

"You had a dream," Eva said when Fred seated himself at the table for a quick spot of tea before he left. "What was it about? You cried out in your sleep." She placed a plate of scones on the table, an added treat that usually appeared the morning before Fred would leave for a crossing. This time, there was even a tiny jar of raspberry preserves, a gift from home that she had been saving for a surprise.

Eva kissed Fred on his cheek before she sat down to join him. How her heart would ache for him while he was gone, even though she knew loving him was a mistake. Sometimes mistakes are the hardest things to abandon, especially for a romantic girl like Eva. As she grew up on Guernsey, her hard-working, practical-minded family had warned against her romantic daydreams. She hadn't listened. Instead, Fred Fleet had stepped, or slipped, into her life one muddy morning.

"I had a dream, is all. I don't remember none of it now."

"But you said a name. A Mister... May, I think it was. And you were talking to him about ice. Do you know a Mr. May?"

***

What had he said that Eva shouldn't have heard?

"Of course not," Fred replied, but he was worried.

"Oh, you must have meant Mr. Ismay! You said Boss to him!"

"That makes no sense. I've never spoken to Mr. Ismay! Why would he talk to the likes of me? He's a fine gentleman. I'm a dock rat."

"You were talking to the boss in your dream. You were telling him yes about something, and you mentioned ice, and you were upset. You sounded like a stranger to me. What did you agree to with Mr. Ismay?"

"I told you, I never talked to him. I agreed to nothin." Fred tried to gauge her mood. Did she believe him? He sat there looking at her, the tea grown cold in his cup. He was unsure what to think.

Fred tried to change the subject. "I'll miss ya when I'm gone, m' love, every single day I will." His words were entirely true. He would miss her, but he chose his words carefully. "You're the fairest lass I've ever seen, the only one for me Eva." She gave him a tentative look, as if she were weighing his words and his affection in the balance.

And he meant what he said, every single word of it, at that instant. Even if, a second later, feeling completely defeated by her lack of response and the sour expression on her face, out of the blue he remembered a girl he had known once, in New York, for a few days between crossings, before he'd met Eva. She was a few years older than him, and very experienced in things he'd never done before. They'd shared a few nights he'd never forget. She was the one girl who stuck in his mind, all this time.

Recently, when he'd been in New York, out on the town with Alf and Horace, he'd been proud that he had resisted the advances of Moira, the girl in the bar. But since then, he'd had stimulating thoughts of the nights spent in the small room with the first girl. Her name was Juliette. They'd laughed that the bed wasn't big enough for two, and then it hadn't mattered at all. Things had been so simple between them.

Lately, whenever he felt Eva slipping away from him, whenever she recited the reasons her brother detested him, whenever she made him feel less of a man, he sought comfort in remembering and reliving those moments in that bedroom with Juliette. In his weakness, he wanted to be there again. He couldn't help himself. If anything, he used Eva and Phil as an easy excuse for his forbidden desires.

At the same time, Fred knew love was more important than whatever the dark-haired girl had had to offer him for those steamy hours in that room with no windows. Love was what he really needed. As a waif, love and acceptance were all twisted up together in his mind. They were what he'd really craved all his life. But when Eva rejected him, he was left wanting. He was unable to go on without filling the void somehow. The passion he might share with a stranger would be intense, but it would be fleeting, and he would be left empty once more. Even so, he remembered the dark-haired girl. He'd come to realize this lately; he had his needs.

And that was the very reason Fred wanted things to be right between him and Eva before he left for New York again. He never wanted to stray from her when he was thousands of miles away, on his own. Eva would never know of his indiscretions, but he would. So, he wasn't looking to be unfaithful, but he needed her assurance, her love, to keep him on the path. He knew he was far from perfect. On his own, it was almost impossible to resist temptation. For good-looking young sailors, there were always invitations from women in the taverns near the docks. He needed the love he shared with his wife to be strong and unblemished to prevent any dalliance on his part. The last thing he needed was for Eva to find out about his deal with Ismay. She would never understand, and it would diminish her already dwindling opinion of him.

Fred took a quick sip and finished his cold tea. He popped the last of the scone into his mouth. "Well, I'm off. Please think good thoughts of me, and please pray for me. After *Titanic*, I need to ask for your prayers whenever I leave. Y'know, I never expected to be on a ship that would sink." He shook his head in amazement. "Will ya pray for me, Eva? It will make all the difference, I know it will."

"Of course I'll pray for you." She stood and wrapped her arms around him. "Be careful then, Fred." She pulled him even closer. "But when you get back, I'll be at Phil's. He'll help me move our few things. But I want you there with me. You're my husband, the only man I want, just you remember that. We need to try a little harder to work out our problems. I know we aren't supposed to talk about your blackouts, but that doesn't mean they haven't happened. I've seen you like that, more than once. And now you are saying crazy things in your sleep. You must see a doctor again when you get back. I won't have it any other way."

"If that's what you want, I will, though I don't know how it can 'elp me. The other times I went, they were of no use. I'll try and find a different one, a better one, if you insist."

The morning was getting away from him and it was time to leave. Fred leaned over and kissed Eva deeply. He never wanted to stop. His lips clung to hers. By the time he returned, Phil would have come between them. He was sure of it.

Chapter 15

Every crossing was the same as the one before, barring the bad weather that could pop up and surround a ship for days on end. And this one, departing So'ton on August 8, 1912, with *Olympic* riding the seas with undeniable majesty, was no different than her many other crossings, except for one thing.

The shadow of her sister ship, her long tentacles reaching from beneath the sea, altered the mood of the ship's officers when they cast their eyes on the surviving crew of *Titanic*, the few who had been chosen for this journey. Most of all, when they looked at Fred Fleet. For it was he who had stood before the Senate in their august chambers of marble, in Washington, DC, and swore under oath that if he'd had binoculars, he would have seen the berg sooner and saved the ship. And, logic had it, who had denied him the glasses? Why, the officers of the *Titanic* of course. And even though only four *Titanic* officers had survived and none of them were assigned to this *Olympic* crossing, all of *Olympic's* officers felt the blame cast their way inadvertently. Fred had only been trying to protect his reputation as lookout, and who could find fault with that? As luck would have it, all of the officers of the White Star Line decided to blame him, and they employed little effort to disguise their resentment.

Back at the hearings, if he'd thought carefully about it, he might have phrased some of his answers differently. But Fred wasn't that smart. Besides, he was already challenged enough, standing there in the poorly fitting, borrowed clothing he'd been instructed to wear, with the stiff celluloid collar and the tie too tight around his neck, his addled brain trying to remember the words Mr. Ismay had put in his mouth, or tried to put in his mouth. Fred was confused and lost once the questioning had begun.

"How far off was the iceberg when first you spotted it? How tall was it?" What was it that Mr. Ismay wanted him to say? He could hardly get the words out. And the way the senators looked at him completely unnerved him, as if he wasn't lost enough to begin with. More than once he was asked to repeat himself. They said no one could understand a word he was saying.

"Was it English?" one of the fancy-dressed men wanted to know. He'd heard a snicker in the room.

Then another one cut in, asking, "Would the binocs have made the difference, really?"

At that moment, he knew he couldn't back down and deny his first response. He'd always used glasses before on the *Oceanic*, so what were they talking about now? He remembered how he'd reached up and scratched his head and there was laughter in the room, until a voice told them to restore some decorum to the hearing. He didn't know what that word meant. *Decorum?* He'd always used glasses in the crow's nest. He'd never spotted an iceberg before, not directly in the ship's path. The earlier ones seen from *Titanic*, the ones Ismay had forbidden him to mention, were best forgotten. He'd been totally out of his element before those fine gentlemen who'd viewed him as a subspecies, at best.

Eventually, he'd reacted the same as if one of the lads had punched him in the schoolyard. He wouldn't let them bully him. Anyway, all of them wanted a piece of him, they wanted to blame him. He could feel their hostility, their dislike and lack of any respect for him as soon as he'd walked into the chamber. They knew he was the dock rat he always assumed he was. So, he'd said what he did about the missing glasses, and he'd incurred the ire of the officers before he'd even stepped on board the *Olympic* this fine, cloudless, morning in August.

On his previous trips these last weeks, the officers had seemed diminished by *Titanic's* tragedy, but they hadn't targeted Fred. Now, Fred sensed they wanted revenge, and he stood before them, the perfect target, which only fed into his own personal guilt. He knew they wanted him to feel uncomfortable in their presence, and so he did.

He kept to himself and thought about Eva. He wondered if Phil had come and moved their things to Norman Road yet. He worried that Eva would stop missing him once she was living in the relative comfort of her brother's house, sharing his table, and listening to his insults directed at Fred. He knew Phil's goal was to convince Eva to undo their marriage, no matter what was required. Maybe the church would be involved. Maybe Phil had already discussed this with the vicar. Then, with Fred out of the way, Phil would insist that Eva return to Guernsey to marry whomever the family chose.

In the evenings, Fred sat on his bunk, avoiding the other crew members as he tried to figure out what he could possibly do to win Eva back. He wrote ardent love letters to her, letters he dropped in the crew's post box, letters that would be mailed once the ship reached New York.

***

Two weeks later, Fred was home at last in Southampton. He gathered his few possessions and hurried off the ship. He wanted to be first in line to receive his pay at the White Star office, and he didn't want to waste time standing in a long queue.

With the money in hand, he headed home, saying a silent prayer that Eva had read, and was touched by, the letters he had sent. He hoped she had received at least some of them before Philip had come to take her away. Most of all, he really hoped she had changed her mind about moving to Phil's. He and Eva, they belonged together, no matter what. He turned off High Street and spotted a display of flowers for sale outside a corner shop. He didn't have money to squander on such things, but flowers seemed like a necessity, not an unneeded and wasteful item. He picked up the smallest bunch and asked the price.

"Is yer missus mad at ya?" the bloke in the shop chuckled as he took in Fred's worn and bedraggled seaman's attire. "Ah, lad, I'll give 'em to ya fer a special price. Gimme six pence and they're yours!"

Fred didn't think that was a very special price, or if anything, it seemed higher than it should be, but he had no real idea how much such blossoms should cost, so he handed over the coins and took the flowers, holding them carefully as he hurried up the street. He couldn't wait to give them to Eva.

For you, my love. That was what he decided he'd say to her. Hopefully, that would work. Hopefully, she would see how sincere he was in his affection. That would be worth any price. He rushed up to their front door and opened it, the flowers, with their heavy fragrance, leading the way in his extended hand. He started to call out to Eva. A rush of warm, stale air greeted him. The room was empty. Their few belongings were gone. Most importantly, Eva was gone.

Fred stood in the doorway, unable to take another step. He saw the hook where he'd toss his cap whenever he came through the door. In place of the warmth he'd clung to within these walls, the room was barren, pitiful and forlorn. Everything good in his life, all his memories with Eva, and their plans for the future, had been stolen away. His face crumbled, and a tear slid down his cheek. Why did he always lose any love that might come his way? He was reluctant to put it all in the past, their happy days in the cottage. He sat on the floor for a moment and closed his eyes. He could almost feel Eva's lips on his for a brief instant. And then the blackout came, another descent into he knew not what, or for how long. He woke with a start and remembered his desolation.

There was nothing for it but to walk over to Phil's house. He didn't want to, but if he didn't, most likely he'd never see Eva again. He'd rather have her in his life, at any cost, than lose her completely. He knew the price to pay would be enduring Phil's insults every day he lived in that house, but there was nothing he could do about that. Slowly, he walked toward Norman Road. There was no joy in his footsteps.

In a few minutes, he stood in front of the house. He hesitated before going in. His eyes were drawn to the building next door, where he had rented a room the last year he was crew on the *Oceanic*. He'd rather have remained on board *Oceanic* and not been switched to *Titanic*.

His early life had been hard enough. Fred didn't fancy change. He looked up at the window of his old room and remembered how alone he had been before he met Eva. The brother and sister had moved in while he was away at sea. They'd come from Guernsey two weeks before he and Eva met that rainy day. Eva was his world from the moment he first caught a glimpse of her.

Now, he was afraid to walk inside and greet his wife, but he couldn't stand out here forever. He tried to straighten his clothes. He took a deep breath. He decided he'd better knock first. After all, this wasn't his home. He was an unwanted boarder here, at best. He tapped on the door.

"It's open," Phil's voice drifted out of a back room. Fred opened the door, but Eva was nowhere to be seen. He was even more uncertain, walking in without his wife standing there as a buffer. *Where could she be?* He remembered he still had the flowers in his hand. Feeling absurd, he dropped them on a small table next to the door.

Eva and Phil walked into the room from different directions. They both stopped dead in their tracks when they saw Fred.

"Oh!" Eva exclaimed, looking over at Phil. He scowled back at her.

"I wasn't sure you would come," Eva said, not exactly the first words he wished to hear from his wife after being gone almost three weeks. *I'm glad to see you, I missed you, would have been more to his liking.*

"Well, I thought you said..." Fred began.

"He's here now, isn't he?" Phil obviously wasn't going to make Fred feel welcome.

Phil ignored Fred and walked out of the room, returning to whatever he was doing before.

"Come upstairs," Eva said as she headed for the staircase on the side of the room. Once upstairs, Eva showed him their room and he started to unpack his clothes. Eva softened up a bit once they were alone and the door was closed.

"I'll do the washing. I'll clean up yer stuff, don't worry about it." She reached over and touched his hand, stopping him from unpacking his duffel. "How was your trip?"

"It would have been fine, the weather was really smooth, but the officers on the ship were nasty to all of us *Titanic* crew, me especially. They don't like me none."

"Why is that?"

"Because I told the truth, at the hearings, about the binoculars. If I'd had me some glasses, I coulda seen the berg sooner and saved the ship. But they don't want ta 'ear the truth. *Titanic's* officers are the reason we had no glasses in the nest that night. The crow's nest glasses were missing, but they could have given us theirs."

"I'm so sorry they treated you like that. Of course, you had to tell the truth. Think of all the trouble you'd be in if you'd lied." Her words grated on his guilt.

"How have you been, Eva? When did you move over here with... him?" Fred hated to say his brother-in-law's name.

"Two weeks ago. I just feel safer here, not alone in that cottage, when you're gone all the time."

"I want to keep you safe, Eva."

"You can't if you're not here. I'm better off with Phil." Fred could think of no reply.

"One more thing Fred..."

"What Eva? Ask me anything." Suddenly he was terrified as to what might be troubling her when he thought they were patching things up between them just a tad.

"All the time you were gone, why didn't you send me a single letter? You say you care, but..."

"I did send you letters! Loads of them." Fred stopped and thought for a moment. And then he knew exactly what had happened. The officers had seen to it that all his mail was tossed in the ocean instead of the post. He was right when he sensed their resentment. He explained what must have happened to his letters.

Eva didn't say a word. Fred could see she was weighing his words to see if she could trust him. She walked over and took his hand. Hope, a tiny hope was born in that moment. If only it could last.

When they came downstairs, Phil stood by the door. "What's this? Where did this come from?" He held up the small bouquet of flowers Fred had forgotten in his discomfort.

"I bought them," Fred said. "They're for Eva."

"Well, did you? You bought these? Did you bring anything useful with you? Nah, I didn't think so." Phil gave Fred no chance to respond.

"They are beautiful, Fred. Let me put them in water." Eva took the flowers from her brother's hand. Lifting the blossoms to her nose, she carefully avoided Phil's exasperated expression.

"You always provide just what we don't need, Fred." Phil almost sounded like he was enjoying himself.

Fred had to hold back from punching the man. That wouldn't help, but it was the only thing that would have made him feel better. Instead, he tried to reach out and connect with Eva.

"I'm back for a while. They will be refitting *Olympic* with more lifeboats. I'm hoping for a few trips on the Union-Castle. I heard there are openings. I'm going to check in at the Hiring Hall tomorrow." Fred took Eva's hand and tried to lead her out of the room. "Let's go for a walk," he suggested.

Phil made a noise of disgust, but Eva accepted Fred's invitation. Once they were alone outside, Fred turned to Eva with a serious look on his face.

"I've been having lots of flashbacks. I can't shake it off, Eva. I can't sleep at night. I hear the people in the water, screaming, before they froze to death." He stopped walking and put his hand up to his face. "I can't go on like this. I'll call 'round to a doctor again."

"You best do that then. So, now it's flashbacks, along with the blackouts and talking in your sleep. Go to the doc as soon as you can. Just don't mention it around Phil. He'll never stop ranting that you're going crazy."

"Sometimes I feel like I am going crazy, if you want to use that word. I don't know what's happening to me. I'll make an appointment tomorrow, right after the Hiring Hall. I will do it, I promise."

And so he did. He got a job for a trip or two as an able-bodied seaman with the Union-Castle line, and then he made an appointment for the following day with the doctor he had seen shortly after the sinking.

The time spent in that office was a waste. The man did little more than say, "Just give it time, young man." It was the same thing he'd heard before. Fred wanted, and needed, more help than that. In the days that followed, he saw two other doctors, but none could help him.

Then it was time for a crossing back to New York, and off he went, no better than he was before.

When he came home, he had another blackout. He could tell Eva's patience was wearing thin. And her affection, if she still had any, was hard to recognize. She and Phil exchanged blatant looks of displeasure every time Fred walked in the door.

***

Time slipped away. Months and then years he hardly remembered. Eventually, Eva didn't offer even the slightest hint of a smile when he returned from the sea, and Phil's anger grew more pronounced. Fred was back with White Star, traveling on the *Olympic* with regular crossings. The small amount of money he earned wasn't enough to win Eva back to his side, or to afford a house on their own. Phil ran Eva's life.

One day, Fred overheard Phil gossiping with a neighbor about him, and how worthless he was, and how mean he was to Eva. Fred knew he was worthless, he had no doubt about that, but he never meant to be mean to his wife. He knew he was often abrupt with her, his mind more focused on how soon he could leave again. Often, he was thinking of some fair lass he'd met when he was here or there, off on a journey. He had long since abandoned his intention of remaining faithful, no matter what. After all, a man had his needs, and Eva had no interest in satisfying his.

On a trip to New York, he'd found his way to the bar he'd visited in the past with Alf and Horace. As luck would have it, Moira still worked there. Instead of the red dress he'd remembered, she wore even less. This time a purple frock revealed even more of her charms.

After a few minutes in a back room, he'd seen the rest. Each time he was in New York, he spent time in that room with her, and others of her trade. He wanted to control his behavior, to win Eva back, but that seemed impossible. And yet, he was deeply wounded by the conversation he wasn't meant to hear. But Fred wondered if Phil purposely spoke in a loud voice, hoping Fred would hear.

To make matters worse, one after another his doctors told him he should simply put his memories aside. And when that didn't work, he lay sleepless on his pillow as time moved on, but he didn't. The doctors had thrown their arms in the air and accused him it seemed, at least that was what he made of it, of seeking attention perhaps, and nothing more than that. That hurt as bad or worse than his feelings of guilt.

But he never mentioned the blackouts, the time he couldn't account for when he was lost, somewhere in the horror of the sinking perhaps. He didn't know where his mind went. He just knew he could never talk about all that, not to the docs. Now, not even with Eva. He had no intention of talking with her anymore about anything related to that night. How could he? They had drifted so far apart. He was such a disappointment as a husband, he knew that. No use making it worse.

One night, in a fit of deep despair, he reached out for Eva in the bed they still shared. This time, to his surprise, she didn't say no. The touch of his fingers on her breast lit a flame. In the morning, they exchanged surprised glances when they woke to the light in the window. Fred felt renewed, strengthened, and so he decided to seek out one more doctor. Maybe there was hope for him after all. And this one, a new, young one, suggested he try something different.

At first, Fred had sat in the office, all talked out, no better for the effort of reliving the *Titanic* night. Then the doctor, touching a match to the bowl of his pipe, had suggested a different tactic. Smoke had drifted in a wreath about his face, bringing a sweet, musty smell to the room.

"Don't try and move forward, Fred. Rather, move back. Back to the loss of lives and find a way, some way, of helping the families of the victims. Bring good from the bad. Give it a try."

He'd kept his eyes on Fred, until Fred could hold his gaze no longer, and he looked down at his hands, wondering why he'd persisted, year after year, in redoing the dark red india ink tattoos on the backs of his hands. Popular as they were with seagoing men his age, he saw them for what they really were. At first, he had paid good money, more than he should have, in a shop in Liverpool, when he saw the tattoos as a way to hide the small red birthmarks he'd been born with, his *mark of the devil*, he'd come to believe.

Now the tattoos looked like blood splotches. He'd never realized this before. Was his guilt expressed in the dark red marks on his hands? He made a decision right then to clean the tattoos and not replace them, and he'd try to seek out the victims whose suffering still haunted him with relentless precision. It was as if a retroactive miracle had been granted to the discarded waif in the foundling hospital thirty-one years ago, and his own parents had come back for him after all these years.

But they had not. But Fred would go back and see what he might do to help the wee lads of the *Titanic*.

At last, he had an idea that might work.

Chapter 16

A few days later, Fred stood outside a red brick building, unsure if he should go in. Oh, he knew he should. The words stenciled on the door, "Southampton Seamen's Relief Society" assured him of that. But it was the thought, *what will 'appen next?* that made his feet stick to the pavement, impeding his forward progress.

The loss of adult life was certainly troubling, but lately, it was the suffering of wee children that gave him new nightmares that never faded. Maybe it was the thought that came to him in the middle of a cold night, the bedroom frosty, the heat from the thruppence dropped in the heater box long since faded in the early morning hours, and Eva once again, sleeping wrapped in her own dreams, as close to the edge of the bed as she could get.

Their one recent night of passion had not been repeated, much to his disappointment. But the thought had come to him, as he stared at the ceiling in the dim light creeping through the window, *It's no different, if'n I forget the lads an' move on, it's no different than when me own parents left me for convenience sake and moved on with their own lives. I can't just let go of these wee ones. They are my burden t' carry t' the grave.*

As the breeze whipped up and the trees swayed in response, Fred looked across the street, his eyes drawn to a small group of children on the pavement. Two lads played what seemed to be a game of conkers. Which made sense, since there was a long row of horse chestnut trees, the source of the conkers, seed pods, littering the ground below. The lads swung the conkers they'd attached to strings, and a chorus of voices erupted with excitement as they went at each other.

Life should be that simple and carefree for all little children. The thought popped into Fred's head unbidden, and so he pushed his way into the building.

The bright lights and crush of people inside surprised him. Lines snaked around the room. Several ships had gone down in the six years since *Titanic*, and families were always in need. There were various desks manned by men, and a few women, with a sign resting on each desk.

"Claims" said one, another offered "Inquiries for the Lost," and another, "Inquiry, Follow up." Voices buzzed amid an odor of unwashed bodies and second-hand clothing that had seen better days. Fred recognized it as the scent of the needy.

Where to begin? he asked himself. But a voice interrupted his thoughts.

"Are you looking for handouts? Are you hungry?" Fred searched for the source and saw a woman, dressed in better clothes than the others, but with a weary look on her face. *Perhaps she got to the box of discards before the rest of them.* Seated at the "Inquiry, Follow Up" desk, she pushed a strand of red hair behind her ear as she watched him.

"May I help you?" she asked.

"I'm not sure," he replied, stepping closer.

"We do have meals being served, if you're hungry, in the back room. Potatoes and some beef today. There's no charge, don't be shy to ask, it's all right. Everyone needs something. We're all in the same boat." Her voice faltered for a moment.

"In the same boat?" he asked. It occurred to him that her voice, her way of speaking indicated a far more privileged background than that of probably anyone he had ever met, and most likely, of anyone in this room right now. "What boat might that be, m'lady?" he asked, because that was what she seemed to be. A lady of some standing, at least, once upon a time. If she were a lady, why would she be sitting here now? In this room of the unwashed with a stack of requests on her desk that will probably go unanswered, no matter her good intentions. Because that was the way the world worked for the unfortunate, Fred was convinced of it.

"The *Titanic,*" she said softly, looking at him to see his reaction. "I was there. But that's not what I meant *now,* rather I meant it as a figure of speech."

"What's that? *A figure of speech?* I 'ave no idea what you're saying, m'lady." He wondered to himself, what does she mean, she was *there?* Certainly *not.* He must have heard her wrong. Those who *were* there, the rich and entitled first-class passengers of the *Titanic,* because that is what she seemed to him now, she was one of those no doubt, those elite passengers who survived, they've all gone their separate ways, years ago. No need for them to linger in the area around the wharves that attach to the fringe of working-class neighborhoods of Southampton. Once they returned to England, off they all went, back to their pampered lives, dancing at balls and hosting afternoon tea. No need to look back. He took a closer look at her clothing. Even if it was badly creased, and her hair in need of a silver brush resting on a dressing table somewhere, with a maid to fix it just so, she was one of *them*, and totally out of place *here*.

"I meant, we all have burdens to bare, so in a sense, we travel in the same boat through life." Her voice was so low, her message so unexpected, that Fred was caught off guard.

"I can't say as I agree, m'lady. We may have troubles, but they are different, we are completely different."

"Can I ask you a question, sir?" Fred was certainly confused now. Why did she refer to him as *sir*? And why did she ask permission of him? She could say whatever she pleased to him, he a working-class bloke, down on his luck, and irreparably damaged by circumstance.

"Of course y'can." He was unsure of what to expect. "Call me Fred, that'll work."

"All right. Where were *you*, Fred, on the night of April 14, 1912?"

"I was, I was..." he struggled to complete the sentence, caught up by the expression on her face, as if she already knew the answer. Her eyes urged him to continue. "I was on board the *Titanic*, I was there. But you knew that, didn't you? How could you?"

"Yes, yes I did. And that changes everything."

"Wha' d'ya mean by that? What changes what?"

"*Titanic* changes everything. There is no difference now, as there used to be, one class to another, man to woman. At least, that's the way I see it. Come, please come and sit down and talk to me. I need you to do that, if you will."

Fred was totally thrown by her comment, shared so freely, and also by her request of him, as if she could have a need of *him*. He slipped into the chair beside her desk. As he looked into her large green eyes, he realized she was younger than he thought at first. She seemed just a few years older than he was, if that. He felt himself drawn to her and he was shocked by the connection that asserted itself between them, all the more so as she returned his glance with the same intensity, which only added to his unease.

"Can I ask you another question?" The intimate tone of her voice wiped away all the other voices, the din of conversation, the whimper of children who clutched their mother's skirts and bemoaned their dissatisfaction. It was as if she and Fred were the only ones in the room. "You suffered a huge loss that night, didn't you?"

"I lost something, but it's not what you think, it's hard to explain. It's hard for me to understand, even after all these years." He was shocked at the sound of his own voice, how could he just *speak* to her, and tell her the hurt in his heart, just like that? He found it impossible to mouth the words or form the thoughts, not to the doctors, and certainly not to his wife, and yet here he was, speaking them to a perfect stranger. But then, there was that connection, again, he'd felt it instantly and it was still here, floating in the air between them, and somehow, they were both aware of it.

"Tell me, please. What did you lose Fred?" She was almost whispering now.

"I won't say it right, I'm no good with words, you see. But, 'ere it is, I didn't *know* I was *safe* before, not ever. But now, I feel like I... I'm *not* safe anymore. I guess what I lost was, I lost my *innocence*." He paused for a moment, as he thought about the word, a word he might have never used before. "I didn't know life could be so *dangerous* in just a few seconds, that was all it took. And on top of that, I feel, so, guilty, *all* the time. I didn't know the ways of the world, although I thought I did. I grew up hard you see. But, is there such a thing as *innocence?* Are we born blind to the possibilities of really bad things? I'm sure you know better than me? Do we 'ave that?" He stared at her, but she didn't respond. She looked lost in her own thoughts.

"Let me start again," Fred said. "I'm not saying it right. To start with, we 'ave a feeling like we are in a certain place, and even if we are never, well, perfect... still, we are protected from the very worst thing that could happen, we just are. But then, something so unexpected, so 'orrible 'appens, and that shield, or wha'ever it was, it just breaks. Like glass in a windowpane, y'see what I mean? And it can't be put back together, no matter what?"

"You mean, once the worst thing possible comes along and surprises us, and takes what we almost never knew we had, that *innocence,* our greatest treasure, then, our peace, that runs deep like a river inside of us, can never come back. Not ever?" she asked.

"Yes, yes, that's *it. Peace like a river*, deep inside, and then it's gone... You *do* see what I mean." Fred couldn't believe the moment. No one else had ever come close to grasping what was buried at the root of his anxiety. In fact, he had never voiced the words to himself before this moment.

"Oh yes, I certainly do. And before, before this happened, we were whole, in more ways than we ever knew. Even if our life wasn't completely perfect, because no one's ever is. But then, then it's gone, that *wholeness.*"

"And we always feel the loss."

"And everything bad, is just one-half step away from another disaster." she whispered.

And then they both spoke at once, their voices melting as one. "Yes."

She reached out and covered his hand with hers.

"Tea. Can we go for a cup?' she asked, inclining her head to be certain her words are private. She stood up, even before he could respond.

"Yes, of course we can. But not the Ritz, please."

"I don't want places like that, not anymore. You can be certain of that," she told him emphatically. More than a few pairs of eyes watched as they left the room, but neither one of them took notice. Out on the street she took the lead, ushering him around the corner into a dimly lit, half empty shop, "Biggley's Tea," the sign announced. They found a table off to the side and she ordered as soon as the waiter appeared.

Once the tea arrived, she poured, never taking her eyes from his face. Fred took a sip, suddenly confused by what was happening. He drank more of the tea from nervousness, not thirst. He placed the cup on the table, spilling a bit in his haste.

"Let me explain, just a wee bit better, if I can." Fred told her all about his growing up years and finally ending up on the *Clio*. "So I know what it's like to be on the *edge* of terrible things about to 'appen to me. That's my life, it's not easy for a lad in those places."

"I'm sure it's not."

"But, this, this *Titanic* night, I never thought somethin' like *that*, and there I was... How could that 'appen, to me, to *you*, to any of us? And 'ow can we make it go away? I wasn't ever in a safe place, but whatever place I *was* in before, I lost that, that night. But how did you know?"

"I knew as soon as you walked into the office, because you carry your loss in your eyes, the suffering. And, I know what that feels like. I wish I didn't."

"Then we are one, aren't we," he told her. "We understand each other, completely." He was shocked at his own words.

Rather than giving her response in words, she lifted her fingers to her lips, kissed them, and reached out, touching his mouth lightly. Their eyes were joined together. Fred had never been here before, not with any other woman, not in any port he's been, in the many brief encounters on unwashed sheets these last years, and certainly not with Eva, not since they've drawn apart. Intimate moments with his wife were hasty, few, and far between. But now, Fred had experienced the most unexpected sensation. He and this stranger, they were one person, joined together. It was no different than if they had lain together, blankets tossed to the floor in their passion, sharing their deepest needs. There was no space between them.

Finally, she spoke. "When will I see you again? I must go back to the relief office, *now*. They will talk if I don't come back at once." She picked up a napkin and pressed it lightly against her mouth.

"Tomorrow? Here? "You see, I must sail on Friday, crossing to New York again, but I'll be back. In two weeks, if you want me."

"I *do* want you, then, and *now*. Yes, I'll see you *tomorrow*. I *need* to see you tomorrow. *Cybil*. My name is Cybil, you didn't even *ask* me."

"A name didn't seem important, all that's important is you, and me, 'ow you feel, 'ow *we feel*..."

"Together," she answered him. Fred realized that she hadn't denied the implication of deep intimacy between them. She looked at him without blinking, and he returned her glance.

"Yes," he said, his voice a whisper. Then, "Here for tea, tomorrow, at three."

"Yes Fred. *Yes*."

"But, Cybil, what did you lose on *Titanic*, or who? You didn't tell me."

"Tomorrow," she said, as she stood up and walked out of the shop, her words leaving him longing for more. Just the way she had said his name, the way she breathed *life* into him as she savored the word *yes*, so much was carried in those simple sounds.

He watched her as she approached the door, his eyes reluctant to let go of her, he watched the way she walked, the way her body moved. Once she was out of sight, he glanced down at the table and noticed her full, untouched teacup. The sight of it filled him with a promise of her return the next day. Wanting more, he took her napkin and slipped it into his pocket. He needed something of her to hold onto. He still felt the brush of her fingers on his lips. The warm sensation lingered. In a few short minutes, Cybil had filled him with a promise of acceptance, and with something else as well. She had awakened a new, unexpected world inside of him, with one simple touch.

Standing beside the table, Fred searched his pockets for some coins for the tea. Finding just enough, he tossed them on the white starched tablecloth and left the shop. It was only once he was out on the street, walking home, that he realized he never asked the question he had in mind when he'd set out for the relief office. *How might he help the children that were left, the ones whose fathers, members of the crew, died in the sinking?* But there was always tomorrow. For the first time in a long time, for the first time in years and years, he felt a rush of excitement when he thought about tomorrow. Up until then, his only thrill had been when the latest ship he was on pulled out of port, the tugs falling back as she headed out to open water, and there *he* was, up in the nest, feeling the wind on his face. With each trip, his blood ran fast with new possibilities, only to melt away soon enough. *But now,* he told himself, *now it's like I'm alive for the first time.* Yes, he couldn't wait to see Cybil again. A new hunger revealed itself as he made his way along the crowded pavement. Men headed home from their jobs, and he felt at ease moving among them, where previously he had felt isolated and alone, disconnected, surrounded by the dark cloud of his disappointing life.

***

"Where have you been?" Eva called out as he came through the door. She stood at the sink, peeling potatoes for dinner.

Phil wasn't home, and Fred was extra glad of that.

"I went to the relief office."

"Well, did they give you any money? I've not got much left, you know. And Phil is tired of buying all the food, and well he should be. And there you are, off to sea again in a few days' time, over and over, and me left behind with no more than a heel of bread in me hand. You've turned me into nothing but a charity case."

"I didn't ask for money," Fred replied, trying not to look at her, lest she see the expression on his face, which he was certain would give away the unexpected treasure he'd found this day in the lady with the green eyes.

"Why did you go there then? If not to ask for money?"

"I went because I want to find a way, I'm not sure how, but I want to help the wee lads left behind, the ones who belong to the men, the crew on *Titanic* who were lost. All this time gone by, ya see, and I just can't get them out of me mind."

"Help the lads? How could you possibly do that? You can't even take care of yer own wife. And the baby that's coming as well?"

"What? What are you tellin' me? You are going to 'ave a wee one, after all these years?"

"Yes, yes, I am. I didn't say a word at first. I wanted to be certain. But the midwife said so. I was looking forward to telling you. That's why I went to see her today. I wanted you to know before you leave on Friday. But you're more concerned about other people's wee ones than your own."

"Eva, that's not so. I didn't even know about the baby up until this minute. How could I?" His voice softened for a moment.

Her news brought back bittersweet memories. At first, right after they married, they had wanted a baby. Rather, Eva had wanted a baby. Fred wanted Eva to have whatever she wanted. But after months of trying, she hadn't gotten pregnant. The doctors had assured them they shouldn't give up. And then the iceberg, and *Titanic* sailed into their lives, unsettling her, as she referred to it, in every possible way. Eva blamed Fred for her inability to conceive, even though the doctors had said nothing of the sort. But now, he was gladdened by her words. The chance of a new beginning seemed possible. He walked toward her, his arms extended, the beginning of a smile pulling at his lips.

"Well, we will see in the months to come," Eva said. "What will you do and where will you be? If you're on the sea again, I'll know you don't care about me or the baby."

The harsh, accusatory tone in her voice bit at Fred and he dropped his arms, standing still. Disappointment welled up in his eyes.

"But Eva, that's not so. How else can I earn any money for the two of you if I'm not on a ship? It's all I know."

"Well, at least they could pay you more money. Can you arrange that?"

"That's why I went for the lookout watch, you know. I got the extra five shillings from that."

"Yes, and look how that's turned out for ya. And for me as well, a regular disgrace, you missing the iceberg, and the ship going down. Some lookout you were, Fred Fleet. And now you cannot even look out for yer own." She stuck her hands on her hips and glared at him. "And it's all on you, all those people lost. None of that has changed in the years since. It's only grown worse. And it's on me too. What's to come of the babe, the wee one soon to be born of a man who's a failure?" Her voice rose to a high, ear-piercing pitch.

"That's enough, Eva. I've told you over and over, it wasn't my fault." He raised his voice at last, and forgetting his warm thoughts of the baby, he screamed at her. When was she ever going to stop this tirade of blame? He could stand it no more. Her attitude increased his own guilt. That was the rub. If only she had supported him and told him none of it was his fault. But she hadn't.

He turned to head for the door, but then he remembered he'd spent the last of his coins for the tea. He pulled open the drawer that kept the small jar with their emergency reserve and helped himself to a few coins with Eva glaring at him, speechless that he would touch the money. Ignoring her exasperated expression, he stormed out, slamming the door as hard as he could behind him. The windowpane in the door shuddered as if it might break.

And indeed, a small crack crept out from the lower corner of the glass. Unseeable yet by the human eye, its presence marked the seed for the future, a point-of-no-return fracture in their lives.

Out on the street, Fred could still hear Eva screaming after him. "We need the money, Fred. The baby will need the money..."

But then he was gone, off to the workingmen's club down the way in Freemantle, where he'd soon sit alone at a table and watch the lads play snooker. He would drink a pint and sulk. He'd done it before when Eva got testy. What was a bloke to do, and Phil always standing there, listening to every word? It was another reason he looked forward to a fresh journey, off to sea once again, a chance to lose his frustration in the stiff wind on the top deck.

The constant travels hadn't lessened his misery, not really, but it was better than a job in a factory, if he could find one. A factory job would leave him living in that house every day, listening to Eva. Anything would be better than that. If only she hadn't chosen Phil over him, but she had.

He thought of Cybil, and a flush of anticipation rose as he wondered what would happen when he saw her the next day. He lifted his hand to his lips, conjuring the sensation aroused by Cybil's touch.

Chapter 17

The next morning, as he sipped his tea, Fred was very quiet. He was thinking of Cybil again and trying to hide his thoughts from his wife.

"Are you off to the ship for a bit this morning?" Eva asked as she pulled back a chair at the table and joined him. "Are you getting her ready for the trip?" Fred was unsettled by her questions. It had been a long time since Eva had expressed any interest in anything he had done, or where he'd gone. Even these last years, with the *Olympic* serving as a troop transport, and the crew in great danger on the seas with the U-boats after them, when there was a good chance he'd never come home, Eva had shown little concern, which hurt his feelings terribly. She had busied herself looking after the house, and taking care of Phil, and helping at the church when asked. But today, of all days, when he was trying to restrain his excitement about Cybil, Eva was curious. Fred worried that the expression on his face had aroused her suspicions.

"Yes, I'm going down to the dock. We have work to do. Don't look for me until the evening." He lifted his cup, hiding his face and his thoughts, he hoped.

"What do you have to do that will take all day? There's no need when the ship isn't going anywhere!" Her voice was mocking, and Fred struggled to restrain himself. He wanted to strike out at her. But today was the last day he wanted to get into a row with his wife.

"I have things to do. And yes, there is a need for someone to keep watch on the ship when she's in port. They're loading cargo. It's important that it not be stolen. But I have other tasks as well. You don't know anything about the preparation when a huge ship like *Olympic* sets out on a journey. We are carrying thousands of troops." He kept his voice as mild as he could, but it wasn't easy... and today, of all days! What was she going to do? Follow him down to the docks and check on his every move?

"You're right, Fred. I have no idea about the ship, and certainly no idea about anything you do, or where you go, for that matter. You keep yourself, well... hidden from me. You've been doing that for years."

"Maybe it's because you judge me so harshly." Fred wished he could take back his words. This couldn't lead anywhere worth going.

"How are you feeling?" he asked, trying to change the mood. "With the baby and all?"

"I didn't think you were interested. But, actually I am feeling all right."

"Not sick? I've heard some women feel very sick..." his voice trailed off. He wanted to show her he's not uncaring and cold, although he has no knowledge of babies and women's business.

"No, I'm not feeling bad. Some of my friends did with their babies. And Maisy felt terrible, and then she lost that wee one, right after she finally got married." Eva let out a heavy sigh. "Oh, I hope that doesn't happen to me. I couldn't bear it if I lost the babe." She reached for a handkerchief and wiped tears from her face.

"I'm sorry I made you think of that sad business with Maisy. Our baby will be fine, you'll see."

"If you don't unsettle me, Fred. Just don't unsettle me." Her words accused him, even as the tone of her voice, soft and vulnerable, broke his heart. As much as the two of them had grown apart and shared nothing but a bed, and rarely touched one another in that bed, now and then, they did. Fred felt a desperate desire for her to have the baby she wanted so much, to hold the wee one in her arms. Maybe the baby could make up for the disappointment he was as a husband. Fred wondered if that was possible.

"I won't do anything to hurt you or the baby. I promise." But even as he spoke the words, he knew he was lying. There was a table in a tea shop on Hurley Street with a fresh linen cloth set upon it, and teacups to be poured, and chairs to be occupied. And he would be there at three. Nothing could stop him. He was, if anything, a restless, needy soul, unfulfilled and searching all his life.

Fred went into the bedroom and looked through his sparse collection of clothes. Eva had already washed all except one of his shirts so he would have clean clothes for his trip. The one remaining shirt is the one he wore, and after a week on the docks, working in the sun, it was hardly clean, and certainly unfit for a tea shop and an assignation with a lady such as Cybil.

He slipped off the dirty shirt and chose a grey one, the one he liked best, out of the four he owned. At the tiny mirror on the wall, he stared at his reflection as he combed his hair. No matter his efforts, it still looked unkempt. Phil kept some dressing for his hair, in his bedroom, among his things. He'd seen him use it. Phil had already left for the day, off to the chemist shop he managed. Fred tiptoed into Phil's room, and quick as he could, he opened the top dresser drawer, hoping to find it. He heard Eva in the kitchen, washing up the plates from breakfast. Fred opened the jar and helped himself to a small dollop. Then he walked back to the mirror and combed the substance into his hair. He had never done something like this before, both the theft and the new look for his hair. He couldn't help but indulge in a little smile as he looked at his reflection.

"I'm off, Eva," he called out as he hastily slipped through the door, careful that she not catch a glimpse of him.

He had nothing to do on the ship, but if he had stayed home until just before three p.m., it might have been difficult to disappear at just the right time. So he went to the *Olympic* and walked about, looking busy. He climbed to the nest and looked out over the port of So'ton. He'd never paid much attention to the houses that dotted the landscape. He knew where he and Eva used to live, before Phil persuaded Eva to move back with him. And he knew exactly where their current house was on Norman Road.

But where did Cybil live? Which one of these houses was hers? Or was it hers? How could that be? Did she live with her family? Wherever it was, it must be a very fine home indeed.

And then he felt the ridiculousness of his situation. Here he was, a lad from an orphanage, a discard with less than nothing, looking forward to drinking tea with a lady like Cybil. What a fool he was. What in the world was he doing here today? And where was Cybil? What was she doing? Was she choosing a special dress to wear when she looked at him with those deep green eyes? It was almost like her eyes were touching his skin. A flash of excitement streaked through his body, and he was helpless. He had to see her. He could hardly wait.

Time came to walk to the tea shop. As he made his way down the gangplank and headed off the pier onto the main road, his heart fluttered. He wasn't nervous yesterday because everything just happened. There had been no preparation. But now he felt unsure of himself. What if he can't think of a word to say? What if he sounds like a fool? He can read and write, but that's about it. Surely, Cybil is used to fine gentlemen, men who have been to universities and come from families with means, men the exact opposite of him. And yet, she wanted to see him again, she was very clear about that. But why?

He paused for a moment as he caught a glimpse of himself reflected in a shop window. French's, it was, the shoe shop. He pulled out the comb he'd saved in his pocket and ran it through his hair. The image of a young man stared back him. Well-built, with deep-set grey eyes, high cheekbones, a straight nose, and lips that a woman he'd met in New York had described as filled with passionate promise. At the time, he'd been full of ale, and he'd laughed and suggested she was leading him on with flattery, and as it turned out, she was. Soon they had found a small, dark room together. Afterwards, as she slipped back into her dress, she'd told him he had fulfilled that promise.

What could Cybil possibly see in him, he wondered, and what she was after? What did she need from him, and how could he possibly leave her satisfied?

Chapter 18

Deep in thought, he stood in front of the tea shop. He realized there was nothing for it but to go in, even though he felt completely out of place. Just as he started to open the door, he heard a voice behind him.

"Fred! There you are!" Cybil hurried up. "I was worried you wouldn't come." Her eyes traveled over his face and his body quickly, coming back to rest on his lips, and then his eyes. "I thought perhaps I'd imagined the whole thing, yesterday, meeting you and..." Fred realized she was embarrassed. Here she was on the street, speaking with a man she hardly knew.

"Let's go in, no need to talk out here." Fred pushed open the door. Now it was his turn to look at her, as she moved past him. She wore a very handsome, very proper dark grey dress, no doubt from the needle of a fine dressmaker. Revealing her attractive figure, it fit her well, while still maintaining her elegance. Her jewel-like red hair was pulled atop her head. She walked with a grace he hadn't noticed when she'd hurried from the shop yesterday. And then they claimed the same table they'd occupied the day before. And the same waiter came to greet them.

"Good afternoon, m'lady... *sir?*" he hesitated, seemingly unsure of the correct form of address for Fred. Surely, he wasn't a gentleman. "Can I serve your tea now?" He looked at Cybil.

"Yes, thank you." Fred pushed himself to appear comfortable, used to giving orders to waiters in places like this. When the waiter left them alone at last, Cybil seemed hesitant to speak.

"How are you today Fred? Did you have a pleasant evening last night?' She was obviously uncomfortable and trying to make conversation.

"I am good, and yes, last night, all is good." Fred struggled as well. This was not what he had expected, but then again, what had he expected? "And you, how are you today, Cybil?" He was suddenly unsure about using her first name, rather it seemed he should address her as Lady. He couldn't recall her last name, if she'd told him.

"Excellent, Fred, I am excellent." Fred realized she was staring at him. He swallowed deeply, trying to hide his discomfort. He wondered if she would just get up and leave. He didn't want her to go, but it seemed they had no concrete reason to be here together at all. He tried to hold on to her with his eyes, he begged her to stay, without saying a word.

"I'm not sure where to start Fred, so I just will... We are the same, you and I." She saw him start to shift in his chair, it was obvious he was about to protest again about them ever being the same. "No, I really mean that. What does social standing, or money, or anything matter after all we went through? Did the money in my family's coffers lessen my experience that night? I can tell you, no, it didn't. If anything, it made things worse. I was very well situated before the journey. I had a very rich husband." Cybil shared the details of her unpleasant marriage, although Fred could see it wasn't an easy thing for her to do. "And then when it was all over, he blamed me, for our loss, of Matthew, and he was right." Her voice cracked and she was unable to continue. Without thinking, Fred reached over and took her hand. Words tumbled out of his mouth.

"Cybil, it could never be your fault, none of it. You see, it was all *my* fault. I know you will want to get up and walk away now, and I don't blame ya' when you do. Everything that 'appened that night was all my fault. You see, *I* was the lookout, the one who didn't see the iceberg in time."

"You are *that* Frederick? Frederick Fleet, that's you?" Her voice betrayed her shock.

"Yes. So, I've been honored to make your acquaintance, m'lady, and I'm so sorry for the loss you suffered. Now you are looking at the man caused it all to 'appen. And I'm truly sorry, although, I know, it's too late. Go, I'll cancel the tea. The bloody bloke has yet ta' bring it." He stood up, waiting to assist her, as he expected her to rise and depart without speaking a word. He couldn't imagine what he was thinking in the first place, coming here to meet her. Now, he knew he couldn't bear to see her cry, and hear her tell him just how terrible a man he was. For a few hours, in his imagination, he had hoped for more from her. Just what, he wasn't sure. But that was all over now, it was obvious. But she remained seated.

"Fred, sit down, I'm not leaving, and I hope you will stay as well. The loss I suffered was because of *my* actions. I wanted to be with my friends, in the ballroom, dining and drinking wine and having a wonderful, exciting time. It was selfish of me." She told him how she'd left Matthew in the cabin with the nurse, and the terrible result. "If I had been below, if I'd been where a mother should be, none of this would have happened." She lifted her napkin and cried into the linen. A couple of people seated at tables across the room, turned and stared at her, and then at Fred.

"Matthew?" It was all Fred could say. He was overcome. It was the first time he'd heard directly from a mother of a lost child. And to think it would be Cybil, was more than he could take.

"Yes. He was four." She talked through her tears. She told him about the loss of her little boy, and the teddy floating in the water.

***

For a few minutes Cybil was back at *Titanic* that dreadful night. Unable to get into a lifeboat, she'd found herself in the water, and it was so cold. Now, she shook her head to dismiss the memory. She opened her eyes and looked around the tearoom. But she couldn't ignore the memory of how both she and Matthew were both in the ocean that night. None of the people in the lifeboats would rescue her, no matter how she'd pleaded with them. But she doesn't talk of that part now. Now, only Matthew mattered. "I never would have let that happen, *never*. If I'd been there in the boat with him, he'd be alive today. So, his loss, is all my fault. Not yours." As soon as she uttered the words, *my fault*, it seemed like heads turned in her direction.

"I don't see it that way," Fred reassured her. "No, absolutely not! It's me! I should 'ave seen that berg sooner."

***

Now it was Fred who was back at *Titanic*. He was thinking how different things would have been if the officers had heeded his very real, earlier warnings of ice in the area, and slowed down. But he still refused to give himself a pass, perhaps he could have sounded the final alarm more quickly, with no tiny hesitation whatsoever, the very instant he saw the ambiguous smudge in their path. It was his deepest secret. But there was more to it. The truth of it was, he was unable to put two and two together about exactly what happened up in the nest. He can't get past believing everything that went wrong that night was his fault and no one else's. Others might not see it that way, if all the pieces were in place. Only Fred could set it right, but the true tragedy was he couldn't see this for himself, just yet. If he ever could remained in question.

"Well, we have so much in common, do we not?" Cybil looked around the room again. People has ceased watching them. "No one else can ever understand all the guilt we feel. But, hear me on this, I *refuse* to blame you Fred. Speed was to blame, and the moonless night, and so many other things, but *not* you. But I understand your pain." She took his other hand, and they sat there, staring at each other intently, their hands clasped. They leaned toward one another. All the grief they'd suffered these past years passed between them, and no one else existed in the world at that precise moment. As they stared into each other's eyes, as their souls touched, they nodded at one another, offering a *unique* forgiveness, a healing filled with peace that no one else could offer, or even understand. Just then the waiter approached with their tray. He looked startled.

"Tea is served." The couple jumped back in their seats. Anxious for him to disappear, they watched in silence as he set the cups on the table. Finally, he was gone. They busied themselves pouring and drinking.

***

"Why *did* you come to the relief office, Fred?" Suddenly Cybil was embarrassed to ask him once again if he needed food. It was far easier to inquire as to his motives yesterday, when he was a complete stranger. She intuitively realized that asking that question now would drive a wedge between them, which was the last thing she wanted. Instead, she willed herself to hold onto the moment of togetherness, of healing.

"I know this makes no sense, because 'ow could I possibly do this? But I want to find a way to 'elp the wee children, who lost their da's on the ship. Maybe if I could do that, it would 'elp me, try ta' get past this. As I 'elp them, I could 'elp me. Do you see what I mean?"

"Yes, yes, I do. Actually, I am doing the same thing. I mean, I hope I am. These last years, since I've been alone, I have worked with the relief committee, helping the children, just as you have expressed. I visit their homes, and bring them food every few weeks, and presents on their birthdays, special treats, so they will know they are not forgotten. The money that was collected for the families after the sinking, from the various charity funds, is starting to run out. And, anyway, I want to give a more personal touch. Maybe you could come, and visit with them, when I go on my outings."

"Oh, I'm not so sure that would work, you see, they, the *Titanic* crew families, they want nothin' ta' do with me. I'm a leper in Southampton ya' see. That's what I am."

"Is it really that bad Fred? How can it be? Quite a bit of time has passed." Cybil shook her head in disbelief.

"Oh, trust me, it's that bad, and more. Me own family, what little I've got, they blame me too."

"But how can they? The report from the Board of Trade didn't blame you at all. Didn't your family read it?"

"Yes, but it made no difference. I think the reason is, the neighbors, they treat me wife so bad, they treat her like *she* missed the iceberg. And every time they look at her, they see their dead sons and 'usbands. At least that's what she tells me."

Up until now, he hadn't mentioned having a wife. Cybil was struck by the surprise and disappointment she felt. Up until now, she hadn't given a thought to whether or not he had a wife. It had made no difference, until she learned he did.

"My wife and I, we really don't get along." As soon as the words were out of his mouth, Cybil sensed that Fred felt guilty for telling her this. It's almost like he was betraying his marriage by bringing his wife into the conversation and sharing the sad truth of it with her. She wanted to stop herself from asking, but she couldn't.

"Do you have any children, Fred, with your, wife?"

"Not now. But very soon." Fred gave her a cautious glance.

Cybil was struck by the fact that he didn't sound particularly happy about this, it was almost like has was apologizing. Or was he saying that so he could hold on to her a little while longer? And then she realized how much she wanted him. She didn't even understand what that meant, but the feeling was there. *Could he feel the same way about me? Even if he wanted the baby? And he should want the baby!* She felt like he held the key to peace for her, peace and so much more. She couldn't let go. Things were getting more complicated than she had ever imagined. One look at his face told her he felt the same.

"We haven't gotten along, ever since the iceberg. She was blaming me before I ever made it back to England, and she's never seen things my way."

"But, you said she read the report, so, I still don't understand." Cybil shook her head.

"Well, she has this bloody brother you see, and he hates me, he always has since first we met." He paused for a moment. Cybil guessed he was trying to decide just what he would tell her. Then he started talking in a rush and told her everything. He told her the truth of the tension with Phil, and his early life as a waif. "And I never knew me dad, he was never in me life. He probably doesn't know I'm alive, I 'ave no idea."

"How terrible Fred. How awful for a boy to grow up knowing all this!"

"Oh, I didn't know it from the start, what makes it worse is, I thought I was an orphan like the rest of the lads." He went on and on, telling her about the foundling hospital and Elm Lodge and his eviction and going to the *Clio*. He told her every bit of it.

"What a cruel place that training ship must have been. What a sad, sad story Fred. But somehow you got a position with White Star Line? How did that happen?"

"There was one man, he was the only person who ever believed in me. But, let me get the story straight. At first, when they threw me out of Elm Lodge on me ear, I was certain everyone thought I was a thief. I couldn't stand that."

"Oh of course you couldn't. You were a fine young man, I'm sure of it."

"No, I wasn't. I was no saint as a lad at the Home. I was always into fighting and making trouble." Cybil put up her hand to stop him.

"Oh, I can't believe that Fred. You seem such a kind man to me."

"Kind? You read me wrong then, m'lady. I 'ave to tell you the truth, tell it as it is, or was. I don't fight anymore. I guess I grew out a' that. But when I was a lad, I was a brawler and a bully, yes. But I never stole no money."

"Of course you wouldn't" Cybil felt she had to interrupt. She wanted to defend him, even the boy he had been years ago.

He told her all about breaking into the office at Elm Lodge, and the box, and the money he didn't take. "I would never do that. But I got accused of the whole thing. And I ended up on the *Clio* as punishment. They beat the boys, all of us, and didn't feed us much. We worked dawn to dusk. But I learned about being on a ship. And then I got a job with White Star Line, as a deck boy, the lowest of the low, but it was a start."

"And what about the man, the one who helped you?" Cybil reached over and took hold of Fred's hand again. He was shocked, and unable to speak for a moment. But her eyes begged him to continue.

"One day, right after my sixteenth birthday on the *Clio* they told me, *this is it, you are done here.* They were sending me out into the world to find a job on a ship on me own, they were tossing me into the world, just like that. They said I was old enough. I was scared, I'll tell you that. I've never told anyone else, but I was. I had to be gone in a week."

"Go on, tell me more, if you want to."

"Three days later, I got a letter from this man, George Killey. He said he was on the Home Committee from Elm Lodge. He said he had discovered, some time back, that I hadn't taken the money, after all. And he wanted to help me if I needed help. He said he had just been informed that I was being sent off from the *Clio*. And he would help me get a job if I came 'round to see him."

"How did he find out you didn't take the money?" The waiter approached their table, fresh teapot in hand. He stopped when he saw Cybil and Fred's hands linked on the table. He backed away with a confused look on his face.

"The morning after I broke into the office, they found out I'd been there. You see, I carried a candle, so I could read me records in the dark room." He shared the story about the hot, dripped wax. "Then they saw the money was missing and decided I had taken it. They searched everywhere for the money and never found it."

Cybil raised her eyebrows and set her cup back on the table. "What happened next?"

"A few months later they learned the new boys had stolen things at the Home they had lived at before Elm Lodge. So, the masters at Elm looked around again, and found some money where these boys had hidden it, but the masters didn't know it was the office money from that night. But then, later on, they found some gold cuff links that were also taken from that box in the office, and the boys finally confessed, they had broken into the office right after I left the room, and they took the money, and the cuff links."

"How did the boys even know there was money in the office? Why did they break in at all?"

"Well, I told you I beat them up pretty bad. Eventually, one of them took a turn for the worse and ended up in hospital." Fred stopped speaking for a moment, watching Cybil's face. She just sat there, her expression unchanged, so he continued. "But getting back to the events of the day of the fight, later on that afternoon, the master had taken the two of them into the office to ask what happened. I'm guessing they didn't really want to talk about the fight at all, because they had started it, and they thought they had the upper hand on me, and well, talking about it would do them no good. They wanted to glower at me, that I was no longer top dog, they wanted me to still *be* there, so they could bully me I think. But when they were in the office meeting with the master, they'd noticed the beautiful box. And later on, they must have decided to go back and check out the contents. They were *already* thieves. That night, they were the ones out in the hallway, they made the noise that made me jump back out the window. Then, they got into the office after I left."

"So, did the man from Elm Lodge apologize to you?"

"No, not really. The committee itself, was never going to say *they* made a mistake. But Mr. Killey, he knew I had been blamed for something I didn't do. He knew I'd been sent to the *Clio*, and he said he was keeping an eye out for me, from a distance. Then, years later, when he heard I was being sent out on my own, he wanted to help me. He said I deserved his help, to make up for what happened. And I went and met with him, and he got me the job with White Star. I was on the Oceanic from that time on. I was trained as a lookout."

"And how did you get hired to *Titanic*?"

"I didn't fancy *Titanic* at all. I don't like change. After all that had happened to me in my life so far, I just wanted to stay where I was. But White Star decided I was going, since I had experience as a lookout. Mr. Killey, he was a good man. We kept in touch for quite a few years, even after *Titanic*. He saw my name on the list of survivors, and he wrote me and said he was overjoyed. He even went so far as to say, I'd always been a good lad! Imagine that! That was very generous of him, I didn't deserve it. But I don't know what's 'appened to him by now, he's probably dead. He wasn't young at the time. But he was kind to me, he thought well of me, he's the only person who ever was."

"*I* think well of you Fred, I..." and then Cybil stopped talking. They sat there staring at each other. No words were needed, their shared feelings for one another were quite apparent. What might happen next wasn't. The waiter watched them from across the room.

"Let's get out of here, let's go for a walk. Would you like that? Does it suit you?" Fred's voice was full of hope.

Chapter 19

"Yes, yes of course." As she stood up, Cybil felt she was discarding the boundaries of convention, and she suddenly knew that was exactly what she wanted to do. Blindly following the path laid out for her in her very proper life hadn't worked out very well, in the past. In fact, convention broke her heart. Fred left some coins on the table for the tea and they left the shop together.

"There's a nice spot down by the wharf. I like to sit there sometimes, before I head home after a crossing. It gives me a chance to ready myself, before I face me wife, and her brother. It's never easy, so I must get my mind ready. I'll show you the spot if you like."

"Yes, that would be lovely." Cybil walked faster, trying to keep up with him.

"Here we are," he said at last. As they came around a corner between buildings, on a street Cybil had never seen before, the whole view of Southampton Water opened up.

"Oh my, it's beautiful! It's so much better than I've ever seen the waterfront before. Why, there's even a tiny patch of grass, an oasis! It's a whole new world, hidden away, right here." She looked up at Fred. *Who is this man?* she wondered. *He is capable of such surprising things, he can find beauty amid the darkest slum it seems. And yet his mind is filled with so many sad thoughts.*

"Here, come sit on the grass if you don't mind. I don't want to dirty your fine dress. I'll take off me jacket, you can sit on it."

"No need to do that. I'm not worried about my dress." She sat down next to Fred. And she realized, for the first time, she *didn't* care what happened to her dress. All at once, she saw the world from a different perspective and she felt the shackles of her past, and the judgment of society, slip away.

Fred asked the question that had to be asked.

"You said you are alone now. What happened when you came back to England?"

"My husband blamed me right away, that Matthew was lost. Actually, he said *many* mean things to me. Fred, it's no use wasting time

"

now, and pretending we were some fairy tale married couple, we weren't. My family insisted I marry him. He was from the right family, and very rich. He knew my father's family, all the same clubs, same public schools, and everything like that. Once we were wed, he had little use for me. He was always gone. And he was very controlling of my life, even when he wasn't there. He traveled a lot, on business I thought."

"How unfair to you," Fred replied. "Of course I leave my wife a lot, because of the sea."

"That's different Fred. You have no choice." Cybil realized it was his low opinion of himself getting in the way of the facts. But she wouldn't allow it. She raised her hand to stop him from saying anything else.

"With my husband, it was another story entirely. Before I lose my courage, I will tell you the way it *really* was. He left me when I arrived back in England, he ended our marriage. He said I *killed* Matthew. His barristers arranged the whole thing, and just like that, it was as if our marriage had never existed. If you throw enough money into it, it's entirely possible to get the deed done. I was disgraced before everyone I knew. You know of course, if a man can show his wife was unfaithful to him, he has grounds. But in this case, that wasn't true. I *hadn't* been unfaithful. But our friends, everyone I knew, assumed the worst of me. And then, a couple of years later, by accident, I found out he'd had a mistress, all along, right from the start. And that was why he traveled so much and had little regard for me. He married me for a business alliance with my father's family. I never meant any more than that, I was a means to enrich his personal wealth, and a source of an heir. It broke my heart. Not that I cared for him, I really *didn't*. But just the idea of being *used* like that, and abandoned."

Cybil started crying, a pitiful cry. Without knowing he would, acting purely on impulse, Fred reached out and put his arm around her, pulling her close to him. And then, suddenly, his lips were on her lips. What had been a tentative, questioning kiss turned into a deep, long, needy one, a kiss that was answered with every bit of passion he could have hoped for. Cybil didn't pull back. She was lost in Fred, and he in her. Finally, she leaned back, until she was lying on the grass with Fred beside her, kissing her again and again. Several minutes went by, the birds flying overhead, as a few sheep-clouds covered the sun. Time passed, and time stood still. Fred's mouth moved down Cybil's neck, brushing against the fabric of her dress. A moan escaped her lips. But then, a sudden cascade of chiming church bells pulled them from their passion. Afternoon was about to slip into evening's grasp.

Fred spoke in a new voice, as now it seemed, all at once and for the first time, all his demons were gone. "I must get home, it's suddenly getting late, better not to raise a fuss, with Eva, and Phil. I hate to go, Cybil, really."

"You've no reason to apologize. Really. As long as I know I'll see you again."

"Of course you will. I need to see you too, can't you tell?" He looked into her eyes.

***

For Fred, reflected back to him was everything he needed to see, and more. More than he ever dreamed he'd find. But he also sensed her confusion as to what would happen next. What could happen next? He had no idea. He knew part of what he'd like to have happen, no surprise there, the fire was burning in him right then. But, acting on it was something else, something he wasn't sure would happen from either of them. And then there was the other part, what could they ever mean to each other? What could ever make sense between the two of them? What could Cybil ultimately be willing to give him? Again, he had no idea. So, reluctantly, he jumped to his feet, leaned over and helped Cybil up. She wrapped her arms around him, as if she would never let go.

"When will I see you?" she asked.

"I leave for New York on Friday." He saw the hurt in her face. "Oh, but Cybil, I'll see you when I get back. In fact, I'll be thinking of you all the time I'm gone." He, was instantly embarrassed. Should he have said that?

"I'm so glad of that Fred. Because I'll be thinking of you too, every minute. In fact, I won't be truly alive until I see you again." After the words escaped her lips, she gave him a shy smile and fell in place beside him as they walked back toward the main road.

Fred was quiet when he got home. He was lost in thoughts of Cybil; their shared kisses were impossible to dismiss. His blood ran fast, he was filled with desire. He knew if he said a word to Eva, his voice would give him away, she would realize that something had happened, something had changed in him. He no longer felt he was Phil's whipping boy, and the man Eva regrets she married, the man who wasn't good enough to please either of them.

***

As the next days passed, and Fred prepared for his trip, Eva was more and more aware that something was different between them, but she could not begin to unravel her husband's new composure, that was the only way she could define this new Fred. He was quiet, and self-assured, no longer begging for love and attention and acceptance. She saw the new Fred in stark contrast to the old one, the man she'd lived with these last years. There was a distance between them, almost as if he didn't need her anymore. On Friday morning, travel bag in hand, he gave her a quick peck on the cheek.

"Well, I'm off. Take care of yourself. See you in two weeks' time." And then he was gone, just like that. She sensed that leaving had cost him no pain whatsoever. The waif she married had found himself at last, and this new man was traveling light, almost as if she, his wife, would be heavy baggage, an unwanted burden that would slow him down.

Chapter 20

Cybil began a new existence as well. For the first time, she was a woman waiting for a sailor to return from the sea. These last years, against her family's wishes, she lived apart from them, in a house of her choosing, and save for her few servants, she lived alone. The family had owned the large, elegant home for years, with staff in place whether the house was occupied or not. Appearances must be kept up.

Cybil, upon the dissolution of her marriage, had sought the freedom of solitude, so she could absorb the sudden collapse of her life. Bringing her ladies' maid, her clothing, her books and little else, she defied her parents, moving to Fairfield House on a clear September morning, after insisting she would have it no other way. As a divorced woman, she was truly an embarrassment in proper society, and so, at last her parents stopped haranguing her to forgo her plans and stay with them. She certainly wasn't a child anymore, with an ex-husband and a dead son, no, not a child. She was hard to explain at dinner parties. So, they let her have her way, as if they had any choice in the matter.

In the first days, out on her own, and freed from the obligation of social calls with her mother, she'd looked about and realized more than ever how empty she felt. Days went by when she didn't leave the house. She'd lie in bed, picking at trays of food her maid begged her to eat.

Finally, she realized she had to take a small step back into the world. All she truly cared about had been taken from her when she lost Matthew. Seeking solace, she had found the volunteer position at the Southampton Seaman's relief office. Her greatest hope was to keep families together, children with their parents, no matter their financial condition. Donations to the relief office, once plentiful, had dwindled over the years since *Titanic* sank, but a small amount of funds were still available, if they were doled out carefully.

Cybil had felt the urgency of her work and it had filled her life. She'd needed nothing more, until Fred walked through the door. She was hard pressed to get him out of her mind. The weeks dragged by as she waited for his return.

This stood in stark contrast to the last years when she had stayed busy with her volunteer work. Her life had become totally predictable, in a pleasing manner. A generous family allowance had been provided. Her parents would have been humiliated if their daughter didn't live in the lap of luxury. They suffered less guilt for not putting up more of a fuss when she moved out.

Cybil guessed her former spouse had been only too happy to send her the vast amounts of money that showed up, as long as she held her tongue about the other women in his life. At first, Cybil had thought it was only the one she'd uncovered. When she discovered two more after the divorce, and mentioned it to her ex in a note, more money showed up on her doorstep. Hush money, no doubt. All she could say to herself was that somehow the fool cared about his reputation. She would never have told anyone, save her parents. And now, years later, Fred. She had to tell him.

As the days of his absence at sea slipped slowly by, Cybil wanted Fred to know everything about her. She tried to make sense of it. She'd known she had an instant connection with him when she'd looked into his eyes, knowing he'd suffered, knowing for a certainty he'd been rescued off *Titanic*, same as she.

She hadn't been in a lifeboat, not at first. She had missed the last of the boats, searching for Matthew, and then the huge wave swept her overboard. But why did she feel this undeniable intimacy with this man? They were from two separate worlds, but there was something else she could not explain, almost as if they'd known each other before they met in the relief office.

To escape from her confusion, she wandered into the library and picked up one of her favorite books. Her grandmother, her dearest relative, had given it to her. She lived most of her life at Chelmsford House, her enormous estate in Ireland. She'd shared the Gaelic lore with Cybil, much to the dislike of Cybil's very proper English mother.

"Oh! The Celts are pagans, Cybil. Don't fill your head with that drool. I forbid it." But like most things her mother tried to persuade Cybil, it was wasted effort.

Cybil loved to hear the old tales and relished every chance she got to sit with her grandmother. On her last trip to Ireland, a few months before her wedding, her grandmother had given her this book. A memory popped into Cybil's head, and she knew she would find the answer among its pages.

"*Anam Cara.*" The Gaelic words slipped from her mouth even before she found the page she was looking for. "The soulmate friend, the one person who lives in you."

Back in Ireland, when she first received the book, Cybil had daydreamed she might find such a partner in her soon-to-be husband. Time would prove her wrong. But now it turned out Fred was that person, her *Anam Cara*. Her heart had recognized his even before they'd spoken their first words. She could feel a piece of his soul buried in hers, no matter the miles that separated them.

She went about her days, nurtured by this presence. She yearned for his arms around her once again.

Chapter 21

This early May voyage on *Olympic* had been unlike any Fred had ever experienced in the eighteen years he'd been on a ship. He had experienced drama and exhilaration at sea, right from the beginning, but this trip would be unique. And it caused him to think back and sum up his years as a sailor. The *Clio* had stayed in port, but starting with his first days as a deck boy at age sixteen on the *Oceanic*, he'd always had a taste for the sea. Whereas some of the crew, in quiet moments, once the ale was having its way with them, confessed they had to grow into the job. They had come to it on their father's prompting, not their own desire. Many of them would get stinking drunk before they boarded the ship each time, the only way they could handle it.

Not so for Fred. One of the happiest moments of his life was when he first stepped onto *Oceanic*. Most likely it was because he was gone at last from the *Clio* and the harsh treatment he'd received there. But it was more than that.

Seeing the sky and the huge expanse of water stretched out before him, he'd experienced a world of possibilities, a freedom he had never imagined, not for him, a lad with literally nothing all his life. The few happy moments he could remember had been Christmases past at Elm Lodge when he was just a wee lad, with the appearance of apples and walnuts on the table, and one year, a small gift for each boy on Christmas morning. But then, he had spoiled all of that and suffered through the bleak years on the *Clio*, the beatings and the fear. The *Oceanic* had been his first taste of freedom. His one opportunity.

He'd decided to make the best of it. He'd watch his money and try to put something by each month. He'd watch the drink, and take less than he used to. He'd surprised himself with these thoughts. It was all due to the man from the Home Committee, Mr. Killey reaching out to him in a note sent to him on board the *Clio*, when he was about to search for a job. Mr. Killey explained that he believed Fred should have a chance with White Star. No one else had ever done that for Fred. As far back as he could remember, everyone in authority had expected the worst of him.

But with Mr. Killey's words, he was borne up, almost as if he'd sprouted wings. He couldn't get it out of his head. He'd called Fred 'A good lad!'

In his four years on the *Oceanic*, he had been just that. He'd become a valued employee to the line, which resulted in the job on the *Titanic*, a posting he didn't seek. But there it was. They'd trusted him, wanted him in the crow's nest of their premier ship.

The iceberg had shattered all of that, and his marriage as well.

And then these war years came along, and the danger on the high seas, with U-boats lurking, and the ship filled to the brim with troops. But Fred was never afraid, not for himself. The soldiers about to step onto the battlefield deserved the privilege of fear. Fred was just a cog in a wheel, doing his job to get the heroes where they needed to be.

At night, lying on his bunk in the crew quarters, stuffed together with forty other men in their common dormitory, he'd think about the rest of the ship, the area reserved for the troops, and wonder if his father might be there, that Frederick Laurence, Private in the Fourth Dragoons. At least that's the way he was listed on Fred's application form into Elm Lodge. That page burned a hole in Fred's memory, even though so many years had passed since he had seen it that one time.

It would make no sense for his father to be here. *Olympic* wasn't transporting British troops at all. Now, in May of 1918, they were headed to Cherbourg, where they would drop off their military passengers. From there, they would travel on, returning at last to Southampton. And yet, he couldn't shake loose the notion of the father he'd never known, right here, in uniform, on this ship. *What would I say to him, if ever we stood face to face?*

An alarm going off on the ship pulled Fred from his dream. Most often the alarms were false, or just tests for the crew. But in an instant, it was obvious this was the real thing. Everyone was running. Fred leaped from his berth. They were just entering the English Channel, about to connect with their escort. Four British vessels were due to arrive, their mission to ensure *Olympic's* safety from German U-boats.

"What's 'appening?" one of Fred's mates called out. "Anyone see anything?"

Fred shook his head. "I was sleeping."

The two men ran up to the boat deck. The U-boat was there on the surface, just one and a half points off the starboard bow. The ship changed course. *Olympic* fired one of her forward guns, but missed. The gun was too high! The U-boat tried to maneuver into a better position.

Fred's heart pounded.

Fred, like the rest of them, was nearly knocked off his feet as the liner swerved in an instant and struck the U-boat. Fred's mind flashed back to the iceberg, and *Titanic*, and how, even up in the crow's nest, he hadn't felt more than a scrape, but this was different. A powerful collision, the resounding shudder on the deck, and the engines throbbing. This was madness, and yet, all at once, it seemed as if the U-boat was about to dive! Was it going to escape? How could it be? Would it fire a torpedo?

The commander of the sub must have thought differently and chose to surface. Diving was certain death for all on board the submarine. *Olympic's* poop deck guns fired in response. Fred watched, his heart in his throat.

The U-boat was disabled, *Olympic* was saved! Fred, along with his mates, stood a moment, watching as the liner changed course yet again, continuing on her way to Cherbourg to complete their mission. She wasn't about to tarry and pluck the enemy from the sea. The task would be done by a destroyer, the *Davis*, which went after the Germans in the water. Then, with their hearts still aflutter, the crew of the *Olympic* resumed their duties of getting the old girl, or majestic lady, as she certainly deserved to be called, home at last.

A day later, Fred finally made his way off the ship, duffel bag over his shoulder. He was glad to feel Southampton pavement under his feet. He glanced about the wharf, everything looked the same, and yet here he was, in a state of shock to have survived another near miss. *What a strange thing, this perilous adventure called life*, he thought to himself.

When he looked up, who did he see but Eva, standing on the wharf, watching him? He hurried his pace, closing the distance between them quickly.

"Hello, Eva! You're here." She never came to meet his ship, save for his first crossing after their wedding.

"Yes, I am. I guess I'm here because of the baby."

"What do you mean? Is everything okay?" Had his longing for Cybil backfired against the poor babe in the womb?

"Oh, yes, everything is fine. But I guess being pregnant has made me feel more protective. It makes me see how much I need you, Fred. I have to be certain nothing happens to you. Do you see?"

"Nothing's going to happen to me." He couldn't shake the realization that he wasn't the real reason for her appearance on the dock. It was because she needed him to be Da to the babe. But all the same, he wanted her to be reassured, and not worried; he had promised not to unsettle her.

He reached out and hugged her. She hugged him back. Overcome in the relief of his survival, he stood there and thought about what might have happened when they'd struck the U-boat. He had no intention of telling Eva anything about the incident. The crew wasn't to say a word to anyone. And sharing the news would, indeed, unsettle her. His mind wandered, as he thought about what, or who, he shouldn't think about. He pulled Eva closer, as his guilt surfaced. *What was he all about anyway? What kind of man was he?* He hugged a pregnant Eva and thought of Cybil.

***

The welcoming crowd stretched across the wharf. At the far end stood another woman, a woman who just wanted a glimpse of Fred, a woman who couldn't talk herself out of hurrying down to the dock on impulse. She'd caught a glimpse from the window of her home, a glimpse that had given her a fine view of *Olympic* steaming up Southampton Water.

Cybil Stuart knew she couldn't greet him in public, surrounded by all his crew members and their families. She just wanted to rest her eyes upon him for a moment. But she hadn't counted on the sight of Fred and his wife in a tight embrace. She struggled to hold back the tears that gathered. Unable to watch any more of this, she ran up High Street, back to her empty house.

***

Fred and Eva also headed home, walking toward Norman Road. Fred hated the thought of seeing Phil Le Gros. His eyes swept the streets ahead, wishing he was going anywhere but home. Out of the corner of his eye, he saw the back of a slim woman with red hair piled on top of her head. The way she moved matched the image he'd clung to, all the moments he'd thought of her and little else these last two weeks. He knew it was his Cybil. *My Cybil.* But had she seen him? Had she caught sight of him and Eva, wrapped in their embrace? Was that why she ran up High Street? He longed to go after her and tell her all that was on his mind, how he wanted her so much.

He followed Eva home and tried to prepare himself for his brother-in-law's nasty greeting.

Chapter 22

The next morning, lying in bed after a restless night, Fred made up his mind. He would go to the relief office and talk to Cybil right away. He must see her and find out if she had indeed seen him on the wharf. He must explain why he had his arms around his wife. The whole thing was pitiful. Of course, he should have hugged his wife, but he had told Cybil that he and Eva were estranged. What would Cybil think of him? He certainly had nothing to be proud of. His behavior was inexcusable all around, to both women. But he was an impetuous man, always acting out his emotions, when many times he shouldn't have. Knowing this didn't stop him though. It rarely had before. He knew what he wanted, and he knew what he needed.

He wanted Cybil. He must have her. He couldn't hold back. He wanted her too much. He threw on his clothes and rushed into the kitchen, looking for a quick cup of tea.

Eva stood by the table, hands on her hips. Obviously she had been waiting for him to wake up, although his abrupt appearance startled her. "Who was the fancy lady you were walking down Above Bar Street with a few weeks ago, just before you left for the crossing? She had red hair. And don't tell me you weren't. Mrs. Ferris saw you. She just told me so when I stepped out the back door to fetch the milk. She's been feeling poorly and staying in her bed, her arthritis acting up again. This was her first chance to warn me."

"Wasn't me. I don't know no fancy ladies. Why would any of them want to speak with me, much less walk with me?" Fred tried to keep his voice steady and his face without expression, a skill he sadly lacked. But the fear helped him succeed this time. "And don't all us seamen look alike in our ship's clothes?"

"And Mrs. Ferris has known you how many years? You used to board next door, in her house, for goodness' sake, Fred!"

"I can't explain her mistake. Maybe she's getting old. She's how many years now? At least sixty, seventy? Who knows? I just know 'twasn't me. I know no fancy ladies, or men either, for that matter."

"Oh, stop that, Fred! She said it was you." Eva raised her voice. Her face was red, and she shook all over.

"And maybe she needs new specs. Did you think of that? When did she get new glasses last? There has to be a reason, because it wasn't me."

"She says it was you. I guess it could be her age, or better yet her glasses. There is that chance." Her voice wavered for a second. "But just to be sure, I am keeping my eye on you, Fred Fleet. I don't want you going anywhere that I can't be sure of. You are staying right here, especially today, and tomorrow... and every day, if I have my way."

"That's ridiculous. I won't be a prisoner in my own house."

"What makes you think this is your house? I could almost laugh if I wasn't so angry. This is Phil's house, or have you forgotten?"

"No, no, I haven't. You and your Phil never let me forget that. Serves you right if I was out walkin' with another woman," Fred yelled back at her. But then he caught himself just in time. "But I wasn't. But the way you treat me, like I'm not a man at all."

Overcome with anger, Fred stalked out of the house, slamming the door behind him. No way was he staying there one more minute, locked up like a misbehaving child. He wanted to make his way to the relief office, but had second thoughts. If people were gossiping, and maybe watching him now, he couldn't go anywhere near Cybil. He was torn in two, because that was all he wanted, what he desperately needed, to see Cybil. To reassure her that he cared for her. He did.

But if he saw her right now, he would say things he shouldn't say. She meant more to him than he should let on, and he wouldn't be able to control himself. He might scare her away. He couldn't go to the office.

He walked around aimlessly until he stood outside the train station. He went in and sat down on an empty bench. *Life is so unfair,* was all he could think. He didn't see how things could ever be any different. He knew he'd be better off dead, but that would be an unkind thing to do to this baby soon to be born. It was no different than his own parents abandoning him.

He closed his eyes, searching for peace. All he really wanted was Cybil, but she was beyond his reach. Never mind how his blood raced at the mere thought of her, how he remembered the feeling of her lips against his, the shape of her body pressed against him as they lay together in the grass.

And there was more to it. Oh yes, there was more. She was the only one who understood his distress over the *Titanic*, the way it had changed his life forever, the loss, the guilt. Only Cybil understood, even shared his guilt in her own way. She didn't deserve any guilt. It was all his fault, every bit of it. And yet, she refused to blame him, not like Eva. Eva blamed him for all of it.

"Mummy, look at that man! Why is he sleeping here, Mummy?"

A little girl's voice cut into his thoughts, and his eyes flew open. They stared at him, a little blonde lass about five years old and her nervous-looking mother. "Mummy, doesn't the man have a house to sleep in?"

"I'm not sleeping, I'm just..." Fred mumbled., Seeing the scared look on their faces as they scooted as far away as they could, he yanked himself to his feet and found the nearest exit. Outside, the streets were crowded, and he could think of nowhere to go. It was lunch time. He'd had nothing to eat since the night before, but he wasn't hungry.

He walked, in no direction really, but as he turned the next corner, and then the one after that, he found himself on the street leading to the special, hidden patch of grass, his secret place near the wharf.

There she stood, under the tree, in the middle of the grassy area. Cybil, his Cybil. He couldn't help himself. He ran.

As he got closer, her face changed from sadness to joy, and he ran faster until he stood in front of her. Without a word, he threw his arms around her. She hugged him back fiercely, her tears wet on his face. He kissed her so hard and with so much passion, for a moment he thought he might frighten her.

But no, she returned his kisses with the same hunger. Finally, she stood back. Her eyes gleamed as she looked at him.

"Let me explain," he said.

Struggling to get her breath, she spoke anyway. "No need to explain Fred. Just come with me."

"Where?" he asked.

"You'll see. Just come."

And so, he followed her. At first, he couldn't imagine where they were going, but as her steps headed toward High Street, he knew. He didn't say a word. He couldn't.

The huge house stood on a hill, and he almost paused upon seeing it, but he couldn't stop. Things had come too far between them. Cybil took his hand, showing him she had no intention of losing him.

At the entrance, she dropped his hand and quickly opened the door. Then she took his hand again and ushered him inside.

"Just follow me, upstairs, and don't say a word," she whispered.

He realized she was shooing him in, hoping to avoid the scrutiny of her butler. She must have one. He could be put off, he thought to himself, but how did any woman with staff in her home have a lover with any degree of privacy? Why should he be insulted?

He followed her upstairs. Her bedroom was at the far end of a long hallway. They entered the room, and Cybil closed the door.

Watching each other in the dim light, they pulled off their clothes without a word.

A few minutes later, Cybil's passionate outcry surprised Fred.

"I just never knew it could be like, like this," she whispered in his ear, mindful of where they were and who else might be in the house. "My husband, he was only interested in himself, it was nothing..."

"Shhh, yes, it's always supposed to be like this," he said, tracing his finger lightly along her lower lip.

She sucked in a breath at his touch. "Oh, Fred," she moaned. "I can't ever let you go."

He wasn't sure what to say. He wasn't sure of anything. He held her in his arms and felt her heart beating fast against him. They clung to each other. He knew she wanted him to make love to her again. He kissed her gently.

"Fred, I've had this feeling, I know it's crazy, but it's almost like I met you before you came into the office that day. It makes no sense."

"No, no it doesn't. On *Titanic*, as you know, the passengers never see any of the ordinary crew. Only the officers in their fine uniforms are visible." He was quiet. But then another possibility occurred to him. "Which lifeboat were you in? Could it be number six? I was rowing that one."

"At first, I wasn't in a boat. I had missed the last one, looking for Matthew. Remember, I told you. But then a huge wave washed me overboard and I was in the sea. And the water was so icy cold. I tried to get one of the boats to pick me up. I pleaded, but they wouldn't."

"Oh no! It can't be!" He couldn't continue.

"What is it?"

"What were you wearing that night, in the water?" Fred was reluctant to ask the question, but he must.

"An emerald-green evening dress, and a necklace. A very special necklace. I'm sorry that piece of jewelry even made it back to shore. It was a diamond necklace my husband bribed me with. I saw that eventually. He bribed me with gifts as a distraction. Why do you ask?"

"Because you —" He stopped. He couldn't bring himself to go on.

"I what? What did I do, Fred?"

"No, not you. Me. I'm the one who did something, or didn't do something. I didn't rescue you from the sea that night. It was my boat you came to. But the man in charge, Hichens, he and I were arguing. He was the helmsman on *Titanic*, and he was put in charge of our lifeboat. I was there to row. Actually, he was fighting with everyone in the boat. I think he had a panic fit and went crazy. He wouldn't let us stop and pick up anyone. There was a big fuss about it later, at the inquiries and everything. But all the same, I didn't rescue you."

"So this man, this Hichens, he wouldn't let you pick me up?"

"No, he wouldn't. He kept screaming that if we tried to pick anyone up, the boat would be swamped by the crowd in the water and we would capsize, and every one of us would die. No, he was having none of it. He was just screaming! One of the ladies, it turned out it was that American socialite lady, a Mrs. Brown, she took control of the boat. She was a first-class passenger, and very pushy. She threatened to throw him overboard at one point."

"Fred, listen to me, you must believe me. I don't blame you at all. And obviously, I got into another boat, and I'm alive. But you and me, we are linked together. It's fate, you and me. And it's more than the lifeboat, it's beyond even that. We were meant to share everything, even though it's hard for me."

She stopped talking, and Fred was confused, afraid. What did she mean? He was afraid to hear what she would say next.

"I love you, Fred. Nothing will ever change my mind. I must tell you, I need you so much, only you. I hope I don't scare you off by saying this. I think I need you too much, that's what frightens me." She pulled him closer and kissed his face and his lips, over and over. And then she kissed his neck and his chest with lingering kisses. A little while later, after they made love again, slowly this time, exploring each other with delight, they fell asleep in each other's arms.

They were awakened by a tap at the door. "Mrs. Stuart, can I be of assistance?" The door handle rattled.

"Fiona, I'll be downstairs shortly. I don't need your help."

"Are you all right? Can I fetch anything? It's teatime. Maybe your tea, up here, if you are unwell?"

"I'm perfectly fine, Fiona. I'll be down for tea very soon." Cybil locked eyes with Fred. Footsteps moved down the hallway and eased the tension in the room.

"Yes, yes, I know," Fred whispered. "I must leave. How shall I get out of here?" He felt back in his place, a working stiff, a nothing, a poor excuse for a man who didn't belong here.

"I'll show you. There's another way out, *Anam Cara*. There's another staircase—"

"What did you say? Anam...?"

"Ah, I'll explain that next time we meet. I have to lure you back somehow."

"You have already done that, lured me. I'll be back, you can be sure of it." They looked at each other for a long moment, lost in a place far away from this room on High Street of Southampton. It was as if they'd sealed themselves for all eternity in that far-off spot.

How would he face Eva? Would she see the change in him? For it was true. He knew he was different. Just like the first time he'd kissed Cybil, except now, his transformation was complete.

Chapter 23

Outside the house on Norman Road, Fred remembered he had walked out on Eva in a fit of rage. It seemed like a lifetime ago after the couple of hours with Cybil. He took a second to compose himself. It seemed he was still caught up in a dream, but he had to break free and enter the real world once again. He took a deep breath and opened the door, not knowing what to expect.

Phil's voice rose in anger from the kitchen.

Fred closed the door quietly and listened.

"It's time you just threw him out. He's worthless. He always has been. Now he's running around with some fancy lady, right here in So'ton! I'm not surprised if he does that sort of thing with countless women when he's in New York, but—"

"Don't say that! I never imagined that! Fred wouldn't!"

"Don't be a fool, Eva. I swear, from the moment you set eyes on that man, you lost all common sense. It's quite simple, you and he don't get along. Ever since he sank *Titanic*, he's been damaged goods. Even before that. And don't tell me how you love him. Face the facts. He has a traveling job and a troubled marriage, at best. And half the time, he acts crazy. So yes, there are bound to be other women, giving him, shall we say, comfort. The only thing he has going for him is his good looks, and you see how that plays out!"

"Fred's not crazy." Eva said the words, but they lacked conviction. "Well, there have been a few times, I wondered..."

"What? You wondered what?" Phil was all worked up.

"He's acted a bit odd sometimes, but I promised I wouldn't say anything."

"There! I knew I was right! I'll kick him out of the house, today! Where is he anyway? Let's sort this out right now."

"No, Phil. You can't do that." Eva's tone had changed. "There's the baby. It would be selfish of me if I deny the baby his father's presence just because Fred and I have our differences. I can't do that."

"The presence of his father? When is the man ever here? Besides, what does he know about being a da? He had none. He has nothing. All the more reason I begged you not to marry him in the first place. And I'll take care of the baby, just like I've taken care of you. Fred's never taken care of you right. And he's mean to you. You can't deny that. I'll be here for both you and the baby."

"I can't kick the father of my child out of his life. I just can't. And that's the end of it. Look what that very situation did to Fred! He never knew his father or his mum. I can't let anything like that happen to this baby." Eva stood up and cleared the cups and the teapot from the table. The conversation was over, for now.

Fred sneaked upstairs. He went into their bedroom and lay down. The events of the day overwhelmed him. He needed to see Cybil again, he needed to hold her in his arms, and at the same time, he needed to be on board *Olympic*, enjoying the freedom of his escape from all the things he could never straighten out. His eyelids grew heavy, and he fell asleep.

When he woke up, he had no idea how much time had passed, but he was terribly hungry. He pulled himself from the bed. Eva had defended him, and she hadn't told Phil about the worst of his bad moments or the blackouts. His guilt over Cybil also figured into his thoughts. He went downstairs, hoping to find her alone.

"Eva!" He spoke her name cheerfully. She sat in the front room, a pile of darning spread out in her lap. "Would you like to go for fish 'n' chips? Down at the pub?"

"What? Are you serious, Fred? Why would you be so sweet to me, I'm wondering?" She looked amazed that he would ask. "Where have you been all day anyway?"

Fred ignored her last question.

"We're going to be parents, together, you and me, aren't we? Let's just go out, and have a little fun, before the babe is here, and things are so busy."

His own words surprised him, but he kind of liked the sound of it. Instead of keeping his few coins for a pint on his own at the Working Men's Club, it made sense to try for a truce. A good idea it would be, and it might help erase the words Phil had spoken to her, true as they were, about Cybil and all the women he'd been with in New York. The less Phil's accusations played about in Eva's mind, the better off he'd be. He needed to set things straight with Eva.

"Have you thought about a name for the baby?" Fred asked once their piping hot food was spread before them on the tiny pub table. He waited for Eva to take the first bite, trying hard to be polite, an effort he'd never made, even in the best of times. But he did take a pull on his pint of ale. No one could blame a bloke for being thirsty.

"If it's a boy, I want to name him for you."

He had expected her to say the babe would be named Philip, or maybe Ernest, the name of the Le Gros patriarch. He'd been trying to decide how to talk her out of both of these names.

"Blimey! I'd really like that. The wee lad named for me! Can we give him a second name, do you think, after your da? Frederick Ernest has a nice ring to it, don't ya think?" He was caught up in the moment.

"I like that. And if it's a girl, I really like Dorothy. What do you think?" Eva took a bite of fish, her eyes on Fred's face.

"Dorothy it is. Eva Ernestine too, to go along with it," he suggested, including part of her full name of Eva Ernestine Mai.

"Even better, how's about Dorothy Frederica Ernestine. That's perfect, I think. Do you like it? She's part of both of us that way."

"Yes, yes, I like that very much." Fred gave his wife a warm smile. Maybe things could work out between them after all, for the sake of the babe. They ate their fish and chips and talked about the baby. But when they made their way home, just as they were about to open the door and walk into the house, there was the nosy neighbor, Mrs. Ferris, standing on her front step, almost as if she had been waiting for them, but it was just bad timing.

"Good evening," she called out. "Good to see you both together." That was all she said.

But to Fred, it sounded as if she had added, *Don't forget what I told you, Eva, he has another woman.* Fred thought of Cybil. And Eva probably was as well, although she didn't know the woman's name.

The months passed with Fred on the sea and back again, Eva watching the increasing girth of her belly and sewing wee clothes for the baby. The air between them was tense at times. It really depended on whether Phil stirred the pot, digging into his sister's mood when he saw her smile at her husband now and then. As for Fred, he ignored the bar girls who flashed invitations when he swaggered into his favorite sailors' tavern in New York, spending his passion in the bed on the Southampton High Street. Neither he nor Cybil could imagine where this was leading, but they were powerless to stop.

At home with Eva, Fred made a concerted effort to get along, chatting about the baby and making easy conversation. But he made no attempt at intimacy. With a shy smile he suggested that, at this point in the pregnancy, he wanted to do what was best for the little one. He'd pointed at Eva's belly and was relieved when she agreed with him. He had no need of his wife to satisfy his desires, and the sight of her changing body didn't appeal to him. But he did care about the babe, there was no duplicity in that.

***

One afternoon, as he was about to rise from Cybil's bed, he leaned over to find his clothes on the floor.

Cybil touched him on the back. "Wait, there's something else."

"What? What can you mean? I thought I'd satisfied everything you could possibly need, m'love." He smiled at her. Just looking at Cybil stirred the fires within, even after two hours in bed. "You certainly seemed very, how shall I say? Very pleased by this afternoon's —"

"Oh, yes, I am, Fred. You are always just what I need, I had no idea before we met. No, it's something else. Something I didn't finish telling you, that day, the first time we —"

"What do you mean?"

"I mentioned then that you are my *Anam Cara*."

"Oh, yes. What is that?"

"It's Gaelic, it means soulmate, soul friend. We are linked. We are one person, closer to each other than we can ever be to anyone else. No one else can ever understand me the way you do. And I, you. I feel in my blood, in my heart, all your pain, all your sadness. I know why you say and do the things you do." Despite her words, she looked at him with a flash of uncertainty. If he couldn't grasp what she was telling him, what would happen? Had she overstepped the bounds, and misjudged? If she had, how would she cope with the loss?

"It seems impossible, Cybil, but I feel the same. Really, I do. To the rest of the world, we couldn't be more unsuited, but here, in this room, I see how true your words are. I see inside you. And I know you see inside me, like no one else ever has. It doesn't make sense, not at all, but it is true. *Anam Cara*." He said the words slowly. "You are mine." He rolled over and pulled her to him with renewed urgency, kissing her deeply. "Let's never walk away from this moment, no matter what the future brings."

"What does that mean? We must be just like this, forever and ever." She whispered, her voice full of doubt and fear.

"I have no idea what it will bring, but I agree with you, we must, even after we walk out of this room this afternoon, we must always, in our souls, still be here together."

"We will be. I promise you that, Fred."

***

Three weeks later, Eva woke Fred in the night. "The pains have started. We need to call the midwife."

"What do you mean? Right now? She told you to wait a few hours and count the pains. I remember you told me that."

"I've been doing just that, while you slept for the last three hours. The pains are coming closer, just ten minutes apart now, and it hurts, really bad." She stopped talking, blinked her eyes, and winced in pain.

"Then it's time," he said, and both of them instantly looked over at the bag of supplies sitting in the corner. The midwife had left it on her last visit. Before, they'd ignored the large rucksack. Now, it took on new meaning.

"Now you see why Phil insisted on getting that new telephone," Eva said. "Can you find the woman's number and ring her up right away? She's part of that convent, St. Agatha's on the next street."

"Yes, yes, of course, I can. You'll be all right if I leave the room?"

"Oh, Fred, I haven't needed you these last hours. I'll be okay. Just *go*, ring her right now, hurry." Eva managed a weak smile.

The smile gave Fred encouragement as they were about to enter a new chapter in their lives. He thought there was a chance she did care for him, in spite of everything. Perhaps Eva was starting to doubt all that Phil had said about him over the years, most of which was untrue. Then the next pain, stronger than all the rest, grabbed hold, and she called out as she shut her eyes.

Fred galloped down the stairs. Eva had left the number on the table next to the telephone. He grabbed the phone and gave the number to the operator. "Hurry, my wife's having a baby!"

"Not to worry, women have babies every day," the operator chuckled. Fred wanted to tell her to be quiet and just do her job, but he held his tongue.

Eva screamed again.

Phil stumbled from his bedroom, ignored Fred, and ran into Eva's room. In what seemed way too long to Fred, but was less than a minute, his call was put through. Fred lost his composure again as he begged for assistance. The midwife assured him she was on her way. He ran his hands through his hair and dashed back upstairs.

As the two men stood on either side of the bed, it was impossible to say which was more nervous. It certainly wasn't Eva. She was too caught up in pain to think straight. And then Sister Catherine entered the room, placing a large rucksack on the table next to the bed. She was the epitome of professional composure.

"Mrs. Fleet, how far apart are the pains now? And how long do they last?"

Eva let out a scream before she could answer. Sister Catherine indicated with a practiced gesture that Fred and Phil should leave the room. "Just bring me a large basin of hot water, that's all I need," she assured them.

They were both more than happy to comply, racing down the stairs, one after the other. Fred returned with the basin, and then was only too glad to leave the women to their work.

In the hours that followed, Fred and Phil sat downstairs in the front room and tried not to look at each other. It was easier that way.

After what seemed a lifetime, the hurried footsteps of the Sister, and Eva's screams followed by the wail of a newborn, indicated their lives had changed forever. Forgetting their earlier resolve, they looked at one another in surprise. And then the Sister called out from the top of the stairs.

"You have a beautiful daughter, Mr. Fleet. Wait just a moment or two while I clean things up, and then you can come upstairs."

Fred broke out in a huge grin, but Phil's reaction was different. After a minute had passed, the two men climbed the stairs. Fred, for once, refused to defer to his brother-in-law, pushing ahead of the younger man with authority.

Phil entered right behind Fred. He wasn't going to allow the couple to share the moment alone with their new babe, as well they should.

"Dorrie," Fred burst out as he caught his first glimpse of the babe in Eva's arms.

"Oh, you've given her a nickname already." Eva smiled at Fred, although her voice was weak. She started to lift little Dorrie toward her father.

Before Fred had hold of her, Phil shoved his way to the bed. "She's a bonny lass. Let me hold her, Eva."

Sister Catherine would have none of that. "Mr. Le Gros, let the babe's father hold her first. Let's do things the proper way, if you please." She frowned at Phil, having no idea of the friction in the family.

Phil stepped back, anger flashing in his eyes.

Fred reached out and cradled Dorrie in his arms. A tear slipped down his cheek. He had never felt such love before. And, at that same instant, he knew what he must do. But he wasn't sure just when, or how, he could do it.

The next weeks passed quickly. Eva nursed the baby, who took to her feedings easily. Fred spent as much time as he could being helpful to his wife and child.

Fred sensed that Phil was angry, very angry. It was obvious this wasn't the way he'd expected things to turn out at all.

Everything would have been perfect for Fred, better than he could have imagined, except for one thing. He remembered the promise he'd made to himself the first moment he'd held his daughter in his arms. His guilt about Cybil grew, even as his love for her refused to die.

He saw her still, and they spent time in bed in the house on the hill. Something was different in the room with them. Fred knew the reason why, and he could sense that Cybil felt his uncertainty, and didn't know what to make of it. He saw a new look on her face but dared not say anything to her. If anything, he was more passionate than ever, but then, there was that look.

Fred's other concern was money. How could he afford to pay any of the cost a new babe brought? He kept his worries to himself, but he needn't have, because Eva was thinking the same thing.

***

Eva had never wanted anything to do with charity, but she knew they needed outside help when little Dorrie was four months old. It seemed better than asking Phil for more money. She hoped he'd never have to know she was taking charity. How could he? How would he? She resolved to look around and see what might be available.

She thought about going to the church, St. Mary's, where she and Fred had married. But she didn't want everyone in the parish knowing she was a charity case. No doubt the vicar would inquire with Phil if everything was okay, which was the last thing she wanted.

With the baby in her tiny pram, Eva walked the streets one sunny day, trying to decide where she should go. She wandered aimlessly, unsure of her destination until her feet brought her to the building that housed the Southampton Seaman's Relief Society.

She stood there, just as Fred had done months before, unsure if she should open the door and go inside. Fresh out of ideas, she decided this was the best place to start.

The place was filled with families, mums with babes in prams and in their arms, and clusters of small children standing about, poking each other and whining and fussing. The air carried a hint of a vegetable stew with a whiff of mutton mixed in.

"Can I help you?" a woman asked.

She looked kind, her eyes fixed on baby Dorrie in the pram with a look of love, even though they had never met. Eva walked over to the desk. Dorrie wailed in protest as if she didn't want to be there at all.

"Hush babe, there's nothing to worry about here," Eva assured her as she picked the infant up and patted her back. "I shouldn't have come."

"We are here to help. Do you need a warm meal? Clothes for the baby? I love babies so much, and yours is really beautiful."

"Do you have one of your own? A baby?" Eva asked. She felt so uncomfortable asking for help, she'd rather talk about babies. Other people's babies.

"I did, once. But I lost him. Please, how can I help you?" The woman pushed a strand of red hair behind one ear.

"It's hard to say this, but what I really need is some money to help pay the bills. You see, I live with my brother, and it's not fair that he has to foot the bill for everything, for me, and Dorrie." She looked down at the baby, who had settled in her arms, a tiny smile on her pink lips.

The woman pointed to the chair beside her desk, so Eva sat, adjusting her coat and sitting in a careful manner, as if she wished to retain some sense of dignity, an item she felt she was losing with every passing second.

"And you have no husband?" The woman asked, a look of concern in her deep green eyes.

"Oh, I do have one of those, but that's part of my problem. He's no use, he's nothing but trouble. Ever since *Titanic* went down..." Eva stopped talking. She hadn't meant to bring that up. She'd shared too much.

"*Titanic*?" the woman asked, with a slight catch in her voice. Her eyes were glued to Eva's face.

"I didn't want to say this, but yes, he's a seaman, a poor excuse for one, if you ask me. He was on *Titanic*. Well, you might as well know," Eva spoke louder, casting caution to the wind. "I mean you will understand, when I tell you his name, so..."

"His name?" the woman asked. "How can that make a difference?"

"Well, no doubt you've heard of Frederick Fleet." Eva spit the words out of her mouth. "He's my husband, and he caused the whole thing with the iceberg." She looked down at the baby in her arms. "Good thing you can't understand what that means yet, Dorrie. I wish you'd never have to know what he done, that worthless man!"

When the woman behind the desk said not a word in reply, Eva looked over at her, baffled. "You mean to tell me you've never heard the name of Fred Fleet? You have no idea who he is?"

"Oh, I know who he is," the woman answered in a strained voice. Again, she ran her eyes over Eva. Her hands were shaking, and she placed them on the desk.

Feeling uncomfortable, as if she had said too much, damning Fred before a perfect stranger, Eva tried to soften her words. "He was the love of my life, Fred was. And I mean, I guess he still is, but it's all become so impossible. He was such a good-looking man, I mean, he still is, he's quite beautiful. When my brother and I moved here from Guernsey and Phil bought a nice little house, well, there was Fred, living in a rented room, right next door. We fell in love. He does have a certain way about him. He... you see, I found him so, irresistible." She paused and looked over at the other woman. "I don't know why I am telling you this."

"You should tell me everything, Mrs. Fleet."

"My brother Phil didn't want me to marry him," Eva began. And then she told the woman how things had progressed between Fred, herself, and Phil.

She ended with, "That sums it up. Fred is a sorry excuse for a man now. He has never provided for me as a man should for his missus, and yes, there's even been talk that he sees other women, if you know what I mean." Eva stopped speaking for a moment. The woman behind the desk caught her breath and reached up, fussing with her hair. Eva could see she was visibly shaken, and Eva was confused. What raw nerve had she touched in the woman with red hair, who had looked so composed when their conversation had begun? "The neighbors have seen things, and suggested things." Eva stopped talking.

"But you don't really know if this is true, do you?"

"I've never seen him with another woman, if that's what you mean, but it really wouldn't surprise me. Fred is very depressed, he's very sad because of *Titanic*. The only thing that makes him smile is when he holds Dorrie, when he walks in the door after a crossing. Then that fades, and he gets all sad and restless all over again. Then he'll be gone for a few hours in the afternoon. I have no idea where he's been. When he shows up, he'll sail through the door and I can see how his mood has changed, how incredibly happy he is. I can find no reason for it. Except for the possibility he's been with his lover. That's the only thing I can think of. You see, in the beginning, before *Titanic*, he was, how can I say this, a very passionate man. But now..." She looked at the floor, her face warm, embarrassed she had said all she had, and yet somehow, she felt she could discuss this with the stranger seated across from her. It made no sense, but she felt she could, almost like she should. It seemed there was a connection between the two of them, although Eva knew that was impossible. A few minutes ticked by, and just when the silence threatened to become unbearable, Eva spoke again.

"Are you married? Do you understand what I mean? About my husband's passion? We were so suited to one another that way, from the first. It delighted both of us, and then..." Eva knew she had gone too far. Her face grew warmer still.

The other woman averted her glance and looked down at her lap. She twisted her fingers about.

"I was married," the woman spoke in a flat voice. "But my husband is gone. And my little boy, yes, he's gone too." She paused, seeming to decide what to say next. "And you need money, that's what you said." She hurried her words, a new strength in her voice. "Here, we do have money for people with babies and unpaid bills."

"Why, thank you, m'lady, I never expected such a bounty!" This wasn't what Eva thought would happen. She gave an awkward laugh. At best, she thought there would be papers to fill out, days to wait, and, if that even worked, she had no idea. She had intended to go home and pray for a good response to her request. But now, this woman handed her a stack of money, from a source that she kept hidden. It was most odd. Almost like she was giving up her own funds. But Eva didn't question it.

"Yes, it's all for you, Mrs. Fleet. You and the baby deserve it." "If you need more, just come back, come back directly to me. I'm Mrs. Stuart, Cybil Stuart."

"I'm so grateful, Mrs. Stuart. I'll be grateful to you all my life, and so will baby Dorrie." Eva secured the pound notes in her purse and put the baby back in the pram. "You are the kindest woman, Mrs. Stuart."

***

As soon as she was gone, Cybil told the man in charge that she was feeling ill and must go home at once.

"You do look poorly, Mrs. Stuart. I hope you feel better tomorrow. See you then, m'lady."

Cybil cleared out her desk and left, knowing she would never go back to the Seaman's Relief office. She had no choice. How could she possibly face Eva Fleet again? As she walked home that day, wiping tears from her eyes, she came to a decision. At last, she understood the uncertainty she'd seen in Fred's eyes of late. She wasn't surprised he hadn't told her about the baby. The poor man was torn in two.

It was time for her to do the one thing, the only thing, she could do for him. It all made sense to her now, and she hoped he would understand. But making sense didn't diminish the pain. If anything, it magnified the pain. Their love for one another was, at best, pointless.

"I'm going to Ireland," she said as Fred walked into her room the next afternoon. He stopped pulling off his jacket and stared at her. "My late grandmother lived in a house there, and it's been empty too long."

"But Cybil," he began. As soon as he said her name, Cybil could sense the relief in his voice, and in his face. He couldn't possibly know she had met his wife, and seen the baby, but it was almost as if he had. Or had he made up his mind that their time together must come to an end? Had she just handed him what he'd wanted of late? But then she saw him seem to change course. "Why now, Cybil? What did I do wrong?"

"Why didn't you tell me about the baby?"

He didn't say anything at first.

"What happened? How did you find out about Dorrie?"

"Eva came to the relief office with the wee baby in her pram. So, there they were, the two of them, with your wife asking me for help. As soon as she said she was Mrs. Fleet, and her husband the lookout on *Titanic*, it was all I could do not to cry out and scream! Fred, how could you do this? Why didn't you tell me? I thought, you and she..." Cybil's face burned, and tears slipped from her eyes.

"We don't, Cybil. We don't get along at all. Except that one night, things just happened. But only that once, just before I met you." Fred's voice trailed off.

"I'm not going to interfere in your life any longer, Fred. You belong to your wife and the wee baby. Don't try to pretend otherwise. You must belong to them. I'm booking passage to Ireland. I should be gone in two weeks' time, if I can arrange it. And I'm not coming back. There's nothing here for me any longer. I'd rather be at Chelmsford House. I should have gone there when my husband divorced me. Oh, how I wish I had."

"How can you say that, Cybil? Don't you love me, even now? Aren't you glad we met?" Cybil sensed Fred was pleading with her now, unable to hold back his true feelings.

"Of course I love you. But this is impossible. I've known so much loss in my life, and losing you, realizing I really had no right to you in the first place... I see that now." She couldn't say another word, her tears got in the way.

"*Anam Cara*," was all Fred could say. As soon as he did, they rushed to each other, throwing their arms about one another. It seemed they would never let go. They stood there a few minutes, lost in each other's embrace, until together, they moved toward the bed.

Slowly, for the last time, they made love. When it was over, Fred covered Cybil's face with careful kisses and left the room. The sound of his footsteps muffled her cries.

Chapter 24

As the years passed, Fred was the best father he could be to Dorrie, or the best any man of the sea who is rarely home, could be. The best father a man could be, when he had no idea how to be a parent at all, since he never had one of his own.

Their relationship was far from perfect. Dorrie was close to her mother, and her head was filled with Phil's complaints about Fred. None of that had changed. If anything, it had festered. With the little regard Dorrie displayed for him, Fred would think how he had given up his happiness with Cybil to be a father to Dorrie, but to what end? She had little use for him.

Most days, he didn't see that he'd any choice. Holding on to Cybil would have meant allowing his lover first place in his heart, the spot that should be reserved for his daughter. What man would do that? But sometimes, sometimes he longed for happiness and a true love that managed to last all his life. Some days, he felt Cybil's arms around him, pressing him close to her body, just as she had in the last hour they'd spent together. And then, he'd shake his head, asking, *Was that too much to hope for?* It seemed it was.

His depression deepened.

He thought about all those who died that icy night so long ago, and how each and every one of them would have made a better stab at life than he had. Despite the huge chunk of ice floating about that night, they had all deserved a chance to live. He'd taken that chance away from them. Last but not least, he revisited the deepest, darkest bit of truth concerning that April night. If only he hadn't done the one thing that night that sealed their fate, the thing he hadn't mentioned in either of the inquiries.

His heart grew heavy, and when the blackouts came, they took him to another place, a place where memory never tagged along. As upsetting as they were, the blackouts provided relief. He never told anyone that eventually he welcomed this escape from reality. The blackouts increased, almost as if he granted them permission. But they never came when he was at sea, or in New York. Whatever brought them on only visited when he was home, in Southampton, with his wife and her brother.

As the 1930s dawned, fewer and fewer passengers filled the decks and the staterooms on the *Olympic*. The crew noticed.

"Do you think we'll still get paid?" was a common question.

"Some people still want to cross the Atlantic, and they haven't got any other way of doin' it, have they?" was the common reply.

But the men worried about their jobs and their fate. Were the passengers choosing other ships? Would the *Olympic* last? If not, what then?

Fred was certainly among those who took notice of the changes on board. The boat rode high in the water, fewer passengers, less cargo, a good reason for concern about the pound notes to drop in his pocket, or maybe not, when they reached the other side.

On that day so long ago, when the finely dressed gentleman with the waxed mustache had pulled him into a private room for a chat before Fred's testimony at the Senate inquiry, Ismay had promised him a bit of a pension once he'd reached retirement. But the man was gone, living in obscurity. Fred had heard he was in Ireland, but who knew? And what difference did that make? Ismay no longer had any say in White Star, even less, since the line had merged with Cunard. What money Fred might receive when his sailing days were over was shaky at best. Or maybe that future was closer than he expected? How long would White Star stay afloat, so to speak?

Walking down the street in New York in 1935, he passed by a news hawker pitching his papers. Fred stood still and tried to undo the words he had just heard, but it was no use.

Olympic was off to the scrap yard.

He reached down instinctively, his fingers pulling out the lining of the pocket in his trousers. The pocket was empty, the lining frayed, his future more uncertain than ever before.

Some weeks later, back in Southampton, he made the rounds of the hiring halls, but no one was interested in him. He tried to convince himself it was his age. At forty-eight, he looked that and more after a life out in the elements. But he really couldn't fool himself. Whomever he spoke with looked like they were about to offer Fred a job, on a large ship or a small one, Fred didn't care.

But when the man looked at Fred's Discharge Book, and read his name, and looked up at Fred again, he shook his head. "We have nothing for you this time, Fleet." It was the same everywhere he went. Sailors were suspicious men. No one wanted the ghost of *Titanic*, much less the lookout, riding their deck. The hiring men knew that better than Fred did. Soon it was obvious. Fred's dream of feeling the wind in his hair, sailing from port, was over. It was time to find a way to pay for his next meal, stuck on the shore, the last place he wanted to be.

Eventually, Harland & Wolff hired him. The irony of the situation wasn't lost on Fred. H&W's name was forever linked to *Titanic*, as was his own, so it seemed only right somehow. He'd be working in the shipyard, even if it was this side of the Irish Sea, and not Belfast, where H&W had brought *Titanic* to life. Rather it was here, in So'ton, where her last birthing pains and the final fitting out had taken place.

Working in the yard was a humdrum life for Fred, but he ate, and slept, and woke in the morning with a job to go to. And when he had a few coins, he made his way to the Freemantle Workingmen's Club to watch the lads at snooker.

One night, he walked through the door on Norman Road. There was Eva and Phil. And Dorrie too, sitting at the kitchen table, doing her homework, with hardly a smile to spare for her da. It summed up his sad situation. But things were about to get worse.

And then, the very next day H&W no longer had need of his services. The boss man handed him his last pay and wished him well in a voice that sounded less an apology, and more a sigh of relief.

"There you go, we're done at last. A shame isn't it, Fred?" Without waiting for Fred's reply, he'd turned away.

Fred rarely drank to excess, partly because he hadn't the money. But this evening he ordered a pint, and then another to follow the first. A shandy, his usual beverage, being half ale and half soda pop, wouldn't do at all tonight. After a couple of hours, he staggered home. Without waiting to join the others at the table, he went into the bedroom, closed the door, and pulled the blanket up around his neck. What he would do next, he had no idea. He started to shake all over. The familiar blackness descended upon him once again, providing relief.

The next morning, he kept his eyes shut tight when Eva got up early. He knew she expected him to follow in a few minutes, pulling on his work clothes, and heading out the door after a few swallows of tea. Eventually, he decided not to prolong the inevitable. A spat was sure to follow his announcement.

"I may as well get this over with and be done with it," he muttered as he pulled himself from the bed.

"Eva, my job is over. They don't need me at the yard anymore." He hardly looked at her as he spoke. Any minute she would degrade him. He'd heard it all before.

Yet she remained silent. She sat at the table, clutching the cup in her hands, instead of being up and about, preparing for the day.

"Eva, are you all right? Did you hear my bad news?"

"Yes, I heard you. I'm just not feeling well." She gave a little shudder and shook her head.

"What do you mean?" His whole mood changed in an instant. "What's wrong?" All the resentment he'd felt toward the words he expected to hear left instantly. It was as if they hadn't quarreled at all over the years. He stood there a moment, taking in the image before him.

Eva always had a certain pride about her, a way of holding herself. All that was missing. She slumped forward in her chair, her hands wrapped around the teacup.

"I went to the doc the other day. He said it's my heart, it's not working like it should." She spoke in a tired, scared voice.

"How can that be?" He didn't want to believe what he heard.

"We're not getting any younger. Neither of us. He gave me some tablets to take. Don't worry, they were cheap. Just pennies really. But doc said they will help. Something called digitalis. It will help my heart pump. He said my heart can't pump strong enough. I just started the tablets yesterday." She looked up at Fred, her eyes begging for reassurance.

He sat next to her, placed his hands on hers, and looked into her eyes.

"Then we will just have to give it a chance. How soon is it supposed to help?"

"Not for a few days. That's what he told me." Her voice shook as she struggled not to cry. "But Fred, I'm so scared."

"I know you are. But you'll be okay. I won't let anything happen to you, Eva." He reached over and smoothed her hair.

"You think you can do that? You think you can protect me?" Any other day, words like these passing between them would have been riddled with sarcasm, but Eva wanted only his reassurance.

"I'll protect you from worrying too much. Think of it this way, if the tablets have helped other people, they'll help you as well, or doc wouldn't have given them to you."

"That's a good way of looking at it. You've helped me more than you know." She gave him a weak attempt at a smile. "Let me get up and pour your tea."

"No, don't even think of it. I'll pour my own. You stay put. I'll rinse the cups afterwards. You should go and lie down once you're done. Maybe it's a good thing that I'm home today. I'll look after you, Eva. Anything you need. From now on, if you aren't feeling well, please tell me right away."

A tentative but tender message passed between them. Fred gave Eva a bittersweet smile. She shook her head slowly in agreement, as if to say, *After all that's happened, Fred, here we are, just the two of us, after all these years.*

For a moment, all the rest didn't count in the least.

After Eva went into the bedroom, Fred rinsed the teacups at the sink, thinking maybe there was still hope to mend all that had been broken. He was counting on it, after all. What else was left in his life but Eva? She was his one connection to life before *Titanic*, to those innocent days before his world turned upside down.

Soon, Fred found a job as a night watchman at Union-Castle. Not what he wanted, but all he could find. He had to take it, uncomfortable work hours and poor pay notwithstanding.

Eva didn't ridicule him, as he'd feared. She seemed relieved. She pointed out she wouldn't be left alone with her weak heart, since Fred would be home all day, while Phil was at work, and then Phil would be there at night. The heart tablets helped her just enough to tend to her housework, if she moved slowly. She was hardly back to herself. She worried about everything it seemed. Her main concern was not being left on her own.

By this time, the late 1940s, Dorrie was married and living her own life, with two children to look after. For Fred and Eva, they had each other, at least for a little while. And so, they limped along together, taking one day at a time.

***

Phil watched every bit of their reconciliation, if that's what it was. He'd mentioned more than once that this recent turn of events was his sister's foolishness disrupting their lives once again, and he was having none of it. He'd sit in a corner and sulk, biding his time until something would go amiss between them, and he could pull Eva back under his control. He wasn't disappointed.

One morning, when Fred should have been home an hour ago, he was still nowhere to be found.

"See? What did I tell you, Eva? He's proving a rotten apple stays rotten. He's probably drunk or off with some gal somewhere. Why haven't you learned? It's a mistake to count on him."

"You know Fred doesn't drink much at all." Eva sat in a chair by the window, where she had been watching for her husband with growing concern over the last half hour.

"Then he's got him a new little chippy. He did like the ladies. You haven't forgotten that, have you?" Phil was smug. Things were finally going the way he'd wished.

"That was only a rumor," Eva answered, although her voice held little conviction.

"A rumor you believed at the time. Or have you forgotten that too?"

"No, I haven't."

"There you go. He's up to no good again. Won't you ever see what's right in front of your nose?"

Eva didn't reply, she didn't want to agree with her brother. But as the minutes ticked off the clock, and Fred nowhere to be seen, she begrudgingly had to agree Phil must be right.

***

Fred left the shipyard the same time as every morning. He was sleepier than usual, looking forward to a nice nap when he got home.

Sometime later, he struggled to prop his eyes open. He glanced about, trying to figure out where he was. He lay on a bench, assaulted by the smell of diesel fumes. He blinked again, as the long row of parked buses came into view.

He was in a bus station. Where it was and how he got there was a total mystery. The blackout had hit without warning.

He pulled himself up and started walking, stumbling over his own feet. He stepped off the curb, almost losing his footing.

"Where ya goin', mate?" a man screamed at him. "Ya wanna step in front of a bus?"

Fred shook his head, trying to wake up, but he was lost in a fog. Slowly he sank down to the ground.

"What's wrong with you, you bloody fool? Do I have to scrape you off the pavement?" The man leaned over and gave Fred a hand up. "Mate, you need to go home and sleep it off."

"I ain't drunk." Fred hardly recognized his own voice.

"Well, ya coulda' fooled me. Get outta here before you do get hit by a bus."

Fred stumbled around until he found the exit. He made his way along the pavement, holding on to buildings and storefronts, his vision cloudy, his steps random, as his feet tried to make contact with the ground. People stopped and watched him, shaking their heads. He got turned around a few times and didn't recognize where he was.

When he finally reached home, his head had cleared, but he was three hours late.

When he walked in the door, Eva wouldn't look at him. He tried to explain, though he wasn't sure what to say.

"Eva, I don't know what happened." She ignored him. "Really, I can't explain it..."

"Don't even try, Fred. I knew it was too good to last. There's nothing left to explain. You are just back to being who you really are. Just leave me alone, I've had more than enough of your excuses over the years. Phil tried to wait for you. He was late to work because you didn't show up. He told me I should never trust you again, and he was right."

"Oh! So, we are back to what Phil said!"

"Shut your mouth and leave me alone. I don't give a damn where you were." Eva picked up a basket of laundry and pulled open the door into the back garden, slamming it behind her as hard as she could.

In the days that followed, they hardly had a civil word between them. The only thing worse than Eva's anger for Fred was Phil. Fred could sense how pleased he was at pulling the strings once again.

Chapter 25

September 1955 brought a fine autumn day, but not for Fred. Although bright sunlight poured into the house, and the sky displayed a promising shade of hyacinth blue, Fred was restless, despondent.

Life's certainly upside down for a night watchman, Fred thought as he sat at the kitchen table sipping a cuppa, with Eva washing clothes and doing her best to ignore him. He didn't have to be at work until eight bells — he still thought of life in ship's time — but he wasn't sleepy. He'd hardly closed his eyes this morning after he got home.

At the Union-Castle shipyard, he was supposed to make several patrols through the night, checking all the possible entry points. Lately, he couldn't force himself to walk his rounds. He'd spend most of the night half-dozing on a wooden chair tipped back against the wall.

Last night, he'd almost fallen over when a noise startled him awake a little after two a.m. Turned out it was a rat. The long tail disappeared behind a work bench. *Oh well,* he'd told himself, as he adjusted the chair back into his favorite position, *I ain't on rat patrol.*

Being a watchman was the last thing he wanted. What he really dreamed of was being back at sea. But no one would hire him. He was too old. He should be upstairs in bed, sleeping, but he couldn't.

"I think I'll take a little stroll. You want to come, Eva? Maybe over to the park? We can sit on a bench."

She looked up at him, the expression on her face showing she thought him quite mad. Her hair slipped into her eyes, and as she lifted a hand to shove it out of the way, soap suds sprayed across the floor.

Unfortunately, once the digitalis tablets had started working, and Eva felt a bit stronger, her old way of looking at things had returned. Phil's distaste for Fred had never waned. He had done his best over time to undo the improvements in their marriage. As luck would have it for Fred, Phil had won out.

"You must be joking, Fred. And who's going to do the laundry? Phil needs clean clothes for work."

"Phil. Always bloody Phil."

"Well, he's got a regular job, in a shop. People see him every day at the chemist's. He's no night rat in a shipyard!" With a look of disgust on her face, Eva turned back to the laundry tub. Funny she should talk of rats!

"Oh, so now I'm a rat, am I? For once, can't you treat me decent?" He got no reply.

"I'm going for a walk on my own then. I'm off to the park. I think I'll sit on a bench all by myself." With a defiant sneer on his face, he slammed the cup down right under Eva's nose. She jumped at the sound, and the last dregs of tea splashed her face. "You're married to yer bloody brother, that's yer damn problem, woman."

She kept her eyes averted. Maybe his words struck too close to the truth.

***

Once he was gone, Eva shook her head in resignation. She wiped the tea from her cheek.

"I don't know how much more I can take of this. The man isn't right in the head." She spoke aloud as she often did once Fred was out of earshot. The minute he'd walked out the door, she felt almost buoyant with relief. "Maybe I should follow Phil's advice at long last. This needs to end, this marriage. The bloke is impossible to live with."

The empty room didn't disagree with her.

***

In the years that followed, increasing dissatisfaction marked their lives.

Eva's heart condition worsened.

Fred's depression deepened until, one day at long last in 1959, he slipped through the trap door of sanity, a hatch that had stood ajar, waiting for him it seemed, ever since that icy April night so long ago.

A new reality, or lack thereof, existed for him in the Royal South Hampshire Hospital, in the area reserved for the insane, in the lockdown ward. Eva never came to visit, not once. Not that he would have known if she had stood there, trying to comprehend that this bundle of skin and bones and dirty clothes was her husband, collapsed on the floor in a corner, in a room he shared with dozens of other lost souls.

Blacked out, in his own world, his body metabolized doses of potassium bromide and little else. When the legal papers arrived dissolving their marriage, he never saw them. They would have made no sense to him. They were simply dropped in his file. Fred Fleet's existence had been reduced to a mere number on a folder in a grey filing cabinet in a dusty office.

Two or three years later, Fred wasn't sure how much time had passed, they deemed him fit to re-enter the world. Cuts in the mental health budget may have been responsible for his impending release, or the mere fact that he could keep his eyes open for at least seven hours a day and repeat his name when urged to do so. Maybe it was the electric shock treatments that had lifted Fred off the table. Maybe they had done some good, along with the harm. But really, who knew why a doctor, or a bureaucrat, suddenly signed his release form?

Fred came out the front door, blinking in the bright sunlight on a warm afternoon in early May. Completely disoriented, he stood there, unable to take a step.

A woman approached him.

"Here, Fred. You're coming with me." She leaned over and gave him a brief, cautious hug. Then she stepped away, sniffing in disgust at the stale smell of the man.

He turned his head. She was familiar in some way. He rubbed his eyes, still trying to figure things out.

"There's a room for you." She walked on, expecting him to follow. He didn't. She stopped and looked at his face, really looked at it.

"Fred. Do you know who I am? It's me, Dorrie. Mum sent me to pick you up." She took a few steps. When he still stood in place, she turned round, staring at him, her hands on her hips. "What?" she asked.

He didn't reply.

"Well, you didn't expect her to come pick you up, did you? Just come with me. Dad, are you able to walk?"

He still didn't move.

"For goodness' sake! Look, I can't relate to this, or to you. I mean, you are my father, I know that. But you can't cope with anything, can you? It's almost like you're the child. So, I'll just call you Fred." She stood there, waiting.

Finally, she extended her hand and spoke with a softer tone. "Here, hold my hand. I'm taking you home, Dad."

As he sat on the bus next to Dorrie, Fred couldn't imagine what he would find when they reached their destination. He had been told a few months ago that he and Eva were no longer legally married. He had listened to this news with little surprise, but nevertheless, the pain he'd felt was real. So how would she receive him, with the court placing her in charge, as was the law, and against her will, no doubt? And then there was Phil.

Fred grew nervous as he and Dorrie climbed off the bus and walked toward the front door. But he needn't have been. Neither Eva nor Phil were home to greet him. Dorrie led the way to a small, dank room that had been set up for him under the stairs at the end of the back hallway. The house smelled of yesterday's cabbage and onions. He took off his jacket slowly, hung it on the back of the only chair in the room, and lay down on the bed. He stared up at the ceiling.

"I'll be going now, Fred," Dorrie said, as she headed out. But just before she opened the front door, she stopped, turned, and retraced her steps. She walked into the room at the end of the hall and leaning over, she placed a kiss on her father's cheek. "I'm glad they let you out of that place, Dad. Please don't mess things up here." And then she was gone.

The years passed. Things between Fred, Eva, and Phil grew worse than ever, if that was possible. Neighbors walking by on the street would hear voices raised in anger all the time. They'd shake their heads, surprised at nothing anymore about the inhabitants of 8 Norman Rd.

Fred had a pitch as a paper seller on the corner of Pound Tree Road. He'd tell people he did it just to help while away the time. But he needed the money. With nothing more than the tiny White Star pension from his days at sea, Fred was all but penniless, and depression rode his back as it always had.

Now and then, when he'd see a woman walking along the way, with red hair piled atop her head, he'd watch, and remembers his *Anam Cara*. If only it were her, he'd think. Even after so many years, if he tried really hard, he could still recall Cybil's face.

He was a solitary ghost of a man, a remnant of a human being, a creature who kept to himself, even when he passed an afternoon at his favorite haunt, the club in Freemantle. He'd sit alone, his eyes fixed once again, on the lads and their game. He'd watch the colored balls as they rolled about on the billiards table. If anyone pulled up a chair to join him, he'd move away and find another spot at an empty table.

He'd sit there for hours, sipping on the same drink. A half glass of shandy, still his favorite beverage, and the only one he could afford. A cane for his arthritic knee rested against the table. At night, sleep would elude him in the tiny back room of Phil's house. Most nights, he'd toss and turn 'til morning.

On this bright sunny day, after selling off his afternoon copies of *The Echo* extra early, Fred sauntered along the street, favoring his bad knee, but determined to keep going. *Maybe if I try and walk fast, I'll get a wee bit tired, and then I can take a real proper nap when I get home.*

He entered the park, surprised to see it quite empty. It seemed the fine weather had beckoned to him and no one else.

A figure in the distance limped along. For some unknown reason, as she came closer, she looked vaguely familiar. *Who could she be?* Suddenly, he realized it was her distinctive limp that had caught his attention.

As the woman drew near, they exchanged a nod and a glance. And then, puzzled more than anything else, they both stopped and stared at each other.

"Is that you, Fred Fleet? From up the crow's nest on *Titanic* then? It is, isn't it? How are you, Fred?" The woman extended her hand in greeting. She looked genuinely glad to see him.

Recognition dawned on Fred. Her youthful good looks had vanished, but still, there was something about her face, and of course, the limp betrayed her identity.

"It's you, isn't it, Mrs. Lightoller? How are you? How's Lights? I hope you don't mind me calling him that. We all did, you know."

"Of course you did, and Lights he is, or was. I'm sorry to say he passed back in '52. Died in his sleep. I still miss him, but I've grown used to things being the way they are, I guess. But how are you, Fred?" Sylvia Lightoller looked at his face carefully.

"I'm... I'm the same, I suppose, m'lady." Fred looked at the ground, a bit uncomfortable. *Who am I to be speaking with the wife of an officer?*

"Come, let's sit down and chat a bit. Catch up, you know." She sounded as if they were old friends! Fred was pleasantly surprised. He followed her over to the bench as she led the way, her limp slowing her progress.

"How have you been?" Fred asked. His outspoken nature overrode his discomfort at speaking to the widow of the second officer of *Titanic*.

"Oh, it would take a long time to answer that." She gave him a quick smile, but then her face grew serious. "Getting older, that's what I am. And there are so few of us left from those old days. Makes it extra nice to meet you, Fred. As you can see, I'm still limping along. When I was younger, I never thought about my limp, not really. I was born this way you see, with a club foot."

"I'm so sorry to hear that," Fred said.

"Well, don't be!" she said with a smile.

Fred gave her a surprised look.

"It was my limp that brought me and Bertie—Lights, to you—together. I was traveling back home to Australia, on the *Suevic*, and he was working that route at the time. I couldn't manage the stairs on the ship, and Bertie took to carrying me about. Can you imagine that?"

Fred laughed. "No, I can't, but it must have been a sight to see."

"It was. He carried me up and down. I fell in love with him instead of falling down the stairs!" They both laughed heartily.

"Why do you call him Bertie? Is it okay for me to ask?"

"His middle name was Herbert. He suggested I call him Bertie, since I would be the only one to do that. It was a private name we could use as part of our love for one another. It was the key to entering our private world together. I treasured being in that spot in his heart."

"So, you had a perfect marriage."

"Yes, we did. Through the years, he was so good to me." She paused for a moment, remembering. "I even forgot about my limp!" Then she added softly, "That's why I never could tell him one thing." She paused again, as if she wished to retract her last sentence.

"And what was that?" It only occurred to Fred after asking that maybe this one time he should have kept his mouth shut. Who was he to push her?

Sylvia didn't respond. She seemed lost in the past. Fred didn't prompt her but looked down at his hands. His gnarly, knotted knuckle bones pulled him back in time to when his hands were young and strong. Tying seaman's knots. And yes, striking a warning bell three times.

"It was in Southampton Water. I've never told anyone about this, Fred. But, for some reason, I feel close to you. I mean, who else is left that remembers *Titanic* and the old days so well? Just you and me. It happened that night, when *Titanic* was coming into So'ton from Belfast. I had a fun idea. You wouldn't know it to look at me now, but I was full of fun and looking for ways to enjoy life when I was young. Bertie said he liked that about me so much! But he wouldn't have liked what I am about to tell you. He would have been furious. Actually, he was furious. Well, I'm getting ahead of myself in the story." She hesitated again.

"Go ahead, you can't stop now!" Fred gave a nervous laugh.

"I thought it would be a great idea to go out in a little boat in Southampton Water, try and get a closeup look at *Titanic*. I convinced a cousin to come with me. We went out in a little sailing dingy. But we got too close to the ship, and *Titanic* blew its whistle at us. I laughed and laughed, I thought it was so funny, I thought it was the best thing that could have happened! The mighty *Titanic* blew its whistle at me! But the next morning at breakfast, Bertie was in a foul mood. I asked him what was wrong. And he said, 'Some fool, some total idiot in a small boat got in *Titanic's* path.' He told me that he and Captain Smith and all the officers on the bridge were angry as could be. They actually had to blow the whistle to get rid of the bloody idiot before there was a chance of a collision and bad publicity, and maybe some damage to the ship. I could never tell him it was me. I wish I'd never gone out in the boat."

"He would have forgiven you. I'm sure he would have."

"No, I'm not so sure he would have, not really. I think in a marriage, no matter how much one person loves another, if you do something bad, really bad in their eyes, something really unacceptable, they never see you again in the same light. So, I couldn't let that happen."

"I know what you mean," Fred said in a quiet voice. "After *Titanic*, my wife Eva, she never saw me the same. She blamed me for the iceberg, she listened to all the neighbors. It ruined our life together. Since you've shared your deep secret with me, I'll tell you mine, if you promise to keep it safe." His voice wavered.

"Of course I will, Fred."

He watched her face as he talked. She had a kind way about her, and so he continued. "I wasn't a true husband to Eva after that. I sought, well, I guess, comfort in other women, in ports when I traveled. Our marriage was broken after *Titanic*. I know that's no excuse, but it's true. Eva never saw me the same. I was worthless to her. I was weak, hardly a man anymore in her eyes. I needed to feel better somehow, and these other women, they made me feel that way. For a few minutes, anyway."

"We know men aren't supposed to do that, but, but... you were hurting so, weren't you? And you said Eva rejected you. And it was only when you were far away from home, so..."

"Yes. Well, actually no. If I'm telling you the truth, it has to be the whole truth." He stopped and thought for a moment before deciding to tell her the whole story It seemed there was no reason not to.

"There was someone else. A woman who lived here in So'ton. We loved each other very much, in every way possible. But when my Dorrie, my daughter was born, I gave her up. I loved Dorrie so much, I couldn't betray her. I broke away from Cybil. Her name was Cybil, or is Cybil. Maybe she's still alive, I don't know. But I've never forgotten her, and I've missed her every day. She was the only one in my life who understood me. You see, I never had parents, not really. My mum gave me up and went to America and I never knew my father." He stopped talking and covered his eyes with his hands, willing himself not to cry, because once he invoked Cybil's name, everything changed. His intense longing for her, even after all these years, flooded back.

"About your parents, that's so like Bertie's life. His mum died when he was born, and his father abandoned him and went to New Zealand. Bertie went to sea when he was thirteen."

"I was twelve when I ended up on the *Clio,* a training ship in Wales. It was a harsh place for a lad, but I learned my trade. But, that's quite amazing, isn't it? I never knew Lights and I had anything in common."

"Is your wife still alive, Fred?"

"She is that, but we are no longer married. I live in her house, or, I should say, I live in her brother's house, with the two of them."

"That's a bit unusual, isn't it?"

"Yes, after I came out of hospital, the court told her she was responsible for me." He spoke in a low voice, barely above a whisper.

"Why were you in hospital? I hope you don't mind my asking." Her voice showed concern, almost a fear of what might come next from the sad man seated next to her.

"I had a break. A blackout. I'd had them on and off for years, but it was no bother, not really. But then it all got worse, and I couldn't cope. I honestly don't remember just before they picked me up and took me away. I woke up, you see, in hospital. I didn't know where I was."

"How long were you there? Again, I hope you don't mind my asking."

"I would tell you if I could, Mrs. Lightoller. I just can't remember some things so good. It was a few years, maybe two, three, I'm not sure. But when I come out, the court said I had to go to Phil's house. He was very angry about that. Still is. He hates me. We never got on. I live in a separate room, kind of like I'm a boarder. Except I have no money to give him."

Fred broke down completely, sobbing and crying. None of it made sense. He certainly wasn't crying because he couldn't pay Phil. Rather, everything was so out of control, there was nothing left to do but cry. Once a fighter, a strong seaman, a lookout, he'd been reduced to a fragile shadow of his old self.

Sylvia hesitated for a moment. "Fred, don't be upset at what I'm about to say, but you need help once again. Have you seen a doctor lately?"

"Yes," he says. "Dr. Ritchie is my doctor, at the Royal South. But he's really no help at all. He just gives me the same tablets to take. I don't think they do anything but make me feel confused. The last time I was there, well, it's been a few months, promise you won't tell no one, he hinted he might, well, lock me up again. For my own good, he said."

"What do you think about that? Do you need to be in hospital Fred?"

Sylvia's voice carried true concern. Fred turned and looked at her. The pretty young woman he vaguely remembered from so long ago was nowhere to be seen in her face, but her caring expression told him all he needed to know about who she really was.

"I'm not sure," he answered quietly.

"What does your wife say about this?" She looked at him cautiously. "About the doctor wanting to send you back to hospital?"

"Oh, I would never tell her that. She thinks I'm bonkers anyway. She would insist Dr. Ritchie throw a net over me fast as he could. She and Phil would love to be rid of me."

"So then, what do you think you need, Fred?"

"What do I think I need? No one's ever asked me that." He mulled over her words for a minute or two. "I think I just need someone to listen, and really understand me, the pain I feel... No one ever does that. They just tell me I have no reason to feel bad about the past, even while they blame me for the sinking. Everyone does, especially my wife, ex-wife."

He stopped and thought again, considering his words. Sylvia was about to say something when he interrupted her. "Well, there was Cybil. She really understood, knew what was in my heart, in my soul, deep inside. But, like I said, I haven't seen her in many years. But I'll never stop loving her. She was my *Anam Cara*. That's a Gaelic thing."

"Oh, I know. I've heard of it."

"You have? Well, me and she, we were lovers, but we were so much more than that. But I had to give her up. It was wrong for me to have her at all. Like I said, I saw that as soon as Dorrie was born." He stopped talking and looked at his hands again. "But, it was also wrong, so wrong... for me to give her up." Neither one of them spoke. They sat there, realizing that both things were true.

"That was very good of you making that decision, for your daughter's sake. You were very brave."

"I don't think I've ever been brave, Mrs. Lightoller."

There was nothing left to say. They sat side by side in silence, each in their own way consumed by the past, lost in their own regret. But then again, what else was regret but a bittersweet byproduct of the passage of time?

***

"There's a letter for you." Eva handed him an envelope as soon as he walked in the door. The look on her face showed she almost resented his getting a letter at all. Fred was aware of this. He even suspected that she resented the fact that he was able to walk about as he pleased, standing on the street corner selling *The Echo*, chatting about the fine weather with passersby, while she, slowed down with increasing heart problems, lived a diminished life. Fred had observed that many days she could barely pull herself from the bed. He wished it were different for Eva.

Fred took the envelope, glancing at the return address. It was totally unfamiliar. He needed a moment to read it off by himself, safe from Eva's prying eyes and sharp tongue. He went out the back door into the garden and eased himself down on the step. Who in the dickens was Leslie Reade? He had no idea. He carefully ripped open the envelope.

The man said he was a reporter, and after all these years, he wanted to talk to Fred about that night. Fred wanted to say no. He wanted to rip up the request and toss it in the trash. But he was curious, and his curiosity got the better of him. He decided he would meet the man and see what he had to say. Why was he reaching out now?

It had been years since Fred has discussed *Titanic* with anyone. He wasn't sure he wanted to again. But something still stuck in his gut, something he couldn't ignore. *Titanic* had ruined his life. The rest of the world, they had eventually picked up the pieces and gone on with their lives. But he hadn't. He couldn't.

Well, it was about time he had his say. They all blamed him for what happened that night. He could still feel their accusations blowing about in the salty Southampton air. The assumption was he hadn't been paying attention to the task as his watch drew to a close. He still resented his place in history, maybe more so since he'd kept it all bottled up inside for so many years. But, most of all, Fred was still an impetuous man. Age had failed to dull his tongue, even if it had weakened his ability to watch out for his own best interests.

Was he about to step into a minefield? The thought never occurred to him.

Chapter 26

The September days were still fair. They would meet in an outdoor café at Reade's suggestion. Fred arrived a bit early.

Reade was already there. Catching sight of Fred, or the man he assumed was Fred, lingering out on the sidewalk, Reade was about to ask the waiter to fetch the man. But he realized this would be the wrong approach.

Fred wore an old, tattered sweater, threadbare trousers, and cheap, yellow spectacles obscured his deep-set eyes. A flat cap, the hallmark of the working-class bloke of the last fifty years, rested on his snowy white hair. He seemed frozen in time and place. No doubt the man was hesitant about being here at all. Reade rose from his seat.

"It's good of you to come, Fred," Reade said as he extended a hand.

"Is that you then, Mr. Reade?"

Reade was surprised to hear the man still spoke with a Liverpool accent. "Yes, yes, it is. Come, sit down. What would you like to drink, mate?"

"A shandy will do."

"Ah now, wouldn't you like a pint of ale? That's what I'm having." Reade hoped more information would flow with a higher alcohol content. Besides, drinking the same brew-built comradery.

"Well then, I can hardly refuse. A pint it will be." Fred smiled, he appeared to relax just a bit, as he followed Reade to the table. He sat in the chair across from Reade, rested his walking stick against the table, and looked about. The people at the table next glanced over at Fred, obviously assessing the man. Fred readjusted himself in his chair. Reade placed their order, adding a basket of pretzels onto the tab. He sensed Fred's unease and hoped to make him stay a while.

Reade leaned forward and gave the man what he hoped was an encouraging smile, so Fred wouldn't feel out of place and regret he had agreed to meet. "What can you tell me about that night? Just tell me whatever pops into your head."

After a slight pause, Fred took a deep breath, screwed his eyes up, and started talking. "It was the beautifullest night I ever seen. The stars were like lamps. I saw this black thing looming up, I didn't know what it was."

Reade was instantly aware that the man was no longer present in the here and now. Rather, he was back there, seeing and feeling all he had that night. "I asked Lee if he knew. What did he think it was? He couldn't say. I thought I ought to ring the bell. I rang it three times."

Reade was speechless, not that he wanted to interrupt. Let the man talk. Especially since Fred just said something he'd never even hinted at during either of the inquiries, or at any other time on public record in the years since. How long did the interval last while he questioned Lee? Was it half a minute, was it only a few seconds? Was it long enough to have sealed the fate of *Titanic*, giving her no time to avoid the berg?

Up until this moment, Fred had always said upon seeing the black smudge, he instantly rang the bell, and then called down to the bridge. It appeared that wasn't completely accurate. Precious moments had been lost.

Reade took a deep breath, observing Fred. He certainly appeared honest. It seemed, after so many years, the man had simply let down his guard and the truth slipped through his lips without warning or fanfare. The funny thing was, as if there could be anything remotely funny about any of this, even though he'd kept the interval a secret up until now, he still bore the blame for the sinking, based on the partial truth that was supposed to save him from all of that.

***

Fred sat in the chair at the table, but his mind was elsewhere. He had a flashback to the iceberg, and the panic that eventually ensued. The panic itself matched his later determination to do the right thing, but then his confusion as to what was the right thing? For himself, and for Eva and their life together, and so many other things he couldn't keep track of? If anything, he was confused, facing this once again after all these years. Age, coupled with his determination to avoid the part of the story that was so much more dangerous in his eyes, had loosened his lips on this one point, the little interval of time. He knew, above all else, he had to skip over any mention of the earlier sightings of ice, the bergs he'd reported to the bridge, the warnings that had been ignored by the officers, the ice sightings that should have slowed or stopped the ship but hadn't. Ismay had based Fred's White Star employment and retirement pension on keeping this biggest secret of all, and even though the pension was totally inadequate, Fred couldn't imagine how he would eat without it. So, he covered up that big truth, the early iceberg sightings, and let slip the "small" truth. He hadn't struck the bell the instant he saw the smudge.

He looked at Reade. The words had slipped out, almost as if someone else had spoken them. Would the man ask him about the length of the conversation with Lee? Fred had no memory of how long it lasted. But it did exist. The chaotic events of the night and the passing of years had wiped away the details, the exact length of time spent, a blur. But would Reade seize upon it and blame Fred, sitting here, face to face? Fred shifted in his chair again. He was sorry he came at all. What was he thinking? Through his thick glasses he stared at Reade, trying to sum him up. Then he truly felt that everything was out of his control. To save his sanity, he tried to pretend he was elsewhere, anywhere but here, facing this truth at long last.

***

The waiter set the tankards of ale and the heaping basket of pretzels on the table. He looked at Reade, about to ask if he could get them anything else. Reade waved his hand, shooing the man away. He didn't want to interrupt the flow of Fred's words.

As it happened, Reade had a different agenda when he'd asked to meet. His interest lay in a different direction. He wanted to know about the *Californian*, the ship that could have helped *Titanic* but didn't. So, for now, he gave Fred a pass.

"I'm writing a book about the *Californian*, and how she refused to come to your aid that night. I know you said you saw her light."

"Then you know I only saw it once we were in the lifeboat. I didn't see any light when we scraped the berg."

"Yes, yes, I recall reading that from your testimony Fred." Reade sought to encourage him.

"But she was there all right. Even if I didn't see the light sooner, Mr. Reade, she was there."

"I'm glad you remember that, Fred. It's important that we get all the facts just right."

"I absolutely remember that. We were told to pull for the light. But the ship never came any closer to us. She just sat there. Eventually, she was just too far away for us, rowing hard as we could. We couldn't possibly reach her. Thank goodness *Carpathia* came and picked us up."

Reade thought about asking Fred more about the time interval, when he'd conferred with Reginald Lee about the strange smudge. But then he reconsidered. The poor man was so totally down on his luck. The whole world has blamed him for the tragedy from that day to this without knowing this last detail. Why make things worse? It wouldn't really change anything for anybody other than this poor, pitiful, wrecked soul sitting in front of him. Reade watched the man take a few tentative sips from his ale, and then a nice, long swallow. *I doubt he's tasted anything that good in many a year. Look at him go at it now, poor bloody bastard.*

So, Reade said nothing more about the sighting of the iceberg. He took a drink of his own beer and offered Fred a pretzel.

After draining their tankards and eating most of the pretzels, the two men parted company. Reade was pleased with the interview. Fleet saw the light of the *Californian* that night. That was the information he'd hoped to hear. Reade had his ax to grind with the skipper of the *Californian.*

***

It wasn't as easy as that for Fred. As he walked away, Fred regretted ever showing up. No sense going home just yet. He didn't want Eva to sense his mood. She was very good at that, prying things out of him and gleaning a nugget, and then throwing it back in his face. Most of all, he didn't want to end up telling her what he just told Leslie Reade about the delay in ringing the bell. In all the years gone by, he'd never told anyone up until now.

He walked along deep in thought. There was more to it. He knew everyone at the Senate inquiry thought he was stupid. Some had laughed out loud at his answers. But he had to word things the way he did. When he was asked if he'd had the binoculars, would they have made a difference? His answer had been, "Enough to get out of the way." And that was true, but there was more to it.

Fred had always had glasses on the *Oceanic.* And so, on this *Titanic* night, if he'd had glasses, as soon as he'd spotted the smudge on the horizon, he would have instantly lifted the glasses to his eyes and identified the iceberg. That's the way glasses were used. You didn't peer through them all the time. You used your naked eye for the wide view, then the binocs helped identify what you'd spotted. Once he had identified the berg through the glasses, a matter of a mere second or two, he would have immediately struck the bell. Fred truly believed, if only he'd had the glasses, the conversation with Lee, and most likely the collision, never would have happened.

If I'd had the glasses. Well, he hadn't. It truly was the missing glasses that caused the chat with Lee and the time delay. And so, as it turned out, all the blame was placed on his supposedly failing to see the berg in time. But that wasn't the true story. But, it was what it was, and all the years gone by had indelibly recorded the history in the books, in the court of public opinion, and most of all, in Fred's own head. He could erase none of it. And even though he could never know whether or not there was time enough for the ship to make a turn if he'd struck the bell immediately, he was guilty.

Never mind that Lights had said at the hearing that the lookout should strike the bell before looking through the glasses, in the interest of time, so the missing glasses made no difference at all in the sinking. Fred had immediately recognized that for what it was, it was Lights's attempt to excuse the *Titanic's* officers for not giving up their own binocs to the lookout crew when the crow's nest glasses went missing. The truth of it was lookouts needed them more than anyone else. Several things offered up at the hearings were coverups and outright lies. Fred was always aware of that. But his own comment, *if I'd had the glasses,* wasn't one of those lies. Since the bridge had ignored his earlier ice warnings, he'd wanted to make absolutely certain this time. So, he'd chatted with Lee. It was as simple as that.

Now he worried that Leslie Reade would eventually say something about the gap in time, but it really seemed as if the man was busy going after this captain of the *Californian,* and well he should. *But ya never know,* Fred said to himself, *I never should have come and sipped his beer. Never.* He wandered back toward *The Echo* offices. He'd see if he could pick up his stack of papers a bit early and then head over to Pound Tree Road.

He was standing on his corner, looking for his first sale, when a friendly face turned up. It was his old mate, Harry Fitzpatrick. He used to work on the docks when Fred was at the shipyards. They'd known each other for years. He often bought an *Echo* from Fred.

"How're you this fine day, Snowy?" Harry asked, calling Fred by a nickname no one knew except for the lads on the docks. Fred had had misgivings at first about the name. Wasn't snow akin to ice? But it was Fred's snowy white hair they referred to, so he smiled at the name as always, and let it pass. Harry handed him some coins for a newspaper.

"I'm all right, I suppose."

"You don't sound all right Fred. What's up? You can tell me."

"I'm upset. I met a bloke, a reporter. He was asking questions about *Titanic*. I wish I hadn't agreed to see him, even though he bought me the best pint I've tasted in years. I don't like to talk about all that, *Titanic*, and that night..."

***

From that day forward, Fred was in a downward tailspin. Talking about the interval of time had brought it all to the forefront. He wouldn't give himself the pass that he'd been extra careful and needed to confer with Lee because of the earlier ignored warnings. That was the absolute truth, but he had such a poor opinion of himself, he easily ignored this bit of reality. He knew a lookout's job was to strike the bell instantly, glasses or not. If a mistake was made, no one would blame him for being too cautious. The fault lay in delay, rather than overreacting. The fault lay in being inadequate. But he had been just that. He still was. Nothing in his years on this earth had ever proved anything to the contrary.

He truly hated his life and hated himself. He should have blamed White Star for preventing him from testifying to his earlier ice warnings ignored by the bridge. Those warnings could have saved the ship. But, from the beginning, he had given in to White Star because he was weak. And knowing that only made him hate himself more.

September limped into October, and by November, Fred was no better than he had been the afternoon of the interview. He continued to deteriorate.

By the beginning of December, he wandered the Dorset-Hampshire bus station once again, not knowing where he was or why he was there. Buses swerved around him at the last second, honking their horns. Drivers yelled at the crazy man, telling him to get out of the way. He lurched through traffic out on the roads. He didn't care what happened. He could find no peace. He was trying to run away from himself, an impossible task.

December 29, 1964, was a cold, rainy day. It was Phil who found Eva dead in her bed of congestive heart failure.

Fred's hopeless dream of winning back his wife's approval was gone. He had always wished it might be so. If Eva had relented, all the blame heaped on him by the rest of the world wouldn't have mattered. With Eva gone, he'd lost his only chance at redemption. He was truly drowning in an unforgiving ocean of blame.

"How soon will you be out of the house?" Phil asked as they walked from the grave in the churchyard three days later on a freezing cold day with an icy drizzle stinging their faces.

Phil had insisted Eva be buried in the LeGros family plot, separating her for all eternity from Fred when his time might come. Dorrie, her husband Mike, Phil, and Fred were the only mourners. The plain wooden casket sat alone, in the open hole in the ground, each of them having lifted a shovelful of the heavy black loam, leaving the rest to the gravediggers.

The rain increased, and Mike snapped open his umbrella, pulling on his wife's arm and pointing toward their car at the curb. Dorrie gave her father a quick peck on the cheek, and her Uncle Phil, a hug. It was obvious she couldn't wait to be gone.

In spite of the rain, Phil stopped walking and turned to face Fred. "You remember the agreement. How soon will you move out?" He wasn't one to mince words, not even at a moment like this. He wanted this business done with as soon as possible.

"I'll visit the welfare office again and see what I can get. Maybe a friend will let me rent a room. I know a couple of people." Fred spoke in an unusually meek tone of voice.

"Better be quick about it then," Phil replied as he briskly walked away, leaving Fred standing there alone.

Fred had left his walking stick in his room, and he moved with a slow, painful limp along the gravel pathway, his knee dragging a bit, the tears on his face mixed with the cold raindrops.

Days later, he faced defeat once again. "We've reviewed your case one more time, Mr. Fleet. But there's no change. You don't qualify for anything. Your work experience and your age don't match up to our requirements. Maybe your family can help?"

The man at the welfare office desk didn't look like he intended to be mean to Fred, but the truth was the truth. If Fred had been born years later, he might have qualified for assistance.

Fred didn't ask for any explanation. He turned around and left, blending into the crowd out on the street, but not really. They moved with purpose, but Fred did not. He had no purpose. He had no destination.

He stumbled over curbstones and he walked out in traffic. Cars and lorries blew their horns, drivers cursing at him and making rude gestures.

Fred noticed someone at his side. A policeman. The man grabbed Fred's arm, preventing him, just in time, from stepping in front of a speeding lorry.

"What's going on with you, mate? You want to get yourself killed?"

"I dunno," Fred responded. He shook his head. "Maybe I do. Maybe that's exactly what I should do." He struggled out of the policeman's grasp. "Yes," he continued, "that's what I want, and the sooner the better." He didn't really want to give an answer, he felt trapped having to talk to anyone. He tried to turn away.

"What's your name, mate?" The policeman stepped closer.

"Fred Fleet." Fred stepped back, keeping his distance.

"Don't you have any family? Must be someone who can help you out?"

"There is one person, but she can't help me."

"Who is that, mate?"

"My daughter, Dorrie Shanley. Dorothy, she is."

The policeman wrote down Dorrie's name.

Fred walked away. They couldn't stop him. He wouldn't let them. He walked onto the sidewalk and headed back to the bus station. He just had to get away.

***

The officer might have thought Dorrie could step in and take control, but she did not. When the police came to her house, she was throwing together tea, and the children were having another squabble. What could she do with her father anyway? He was a difficult man, always had been. And he liked the attention, Dorrie had decided, possibly to make herself feel better. Most of all, she wanted to be done with the problem her father had been all her life. She didn't wish him bad, but there was nothing to be done with him. He wasn't right in the head, never had been, as far as she could remember.

"We are concerned about your father, Mrs. Shanley. He's threatened to harm himself. He is your father, this man, Frederick Fleet? We stopped him walking about in traffic. He almost got hit by a lorry. And he didn't care in the least."

"Oh, he doesn't mean it," she told the policeman at her door. "Fred won't hurt himself. You'll see. In the end, he'll take care of himself. It's what he's always done. He's a survivor."

The policeman rocked back on his heels. "Is he now? Why do you say that, missus?"

"He's the lookout from *Titanic*. Didn't you recognize his name?"

"No, no, I didn't. Is he the bloke missed the iceberg?" The man sounded surprised. "When all those people died? He was the one then?"

"Yes, the very same." Dorrie looked away in embarrassment.

"You say he's pulled this before? This crazy walking 'round in traffic?"

"Oh, he's always doing crazy things. He was in hospital once, for years, the psych ward. They turned him out. There's nothing can be done for him. But one thing's for sure, in the end, he always looks out for himself, if you get what I mean."

The policeman left, and Dorrie slammed the door, hurrying back inside to swat at the children who had been screaming and bickering long enough.

Chapter 27

Eva was gone, the happiness they'd shared for a brief time before *Titanic* but a flickering memory. Fred had no place to go, no place to live. Out of options, and too sad and depressed to look for any. He didn't expect anything from Dorrie, but he loved her. Late Saturday morning, January 9, he paid his daughter a visit.

"Dorrie," he cried out when she opened the door and stood there, watching him, taking in his disheveled appearance. Without waiting to be asked, he pushed through into the room.

"I'm lost." Tears poured down his face. "Dorrie, I have nowhere to go, I can't go on any longer. Say goodbye to everyone for me. Here." He reached in his pocket and handed her an old, ripped up relic of a wallet. "There's five pounds in there, lass. Look after it if you will."

"What do you mean, Dad? What's going on?"

"I don't know what's going to happen to me. I might get hit by a car, a bus, who knows, who cares?"

The tears continued to flow down his cheeks. Their conversation went back and forth as she tried to tell him everything will work out in the end, but never offering any real solution. He stayed about forty-five minutes, never agreeing with her that anything would work out, not ever. Then he left.

***

Dorrie put the wallet in a drawer. "He's nuts," she said to the empty room. "He'll never change."

She couldn't see how he ever would change, and didn't even want to contemplate what was really going on. It was just her difficult, crazy dad being himself all over again. She was tired of it. *I'm so tired of it, and him.*

***

Fred took the couple of shillings he had saved to a shop, where he bought a length of rope, the type he'd held in his hands many times in the past. A strong piece of rope, the type he knew how to tie into a good, solid seaman's knot. *This will do just fine,* he told himself as he paid for his purchase and headed back to the house on Norman Road. Fate had come to make a little collection, it seemed. Fate spoke to him now. The conversation was long overdue.

***

Hours later, Phil wondered where Fred was. *He's such a nuisance. Why did God ever visit that sorry man upon our family?* Phil walked down the hallway toward Fred's room. The door was open, the bed empty.

Good, he's gone to stay with those people he mentioned. Perhaps they will let him move in after all. Maybe things are looking up.

He locked up the house and went upstairs to his own room, turned out the light, and settled into bed for the night. In a few minutes, his thoughts turned to dreams.

***

In the morning, the house on Norman Road was unusually quiet. Phil prepared a pot of tea, thinking how relieved he was to not have to gaze on his ex-brother-in-law's face this morning.

Something caught his eye through the window. There was Fred, standing there in the garden!

What in the world is that man doing out there? Besides, it's cold. Least I can do is offer him a cuppa, and then I can send him on his way, once and for all. Best be done with him now.

He opened the door and walked down the steps. He started to call out to Fred. But something seemed odd.

"Fred. Fred, whatcha doin' over there? You want a cuppa? I just made a fresh pot." Phil stopped talking. Something was terribly wrong. He started running, and then ran faster to the pear tree.

He was too late.

***

In Ireland, an old, elegantly attired lady lay in her bed, lost in her dreams. White satin she wore, almost like a bride, but it was, in truth, a frilly dressing gown.

Cybil Stuart awoke with a start. *What was that?* A dog barking? But whose dog? Something wasn't right.

She rushed down the stairs, moving faster than she had in years, and much more disturbed than she should have been for a barking dog in the night, if that's what it was. She threw open the door and peered into the darkness, across the vast park of the estate. She listened, for what, she wasn't sure. It was quiet, and she could see nothing amiss.

She climbed the stairs and settled back under the featherbed. *Don't be foolish*, she told herself. *It was nothing, nothing at all.* As her eyes closed, she felt a kiss, gentle on her mouth. These words were planted in her heart: *Anam Cara, I will always love you.*

***

While Dorrie thought her father would never change, he has. He's thousands of miles away, his soul that is, in its intended spot. There's little left of the crow's nest in the dark cold water, just room enough for his feet. And really, that's all he needs. He's quite amorphous now.

A woman who bears him great resemblance rushes to greet him, a loving smile and tears of joy on her face. It seems the soul always looks the same, whether a discarded babe in a foundling hospital, or a desperate old man. We are easily recognized by the one who gave us life. And heaven, it seems, is here and there, and everywhere. Love and forgiveness crowd heaven, leaving no place for blame.

The End

Book Club Guide

1. Is Fred a sympathetic character? Do you like him? Is it possible to like a character who does the wrong thing?

2. When you were reading Fred's answers at the Senate investigation, did you think he was lying? Can you blame him if he was?

3. Should Fred have defied Ismay's rules and said what he really wanted to say?

4. The sinking of *Titanic* occurred as the Edwardian Age was drawing to a close, and shortly before the outbreak of WWI. How did society change? How does the sinking of *Titanic* mirror this?

5. Should Dorrie have realized her father was at his wits end? What were the clues she ignored in his words and his recent actions? What should she have done, instead of turning away from the situation?

6. Is it understandable that Eva blamed Fred for the sinking?

7. Should Eva have rejected her brother Phil's dislike of Fred and defended him in their conversations? Or was it realistic that she was easily persuaded? Or did Phil size Fred up correctly? Do you think that having a bad opinion of a person can be a self-fulfilling prophecy?

8. Do you believe that survivor's guilt is always inevitable in a great tragedy? Or, how can it be averted?

9. What, if any, blame do you place on Fred?

10. If you could ask Fred a question, what would it be?

11. If you were unaware of Fred's eventual suicide before you read the book, did you think he would go through with it as you were reading?

12. Did you like the ending, in that, did you realize that Fred meets his mother in Heaven? Did you like the kiss Cybil received?

Interview with the Author

Q. How did you decide to write this book?
A. I was listening to an "On this Day in History" on the radio, and mention was made of three events in the life of Frederick Fleet, the *Titanic* lookout who first spotted the iceberg, and I was instantly fascinated. I was immediately sympathetic to him as a person who had lived a tragic life, and I wanted to defend him from any blame he might have endured.

Q. Was it easy to defend Fred?
A. Things got sticky when I made the shocking discovery that he didn't strike the warning bell immediately, even though he testified otherwise. But for all these years no one knew that, except for Leslie Reade when he interviewed Fred in 1964. Reade was writing a book for another purpose, so even though he was shocked by Fred's confession, no one else took note of it. But I did, when I started reading Reade's book. Now the readers of my book, *An Ocean of Blame*, will finally know the truth about that *Titanic* night. But most of all, I hope I've been fair to Fred and fair to history. Everything that happened that night revolves around the consequences of that unknown, ill-defined time gap between the first sighting, and the actual ringing of the bell.

Q. What's an interesting point people may question?
A. It's been argued that the presence of the missing crow's nest binoculars wouldn't have made a difference in the outcome. But, if Fred had the glasses he would have lifted them to his eyes and taken a quick glance to identify the smudge on the horizon. Instead, minus the glasses, more time elapsed as he paused, and had a conversation with Reginald Lee, his fellow lookout in the nest.

Q. What was a bit unusual about the writing of this book?
A. I have several large photos of Fred around my house so I can stay in touch with him and that period of history. I think he helped me write the book.

Q. What do you enjoy most about writing?
A. Listening to the voices in my head; they write the book, not me. Sometimes the characters force me to write something I really don't want to. I can't see how it will fit into the plot. But I always do what they want, and it always works out right in the end, to my surprise and delight.

Q. What was the most difficult thing about writing this book?
A. I learned to be on the lookout for all the faulty information out there about *Titanic* and Fred Fleet. Only prime sources can be trusted.

Q. What's an example of misleading information you found?
A. It was widely reported that Fred didn't have a job on a ship after August 1912, but I found that wasn't true at all when I searched ship manifests on Ancestry.

Q. Why did you create the character of Cybil?
A. I felt great sympathy for Fred having been abandoned by his mother, and having an unhappy marriage, with the divorce coming when he was in the mental hospital. I wanted him to have some love and happiness in his life, but also, I felt like his relationship with Cybil enabled me to show more of his personality, because she was always willing to listen to him discuss his painful life. He was a very needy person, which is, of course, understandable.

Q. What was the challenge in writing the ending of the book?
A. Of course, I knew Fred took his own life and I wanted to add an uplifting touch. So, in the end, he kisses Cybil and meets his mother in Heaven.

Acknowledgements

As odd as it might seem, first and foremost, I must thank Frederick Fleet for whispering in my ear and showing me all the places I needed to look in my research as I prepared to tell his story. When I wondered about his personality, he showed me his records from the foundling hospital and the orphanage, Elm Lodge. He directed me to check out The Waifs and Strays Society of the Church of England. It's true, so many of the heretofore unknown details of Fred's life were revealed to me through persistent research. But really, when I think about it, I attribute it all to Fred, and his relentless input. In effect, this is a book written by a ghost.

There are others who've played a role, of course, and to all of them I owe my immense gratitude.

Paul Lee: for his invaluable *Titanic* research.

George Behe: for all of his wonderful *Titanic*-related books, most especially, *Titanic Safety Speed and Sacrifice*.

Don Lynch: for encouragement in telling Fred's story.

Joshua Noble: for lunches and *Titanic* conversations, and showing me his spectacular *Titanic* collection.

William Broward: for advocating for the writing community.

Mark Richardson: who keeps me up in the wee small hours of the morning, reflecting on why and how we choose to write, and everything else related to drawing breath.

Leslie Reade: for *The Ship That Stood Still*.

Sonja Foster Allen: my BFF, because no way I could do life without her.

Susan Crawford: writing buddy par excellence since that day in the library.

Dr. Chrys Bruno: dear friend, who shares my "question everything" approach to life, of great value when one is engaged in book research, and everything else.

Robb Grindstaff: my peerless editor, who helped me face reality, more than once. For that, I am truly grateful.

And last but not least, I would be remiss not to point out a few deviations from history. My early research listed Frederick Fleet as a married man. It was only after I was well into the plot that I uncovered the date of this marriage to Eva, which was after the sinking. I didn't go back and rewrite based on this, but it is true that her brother Phil disliked Fred intensely, and influenced Eva against him. When Fred was in hospital years later, they were divorced, but the divorce law at the time held Eva responsible for Fred, and so he lived with them, which was, of course, as uncomfortable situation.

Cybil Stewart never existed. She was a gift I gave Fred as a person who understood his pain and was always sympathetic to his suffering as a result of the encounter with the iceberg. My gut feeling was, given the state of his marriage and his traveling job for so many years as Olympic crew, there may very well have been a Cybil. But that is mere speculation.

I don't know the nature of the exact bad behavior that resulted in Fred's expulsion from Elm Lodge, but existing letters relating to the incident show it was serious enough that Tottenhall Farm would not have him, and so he was sent to the *Clio* training ship instead. That said, the other details in Fred's life are true. Most "striking" of all, is his 1964 confession to Leslie Reade that, in fact, he didn't strike the warning bell the very instant he spotted the smudge on the horizon. Minus the binoculars, he paused and asked Reginald Lee for his opinion. How long did their conversation last? No one knows. Was it long enough to prevent an effective change of course that might have saved the ship from striking the berg? No one knows. And the rest is history.

About the Author

A graduate of Columbia University, Margaret lives in Atlanta with a bossy Cavalier King Charles Spaniel named Wesley, and a backyard full of very rude and hungry deer! Weekends may bring visits to her log cabin atop its own mountain, the perfect writing retreat. Previously a poet and short story author, her main focus now is on historical fiction.

As the mother of a September 11 survivor of the South Tower WTC, the loss of innocence is a frequently addressed topic of her writing, coupled with her lifelong love of history. Occasional visits to house museums have been known to produce a ghost story or two. If the voices are speaking, she's listening.

More from Evolved Publishing

We offer great books across multiple genres, featuring high-quality editing (which we believe is second-to-none) and fantastic covers.

As a hybrid small press, your support as loyal readers is so important to us, and we have strived, with tireless dedication and sheer determination, to deliver on the promise of our motto: **QUALITY IS PRIORITY #1!**

Please check out all of our great books, which you can find at this link: **www.EvolvedPub.com/Catalog/**

Thank you!

9 798890 250292